HI

PERFECT

SECRET

A totally gripping psychological thriller

T.J. BREARTON

Joffe Books, London
www.joffebooks.com

First published in Great Britain in 2021

Cover art by Stuart Bache

ISBN: 978-1-80405-029-3

PART ONE

CHAPTER ONE | FRIDAY

It's him.

I recognize the sharp nose and flare to the nostrils. His thick eyebrows and defined cheekbones. But mostly it's the eyes. Sea green.

There's no question that he's a handsome man. The child I remember, just eight or nine, was becoming handsome, too.

The boy's name was Tom.

"Mom, Dad," my daughter says, "I want you to meet Michael."

Michael.

Not him, then. Just a close resemblance. A trick of the light.

"Michael and I are getting married," she says.

My husband, beside me, coughs, like he's just choked on something. We're standing halfway between the house and the lake, on the gently sloping lawn. The sun is beaming down. "Really?" my husband says. "Married? Wow . . ."

He's trying to sound upbeat. He glances at me; everything is in that glance. More than you could put into words. The turbulent history of our daughter, Joni. The girl who ran away from two preparatory schools. The girl we spent nights searching for, on dismal city streets, wondering if we'd find her dead or alive.

She's not a teenager anymore, I remind myself. She's a young woman. We knew she was bringing someone, but the engagement is a huge surprise.

I try not to stare at Michael, the man holding her hand as they stand just slightly downslope of us in the yard. The lake shimmers behind them, a gunmetal blue, scattered with sun diamonds. Somewhere in the distance a motorboat is buzzing. I ask Joni, "When did this happen?"

"Just two weeks ago," she says, tucking her wavy blond hair behind her ears.

I hear it in the curt tone and see it in her body language — my question has kick-started her defenses.

"We wanted to tell you *here*. Coming to the lake house was already in the plan, and then, when he asked me . . ." Joni squeezes Michael's hand as she trails off. She's deferring to him.

Michael takes a subtle step forward. He's concentrating more on my husband, Paul, than me. "I would've liked to ask you in the traditional way, sir." He glances at Joni before finishing. "But we wanted it to be a surprise."

I'm aware of my folded arms; my own defenses are up. I try smiling. "How long have you two been . . . ?"

"Mom," Joni says, "things have been busy."

"I'm just asking how long you've been dating. I've never . . . you've never . . ."

"We're going to talk about all of that."

"Okay."

"But I wanted to . . ." Joni chews her lip and looks away. After a moment of gathering her thoughts: "I wanted to tell you as soon as we got here. So you could get used to it. Because I thought that if I just introduced him as my boyfriend, and then at the end of the weekend told you about our engagement, things might . . ."

End on a bad note, she might've said. I get where she's going.

She'd been vague on the phone: *someone I can't wait for you to meet.* We knew what that meant. Joni had been bringing home *someone I can't wait for you to meet* since she was seventeen. Five years of new faces, flash-in-the-pan relationships. She brought them to us because she sought our approval. Almost like a cat, dropping the dead mouse on the doorstep. I never understood why, when she was so rebellious about everything else.

As a psychotherapist, I should have some insight. But perhaps my being her parent clouds my judgment.

Joni finishes her thought: "If we waited until the end of the weekend, you wouldn't have time to get used to it. So, we're doing it like this." She draws a breath. "Mom, Dad, this is my fiancé. Michael Rand."

He grins and blushes at the same time. He's good with eye contact, though, and his own body language implies openness. He holds Joni's hand, and his other arm hangs at his side. I try not to study his features in an obvious way, comparing him to that boy from fifteen years ago.

It's hard not to; the likeness is uncanny. The eyes, the nose. Even the dark hair — cut into a contemporary medium-length layered look — is similar. It's thicker than I remember, but then he's so much older.

"Well," Paul says, sticking out his hand, "welcome to the family, Michael."

They shake. "Thank you, Mr. Lindman."

"Call me Paul."

Michael faces me and holds out his hand. "Mrs. Lindman."

For a moment, I can't move. Locked on his eyes, it strikes me again that Tom's were the same exact color. But how can I really remember that? It doesn't seem to matter, because I'm suddenly thrust back fifteen years, flicking through photos of a violent and bloody crime scene. The man on the floor of the kitchen, his head beaten in, a shining pool of dark blood surrounding him.

4

I blink and pull back from the memory. I shake Michael's hand, trying not to withdraw too quickly, marshaling the effort to maintain eye contact long enough.

It's him.

It's not. It can't be.

But even if it were — what could I say? What could I do? Everything that happened during those five sessions with eight-year-old Tom Bishop is held in confidence. Even if I were sure, I'd be ethically bound to keep it to myself. Telling Joni would not only be unprofessional. I could lose my license to practice psychology. My daughter's engagement hanging in the balance or not.

"Well," Paul says. "Should we have a drink to celebrate?"

"Dad. It's eleven in the morning," Joni says.

"So? This is vacation, isn't it?"

"I'll make mimosas," I blurt out, eager to get away. "Why don't the three of you sit down at the lake? I'll be right back."

I turn and start walking up to the house before anyone can object.

"Mrs. Lindman?"

Not fast enough.

I slow and turn. "Yes?"

Michael says, "Can you make mine a virgin? I don't really drink."

For a moment, I can't find my voice. Then, "Of course. No problem." I continue along, trying not to run. I might not be able to say anything, but I can satisfy my own curiosity. I can do a quick search online. Nothing unethical about that.

Just before I reach the front door, I glance back toward the lake. Paul is walking down to the dock, Joni and Michael beside him, their hands still interlocked. I grasp the door handle and am about to step inside when Michael looks over his shoulder at me.

He smiles, then turns away.

CHAPTER TWO

Tom Bishop is a semi-famous triathlete. He's also the owner of a company that presents "the world's finest dollhouse miniature shows." I google *Thomas Bishop* with no better results. And then it hits me: little eight-year-old Tom was rarely in the media. When he was mentioned, his identity was concealed.

Laura Bishop is a different story. I find ample stories about the woman who killed her husband and then blamed someone else. She almost got away with it, too — if it weren't for the witness statement provided by her own son, she just might have.

For a few minutes, I click through the articles, devouring images of the Bishop home, police tape across the door. Laura Bishop's mugshot — an art-world socialite caught without makeup, her hair scraped back into a ponytail, her eyes dark and vacant. So different from the posed shots that would follow in longer news stories about the murder. I snap the laptop shut.

This is crazy.

I take the laptop from the kitchen island and bring it back into the living room, set it on the desk overlooking the front deck and the lake beyond. The three of them are down there, sitting in the Adirondack chairs, talking. Joni tosses her head back, laughing.

I'm being ridiculous. The odds of my daughter's fiancé being the grown-up version of a boy I treated fifteen years ago are astronomical. But while a Facebook search yields plenty of Michael Rands, none look like the young man on my front lawn. Still, it doesn't mean anything. My daughter's fiancé is a millennial, and lots of millennials eschew Facebook.

I try Instagram and Snapchat, but no luck.

I'm overtired; maybe that's the problem. Paul and I drove up to the lake house on Thursday, hoping to beat the traffic but not succeeding. Apparently a few thousand other people had the same idea. A four-and-a-half-hour drive under optimal conditions took us more than six. And I didn't sleep well last night. It's been hot and aggressively humid, and the house has no A/C.

"First-world problems," Joni would call these concerns. And she'd be right. But on top of everything, I had to leave several of my active patients behind, including one of them who's been especially troubling. Maggie Lewis. A bright and beautiful young woman stricken with chronic depression and anxiety. When she's off her meds, she's a wreck. When she's on them, she's lethargic and gaining weight. Recently, she's threatening to stop them again. I fear she might have already. So that's bothering me, if I'm honest.

It's always hard to break away in August. But Paul and I both work a lot — probably too much — and it's vital to escape. And now, with our two kids grown, it's some of the only time we all get to spend together. Still, it's never easy.

As I gather the ingredients to make four mimosas — one of them a virgin, meaning just orange juice, since I don't have any non-alcoholic sparkling wine — I realize I'm not just tired: I'm exhausted.

I'm a fifty-three-year-old woman who's been going non-stop for thirty years. Paul and I have been discussing this. It's time for both of us to slow down. At least, a little.

I mix the drinks, have a taste-test of mine, then end up drinking three-quarters of it. Oh well. I add more orange juice and a healthy splash of dry sparkling wine and pick up the tray. Halfway to the door, I stop. Though Joni just dropped the marriage bomb outside on the front lawn, they've really only been here a few minutes. They came into the house upon arrival and set down their bags. Right there, in the entryway.

I know Joni's suitcase — she's had it for years: a battered purple bag on wheels. The dark leather bag beside it must be Michael's. And it's partly unzipped.

CHAPTER THREE

Just a quick peek. Just to see if there's anything obvious on top. Like a wallet.

There's not. I start digging past folded shirts and pants. My hand bumps something hard and plastic, like a deodorant stick. I grasp what might be a toiletry kit. A little more rummaging, and now I'm sweating and feeling like a criminal. This isn't right. The way to understanding Michael's identity — or my conflation of his identity — is not by sneaking around and being underhanded. The way is conversation, direct interaction.

I pick up the drink tray off the floor and am about to stand up.

"Help you with that?"

The voice is so close I let out a little yelp. The main door is open and Michael is standing behind the screen that keeps out the bugs. He pushes it open as I stand with the tray. "Sorry," he says, "I thought I'd come up and see if I could give you a hand. Here, let me take it."

"Thank you. And that's okay. I just didn't hear you."

I almost drop the tray it as I hand it over.

Come on. For God's sake, Emily . . .

After a smile, I push my bangs aside and run my hands through my shoulder-length hair.

"You all right?" Michael looks concerned.

"I'm good. Thanks for your help." I gesture for him to back out through the door as I push it open.

Together we walk along the flagstone walkway, then to the sloping yard. Partway to the dock, a flagpole pierces the earth, the United States flag gently rippling in the humid breeze high above. At the bottom of the lawn, three docks form a U-shape. The two-bay boathouse sits to the left of the U. In it are our sailboat and small rowboat with a trolling motor.

Michael is admiring it all as we walk. "This place is just gorgeous." He's handling the drink tray well, like a waiter would, up on his fingers, his other hand gripping the edge.

"Have you ever been to Lake Placid before?"

"No. Always wanted to, though."

"Oh yeah?"

"I've read about it. The tuberculosis, the cure cottages. Joni drove me around a little bit this morning so I could see some of the houses. The big porches and everything." He pauses. "It's just fascinating. Thinking of all these city people coming here for the fresh air. Hoping it would cure them. Or at least help them."

I don't have time to respond or ask questions since we're almost to the dock. But my mind is running in multiple directions. Lake Placid is a long ways from where Joni is living. How early did they have to start their journey if Joni had time to give Michael a tour this morning? When did my daughter ever show any interest in, or knowledge of, the history of Lake Placid? More importantly, where did she meet this man and why are they rushing into marriage?

"Ah, they've returned with refreshments," Paul says. He's leaned back in one of the wooden Adirondack chairs. My husband is quite like you might picture an architect in his mid-fifties from Westchester County who owns a lake house in the Adirondacks. He's in white slacks and a navy polo T-shirt. His legs are crossed and he's dangling one of his boat shoes from his big toe. If anything, he's acting extra casual. Working a bit to exude calm.

Joni is dressed atypically — for her. The khaki shorts are preppy, the white top is a button-down blouse. She wears pretty sandals on her feet, toes painted lavender. She wants to appear responsible, given this sudden and overwhelming announcement. She's laying it on a bit, too.

Michael looks for a place to set the drink tray, but there's no small table handy.

"Here — let me." I hand off drinks to Paul and Joni and set mine on the arm of my chair, leaving Michael the one on the tray with the red straw.

Paul has arranged the chairs in a circle. There's just enough room on the wide dock that runs along the shore. Once we're all seated, he says, "Okay," and he stretches forward with his drink. "To Joni and Michael." He looks between them, then catches my eye. "May they have lasting happiness."

"Cheers." My toast sounds too quick and eager, but we all touch glasses. Everyone then sits back and sips.

For a moment, nobody speaks.

Michael gazes out at the water. "This is a beautiful lake. Nice and dark blue, almost black. Do you know how deep it gets?"

"A hundred and fifty feet." Paul points to a spot in the distance. "Right in there? That's seventy feet. It's a good-sized lake. Over two thousand acres. Three islands out in the middle. See that?"

Michael shields his eyes with his hand. "I thought that was the other shoreline."

"No, that's Buck Island."

"Wow. Beautiful."

I sneak looks at Joni as they talk. She follows their conversation, seemingly oblivious of me. But I know that's not true. She's afraid. Joni has always been a tough kid, a real firebrand when she was a girl. As a teenager . . . well, we went through it all. And she emerged intact. Strong, even. But there's one area where she's fragile, and that's my approval. I never intended it to be that way, but it's her Achilles' heel.

I need to proceed with a soft touch. "So. Any other surprises? How many weeks pregnant are you?"

"Mom." Joni balks, but there's a smile beneath.

"I'm just kidding."

Joni and Michael look at each other for a long moment. Then Joni pulls a deep breath. "We just know that it's right."

"There you go. That's good."

She pushes on, ignoring me. "I know it seems crazy. It's like a movie. Like those corny movies. But it happens in real life. We're vibrating on the same frequency." She takes a quick sip of her drink — a little liquid courage maybe. "He knows me. And I told him . . . I told him everything."

Everything?

I watch Michael. It's so hard not to stare at him. The nose, the flat eyebrows. The way his dark hair falls in front of his eyes when he leans forward. Joni is about to say more, but I interrupt. I can't help it.

"What about you, Michael?"

His eyes flick to mine. "What about me what, ma'am?"

"Call me Emily."

Joni answers for him. "I know all about Michael, too."

Michael leans on his hand and stares at my daughter with adoration. Then he sits back, looking thoughtful. "My childhood wasn't the easiest, but whose is? When I met Joni, and we got to know each other, and she told me about her . . . rebellious streak . . ." He smiles, and so does she. Then he continues, "I was open with her, that there was a lot of loss and grief in my past. Some pretty bad stuff."

"I'm sorry to hear that." I glance at Paul, but his eyes are on Michael, rapt with attention.

I want Paul to ask Michael what happened, but he doesn't. And neither do I.

For one thing, I probably already know.

CHAPTER FOUR

Fifteen years ago, in Bronxville, New York, in the middle of the night, a man named David Bishop was beaten to death with a hammer. In his own kitchen.

Police, arriving on scene, found a back door broken into, the alarm tripped. They also found David's wife, distraught — hysterical — her hands covered in her husband's blood.

"We heard a noise," she told police. "David came downstairs. About — I don't know, a minute — went by. Then I heard voices. I heard David shouting . . . and then . . . then he was . . ." She couldn't finish.

Police also found David's son, eight-year-old Thomas Bishop, in the house. When they spoke to young Tom, he explained that he'd awakened to noises. Angry voices, he said, "bad fighting," and then screams.

"Who was screaming?"

"My mom was."

He'd come upon her in the kitchen holding his father in her lap, covered in blood. And she'd shouted at Thomas to dial 911, and he did.

The investigation began. Thomas Bishop's emergency call was listened to repeatedly. The back door was studied, the exterior searched for evidence of the attacker, the home dusted for prints. The Bishops had a security alarm system, but no cameras. The house was big, almost mansion-like, surrounded by ample lawn and privacy hedging. Residents of the affluent neighborhood saw nothing unusual, heard nothing unusual until the arrival of the ambulance and police.

Laura Bishop was likewise unable to provide help. She hadn't seen the attacker. The voice she'd heard, she said, was muffled, through the walls. Male, perhaps in his thirties or forties, but impossible to say for sure.

The detective from the Bronxville Police Department soon kicked it up the chain to the New York State Police Bureau of Criminal Investigation. Six months later, the BCI investigation was going cold. Pressure was on the two people heading it up, Investigators Rebecca Mooney and Stephen Starzyk. They had gotten some conflicting statements from young Tom Bishop, and his family was worried that the repeated questioning by law enforcement was only adding to his trauma.

The investigators went to the DA, who went to a judge for a court-ordered evaluation.

That's when I was contacted. Normally something like that might go to a forensic child psychologist, but I'd consulted with law enforcement before as a clinician. My name apparently topped a list somewhere at BCI headquarters. I don't really remember getting the call, but I remember the first time Rebecca Mooney and I met, since, after chatting for about a minute, she looked at me with steely blue eyes and said, "I think the boy is not telling us something."

"Okay . . ."

"I've gone over his statements, watched the videos a dozen times. What I can't tell — is he traumatized, and that's what's coming across? Or is he scared of something? Something he saw?"

I was reluctant. Extremely. Every police officer and investigator I've met in my career has been an above-board public servant. They're just people, and some are nicer than others — that's the way people are — but they can get desperate when the pressure is on and police captains and district attorneys are breathing down their necks. They have something called a solve-rate, too, which is how many cases they've brought to a satisfying conclusion, with someone guilty behind bars.

The last thing I wanted was to help pressure some little boy into saying he saw something.

Like what? If he'd seen the assailant, why hide it?

After some back and forth, I finally agreed to three sessions minimum, five at the most. We would just talk, maybe do some play therapy. I made it clear with Mooney that my interest was in the boy's well-being, that I would be *his* advocate, not the state's. That after my sessions, and possible contact with collaterals — Tom's teacher, primary caregiver, and any previous therapists — I'd turn in my report.

"That's absolutely fine," Mooney said. "That's the way it should be. But we might need to talk to the boy independently at certain points between your sessions. If any new evidence comes to light."

I didn't like it, but those were the conditions. And a week later, I met with Tom Bishop for the first time.

* * *

"My parents died in a car accident," Michael Rand says.

I snap back into the present moment.

Michael falls silent as I try to absorb what he's just said. *A car accident?*

Michael says, "My father, he, ah . . . My father was an alcoholic. He was drunk. That's why I . . ." Michael looks at me and lifts his virgin mimosa. *That's why I don't drink.*

A car accident, I think, *not a murder after all*. "I'm sorry," I say, "I didn't know . . ."

He frowns and shakes his head. "No, please, not at all. You were just being hospitable. It's an occasion to celebrate."

I check my husband's expression. He's looking thoughtful. I love Paul, but his mind works quite differently than mine — perhaps that's part of why our marriage has worked for thirty years despite the rough patches. After Michael's disclosing of this traumatic past to us, Paul's question is: "So, Michael, what do you do for a living?"

Michael seems happy to change the subject. "Well, I'm still in school now. Got a late start. But I do carpentry for work. Anything to do with building."

Paul has lit up like a Christmas tree. He edges forward in his seat. "I'm an architect, you know. And I'm building my own boat."

Michael laughs. "Yeah. Joni said."

"I *did* talk about you guys," Joni says. And, unexpectedly, she reaches for me and takes my hand. "I talked you up."

Michael is smiling benignly at me. He knows I'm a psychologist. God, it's so hard to know whether he's hiding something or I'm just wrong. A car accident? And his physical likeness is just that — a likeness?

Or, a third option: maybe that little boy who was so good at compartmentalizing, maybe he's become a man who's even better at it. Better to the point that he's invented this other past for himself: one in which his parents died in an auto wreck. One in which, even, he doesn't drink.

Convenient, since drinking tends to lower inhibitions. Maybe it was an unconscious strategy, but it's a smart element. No drinking equals minimizing risk of accidental disclosure of truth.

You're losing your mind. For God's sake. He's not Tom Bishop.
Maybe.

For now, anyway, I'll take Michael Rand at face value. My daughter is still smiling at me — I think she's just relieved I haven't shown any outward disapproval so far — and Michael and Paul are caught up in a discussion of the building trades.

I focus on my daughter. After all, I haven't seen her for six months. Not since Christmas. I tell her I like her hair — she's added some blonde highlights. "I like yours too," she says. "That's a good length on you." After a few seconds, we're lost in chitchat and Michael and Paul have wandered over to the boathouse. They're going to take out the rowboat, have a look around the lake.

Joni and I watch them embark, and wave as they putter away with the trolling motor. Michael waves back. He is handsome even from a distance. Paul's back is to the shore as he steers the boat away from us.

Joni and I head up to the house. It's going on noon and everybody's going to be hungry. We talk a little about Sean, Joni's older brother. "He should be here tomorrow," I say. "But you know how Sean is."

She rolls her eyes. "Yeah."

Inside, she notes the bags on the floor. "I'll take these up to the room." But she stops and cocks an eyebrow at me. "Are you going to be okay with us sleeping in the same room even if we're not officially hitched yet?"

Her voice is playful, but I can sense the tension underneath.

Before I can offer a reply, Joni bends down to Michael's unzipped bag. "Oh," she says, affection in her voice. After a moment of fishing around in a side pocket, she pulls out a leather-bound notebook and holds it up for me. "He keeps a diary, Mom. Isn't that cute?"

Then she tucks it back into the bag and zips it up.

"Cute," I say.

Carrying his bag and her suitcase toward the stairs, Joni says, "What could be wrong with a guy who keeps a diary?"

CHAPTER FIVE

Tom was quiet at first. He ignored the toys in my office and studied his shoes. Nikes, I remember. Blue with gold emblems. His dark fall of hair covered his eyes. Occasionally he brushed it aside, then kept staring at his feet. Or turned to look out the window at the buildings across the street.

I remember our third session together. We'd talked about everything but the crime so far. Tom liked Wolverine the best, out of the X-Men. *Pokémon Dash* was his favorite video game.

I wasn't too familiar with *Pokémon* — my son, Sean, who was just two years older than Tom at the time, never showed much interest in video games. But the thought of the characters, perhaps, reminded me of our two cats. Tom's family had also kept cats.

"Tom? Where are your cats now?"

He gazed down at the floor. "With my Aunt Alice."

"Are they calicos?"

He shrugged.

I said, "We have two calicos. They have pretty patterns. Though our boy cat, he's just two colors, black and white. So you know what we named him? Cow."

Tom looked up. When he smiled, I felt an expanding in my chest, a tingling at the back of my neck. It wasn't always this way, but occasionally, when you broke through for a moment, when you saw a person's light shine back at you, it could be incredible.

His smile faltered. "What's the other cat's name?"

"Rosie. She's the girl cat."

"Is she red, like a rose?"

"No, not really. She's three colors."

"Oh." His eyes drifted down again.

"Tom?"

"Mm?"

"I know you miss your father."

It was the first I'd mentioned it.

"Yeah," Tom said.

"My father passed away, too. It was a long time ago, but I still miss him. I felt all kinds of feelings when he died. I felt sad, but I felt angry, too. And you know what? That's normal. It's normal to feel all kinds of things . . ."

I waited. Then slowly, carefully, I asked a few questions, and Tom recalled things from the night in question. But, unable to conclude with what had happened to his father, Tom looked down.

"I'm scared," he said.

"Why?"

He wouldn't say. I watched as a single tear slipped down his cheek. And then I got up from my chair and crossed the room to him. I put one hand on his shoulder, another on his head. "I'm sorry you feel scared."

A subtle sensation, like a tremor, vibrated beneath my feet. I heard a muffled door close. A second later, someone was knocking to enter the room. My assistant, Mena, who never interrupted me during a session unless it was an emergency, stood in the doorway, wringing her hands. Over her shoulder were Mooney and Starzyk, the two state investigators.

"I'm so sorry," Mena whispered.

I made a decision and turned to Tom. "Tom? Let's take a really quick break, okay? You need to go to the bathroom?"

He shook his head.

"Want a snack or anything?"

He nodded.

I smiled and told him Mena would get him something. "I'm just going to be in the next room, right outside this door, okay?"

"Okay."

I stepped out of my office, wanting to give the investigators a few choice words. You don't just interrupt a session like that. This had better be good.

After Mena went into my office and shut the door, Mooney locked her gaze on me. "We need this to move along a little bit."

"Move it along?"

"Listen, I'm sorry, I know. Things are developing."

"What does that mean?" I was used to working with law enforcement, and understood the need for discretion. But this was making me nervous.

"It means this is delicate right now," Mooney said. "I've spoken to someone close to the family. Things are . . . There are just some things that have come to our attention."

Starzyk stood back by the door to the hallway, checking out the room the way cops do. He wore a gray suit and aviator sunglasses.

It was vague. Vaguer than vague. I shook my head. "All I can tell you is that I have a severely traumatized little boy in there who saw his father dead on the floor of his kitchen. And I need him to talk about that on his own. I can't force him."

"You said three sessions."

"I said three minimum, but maybe five." I kept my voice low, but forceful. "I think he needs to tell me something. I think it's bottled up in him. This boy has an unsettling knack for compartmentalizing. He's highly intelligent, but he has PTSD. He's walled off the memory of that night — seeing his mother and father in the kitchen, his mother cradling her dead husband's head in her hands — he only remembers what won't hurt him."

I was breathing hard by the time I finished.

Mooney, who was half a foot shorter, looked up at me with intensity. "That may not be all he saw."

"What?"

I glanced at Starzyk, no longer checking out the room but watching me from behind his reflective lenses.

"The boy's mother has made plans to leave the state," he said. "They're moving. She's getting on a plane in less than a week, with plans to take him with her."

Mooney stepped closer. "Dr. Lindman, we know it's not your job to work this case for us. You need to submit your evaluation. We just need you to do it as soon as you can. We're out of time."

It seemed that what they were talking about was more than getting the description of a murdering intruder. My throat felt dry.

"I'll do the best I can. When he's ready, he'll tell me what he saw. But only when he's ready."

CHAPTER SIX

I wait for Paul and Michael to return from the lake. They're gone about an hour. After they dock and walk up the hill toward the house, they're shoulder to shoulder, like a couple of old buddies. You could say Paul has a way with people, and he does. It's what makes him a good friend of many, but it would make him a lousy therapist. To do therapy, you have to keep a certain distance. You have to have boundaries. Without boundaries, not only do you lose objectivity, but you can lose compassion.

I've seen young therapists fall into that trap. They think getting close is the way into the healing. But it can lead to complication, even harm.

"Hi there, wife," Paul says as he reaches me. They're both wet around the cuffs of their pants.

"You guys have fun?"

"Michael really likes it out there," Paul says with pride.

"I grew up near the ocean, which is great, but there's something about these glacial lakes," Michael says. "Cold and dark and deep."

They're both smiling. There's no hint that any tough words were shared; it's all good vibes and bonding. But each time I look at Michael, his gaze seems to shift just before I see something he doesn't want me to see. "Well," he says, "I guess I'll go find Joni. She inside?"

"She's upstairs, yeah."

"Go on in," Paul says. "Make yourself comfortable."

"Okay, thanks." He flashes us another quick smile before moving on.

We watch as he approaches and enters the house.

I can't keep it quiet any longer. Paul must read it in my face because his mouth turns down, eyebrows knitted with concern. "What?"

I take him by the arm, trying to be casual, and walk him toward the driveway. Our Range Rover is there, plus the old Ford pickup truck we leave at the house. Behind them both is Joni's Subaru. The garage, where cars usually go, has been serving as Paul's workshop. He's building a boat, a process that's spanned four summers now. He swears it will be done before we return home at the end of next week.

I lead him inside, the smell of sanded wood filling my nose. We're out of view of the house, out of hearing range, too.

"Em? What're you doing? What's going on?"

We stand together beside the boat he's making. It's upside down, the wood bare and smooth. Paul can't help it — he looks at his creation and then runs his hand over it. But his eyes come back to mine. "I know," he says. "It's nuts. But it's Joni. Par for the course. 'You just gotta laugh because it's all so crazy.' Right? He seems like a good guy, Em. I know you think I just like everybody. But he really cares about her. He—"

"I think he was a former patient."

Paul's hand stops. He looks at me, brushes his palms together absently, kicking off a little dust. "What?"

"Fifteen years ago."

"In what . . . ? I mean . . ."

"A murder case. An evaluation I did for the New York State Police. Remember? Investigator Mooney?"

I see the memory hit his eyes, changing his gaze. "The Bishops," he says.

"Yeah."

He points towards the house. "That's him? That's the boy?"

"I think so."

Paul's hand drops. He takes a step closer. "You think so? Or you know?"

"I think I remember him. He looks exactly like Tom Bishop would look if he were now twenty-three. I mean, exactly."

"But he's . . . Michael Rand . . ."

I wait, lifting my eyebrows at my husband, inviting him to work it out.

"Maybe he changed his name? Because of everything that happened?"

"Wouldn't you?"

"I mean, he was a kid . . ."

"He had people looking out for him. His aunt and uncle, for one thing. David Bishop's sister and her husband. The ones who took Tom in after it all . . . after the trial."

Paul has been staring off, but now he focuses on me. "What are their names?"

"I thought of that. I'm not sure I remember, but I don't think it was Rand."

"Can you check? Is there some way you can find out?"

"Well, maybe. My files, but those are back at my office. And I didn't write much down, just some notes for myself and then the report, which went under judicial seal. Because he was a minor."

I'm quiet, contemplating, and notice Paul has gone kind of lifeless again.

"So," I say.

Suddenly Paul shakes his head. "I don't know. I mean, you're not even sure."

"Not a hundred percent."

"It's just a lookalike thing."

"Well, that and . . ." *The way he makes me feel.*

Paul shakes his head again. "Honey, I don't think so. I just spent an hour with that guy. I'm a pretty good judge of character. And he told us what happened to his parents. You know, changing your name is one thing, but concocting a false past?" Paul shook his head. "It's a resemblance, nothing else."

I don't want to argue, even if it feels as much like denial as logic coming from my husband. But in truth, all I have is a feeling.

Pieces of a memory.

A trace of a boy who saw something horrible.

* * *

There were ten minutes left in our fifth and final session. Mooney's words had been ringing in my mind ever since she and Starzyk interrupted us. *That may not be all he saw.* The sense of urgency. I didn't like it; it was anathema to my practice, but I understood it.

And then I asked the question.

"Tom?"

He looked at me. Maybe he heard it in my voice: I needed something from him.

Or, his father did.

And that's how I approached it.

"If your dad could talk to you right now, what would he tell you to do? If you saw something, if you saw what happened to him — not afterward, but *when* it happened — don't you think he would want you to tell?"

Tom gazed at me, impassively at first. I suppressed the urge to say more, I fought to give him space. And then his face changed — it started to crumble.

And the noise — at first, I wasn't sure where it was coming from. A terrible sound, like a moan, at once both inhuman and utterly human. It was coming from him.

Tom opened his mouth, and he took a breath, and that moan escaped him again. Tears filled his eyes, then spilled over the lids, ran down his reddened cheeks.

I stood, my heart rate going up. *What is this? What do I do?* But that was foolish. I'd seen people cry, scream, go on a tear — I'd seen every emotion.

Okay, maybe not like this. Maybe not an eight-year-old boy with the sound of pure heartache issuing from his open mouth. Because that's what it was. A depthless anguish.

"Tom . . ." I said, trying to soothe. I resisted going to him but reached out, fingers in the air just a yard from his face.

"I saw," he managed.

"Okay." I released a pent-up breath. "Okay, Tom. You saw . . . You saw what happened to your father?"

Tom moaned again, the pitch even lower. He gave a sidelong look at the door, exposing the whites of his eyes. Like he was remembering the police on the other side of it, wondering if they'd come back. If they were listening now.

"I saw *her*," he said next.

"You saw her? Your mother?"

He was still describing his discovery of his father's death, it seemed.

"I heard them." Tom whimpered a little between each sentence. Like the words physically hurt. "They were yelling at each other."

I didn't interrupt. The police had said there were signs of forced entry. That someone had broken into the Bishop home and David Bishop had confronted them, had words.

"They were yelling and it woke me up and I went downstairs."

But this was different. I couldn't tell if he was talking about the assailant or his mother. We were in different territory from what he'd told the police.

"I went down and . . . I went down and I saw them fighting."

I had to speak. To clarify. "The intruder and your daddy?"

Tom looked at me — I'll never forget the haunting in his light-colored eyes — and he shook his head. He moaned one last time, swallowed, and said, "Mommy and Daddy. Fighting. And Mommy had a hammer."

PART TWO

CHAPTER SEVEN

I have to know.

First of all, the resemblance is uncanny. We've all heard stories that everyone has a double in the world — maybe this is what that is. Or perhaps time has distorted my memory. That would be fine. I prefer the possibility of dementia or confabulation to the alternative: Michael has sought us out for some reason. Revenge? Because I unlocked the truth that had his mother convicted of capital murder?

But the odds that Michael is Tom, and Michael just happened to meet and date my daughter — then *propose marriage* — all the while innocently disremembering our time together — those are stacked too high. Too many coincidences. And I've learned from both my time spent working with law enforcement and my own experiences as a psychologist that coincidence rarely exists. There's always a connection.

The last possibility is this: Michael is acting unconsciously, or at least semi-consciously. Memory is a wild place. I've had patients who'd forgotten whole chunks of their lives. Patients who misremembered things substantially — swapping out characters from their past, switching family members, confusing strangers with friends. Mostly, we humans compartmentalize. Especially when traumatized. We quickly and carefully hide away painful experiences in a mental room, lock the door and drop the key down a deep well.

I drink coffee as I contemplate, watching the lake through the picture window in the living room. Paul is out there now, using our push mower on the sloping front lawn. We have a caretaker, but we give him an August vacation. Paul likes to do his own mowing, especially when he has something to think about. And I suppose I've given him just that.

We're not in agreement at the moment, Paul and me. He thinks it's coincidence. But he knows me and knows where I'm headed. That I'm not going to be able to relax until I figure this out.

I wait, as patiently as I can, until Joni and Michael come downstairs. They've been up there for a half an hour, and they're both looking a bit glowy. Joni has changed into a bathing suit, and Michael is wearing trunks.

"We're going to take a dip, Mom. Then we're going into town. Okay?"

"Sure." I wrap my hands around my mug of coffee. "Have fun."

They're out the door like a couple of kids. And they are kids, really. Barely into their twenties. I watch them run down the lawn. Paul smiles and gives a wave. Once they reach the dock, Michael sweeps Joni off her feet. He carries her, like the bride over the threshold, to the end of the dock, where he pretends to toss her in. She makes a big show of it, kicking her legs and throwing her head back, which fans her long, highlighted hair. Then he sets her down and she promptly dives in off the end of the dock. Michael waits for her to re-emerge.

Our kids, Joni and Sean, grew up coming here. Paul bought the place when Sean was just two and Joni not yet conceived. She learned to swim in the lake when she was five years old. I watch her break the surface now — she was underwater for several seconds and she's out a good ways — and then Michael jumps in.

Now's the time. I turn from the window and head upstairs. I'm not proud of what I'm about to do, but I make a deal with myself: I'm only looking for identifying information. I'm not going to read Michael's personal thoughts.

The stairs creak beneath my weight. Paul hates that the stairs creak and considers it a design flaw. He's funny, my husband: laid-back in life, slow to act, but a ruthless perfectionist when it comes to his work. Maybe since he's so tough on himself that way, he's got to go easy elsewhere in order to stay sane.

It smells like sex in my daughter's room. The bed is still made, but the comforter is rumpled. Wrinkling my nose, I crank open the casement windows to let in a bit of air. Luckily, the room is on the backside of the house — no one will spot me from the lake. The forest is in the back, thick with pines and hemlocks and birch trees. There's a walking trail that disappears into the lush greenery. Barely visible is an old shed that was part of the original construction.

Lake Placid and its neighbor, Saranac Lake, were mainly developed as early fashionable resort centers. As Michael mentioned, for the affluent who came to escape the city smog, to draw in the fresh mountain air in the hopes they wouldn't die of consumption.

Many did. They spent months — years — sitting out on large porches, bundled in blankets, heads covered with knitted winter hats, as they shrank away into death.

But they couldn't stop the tide of vacationers, attracted by the chance to get back to basics without sacrificing the luxury to which they were accustomed. Men with hunting and fishing skills became guides for the rich, taking the city folk deep into the woods, cooking their trout dinner over an open fire, regaling them with stories of the "north country," playing the banjo or guitar. People built huge log cabins and decorated them with deer heads and stuffed black bears and colorful, hand-woven Native American rugs. They hung pack baskets and snowshoes and black powder rifles. They called these places "Great Camps."

When we bought our property, it contained a Great Camp that had fallen into disrepair. Paul estimated the cost of restoring it was greater than razing it and building a new, more modern home. He relished the challenge of designing his own place.

Michael's duffel bag is on the floor near the bedroom closet. The main zipper is shut, but the side pocket where Joni returned the diary hangs open. I squat down beside the bag and, feeling a bit like a TV detective handling evidence, use the pen I've brought to push the fabric farther open. The leather-bound notebook is where it was. The pen won't help me now. Glancing over my shoulder at the bedroom door, I pull it out, unwind the rope holding the book closed, then open it.

My breath suspended, I check the first couple of pages, catching pieces of sentences, dates. I make an effort to skim these, not to comprehend. Michael deserves privacy, though I can't help but consider the handwriting — big, blocky, exuberant, really — along with the use of both black and blue ink, even pencil.

I flip to where the text ends, about two-thirds of the way through. It looks like he's been keeping this journal for just about six months and has written a fair amount in that time. It's not unheard of for a young man to keep a journal, but it does seem unusual, especially in this day and age.

Occasionally, I have a patient who I think might benefit from journaling and encourage them to do so. But it's not for everybody. Some struggle mightily to put pen to paper, either because it's just not natural to them — they're more mathematical or mechanical than verbal — or because it's too painful. It calls them to fish the key out of that deep well, to unlock their tucked-away mental room.

Michael's prose seems to flow. As much as I'm trying to only look for identifying information — numbers, addresses — it's impossible not to glean a few things . . .

Monday, April 4 — Having a hard time getting going today. Sitting here on the train, watching the commuters — everybody has their face stuck behind either a newspaper, tablet, or phone. Mostly it's the phones. Even people whom I watched board together and sit down don't talk, just poke at their phones. Does anyone just stare out the window anymore?

So, he's a romantic, I think. An idealist, maybe. Not exactly original in his observations. I'm nevertheless charmed. It makes sense my Joni is drawn to a man with the heart of a poet.

I'm about to close the journal — the longer I look, the guiltier I feel — but something stops me.

Sitting here on the train, he writes.

Which train? I flip through the pages, looking for any mention of a place. It takes a few minutes. I'm about to give up, but then:

. . . which is part of what's so fascinating about this place. It's part suburb and part city. And how location shapes people. Even after just a couple of generations. Long Island people are practically their own species . . .

I've noticed the journal is filled with lots of philosophical observations like this, but this is the first I've seen announcing a location. He just now mentioned growing up by the ocean, and I'll be damned if Long Island doesn't trigger a memory. A name.

Bleeker.

Arnold Bleeker, I think, and his wife — I forget her first name. But they were the uncle and aunt who took in Tom while his mother awaited trial. And, as far as I know, they kept him afterwards.

I quickly wind the journal's string, then tuck it back into the duffel, making sure it looks just as it was. What I've found is nothing definitive — Long Island is a huge place, its shoreline hundreds of miles long — but another coincidence?

They're really piling up.

About to leave the room, I stop, hearing music, vibration. The popular song is emanating from Michael's phone, half-tucked under the pillow. It's an incoming call, the number displayed on screen. 315. A Central New York number.

I wait, feeling my heart beat a little harder. I chide myself for being foolish.

The ringing stops. I linger just another moment, and the phone buzzes with a text.

Despite the phone being in lock-mode, the text shows up on screen.

Hey. You there yet? How did it go?

Then, a second later:

Did they buy it?

CHAPTER EIGHT

Outside, Paul's lawnmower has just quit. Is he finished? Returning inside? Leaving the phone, I walk swiftly out of the bedroom and into the master bedroom across the hall. This is where Paul and I sleep, overlooking the lake. I see him down there — he's removing some clotted grass from beneath the machine.

My gaze seeks Joni and Michael, swimming in the lake, but I can't find them. Their towels are piled on the dock; they haven't finished and headed back for the house yet. Then I see it: a ripple of water near the corner of the boat-house, signs of people swimming just out of sight. I breathe a little easier, then trot back into Joni's bedroom.

I pick up the phone.

Did they buy it?

Did they buy what? I infer the rest:

Did they buy your fake story, Michael? The fabricated past about your parents dead in a car wreck? Did they buy that you were nice, sincere, and not sociopathic? Not planning to get some sort of revenge on the woman who aided your mother's prosecution fifteen years ago?

Maybe. Maybe that's what's unsaid, but I can't be sure.

You there yet?

How did it go?

These are innocuous. They could easily be about the marriage proposal. Telling your fiancée's parents.

But:

Did they buy it?

This is so loaded. A phrase with specific connotations. It refers to someone running a con.

I set the phone down but don't move for a moment, recalling the headlines from back then, the chyrons on the cable news: *Bronxville Woman Pleads Guilty to Husband Murder.*

Bronxville. One of the richest cities in one of the richest counties in the United States. So why did she do it? Money, of course. That was the principal speculation. Even left-of-center and right-of-center media outlets could agree: this was a murderous, gold-digging woman. When her husband didn't give her a large enough allowance, buy her enough things, she staged a break-in and killed him for the insurance.

There was little dissent. Just a reporter here or there who pointed out that Laura Bishop actually worked — she was an artist's manager and had some high-profile clients, whose work was displayed at the MOMA, at the Tate Modern, and so on.

Ah, there's no money in that, people argued.

But if Laura's finances were ever parsed — and I'm sure they were — I never saw the data.

Besides, in the end, Laura Bishop took a deal. She pled guilty to a lesser charge — murder in the second degree, meaning it was spur-of-the-moment crime and not premeditated. She was given twenty-five years in prison. When she got out, she'd be in her sixties. Her prime years would be behind her, never to return.

She didn't fight it. Laura Bishop stood up in court and, claiming she was of sound mind and that she understood what she was doing, she entered her guilty plea. Case closed.

That day, when I sat in the back of the courtroom, returns to me fully now. Tom wasn't there, thank God. He was off with his aunt somewhere. But his uncle came to court, the name I've just remembered: Arnold Bleeker. A tall and narrow man;

Laura's brother-in-law. I recall that we met eyes, Bleeker and I, just once. It was after Laura, standing in her orange DOC jumpsuit, had admitted her guilt. He looked at me through the slow-moving sea of people leaving the courtroom. It seemed like he knew me, like he knew I'd been the one to get the truth from his nephew. But of course he couldn't; everything that happened with me and Tom was held in confidence.

Unless Tom had said something? How much did an eight-year-old understand? He'd moaned and cried and confessed his secret to me. Shortly after, the police had taken a statement from him. I knew that such a statement would be critical, and it had turned out to be the cornerstone of the prosecutor's case against Laura Bishop — but such a young boy wouldn't know that. Plus, many days had passed between his aching confession to me and the hearing in which Laura pled guilty. When he was finally told that his mother was going to prison, even more time had elapsed.

What would a young boy know about the criminal justice system? He might've recognized that he'd had a role to play, but no more than that.

Did they buy it?

I'm still standing in Joni's bedroom, holding Michael's phone, staring at this text.

Enough, I think. I replace the phone under a ripple of bed covering and turn to leave the room. My heart jumps and my breath catches in my throat.

Paul is standing there. He's sweaty and smells like cut grass. He frowns at me. "What're you doing?"

"Nothing." I push past him and into the hallway, then start down the stairs.

"I was calling for you," he says.

I stop halfway down the staircase. "Oh yeah?"

"Yeah. I came in the house, couldn't find you."

I wait.

Paul cocks his head. "Find anything?"

"No," I say quickly. And it's mostly true. I didn't find anything concrete, just memories that have got me wanting to locate Arnold Bleeker and his wife. What was her first name?

Alice.

Paul says, "Okay, well, is there a plan? Lunch? Dinner? Should we go out tonight, celebrate?"

In my distractedness, I haven't given any thought to how we're going to officially respond to our daughter's wedding engagement. Even if I'm scrounging around in the background, trying to get some answers, it's best to keep up appearances. Especially if what I turn up ends up being nothing.

Paul remains at the top of the stairs. He's removed his shoes, and the white socks are stained green around the ankles. "How about the Interlaken for dinner?" He's suggesting our favorite restaurant. "Unless you're thinking of going out for lunch instead. Which is, I guess, the point I'm making . . ."

"Let me think about dinner." I turn and continue down the stairs. Before I leave Paul's earshot I say, "But there's cold cuts in the fridge for lunch, if you're too hungry to wait: bread, pickles. Make yourself a sandwich. I'll be right back. I have to run out."

CHAPTER NINE

Cell service is typically terrible by the lake, so I've jumped into the Range Rover and taken off down the bumpy, unimproved road. I'd glanced at the dock, only to see the towels but still no sign of the kids.

The dirt road lets out on a narrow, paved road. I drive slowly. The road bisects a long thicket of bushes — there's some nice wild raspberries in there. This road meets with a third, which leads into town. I don't have to go very far before I can pick up a signal, and so I pull over to the shoulder and make my call.

Mena has been my assistant for years. She's one in a million. Paul once remarked that I'm so fond of Mena because she's never seemed to have any ambitions beyond helping me. "It's true," I admitted, "I'm fascinated with people who seem to have their ego under such control."

But Mena's phone goes to voicemail.

"Hi," I say, "it's me. I hope you're doing well, and I wonder if you could grab something for me from the back room. A file on Tom Bishop; I'm not sure if you remember. I just, um . . . Everything's fine, it's just a little something that came up and—"

There's a strange beep in my ear. Now that my phone is back in service, it's registering a voicemail. And I know the number.

Still talking to Mena's mailbox, I finish: "Oh, I see I've actually got a voicemail from you. Weird. Let me check that and I'll . . . oh, hell."

I stop talking and wait for the automated voice to ask me if I'm satisfied with my message. When prompted, I choose to cancel it. Good grief, I sounded tongue-tied.

Did they buy it?

I'm nervous, that's what. No shame in that. It's been a weird morning. Unexpected. I'm on the horns of a dilemma — or I can see them approaching. If I can confirm Michael Rand is who I think he is, what can I even tell my daughter? Nothing specific, obviously. Just the basics. But I'm not relishing the prospect of that, either. All I'd be able to give is some vague reason for why I think Michael is wrong for her. For why I'm *insistent* he is. Not a chance in hell it would work.

I pull the message from Mena and listen.

"Hi, Mrs. Lindman."

She's always called me that. After eleven years she's called me that. That's not what bothers me — it's the tone of her voice. And while she's talking, there's more beeps — I've got multiple voicemails.

Mena says, "I have some bad news. I thought you'd want to know right away. I tried your landline at the lake house, but no one answered. So okay . . . here goes: Maggie Lewis is dead. She completed a suicide last night. Her landlord found her this morning."

My hand floats to my lips and covers my mouth. *Oh no . . .*

"Everybody knows you're away on vacation," Mena says. "It was a policeman who called the office — Sergeant Rhames — and he said your name was in her phone, he knew you were her therapist, and just wanted to follow up with you. He said that you can call him anytime, and he left his personal cell number."

After she relays the number and says again how sorry she is, I write it down.

Poor Maggie Lewis. It's always terrible when a patient succumbs to diseases of despair. We do our utmost to get them the help they need, to make a plan for their health, to work with their physicians and psychiatrists — but we can't control everything. Maggie was very sick.

I just didn't see this coming.

After sitting there a minute to process the news, I remember the other missed calls. One that precedes Mena's message is also a Westchester area code. It looks like Bronxville Police. Either Rhames called from the office or it was a duty officer seeking contact. I know Sergeant Rhames — we've had a few occasions to speak. But before I give him a call, I analyze a third number.

This one's an unknown caller. It's last in the sequence, but since my phone was out of service, it didn't log the time.

The message appears to last fourteen seconds. Just long enough for someone to leave their name and a brief reason for calling. But when I click on it and put the phone to my ear, I register only silence. I plug my free ear and strain to hear. Nothing, just white noise.

Maybe . . . *maybe* the faintest whisper of a voice in the background.

But I can't make it out.

The message ends.

The Range Rover windows are rolled up, but the air is on. I dial down the vents and kill the engine.

Now it's perfectly quiet. The road I'm on is isolated. After waiting for one lone pickup truck to pass, I replay the message. Finger in ear, hunching forward, straining.

Silence, a kind of background hiss.

And then the voice. As if coming from a distance. Or muffled.

Through a door, perhaps:

"*I want my mommy back . . .*"

CHAPTER TEN

"Dr. Lindman," says Sergeant Rhames. "Thanks for returning my call."

"Of course."

"I understand you're away."

"Yes. We're upstate. My husband and I — we take this trip annually."

"That's fine. Listen, this will only take a moment. Just a few questions."

"This is such a tragedy," I say. "I'm so sorry to hear about it."

"It's a terrible thing. She was a beautiful young woman. Lots ahead of her. Now, you were her therapist, is that correct?"

"Her clinical psychologist."

"You're not her, ah, psychiatrist?"

"No. I have a doctorate, but I'm not a medical doctor. I don't prescribe her any medication. What I do is called 'the talking cure.'" It's more explanation than he needs, but I'm feeling anxious.

"Right. Okay. But she had one of those, isn't that right? A psychiatrist?"

"Yes. Well . . . it's complicated." I take him through a quick, highly discreet version of the story — Maggie

Lewis didn't like being medicated and frequently switched psychiatrists.

What I don't say is that the last one prescribed her the same SSRI — or antidepressant drug — as the previous one, precipitating some of her more recent frustrations, which she had expressed to me. Since I wasn't involved with the drug part of it, Maggie had felt more allied with me. Not that I have anything against medication nor ever tried to steer her away from it. My job had been to help Maggie get what she needs to be as healthy as she could be. That's always my job.

"I understand," Sergeant Rhames says, a little bit of that cop-tone creeping into his voice. As if things like switching psychiatrists are beyond his blue collar, do-the-crime-do-the-time paygrade. "Well, Dr. Lindman, as far as we're concerned, this looks like suicide."

"Can I ask . . . how did she . . . ?"

"The victim hung herself. Medical examiner has already indicated that her injuries are consistent with that. It wasn't staged. But we're following up, just to get the fullest picture we can. You said you were her therapist for how long?"

"A little under two years." It's getting hot in the car, so I turn the engine back on and crank the air.

Rhames is silent, and I get the sense he's hearing the background noises on my end.

I want my mommy back . . .

Did that voice sound like Tom Bishop? Like a recording of something he said during a police interview? Am I going crazy?

A patient has died. Stop this nonsense.

My own internal admonition bears striking similarity to the cadence of my father's voice.

"Not quite two years," Rhames repeats about my time with Maggie. "And during that time . . . ?"

"Ms. Lewis presented no suicidal ideation. That I can tell you. We discussed it, but only in an objective way. The concept of it."

"When was this?"

42

"I'd have to look at my notes. Maybe two months ago."

"What was the nature of that conversation? I mean, how did it come up?"

"Sergeant Rhames . . . I can't divulge any specific conversations I had with Maggie Lewis. Not even in the event of her death. What I can tell you is that she had no plan, to my knowledge, to do this. I assessed her as not at risk to harming herself or others."

Rhames gives a thoughtful grunt. "Yeah, these things are . . . Well, listen, Dr. Lindman, I understand the confidentiality. But the victim didn't leave a note. She didn't tell anyone she was going to do this. I, ah . . ."

I suddenly put the car in drive, keeping my foot on the brake. "Sergeant, I'll tell you what — I'm going to come down there and speak to you in person. I'll have something for you, something that protects Maggie's privacy, but can maybe give you — and her loved ones — some of the insight they're looking for."

He sounds relieved. "That would be much appreciated." He adds, "Sorry to spoil your vacation."

I hang up and turn around on the road, thinking, *It was already going downhill.*

CHAPTER ELEVEN

Rhames is covering his butt, plain and simple. Sometimes a homicide can be manipulated to look like a suicide, even a hanging. Maggie had a child, for one thing — what if that child was threatened? It's an incredible longshot and a scenario I'm sure in my gut isn't so. But for a thorough guy like Rhames to get the word from the decedent's therapist that she was depressed and batted around the suicide idea from time to time? It could help him close out a case.

Paul questions me and Joni seems to pout, but Michael is genuinely concerned. "That's a terrible situation. I'm sorry."

"Thank you." I look at the three of them, my husband in his grass-stained white socks, my daughter and her fiancé still in their bathing suits, wrapped in beach towels. "We'll celebrate when I get back, all right? I'm so sorry."

Paul looks at his watch. "When do you think that will be?"

"Well, it's what — two o'clock now? By the time I drive down there, go to the station, give my statement and all of that, it will be too late to drive back. I'll get up and come back early in the morning."

I already thought about this. I could come back tonight, and under different conditions, I probably would. But

Rhames's conscience and close-out rate isn't the only reason I'm going. The tragic situation provides me an opportunity — to look through my notes on Tom Bishop and make a couple more calls. Maybe even talk to the Bleekers.

Paul glances at the kids. "I guess we'll have to survive without you for a little while." He comes forward and gives me a hug, busses my cheek. "Love you, honey."

Joni is next, throwing her arms around my neck. She's like a cold fish, goosebumps on her skin. For a moment, she hangs some of her weight on me, and I'm transported back to her early childhood. "I'm sorry, Mom."

"*I'm* sorry," I say. "We should be celebrating tonight. But we will as soon as I get back."

Joni lets go and Michael gives me a pursed-lip smile. I move closer and pat his arm. "Lucky for you, my daughter can cook."

"Michael is actually great in the kitchen," Joni says. "He'll probably be the one cooking tonight." She stares at him with pure adoration.

Michael is an enigma. There's no discerning deceit in his sea glass–colored eyes. But something about their sheen, the way his skin frames them beneath the heavy eyebrows, it's like they're designed to be provocative.

I just can't register his intent, and I'm usually pretty good at reading people.

How much is he aware of? How much is intentional? Does he know what I'm planning to do right now?

Give it a rest. He can't read your mind.

"All right, here I go."

I've changed clothes and packed a small bag. My phone in hand, bag in the other, I walk to the Range Rover. Once inside it, I'm backing out and waving as I do. The three of them have come to the doorway to see me off.

When I turn around and begin trundling down the dirt driveway, I'm almost relieved to be away from them.

Why? Because I feel guilty. Because I was raised to believe that even a small untruth — whether by omission or a little white lie — dirties the soul. At least, an unclear conscience can be a troubling thing.

That doesn't mean anyone should expect themselves to be perfect. Part of the trick is to forgive ourselves the transgressions, especially when they're truly meant to serve a greater good. The problem is, for some people, such transgressions are not always for a nobler cause. They're a means to avoid something or hide something.

And sometimes — oftentimes, really — the transgressions that get buried stay buried. And lost. That's what therapy — the talking cure — is about. Waking up those memories, digging through the past to ferret out the unclean moments.

Not to get too grandiose about it, but it's a lot like religious confession. The patient is the sinner, seeking forgiveness.

Only, if you don't know your sins or you're in denial of them, it's hard for the cleansing to work. Impossible, really.

So therapy frequently begins with that examination of one's past. It's how it began with me, anyway. Like many therapists, I started out as a patient, wrestling with my own troubled soul. My father, before his untimely death, had grown up an only child. By his teens, he was drinking and smoking and falling in with the wrong crowd. His father had died young too, in the war, to leave my father and his mother in a crowded apartment complex in Yonkers. Roy started drinking in his teens and was a problem drinker by twenty, though he managed to get a decent job and marry my mother, Eloise — a much more sheltered person, but also an only child.

Eloise never learned how to stand up for herself. Roy's descent into drinking and health problems took its toll on her and on me. By the time I was ready to start dating, I'd already decided men were scary and unpredictable, and I wasn't safe around them.

I met Paul at the New School in Manhattan. He was so easygoing and unassuming I thought it had to be an act. For the first six months that we dated, I was on pins and needles, waiting for the facade to drop and Paul to pick up a bottle — to start talking with his fists.

But he never did.

Paul's easiness didn't convince me of what it should have — that not all men are horrible. Instead, the incongruence had a different effect. Paul made my father seem worse than he already was. The more men I encountered who were less afflicted and temperamental, the more they seemed like anomalies.

I didn't know where to put that. I didn't know how to deal with it, so I rejected Paul. One night, a time I'll never forget, he stood outside my apartment in the pouring rain. Just like in the movies. And he pleaded with me, water running down his thin face, his eyelids fluttering. He begged me to reconsider. Whatever he'd done wrong, he said, he'd fix it.

His behavior turned something in me cold and furious. Seeing him like that, I suddenly judged him as weak. As pathetic. I didn't want anything to do with a man like that. I needed someone strong, like my father. And to show my own strength, I lashed out. I hit Paul. The one and only time I'd hit another adult human being.

Shocked, bewildered, Paul stumbled back. Blood from the corner of his mouth mixed with rainwater and coursed down his jaw and dripped. He touched the blood, looked at it, looked at me, and left.

That night, alone in my apartment with the rain slamming down, I contemplated my life's worth. What had I done? I was becoming my father. Violent and obsessed with vigilance.

Somewhere near the end of my purgatory, I got a phone call. It was my mother. My father had suffered a major heart attack in the night and died.

The timing, it seemed, was auspicious. Here I was going through this painful realization — a kind of metamorphosis — that I had to grow out of my father's influence. And in the midst of that, he had departed.

It sent me into a deeper spiral. I raided my roommate's drug stash and took everything I could find. If it was a pill, I swallowed it. But it wasn't enough.

I spent the next few days struggling on the fringes of a private hell, sneaking out to take drugs and carouse the city in an addled haze. I wanted to die. Somehow, though, I stayed alive. I skirted the edge but never went beyond it. And then a friend gave me the name of a trusted therapist.

Sarah was in her fifties, as I am now. She kept her hair natural and it had a lovely silver sheen. She wore simple earrings, two sterling silver hoops, and dressed in elegant, comfortable, earthy clothes. Her office always smelled like jasmine, and she had a therapeutic bag of tricks that worked wonders. Progression, regression, EMDR — you name it, she did it. Through her, I was able to get myself under control and start living my life again.

I visited Sarah once a week for eight months, and then twice a month for about a year after that, gradually reducing it to an as-needed basis. By the time Paul and I were married, I was already considering my own practice. I wanted to help people the way Sarah had helped me. My practice would span from young to old. I would become adept at guiding my patients as they hunted down their traumas and their shames. To get at the roots of their guilty feelings, their anxiety, and often, depression.

Not everyone could trace back their mental discomfiture to some inciting incident, however. I know this. Maggie Lewis had been abused at a young age. That trauma had gone undigested for over a decade. When I first began to see her, she was just twenty-one and had already been on anti-depressants for five years. She wanted out. She said that they ruined her creativity — she was a dancer, and her meds wreaked havoc on her motivation, body, and form.

In order to help her, I knew we needed to get to the trauma of her abuse. We had to do it slowly and carefully. I could only gently guide her — she had to confront it when she was ready.

But we never quite got there.

I tell as much to Sergeant Rhames once I arrive in Westchester and am sitting across from him and another plainclothes officer at the White Plains Police Department.

"And you can't discuss the . . . nature of the abuse with us?" the plainclothes cop asks.

"Not in any detail. Not other than what I've already stated."

The plainclothes cop, an investigator, taps a pen against his lip. "But you're pretty sure that's what drove her to do it. To commit suicide."

"We say 'complete a suicide.'"

He lowers the pen. "Come again?"

"In the mental health field, suicide is part of the diseases of despair. Alcoholism, drug addiction, suicidal ideation. It's a physical health condition. We don't 'commit' a heart attack. Saying it associates blame, like committing a crime or a sin. The stigma can deter people from coming forward who are contemplating suicide. And also, a person may attempt a suicide, but they may not complete it."

The investigator gives Sergeant Rhames a long look, like, *Are you hearing this?*

Rhames is thoughtful, though. "And you said you're pretty sure she wasn't contemplating . . . ah, attempting or completing a suicide."

"In our discussions, no."

"But you could see how she might. The stresses she was under."

"If you're wondering what to tell the family, it's this: Maggie Lewis was an incredibly brave woman. She was fighting to overcome something almost insurmountable. At the same time, she was trying to live her life to her fullest potential. To be an artist, to dance."

Rhames is taking notes.

"She was fighting a disease of despair not of her own making. She didn't ask for her circumstances. But she was doing everything in her power to overcome them. Sometimes we don't make it. But that's not the important part. What's important is how hard we try."

The investigator has his mouth hanging half-open. He suddenly becomes aware of this, closes it and sits up straighter. Rhames finishes his notes, stands, and reaches his hand across the table. "Dr. Lindman, thank you so much."

I shake with him as the investigator stands and offers his own hand. "Yeah, er, ah, if there's anything else, I'll be in touch."

I'm sure.

I leave and head straight for my next destination. Maggie's funeral won't be for a couple of days. If I attend, it will be just by slipping into the back of the church during the service. But I won't go to the wake or burial or mingle at any reception afterwards. To me, that's unprofessional.

Not that what I'm about to do is incredibly high up there on the list of ethical standards. But making a few discreet phone calls to get a little background on my daughter's fiancé, that's understandable, isn't it? Especially if I suspect he's a former patient who witnessed one parent kill another?

Any mother would do the same.

Right?

CHAPTER TWELVE

White Plains is a medium-sized city in the center of Westchester County, just north of New York City. My office shares the third floor of a five-story building with two other offices: a dentist and a realtor. The building is dark, everyone gone home to start the weekend.

The door from the corridor opens onto the room where Mena typically receives my clients, helps with billing, and attends to other administrative duties.

I move through to my office, which fronts Mamaroneck Avenue below. For some reason, I keep the lights off. It's as if I don't want anyone to know I'm here. As if somehow they'll see through to the duplicity.

I'm supposed to be here for Maggie Lewis, but right now, I don't have time to go through two years of notes. And the real reason I'm here, anyway, is the Bishop case.

I sit down hard in my desk chair, the guilt weighting me.

I'm sorry, Maggie . . .

Tears prick the backs of my eyes. I wasn't expecting this, but being in the office has opened me up. I let the emotion wash through me and run its course.

The space is simply arranged: my desk and chair to one side, a pair of facing chairs to the other, and one couch against the back wall. Most patients prefer the chair. Maggie liked the couch — she sat just feet away from where I am now, and not long ago.

I'm so sorry, honey . . .

Maggie was a smoker, and while I didn't allow smoking in my office, I'd let her hold a cigarette. She'd wedge it between her fingers as she talked and waved her hands. When I'd seen her this last time, I'd thought maybe she was cloaking some feelings about her son. She'd left when he was a baby. Instead of being given up for adoption, he'd stayed with the father and the father's family, who helped raise the boy. Maggie never resumed a motherly role. He was now five, and she'd described him almost casually, as if she saw him much more often. How big he was, what he was like.

But never once did Maggie indicate a plan for suicide. It wasn't anywhere on my radar. I'm sure of it. Over the years, I've learned to separate signal from noise with patients, and her signal was clear to me: she was safe from self-harm.

So then — what had I missed?

The answer: I don't know. Maybe nothing. Therapists aren't omniscient. We're certainly not omnipresent; I was in Maggie's life roughly once a month for two years. I have to let it go. I have to get down to what I'm here for.

I wipe the drying tears from my face and return to Mena's room. In the back is a small walk-in closet, choked with file cabinets and boxes. It's hot in there, no windows and no AC, and smells like paper and mildew. It takes me a few minutes to move things around, dig out the box from fifteen years ago.

I take it to my office and start finger-walking through the file tabs until I find it — Bishop.

My official evaluation isn't here, nor are records of Tom Bishop's final statement to police, because they've been sealed by a judge, so I'm not expecting those. But I've got five sessions annotated and accounted for. And I've got a list of collaterals, meaning other people in Tom's life. The Bleekers are there.

I'm not sure whether to be glad or worried about that.

Seated back at my desk, I dial the number. The other end rings.

And rings, and rings. No voicemail or answering machine, just an endless ringing.

I hang up, check that I've got the right number, and try again.

While I'm listening through the second round, my gaze falls on the file.

There's an address.

It looks like my road trip will extend a bit farther.

* * *

It starts to rain as I drive out to Long Island. Paul has checked in with me twice via text: *Everything all right?* And later, *Things still good?*

I have to dial up my wipers as the rain comes harder. Driving out to Long Island is always an adventure. As the name suggests, it's one long island, but there always seem to be a million lane changes and highway switches to get to any one destination from Westchester. It's already going on seven p.m. — getting late to be showing up at someone's door. And I have no idea what awaits. Will Arnold Bleeker remember me from the courtroom? Will he tell me that a grown-up Tom lives on the other side of the world somewhere? Or that he's maybe living happily nearby with a couple of kids and wife who bakes and sews?

The drive takes over an hour, plenty of time for me to cycle through a dozen scenarios and rehearse what I'm going to say when I get — I hope — the reasoned answer I'm seeking. The GPS guides me to the small seaside town of Sayville, then through a residential neighborhood. The homes are charming, simple two-story structures at first, but become more expansive as I near the water. Greene Ave comes to an end at the water's edge: the Atlantic Ocean. I know I'm facing south, and somewhere in the distance is Fire

Island, known for its wild summer parties. But now, in the overcast and rain twilight, the sea is rough; frothy and dark.

I don't move, letting the rain drum on the car.

The house is large but quaint. The main structure has a gambrel roof, like a barn's. It's a common style in the region, arguably made famous by the movie *Amityville Horror*. In the daylight, the siding might be a dusty blue. A good color for a beach home, which the house tries to be, despite its multiple additions and two-car garage.

The windows are dark. Not a good sign. The Bleekers are not much older than I am, but some people like to go to bed early.

It's now or never. I leave the car and lock it up. I'm almost instantly soaked as I cut across the lawn and up the short steps to the small porch framing the entryway. There's a doorbell, but I decide to knock first. I strain to listen, hearing nothing but the pounding surf to my left, the rain hitting the roof above me.

This is crazy.

What in God's name are you doing here?

I knock again and wait. No reaction. Not a light that's come on, nor the vibration of movement. Just the rhythmic white noise of the ocean . . .

I want my mommy back . . .

My heart skips a beat and my breath trembles. I know what I've just heard is a memory of the strange message on my phone — or a memory of the voice I *thought* I heard in the message on my phone. But it takes me a moment to banish my nerves. To help restore a sense of reality, I reach out and hit the doorbell.

It does the trick, piercing my delusion. The ringing is loud inside — maybe one of the Bleekers is hard of hearing? The neighborhood seems middle class with year-round, not seasonal, residents. But homes like this one nearer the water are a bit more expensive, so it could be seasonal, and no one is here now.

I give it one more ring, letting my finger hold the button just a hair past comfortable. The rain, at least, has let up a little since I've been standing here. Suddenly, I'm self-con-scious. I study the New Balance sneakers on my feet, blue and gray. I'm in twill shorts and a linen blouse. Casual but respectable. An unthreatening, sopping wet woman; but one who's, in the moment, also grippingly paranoid.

Because this is lunacy. You need to ask Michael about himself, not sneak around like some private investigator.

It gives me an idea.

I'm about to turn away, thinking of someone I ought to call, when a light snaps on over my head.

CHAPTER THIRTEEN

Arnold Bleeker peers out at me with dark eyes hooded by sagging skin. He's even older than I expected, and frail. "Hello? Can I help you?"

"Mr. Bleeker?"

"Yes?"

"Arnold Bleeker?"

"Have I won something?"

His delivery is so dry, I take the question at face value. "No, I'm sorry I . . ."

Then he cracks a smile, and the expression de-ages him. He's not so old now. Maybe it was the porch light shining down, creating shadows. "I'm just kidding. What can I do for you? Who are you?"

"Mr. Bleeker, I know this is highly unusual. I'm Doctor Emily Lindman."

I wait for a sign of recognition. Bleeker wears sweatpants and a sagging, oversized polo shirt. I get the sense he's been sick. Or maybe just lost a lot of weight.

When he doesn't seem to recall my name I say, "I'm a psychologist. I work in White Plains."

He blinks. It's unclear whether the additional information has jogged any memory of me. But he says, "You're soaking wet. Let's get off the porch."

"Oh, thank you."

He opens the door wider so I can enter. "Quite a storm," he says. "I'd take your coat, but you don't have one. How about a towel?"

"Sure. That would be great. I'm so sorry to intrude. And I really hope I didn't wake you . . ."

I'm not sure if he hears me. He's moving deeper into the house, and he turns on a lamp as he goes. It's ornate, stained glass but doesn't offer much light. It sits on a table that's behind a couch. The couch is part of an arrangement of furniture forming a living room heavy with shelves and bric-a-brac. Figurines. Dozens of them. Easing a little closer, I can make them out — all manner of pigs.

Bleeker has disappeared down a hallway. Another light comes on, presumably in the bathroom. Stairs go up to a second floor. Directly to my left is a dining room, an elegant table with high-backed chairs. More shelves of knick-knacks (more pigs) surround it, but there's also a double window overlooking the ocean. It must be cracked open, since the curtains are blowing.

The smell of sea air rides the intermittent breeze coming in, but it's not enough to cut through the mildew. The place is gloomy. I imagine Tom Bishop coming here after his father's death and his mother's imprisonment. One day, he's a happy boy in a normal life. The next he's a witness to mariticide and shortly thereafter starts a new life with virtual strangers. At least, that's the information I've been working with.

Bleeker comes shuffling back. Once again, he strikes me as frail. Unwell. He's got a towel in his grip, and he's staring at it like he's perplexed. "I'm not sure what condition this is in," he says, then hands it to me.

I hesitate. *Condition*?

Smiling sheepishly, he explains, "I didn't want to give you one of the ones hanging in there. But Candace does the laundry. That one's clean; it just might be a little mildewed. Tough here to keep things dry, living so close to the water."

I wonder who Candace is — housekeeper? Daughter? — as I blot my face with the towel. It does smell a little musty, but there's a fresh detergent scent beneath. I dry my hair, dab along my arms and bare legs. "Thank you so much."

"I didn't hear you," he said. "I was in the back. I like to listen to music. We don't . . . Alice took care of all of that. How to use these listening gadgets. We sold the old component system. I still have the record player, but no speakers for it, no amp. She got into playing music on the internet. Had some kind of hook up, and Candace has tried to show me. But I just use my phone." He pulls it out of his pocket, ear buds still attached.

He looks at me with his dark, shining eyes. "Alice died. Two years ago."

"Oh . . . I'm so sorry."

"Did you know her?"

"I . . . Can we sit down?"

"Of course, here, this way."

He leads me to the living room, where I sit on the edge of the coffee table to keep the furniture dry. He takes the chair between two couches. There are pigs embroidered on the throw pillows. I give myself a little shake and focus on him.

"Mr. Bleeker, I was your nephew's therapist once — very briefly."

Bleeker's mouth opens a little. A soft breath escapes him. For a moment, he just stares, unresponsive. "Oh . . . Dr. Lindman, you said?"

I nod. I'm fairly certain we never spoke before this, but he surely must've learned my name back then.

His brow creases with concern. "What brings you all the way here? Is Thomas all right?"

I place the towel in my lap. "Have you heard from him recently?"

"No. Not for a long time."

"He just . . . left?"

"Well, you could say that. Thomas and Alice — my wife — they had a hard time getting along. He sort of . . . He left just after he turned eighteen."

"I'm sorry to hear there was trouble. And then — did you correspond with him at all?"

Bleeker looks down at his enfolded hands. "No. Which was very hard. I wanted to reach out to him, but Alice got sick. We thought it was early onset dementia, but it was Alzheimer's. It devastated us. Even her sister — Laura. They were very close. Both of them liked to collect things." He studies the pigs a moment, finally concluding, "It was a terrible time, but at least it went quickly at the end."

I tell Bleeker again how sorry I am. The gloom in this house is starting to feel like a living thing. I have the need to hurry along; I'm poking around where I don't belong. I want to ask about Laura — I want to ask a lot of things, but I settle on what seems most prescient. "You call him Thomas," I say. "Did you ever hear that he changed his name?"

"Changed his name?"

"Yes. First and last."

"We changed his name. I adopted him and he was Thomas Bleeker . . ." Arnold Bleeker gets a worried look, a suspicion in his squint. "What's this? Has something happened? I've tried for a couple of years to find him, but Laura didn't know, and the Thomas Bleekers I can locate on the computer always turn out to be someone else."

I raise my hands in peace. "I'm sorry, the last thing I want to do is alarm you. I have no reason to believe anything bad happened to your nephew. I'm here because a young man recently showed up in my life and he reminds me of him. Very much. But he said he was someone else. Michael Rand."

That's it. That's what I rehearsed for an hour. Best, I decided, to stay simple. And as close to the truth as possible.

Bleeker's scowl deepens. "He said he was *who*?"

"He called himself Michael Rand." My next move is quick. "Mr. Bleeker, do you have any photo albums I could look through? Anything recent — before Tom left?"

But Bleeker makes no reply. Instead he just stares at me, one of his eyes twitchy. "What are you doing here?"

The question throws me for a moment. "I'm trying to confirm if the man I know as Michael Rand is your adopted son, Thomas, or if this is all just a big coincidence. If I'm staking way too much on the way I remember someone looking. I know it's inappropriate, and I'm sorry. This situation just arose this morning and I'm . . . I'm just trying to sort things out so I can move on." I smile, hoping for empathy.

Bleeker stays eye-locked on me. His Adam's apple bobs with a dry swallow. Then he points. "You're the one."

"I'm sorry?"

"Why are you here?"

"I'm sorry. I don't understand. I told you that I'm . . ."

Bleeker stands, still pointing a crooked finger at me. His whole demeanor has changed; he's now rigid and hostile. "You need to go."

I stand too, slowly, cautiously, so as not to alarm him further. "Mr. Bleeker, I'm very sorry if I've upset you . . . As I told you, I was the psychologist who worked with Tom after his father's death. Is that what you mean? I'm 'the one?'"

Bleeker's mouth quivers with emotion. He can barely get out the words. "It took me a minute, but I recognize you. And I remember what happened." Bleeker suddenly straightens his spine and puffs his bony chest. "You need to get out right now. What is the reason for this? You want to check on me, see what I might remember? Just get out."

"Sir — I'm so sorry if I've upset you. I don't know what I've said or done that . . . If I could just leave my card, it has my number on it . . ."

"Out!"

His voice is like a crack of thunder in the humid house. I quickly leave the card, drop the towel on the nearest chair, and get moving. I reach the door and grab the handle, turn back for one more try. "I really think there's been a mist—"

"Get out of my house!" Bleeker bellows. "Get out or I'm calling the police!"

You don't have to tell me twice. Or three times. I'm out the door, and I leave it swinging in the breeze. I take the wet steps carefully, trying not to slip, and I'm about to cross the lawn to my car when I'm captured by bright lights.

I stop abruptly and put my hand in the air.

"Hey!" It's a younger man's voice. I can hear an engine. Someone has just pulled into the driveway, but I can't see past the blinding lights. A door slams. There's a flash of a silhouette and footfalls approaching fast.

My heart leaps into my throat and I rush for my car.

But I don't make it. The man grabs me, and I scream.

CHAPTER FOURTEEN

POLICE REPORT
INVESTIGATORS R. MOONEY and S. STARZYK
WITNESS INTERVIEW TRANSCRIPT (PARTIAL):
THOMAS BRADLEY BISHOP
APRIL 29

Mooney: And then what did you see? You snuck out of your room to—

Tom: I heard bad fighting.

Mooney: Right. Yes. Did you go to the kitchen? Is that where the fighting sounds were coming from?

[Silence.]

Planski: Go ahead, honey.

Tom: It was coming from different places.

Mooney: The fighting?

[Silence.]

Mooney: You can't nod, okay, Tommy? We need you to say "yes."

Tom: Yes.

Mooney: Do you mean you think there were multiple people? Tom? Do you think more than one person was fighting with your dad?

[*Silence.*]

Mooney: Did you see them? Tom, it's very important . . . Did you see who was fighting with your dad?

[*Silence.*]

Mooney: For the tape, the witness has indicated in the negative. Okay, Tom . . . So then what happened? Try to tell me. You left your room when you heard the fighting. Right? Where did you go first?

Tom: I don't remember.

Mooney: You don't rem—

Tom: The stairs.

Mooney: You went to the stairs?

Tom: The top of the stairs. I can look down from the top of the stairs.

Mooney: You're talking about the stairs that come down from your bedroom, right? They go into the kitchen?

Tom: They have all the clocks. All the clocks are on the stairs.

Mooney: Right . . . hanging on the wall going down the stairs. Your dad liked clocks?

Tom: My mom does.

Mooney: Oh, your mom. Okay. So from the stairs, you can see the clocks. And also, a little bit, the open doorway into the kitchen. Isn't that right?

Tom: Uh-huh.

Mooney: Did you see anything? Did you go the rest of the—

Tom: I went the rest of the way down. I was quiet.

Mooney: Yeah, you were kind of sneaking?

Tom: Yeah.

Mooney: And then what happened? I know we've done this a couple of times already. And now it's been a while. But it's very important — it's so important, Tom — that we know what happened to your daddy. He would want you to—

Planski: Investigator Mooney, if you could please stick to the line of questioning.

Mooney: I just need you to tell me what you remember, as best as you can. Okay?

[Silence.]

Tom: I sat on the stairs. It sounded like people were fighting all over. And I looked into the kitchen but didn't see anyone. Then I came all the way down the stairs. Everything got quiet. But I . . . And then I . . .

[Indistinguishable noises.]

Planski: It's okay, Tom. Here, I have some Kleenex somewhere . . . All right, I think we're going to have to—

Mooney: What, Tom? And then you what?

Tom: I don't know. My mom . . .

Mooney: What about your mom?

Planski: I'm going to ask that we end this interview. Tom is clearly upset.

Mooney: Okay, okay. I know. You're right. But he's . . . It's right there. Tom? Did you see who hurt your father?

Tom: He was on the ground. Like he was sleeping. But there was blood everywhere.

Planski: Detective Mooney? I'm asking—

Mooney: And your mother?

Tom: Holding him. Like he was a baby.

Mooney: Oh, Christ. Tom, I'm sorry, Tom. Don't you have any more of those tissues?

Planski: Okay. Okay, that's it. Officer Mooney? That's it.

Mooney: I'm sorry — okay. Tom . . . it's okay, Tom . . .

* * *

ACCOMPANYING MEMO TO DISTRICT ATTORNEY'S OFFICE

INVESTIGATOR R. MOONEY

APRIL 29

It is the opinion of this investigator that either the witness, Thomas Bishop, is afraid to express what he saw in the final moments of his father's life or, having seen something particularly upsetting, he's blocked it out. It is my strong rec-ommendation, in light of this, that we hire an outside coun-selor or therapist to evaluate Tom. Perhaps work with him to unearth any repressed memories. As our only witness to the murder of David Bishop, Tom is critical to the prosecution.

Signed,
Rebecca Mooney

CHAPTER FIFTEEN

When the man grabs me, I go for my pepper spray — but of course I don't have it. I haven't carried it since my days attending college in the city, decades ago. Instead, I wrench free of his grip and keep going for my car.

The rain has slowed but the front lawn is soaked, my quick feet squishing the wet grass. To my right, past the end of the road, the ocean pounds. Harder than before, it seems, with fury.

I reach the car and I dig for my keys in the pocket of my shorts. It's only as I unlock and open the car door that I risk looking back.

The man is standing in the drizzle. He's not much older than my Sean, maybe thirty. A young woman grips his arm, as if holding him back. The details of their faces are hard to make out — but I think I've seen her before.

Candace.

Old man Bleeker stands just outside the front entrance. I hear his voice but can't make out the words over the angry surf. Whatever he says, it gets the attention of the two on the lawn, and they start toward him. The man looks over his shoulder at me as they go.

Part of me — the rational part, you might say, the part who was raised by parents big on manners and etiquette and which-fork-goes-with-which-dish — wants to walk back across the lawn and make amends. But clearly I've upset Arnold Bleeker. I've upset him to the point of him kicking me out. So maybe now is not the time.

And here I am, in Sayville, on Long Island, when my family is in Upstate New York. I'm supposed to have left them to assist police in understanding the suicide of a young woman who happened to be one of my patients.

It's over. Time to go.

I get into the Range Rover, start the engine, and pull a U-turn in the road. I glance at the house as I roar past in the other direction. The three of them are all still standing there; their heads turn in unison as they watch me leave. At the last second, Candace gives me a one-finger salute.

* * *

With a little time and distance — ten minutes and fifteen miles — I'm thinking more clearly. Arnold Bleeker seems to have confused my inquiries about Tom with something else, perhaps some kind of conspiracy playing in his head. Given the difficult subject matter — having your sister-in-law sent to prison for murdering her husband, then raising her son, which led to conflict with your now-departed wife — anyone could understand that. Bleeker needs someone to blame.

The other thing that comes to me: *Candace does the laundry.*

I hadn't remembered about the Bleekers having a daughter, but that was likely her. Maybe the man was her husband, and he was just being protective. I could see how it looks: It's dark and rainy, and I'm some stranger running from the house while their frail father stands in the doorway, visibly upset.

Still — the way the man grabbed me . . .

67

I rub my arm and give it a quick glance. I might even have a bruise there. How am I going to explain that to Paul?

After another minute of sulking, I pick up my phone from the passenger seat and plug it in. The Range Rover has a hands-free system, and in seconds, I'm listening to a phone ring through the speakers.

After the fifth ring: "Hello? Emmy?"

"Hi, Frank," I say. "Didn't think you were going to pick up, so I was planning out my message."

"If you want, you can call back and I won't answer."

His humor is dry, reminding me of Arnold Bleeker — *Have I won something?*

I chuckle; it sounds a little more manic than I'd like. "I think I can improvise," I say. "How are you doing?"

"Ah, can't complain. Busy. You?"

"Yeah, busy. We're on vacation, though. Taking our week up at the lake house."

"Oh, good for you . . . You sound like you're driving, though."

"You are quite the investigator." It's an attempt at a joke that winds up sounding sarcastic. "Sorry," I say quickly. "I'm just . . . I'm not up there, actually. I had to come back down to the office."

"Uh-oh."

"I had a patient die from suicide."

"Ah, man."

"It's a terrible thing. And I needed to speak to White Plains Police about it."

"Yeah, right. Sure."

"But listen — everything's good with you? How are the wife and kids?"

This joke lands better; Frank has never been married.

"Just the way I like 'em," he says.

"Ah, someday, Frank. Someday. You'll meet the right one."

He laughs. "I'm almost sixty."

"Sixty is the new twenty."

"Jesus," he says, "isn't that a sobering thought?"

It's enough small talk. I'm feeling a little more comfortable. My hands on the wheel, ten and two, I drive the Long Island Expressway, the road shining wet, post-downpour. Traffic is surprisingly light for eight p.m. on a Friday, headed toward the city. Like everyone is somewhere else.

"Hey, so, I'm wondering if you can check on a phone number for me. A weird call I got. Are you . . . Think you can swing that?"

"I'll give it a shot. What's the number?"

I give him the digits, and he says, "Okay. I'll let you know. That it?"

I've known Frank Mills for over thirty years, and he's known me. He knows that's not it.

We met when he was a rookie New York cop and I was a graduate student in the city. For the last several years, he's been on his own as a private investigator. He says he does it for the money, but I know how good a New York cop's pension is and how little money Frank, a perennial bachelor with cheap tastes, needs to live. Frank does it because it's in his blood. Without the occasional gig for a divorce lawyer, or running down cheating husbands, or the odd job to see if a workman's comp claimant was waterskiing in the Bahamas instead of hobbling around on crutches, Frank would go stir crazy.

"No," I say. "That's not it."

He listens to my story — it doesn't take long, maybe just a minute, to tell — and then says, "Yeah. Wow. That's a pickle."

Only Frank would say *that's a pickle.* He's born-and-bred New York, with an old-school heart.

"It's driving me crazy," I say.

"I mean . . . You could always ask him."

"Gee, ya think?"

"Well, I'm not saying it would be easy. Maybe he doesn't remember. Anyway, the real question is, does it matter? Does Joni seem happy?"

69

"It's Joni. She's seemed happy with every guy she's brought home."

"Yeah, but she hasn't been engaged to any of them."

"Not that I'm aware of." I suddenly feel like having a cigarette. It's been over ten years, but I can taste it. Maybe it's talking to Frank. His gravelly voice. I think I can hear him puffing on his own — it's in the pauses, the exhalations.

"So you think the phone call is related?"

"It could be. Yeah, for sure."

"Listen," he says, "I'll check into it."

"Yeah?"

"Yeah."

"Frank, you're a good friend."

"I'll give you my 'good friend' rate." He laughs, because he's not going to charge me anything.

"It'll just be quick," I say, suddenly needing to reassure him. Or maybe myself.

"One thing I've learned in this business? Everything takes longer than expected."

"I hear you. Of course, that's life in general, isn't it?"

"Yeah, true."

The conversation is winding down. Then Frank says, "You know, I remember that whole thing. That was a heck of a case. Mooney worked that one, right? Rebecca Mooney? And maybe Steve Starzyk. They seemed to have it in for the wife. There was all this other stuff — neighbor saw an unfamiliar car, the back gate was broken from the outside, and then the rear entrance jimmied open. Said it took a lot of strength."

"I guess that was all staged. By her."

Frank is quiet. "What was her name . . . Lori?"

"Laura."

"Laura, right. So it was her? She beat him up with a bat?"

"Hammer."

"Oh, right. And so . . . and so that's it, huh? Oh, man — the kid saw it?"

"Frank . . ."

He hears it in my voice: I can't discuss those details. Even now. And naming his mother as the murderer is under judicial seal. Sworn testimony. There was no courtroom moment when he pointed her out; it was all behind the scenes. Deals made in cool offices by men and women in stiff suits.

"Yeah," Frank says about confidentiality. "Of course. Sorry. I—"

He's cut off by an incoming call on my end, another number I don't recognize. I tell Frank I need to take it. But before switching over, I get in one last quick question. "You said a neighbor saw a strange car? Were there any more details than that?"

"Nah, I don't think so. Just that there was supposedly this guy outside, sitting in his car, right around the time of the murder."

"Where'd you hear it?"

"You know . . . around. Now we're talking about confidentiality on *my* end."

"Maybe it was a friend of Laura Bishop's who did the staging part."

"There ya go." He pauses, then, "Hey, keep your chin up, kiddo. I'll be in touch."

"Thanks, Frank."

I switch calls, my intuition up: I think I know who this is going to be.

"Hello?"

"Is this Dr. Lindman?"

"Yes."

A pause. Then, "It took us twenty minutes to calm my father down — he's not a well man to begin with. What exactly did you say to him? What were you even doing at my *house*? Who sent you?"

It must be Candace. I left my business card in the living room . . .

"I'm very sorry," I begin. "I had a few questions that—"

"You come near my family again, I'll have you arrested. You understand me? Leave us alone, you *bitch*."

She hangs up.

CHAPTER SIXTEEN

The Bleeker family thinks I've done something. Sure, they're a bit weird — all those ceramic pigs in that house on the edge of oblivion, sea air making everything damp and baggy. They've been through a lot — anyone could understand that. Arnold Bleeker even seems unwell, perhaps turning his daughter overprotective . . .

But they definitely think I did something.

Me and some other people.

I'm part of "them."

It's troubling, but it's also very interesting, giving me the beginnings of a direction. How, perhaps, to proceed with this thing.

When I get back to my office in White Plains, I raid the cabinet in the kitchenette and find a bottle of gin. Tanqueray. What my mother used to drink. I pour myself a stiff one. Leaving the lights off, I sit on the leather couch in the dark. The blinds on the window make slatted shadows across the floor. Outside, the traffic rolls up and down Mamaroneck Avenue.

The sudden knock on the door startles me. Someone is in the corridor. I set my drink down and rise to my feet. As I approach, I hear the jingle of keys. I unlock the bolt but keep the chain on. With the door ajar, I peer out.

"What are you doing here?" I say, sliding back the chain.

Mena comes in when I open up, her shoulders hunched, full of tension. But that's just kind of how she moves about.

"I saw your car in front," she says.

We walk together into the main office. I struggle with the question: "So, what . . . what are you . . . ?"

"I couldn't sleep," Mena says.

I offer her to sit on the couch. She glances at my drink on the side table. "Would you like one?"

"Oh, no," she says, her hands on her knees. "No, thank you. Or maybe a little one. Just a little."

The kitchenette is next to the bathroom; a sink and two cupboards, a microwave. *This is completely odd.* I unscrew the cap, get a glass from the cupboard and ice from the small fridge. I pour a finger, then walk it over to Mena. "You sure you're all right?"

"I'm okay. Yes. Thank you." She pushes her straight black hair back from her face and takes the glass. She sips primly. Mena is Filipina. Perfect dark hair and large dark eyes. Her bone structure is exquisite, with wide cheekbones and a tapered chin. She's small, barely five foot five, and is often fragrant with some coconut perfume or deodorant, as she is tonight, though I can see the dampness around her hair line, and her upper lip — she's also been perspiring. She asks, "Were you able to find Mr. Bleeker?"

"I did," I say, sitting down in my chair. I cross my legs and take another drink. Despite Mena's uncharacteristic behavior, I'm feeling more comfortable now. This is my usual role.

"What did he say?" Mena asked.

I tell her the story while minimizing the emotional impact it had on me. Still, she listens with wide eyes. When I'm finished, she drinks her gin with both hands and sets the empty glass on the coffee table in front of her. Not only is it unusual for Mena to be up at this hour, it's rare for her to drink. She has difficulty metabolizing alcohol — too much raises her blood pressure and fatigues her.

"Okay," I say. "What's going on?"

"It's just . . . I feel terrible."

"About?"

"What happened to Maggie."

"I know. I do, too."

Mena says it's why she's not at home in bed. She's been out driving through the city, and she made her way back to the office without thinking too much about it.

As she says it, her eyes flick to the file box on my desk. I've left it out from earlier. Files on the Bleekers, not Maggie.

"Anyway," she says. "I'm feeling better now." She lifts her thin eyebrows. "Did you find the case notes you were looking for?"

"I did. Mena . . . do you want to talk about it? Maggie?"

Her otherwise smooth brown skin dimples with a frown. "No. I don't think so. But what about you? Can I help *you* with anything?"

"I'm fine. You should go home, though. Don't worry about me."

She's dubious, but gets to her feet. "All right . . ."

After assuring her again that everything is going to be all right and thanking her, I walk her down to the street and see her off.

And maybe I don't know if things are going to be all right, and maybe I feel a little bit bad for not including Mena in more of what's going on. But I've become good at compartmentalizing.

* * *

The night has cooled some but is still thick with humidity. I have a couple of texts from Paul I need to answer, but they can wait. It's my turn to wander the city — though I'm more conscious of where I'm going once I get back to the car and get moving. The Bronx River Parkway has light traffic. The Range Rover's headlights probe the semidarkness as it hugs the serpentine, southbound highway. I know this route like the back of my hand.

As I drive, I contemplate the way we compartmentalize ourselves. "Dissociate" is the word. As in "dissociative identity disorder." DID. At a recent training I attended, the keynote speaker theorized that all of us are actually on a spectrum of DID, in a sense. We all dissociate from things in our lives, from memories and past traumas, to some extent. Most of the time, we're completely unaware we're doing it. By how much, that varies among us.

A little later, I'm driving through sleepy Bronxville, the Tom Bishop file on the seat beside me. The stores are dark along the main drag. I make a left turn up the hill into one of the residential areas. Pondfield Road. In about a mile, I'm slowing down in front of a house.

But it's not my house. Instead, I've driven to the place that once belonged to David and Laura Bishop. Two managers: a hedge fund manager and an artists' manager. Both working in Manhattan.

The house is big, white with black shutters. Only the upper story is visible over the juniper penning the yard.

It's been fifteen years since the Bishops lived here with their son, Tom. The boy who saw his mother brain his father with a hammer, killing him.

At least, that's what Tom eventually told me.

And it's what sent Laura Bishop to prison for murder.

But — maybe it was the look in Arnold Bleeker's eyes, or Frank's memory of a man sitting outside the Bishop house in a car, just about where I am now — I'm starting to see a whole new picture forming.

CHAPTER SEVENTEEN

I sit watching the house for a minute. A few upstairs windows are softly lit. A walkway winds out of sight, decorated with ground lights. I find myself drifting back in time, back to when Tom first entered my office, and my life. His downcast eyes, his shoulders slumped. It had been six months since his father's murder. Where had he been all that time? I try to remember if he'd gone to stay with the Bleekers straightaway or if there was a time he'd still been with his mother.

Maybe it was both. Laura Bishop, before she was arrested, might have gone to Long Island herself. Her Bronxville home would have now been a crime scene, the kitchen floor stained from the brutal slaying of her husband. Splatters of blood would have peppered the kitchen clocks, more flecks dotting the clocks on the staircase wall . . .

You wouldn't stay there with your child. You'd take refuge with family. I just couldn't recall who had been the one to drop Tom off for his sessions. I think I remember a woman.

Alice Bleeker. Dead now, from cancer.

I pick up the file on the passenger seat and leaf through it. Case notes, police reports, even a copy of David Bishop's autopsy . . . I don't remember having that. I slide it out for a closer look and find pictures clipped to the back. It's not pretty. Bishop was hit in the head with a hammer, but not just once. Five times, caving in his skull.

The pictures are the stuff of nightmares. His head, shaved postmortem, looks like cratered asphalt.

I quickly shove the images and documents back in the file and close it up.

Why does an autopsy report accompany my notes on Tom Bishop? It must've been that the police had provided me a copy for context. *This is what the boy saw.*

As I sit there contemplating the horror of it, I get the sense that I'm being watched.

I first check the house, but nothing seems to have changed. The same windows are lighted, and one upstairs window flickers a bit, as if with TV light. The street ahead of me is empty: no one parks on the streets in Bronxville at night.

But then I see it. In the rearview mirror, a car is stopped behind me about forty yards, headlights off. A streetlamp in proximity reveals the shape of a driver at the wheel.

Gut reaction: I grab the shifter and put the car in drive. But before my foot leaves the brake and hits the gas, the door of the car behind me opens and a man steps out.

I'm trapped, too curious to just drive away, even if my heart is now banging my ribs.

The man comes up alongside the driver's side of my car. I let out a shuddering breath, then buzz down the window.

"Evening," he says.

"Hello."

For a few long seconds, we just stare at each other. It's been fifteen years, but both of us are calculating what we see — *whom* we see. He's familiar. He's Mooney's partner.

"Detective Steven Starzyk," he says, holding his hand up to the window.

Of course. I realize the car looks familiar. The shape of it, anyway; the make. Like an unmarked police car.

"You're Dr. Lindman?"

"I am."

We shake and he continues to give me cop-eyes, hunting for my agenda. But he seems satisfied a moment later when he says, "Guess we had the same idea. Or feeling."

I'm not sure what he means. "I haven't been here in a long time."

"Me neither."

He's only kind of handsome, if a little weaselly, his eyes close-set and his nose a bit pinched. His hair is wispy and blond, cut like an aging surfer's. He glances at the house, and his eyes come back to me.

I feel like I'm supposed to say something else. Something better. But before I do, he's looking past me at the passenger seat. "That a file on, ah, the Bishop boy?"

"It is." This is feeling awkward now.

Starzyk's eyes narrow and his tone grows authoritative. "Mind if I ask what you're doing here?"

Fine. I give him a version of the story: I'm on vacation upstate, and I just met the man my daughter is dating, Michael Rand, who looks remarkably like an older version of Tom Bishop. The story includes me coming down because of Maggie Lewis, but skips the trip to the Bleeker house on Long Island. "I just . . . I was in my office. I picked up the file. Then I just came by. Trying to remember, I guess."

When I look at his face, I expect Starzyk to give me the expression I've been getting, you know, *stranger things* and *what a coincidence*, but I don't. Starzyk looks a shade paler, his eyes a hue darker. He even takes a half-step back from the vehicle.

"It sounds like you're not aware of it?"

"Aware of what?"

He glances at the house and then resumes in a low, grave tone: "Laura Bishop was granted parole. They're letting her out."

It feels like a bomb going off somewhere in the back of my brain. I actually see a hammer swinging down, arcing through the air, blood trailing. David Bishop on the morgue slab, half of his skull bashed in. Little Tom, head hanging, shoulders rounded, as he walked into my office the first day, six months later.

"She's getting *out*?"

Starzyk nods. "The hearing was two months ago. The board reviewed her case and recommended parole."

"Really? So when exactly is she released?" The nuances of parole have always eluded me.

"It's not an exact science," he says. "But today's the eligibility date. I know that much because I had it written down. And it was in the paper this morning. Big headline."

"I didn't, ah . . . We're out of town. I've kind of turned off the world."

"Sure, I get that. But, so, you're telling me Laura Bishop's son is dating your *daughter*?"

"Well, I don't know that it's—"

"And you just met him this morning? I mean, that's something, isn't it? That's *more* than something." His eyes are getting intense, probing me.

"I don't know that it's him," I explain. "Which is the whole thing."

Starzyk makes a face, like *yeah, right*. He gives me the same line about long odds I've been telling myself. And he's talking some more about how Laura Bishop must've charmed the parole board, that she's got all the hallmarks of a psychopath, that she's smart and clever and manipulative.

I let him talk, not saying much myself. Until my own question forms. "And what brings you here tonight, Mr. Starzyk?"

"Like I said, it was in the paper."

"Right, but still . . ."

He shrugs. "I live only thirty minutes from here. And I don't take an August vacation." He looks off, up the street. "Half these houses are empty right now. Not me. I don't have any place to go." When his gaze comes back, he takes out his wallet and hands me a business card. Bureau of Criminal Investigation. "Would you mind doing me a favor? Let me know, okay? Let me know what you find out? If this is the boy."

"Of course." I tuck it into the file, adding, "I hear what you're saying, but it doesn't seem possible. I think I've just been under a lot of pressure. This was a much-needed vacation. I should get back to it."

He looks at me with half-lidded eyes, like he can smell the bullshit. "Sure," he says.

"And what about Detective Mooney?" I ask, smiling. I should stop talking now and leave, but I'm curious. "How come she's not here with us, reliving the old days?"

My smile is not reflected back. "Mooney is no longer with the New York State Police." Starzyk doesn't elaborate. Instead, he pats the side of my car. "Good luck, Dr. Lindman. Keep in touch, okay?"

He walks back to his vehicle.

It's all I can do not to tear on the gas and squeal the tires. Instead, I pull away from the curb as calmly as I can. My own home is nearby, and I'm there in minutes.

The encounter with Starzyk has shaken me up. Once inside, I have a glass of wine to cool my nerves. As I drink, I wonder if Starzyk smelled the alcohol on my breath — the gin from my office.

The urge to smoke hits me again. I wonder if there's a pack of cigarettes hidden somewhere in my large, stately home. Maybe Paul? He quit when I quit. We've left some lights on and I flick on a few more, trying to chase away the bad feelings. I hunt through drawers and cabinets, jacket pockets and basement bins, but come up empty.

"Fuck you," I say suddenly, thinking about Starzyk. I'm normally not profane, even in private, but he really got to me.

My phone buzzes in my pocket. It's so unexpected, I feel my heart pound. A text has just come through.

It's from Frank Mills: *Sent you an email. Check it out.*

CHAPTER EIGHTEEN

Paul and I share a spare bedroom converted into a home office. We've meant to update either Sean's old room or Joni's so we can have separate spaces in the home, but we haven't gotten around to it. I open my laptop, bring up Gmail and check the inbox. The subject line of Frank's message reads *Arizona?*

As a former cop, Frank can pull favors here and there and get access to databases I can't, like the Departments of Public Safety in various municipalities. The best I can to do on my own is check social networks for Michael Rand and Tom Bishop, which didn't yield much.

Frank has already found something more: Thomas R. Bishop, residing in Tucson, Arizona. Twenty-three years old, born on March 4.

It's the right birthday and age. I check the picture — an employee photo, and the quality is less than superb. But, squinting at the screen, I study the young man's face. He's a dead ringer for Michael. And just like Michael, he looks quite plausibly like the grown-up version of the boy I treated fifteen years ago.

Thomas Bishop works for an Amazon shipment facility, primarily driving a forklift. In the photo, he's unsmiling, wearing a bright yellow vest.

Below this, Frank has written: *Arrest record and DMV info forthcoming. — F*

Well, I think, sitting back. *Maybe that's that.*

I wait for the feeling of relief, but it doesn't arrive. My father was often telling me I think too much. It seems an absurd thing to say to someone — how could a person *think* too much — and Roy Graber wasn't exactly the epitome of a calm, unfettered mind.

But I know my thoughts are busy. And right now they won't let go of the encounter with Starzyk, or the fact that Laura Bishop is getting out on parole, and what any of that might mean. Nor can I let go of what Frank said when we reminisced about the Bishop murder case: *They seemed to have it in for the wife.*

If Frank just texted me, he's up. I'm loath to push too hard when he's already doing this for free, but I just need a couple of minutes.

I call Frank, and he answers on the second ring.

"Hey there. Looks like we might be all good?"

"I hope so. I hope so, yeah."

Frank is intuitive. "Uh-oh. What's up?"

I tell him about the encounter with Detective Starzyk and the news about Laura Bishop getting out on parole. "Jeez," Frank says. "Yeah, that is crazy timing. She's out, and this kid who looks like her son shows up right around the same time?"

"I know."

"Hey," Frank says, "You're the head doctor, but let me ask you — is it possible you just read about Bishop getting out? Like you saw it online or at a newsstand, barely registered it, and now you're . . . I don't know the technical term."

"Projecting?" I laugh, but it sounds a bit desperate. "It's a good theory, but I don't think so. I'm not seeing things."

"No, I don't mean that—"

"I know. But there's still the phone call."

"Sorry, yeah, I did check that. I should've included it in the email — the number came back as a prepaid. I can't track it or anything like that, I can only get the carrier and the type. It's a Verizon phone, pay-as-you go. The type used for spam."

I sigh. "All right. I guess that's that. I just . . . Can I ask you one thing?"

"Sure."

"Would it be hard to . . . fake what you showed me? To have a profile of yourself that's made up, got you living in Arizona and all of that?"

"I mean, I've just been on this for a couple of hours. And that was what was there." He pauses. "But it's pretty hard to forge Department of Public Safety records. You'd have to hack into the system. Or maybe know someone inside. It is possible, though."

I nod my head. I become aware I'm biting my fingernails and stop. "All right, well, it sounds like I'm just . . . that this just is some kind of weird coincidence."

When he doesn't answer, I check the phone connection. "Frank?"

"Yeah, sorry . . ."

"What is it?"

"While we're talking, I'm sitting here on my computer. Just for shits and giggles, I checked out where Laura Bishop has been in prison for the past fifteen years."

"And?"

"They bopped her around a bit at the beginning, but she did her last stretch of eleven at the same place. SCI Cold Brook. It's, ah, right up by you."

I know exactly where it is. It's a minimum-security women's prison that's fifteen minutes from the lake house.

"Jesus, Frank."

"Yeah, that's . . ."

He doesn't know what to say, and neither do I. I'm already moving, closing the laptop, shutting off the light, heading downstairs to gather my things.

"Frank," I say as I quickly descend the stairs, "I gotta go."

"Yeah. I guess — wow. Maybe there's something to this."

"Yeah. Thanks."

"Hey — be careful. I'm here if you need me."

"Thank you, Frank."

I hang up as I come into the kitchen. My empty glass of wine sits on the kitchen island. I fill it again as I tell my phone to call the lake house.

"*Calling lake house*," the phone says, and the line starts to ring.

I listen until the machine picks up. The outgoing message was recorded years ago, and Joni's voice has a high, pre-teen pitch. "You've reached the Lindman residence . . . um, please leave a message." Instead of leaving one, I try Paul's cell phone next. He won't have reception at the house, but it seems like they might be out.

His phone goes to voicemail. So does Joni's.

* * *

I'm back on the interstate minutes later, headed north, going as fast as I dare.

A cast of characters caper through my mind as I make the drive back to Lake Placid: Little Tom Bishop, his mother, his dead father. I have the autopsy report, complete with graphic photos of his obliterated head. Like something from some scary gore-fest magazine kids at grade school used to bring around.

With the phone hooked into the vehicle, I try the lake house again. For the third time.

This time, Paul answers. "Hey," he says, sounding sleepy. "How's it going?"

"Where have you been?"

"Huh? Right here. Well — I was working on the boat."

"Where are the kids?"

"What's the matter?" It sounds like he's fully awake now. I picture him sitting up in bed.

"Laura Bishop just got out of prison," I blurt.

84

"She got out of prison? What do you mean? You mean parole?"

"Guess how I found out?" I tell him about Starzyk and even get into what Bleeker told me about the police maybe targeting the wife for the wrong reasons. But Paul isn't as caught up as I am — he's more focused on me.

"Are you driving?"

"Yes. I'm coming home tonight. I'm already past Albany, so don't try and talk me out of it."

"It's after one o'clock, Em. You won't — here — three in the — ning," he says.

"Paul, I'm losing you. Going through a bad spot. But everything is okay?"

I can't make out his reply. "I'll call you back," I say, and then add, loudly — "Just check on Joni, okay?"

I think I hear him affirm that he will, but I can't be sure. I curse the spotty cellular service and hang up. Well, this is what people want when they come up here, anyway. At least some people. Time away from the world. Time to unwind and unplug.

I try to focus on driving. Out here, towns and villages are fewer and farther between, everything growing darker and colder. Before I know it, I'm off the interstate and heading deeper into the mountains.

Joni and Michael have probably been out at some bar, I figure. While our lake house is in a relatively remote location, it's not the Yukon Territory. Lake Placid is touristy and popular, especially in the summer. Paul, who's not really into hiking or camping, likes it for the rustic aspects. Building a boat, chopping some firewood, and he thinks he's Paul Bun—

I slam on the brakes when the shape jumps out at me, but it's too late. The deer is in mid-leap across the winding mountain road when I hit it with the Range Rover. The collision sends it flying up over the hood where it cracks the windshield. I'm flung forward, my arms up to shield my face as the airbag deploys.

The airbag is so powerful, it drives my arms back towards my head, and my watch jams into my cheekbone and scrapes across my skin, drawing blood.

The momentum sends the deer off to my left somewhere — but I can't see anything anyway, not with the airbag filling my vision. All I know is that my foot is still on the brake and the tires are making screeching sounds, but I'm still going forward. Then it feels like the road drops away, and for a moment the Range Rover is airborne. It connects hard with a guard rail, sending me slapping back against the seat, my head whipping against the headrest.

The vehicle thumps over an uneven shoulder as it scrapes along the guard rail and finally comes to a stop.

Somehow, my turn indicator was activated in the commotion, because it's going "tick — tick — tick," while all else goes dead quiet.

The whole thing took two, maybe three seconds, but it seemed to happen both in real time and slow-motion.

I pass out.

PART THREE

CHAPTER NINETEEN

DR EMILY LINDMAN
CASE NOTES
MAY 14
Session 1

Met with Thomas Bishop today for one hour, our first session. I am recording the session as per my usual, plus taking notes, and all will go into the submitted evaluation.

Thomas is eight. He prefers to be called Tom. He is an only child, his parents well-off. He has no history of mental illness and no history of medical issues. From his medical report, Tom scored a ten out of ten on the APGAR scale when born. When he was five, he broke two bones in his left arm after falling from a treehouse on his property. And there's a scar on his inner thigh from falling off a guard rail.

His father has recently been killed in what was apparently an attempted burglary.

Police believe Tom not only saw his father soon after his father succumbed to blunt force trauma to the head, but that he may have witnessed the actual assault. This is due to Tom's own conflicting statements, from when police first spoke with him and his mother on the night of, to an interview the next day with an ad litem present but no mother, to a third interview several months later, again with the ad litem and without his mother. These discrepancies are in the police report and describe that Tom first indicated hearing a commotion and getting out of bed. Later, he states he awoke to the sound of his mother's crying and found her in the kitchen with his father, recently deceased. Finally, Tom states again that he was awakened by what he called "bad fighting" and snuck out of his room.

What I see is a boy in a great deal of grief, who has not yet processed a major trauma in his life. My job here, ultimately, is to determine his state and whether the trauma has overwhelmed him to the point he's either unwilling or unable to consistently recall the events of that night. But I also very much aim to provide Tom with some basic tools to help him begin a healing process.

This first session was a chance for us to get to know each other a bit. I've not given Tom any assignments. He is clearly troubled, but he's not showing any outward signs of phobias, any loss of social function. He's able to answer and ask questions. He makes eye contact, though his gaze skips around. He's nervous, as if he knows that being here could lead to something uncomfortable.

* * *

A concerned motorist is knocking on the glass. "Ma'am? Ma'am, can you hear me?"

I try to speak, but it's as if my lips are numb. I blink at him and nod. The air bag remains inflated in front of me, restricting my movements. Something drips from above my left eye.

The motorist speaks again. "I'm going to open the door, okay?"

My head is throbbing with pulses of dark energy. My neck is stiff, and just the act of nodding has sent bolts of pain down my spine and up to the base of my skull, scorching around my ears. The motorist grabs the door handle and lifts. The door doesn't budge. He's in his twenties, with a beard.

Where am I?

I hit something . . .

"It's stuck," he says. Then he tries again. No good. He looks through the glass at me, desperation filling his eyes in the refracted light of vehicle headlamps. "I can't get a signal," he says, showing me his phone. He starts to say something else but is distracted, looking off. I think I hear an engine, see more headlights.

"Hang on," he says.

Moments later, the sound of shrieking metal brings me back from a kind of shocked stupor. The motorist, along with someone else, is prying open the door with a crowbar. After a minute of work, it finally gives. The door pops open and the fresh night air rushes in.

The motorist reaches for me. The man beside him is older, with white hair and glasses. "Wait a minute," the older man says. "We shouldn't move her." He focuses on me and raises his voice. I can smell mint gum on his breath. And something else, too. A coppery smell, but not on him. On me. Blood.

"Ma'am? Can you move your head?"

I gingerly twist my neck back and forth. The pain is strong, but it feels like strained ligaments, not vertebral. "I think so," I say. My voice surprises me. It sounds like someone else's. Like me, twenty years ago.

Fifteen, maybe.

"Okay," the older man says. "But do you feel like your head and neck . . . ? We don't want to move you if there's any issue . . ."

I start to wriggle out of the car.

The older man steps back. So does the young motorist. I can't spend another minute in this car. The airbag has deflated, at last, and I'm able to swing my legs over and step down, toes to the ground. The two men hover close, arms out, not sure if they should touch me or help me. Finally the younger man gets a hand under my elbow to help steady me.

"You took quite a hit," he says. "I think hitting the guard rail like you did put pressure on the doors, cinching them shut."

I'm listening to him, but I'm also staring across the road. The deer is there, on the far shoulder, lying on its side. Its head is thrown back, as if in ecstasy. A small pink tongue pokes from the black seams of its mouth. One eye, glassy and black, stares back across the asphalt at me.

"My wife went on ahead," the older man says. "She was going to drive until she got a signal, then call police."

I get my bearings. The spot is probably just a mile or two off of I-87. It's the windy mountain pass that precedes Lake Placid. Beyond the guard rail, the land plummets into a steep ravine, punctuated with pointy pine trees. The headlights of the Range Rover, still on, stab out into the air over the massive drop.

"Pretty close to the edge," the young man says.

My mind was spinning at first, but now it's settling, thoughts forming clear and simple: The cops are coming. It will be state police. An accident report. An insurance claim. And judging by the look of me in the reflection of the sideview mirror, likely a trip to the hospital.

And I've been drinking all night. Two gins at the office, and a couple of healthy glasses of wine at home. It's been hours, most of it likely metabolized, but still . . .

"Ma'am?"

I get back into the driver's seat. The keys are still in the ignition. A safety feature has rotated the key chuck back into the pre-ignition position, so I twist the keys to test the battery, the starter — whatever gets this thing going. The engine, surprisingly, fires up.

The two men take another couple of steps back. They're almost in the road, and so they walk around in front of the Range Rover, watching helplessly as I put the vehicle in reverse and hit the gas. With a couple of bumps and a jarring jump back onto the asphalt, I'm on the road again. The Rover sounds okay — the only problem is my door is still open.

Leaning over, I catch the handle and give it a hard pull. With a loud wrenching of metal, the door closes. The dooropen indicator light stays on, however. It's good enough.

The men exchange glances. The older one is talking, jaw wagging, but I can't hear. Finally, he faces me and waves his arms in the air. He's shouting, "Ma'am! Ma'am!"

I put the Rover in park. The power window works, but only partway. Pressing the button lowers it by about half. The white-haired man is there, talking at me through the gap. "Ma'am. I don't think you should."

"Thanks for your help. I appreciate it."

"Ma'am — I think you're in shock. It might be best to just . . . get out of the vehicle. Let the police handle it."

I stare past the white-haired man at the deer on the far side of the road. I feel like we're in it together, the deer and me. That these people are interlopers.

"Ma'am? Really . . ."

And yet a part of me knows he's right.

In the end, it doesn't matter, since I can see the blue and red lights starting to pulse in the dark forest as a state trooper car comes up the mountain road and around the bend.

CHAPTER TWENTY | SATURDAY

I'm brought to the hospital in Lake Placid. The facility is small but functional. Paul has been notified and is waiting when we get there. Once I'm out of the ambulance and in a bed in the small ER, Paul fawns over me, touching me, wincing as he takes stock of my injuries as if he can feel my pain.

Within half an hour, I'm released. I have a cut over my left eye — from my watch — and some bruising of my forearms. It had seemed worse at the time, but I'm told I'm lucky. Very lucky. Paul brings me home in the pickup truck — the Rover is being towed. We'll have to get a rental while we work out the insurance claim and repairs.

Dawn turns the sky red and gold. Paul glances at me as we drive along. "The trooper I spoke to said you kept asking about the deer. He said they have hunters, or butchers, one of those. People who will take it and make use of it."

I can still see the eye looking at me over the sloping, dark road. Deer are actually quite common in Westchester, something of a nuisance. We see them in our backyard all the time. But northern deer, Adirondack deer — they're different. Elusive. Less domesticated, and more wild and mysterious.

My head feels off. I have that same sort of preternatural calm as before, but something is wrong. Subsurface. It's not the booze either — despite my worries, the police never checked my blood alcohol level and I've certainly burned it all off by now anyway. Maybe I'm still in shock. Certainly I'm overtired.

I do a mental check of what I can recall from the past twenty-four hours. Has it been just that? Not even. It's only five in the morning now, but Joni didn't show up with Michael until eleven yesterday. She announced their engagement thirty minutes later. I was more dumbstruck by his resemblance to a long-ago patient than the marriage proposal. Soon after their arrival, I was told that Maggie Lewis died. I returned home, a four-hour drive, to speak to local police and look through my files — not for her, but for Tom Bishop. I found the address for the uncle who took him in and raised him. Arnold Bleeker was hospitable at first, but then chased me out of the house. His daughter and her husband showed up and flipped me off. I went to the Bishop home only to discover Detective Starzyk haunting the place, telling me that Laura Bishop was out. Finally, Frank Mills pulled information that showed Tom Bishop lives on the other side of the country, but the jail where Laura Bishop did time is around the corner from my vacation home in the mountains.

I think that about sums it up.

"So talk to me," Paul says. "If you can. What's with this cop? Why was he there? Why's he telling you about Laura Bishop getting paroled?"

I realize I never mentioned to Paul the prison's proximity to our home.

"You're shitting me," he says. "Okay. So something is definitely going on here. Is that what you think?"

Paul's line of questioning strikes me as kind of dopey, like he's some bumbling gumshoe. But that's probably because I'm tired and my head hurts. "I don't know what I think." Closing my eyes, I rest my head on the seatback. "What did you guys do last night?"

"What did we do? The two of them went into town. Picked up some Chinese food, brought it back. After we ate, I went out to work on the boat and they left."

"When?"

"I dunno. It was getting late. Maybe eleven? I'm sorry I didn't hear the phone right away. I always meant to put a line in the garage."

"Anything weird happen?"

"Aside from you hitting a deer after deciding to drive all the way back here in the middle of the night? No."

I ignore it. Keeping my eye closed, I ask, "What time did they get back?"

"They weren't back."

My eyelids fly open. "They weren't?"

"No, her car wasn't there . . . Em, do you know something you aren't telling me?"

"What? No . . ." Fully awake now, I call the house and wait while it rings. When Joni answers, I exhale with relief.

"Mom?" She sounds like the call woke her up. "What's the matter?"

"Go back to sleep. Everything's fine. I'll talk to you in a bit."

"Okay . . ."

I hang up. Paul is watching me carefully. He continues to strike me as goofy, ham-handed. For some reason, I think of hitting him that day in the rain, all those years ago.

"I don't know," I say, "what do *you* think about Laura Bishop getting out of prison?"

He scowls as he drives. "What do *I* think? I have no idea what to think."

I stare a moment, then ease back. "It's just been a tough couple of days. A lot of heavy lifting."

"What? What do you mean?"

"Everything is going to be fine. I just need to rest."

He's silent, mulling it over.

I touch his arm. "Hey. We'll figure it all out. All right? We will."

* * *

95

I sleep until noon. When I wake up, it's with a start, yanking off my eye mask. I'm hot — sweating in the sun that pours into the room. Having spent the time unconscious dreaming about a deer with its head bashed open, I'm disoriented.

"Joni," I say, and then I get up too fast and tumble out of the bed.

As I catch my breath on the floor, I hear footfalls hurrying below. Someone pounds up the stairs. It's Paul. He barges into the room and kneels down beside me, getting his arms under me. "Honey. Honey . . . what?"

"I'm okay." I let him help me up. We sit on the edge of the bed. "I just slipped."

He looks me over carefully. Then we have a quick kiss, and I wave him off. "I'm fine." I walk to the en suite bathroom and flip on the light.

Well, I don't *look* fine. I've got a big red welt on the side of my cheek where I struck my own face and the cut over my eye. My skin looks waxy and pale, glistening with perspiration. I start the shower.

Paul calls for me, "You're really all right?"

"Yes."

"Can I get you something?"

I run the tap for some water — Lake Placid has pristine drinking water — and gulp some down from a cup. "I'm starving," I tell Paul.

"Say no more."

But I poke my head out. "Where's Joni now?"

Paul stops halfway out of the room. "Went into town. To grab some lunch."

"They just went into town yesterday."

Worry furrows his brow. Then it clears, and Paul gets a face I've come to know well all after these years — he's about to be as sensible as sensible gets. "Listen, I did some thinking while you were asleep."

"Uh-oh."

"And I guess I'm of two minds about this whole thing."

I get out my toothbrush and squeeze some paste on it. "Okay . . ."

"On the one hand, I'm thinking maybe you should do whatever it takes to satisfy your concerns about Michael. You know, hire someone to do a background check."

Brushing, I spit, but don't mention Frank Mills. "And your other mind?"

"My other mind tells me there's something else going on." "Like what?"

Paul gives me a sympathetic smile that's a little bit condescending. Like I can't see the obvious thing staring me in the face. "Our daughter is going to marry someone. After all of this time, all of our worry about her, everything we went through. It's a lot to process. You of all people know this."

I rinse the toothbrush and put it away.

Paul comes closer. He needn't remind me of the nights we spent awake, searching for her, worrying.

"She put us to the test," he says. "And now that this thing is happening . . . I mean, think about it, Em. The way you reacted to her not being here last night. The way you've been since Michael showed up. It's post-traumatic stress. The whole thing."

I square my shoulders with him. "I'll admit you might be onto something."

"I worry about her, too. But she seems really happy."

"We'll see what Sean thinks," I say, turning back toward the shower. I let my robe fall from my shoulders and softly hit the ground. "He's always been a good judge of Joni's boyfriends."

"He hasn't really liked any of them," Paul says, right behind me.

"Exactly."

Paul's touch is light, the tips of his fingers feathering over the skin of my upper arms.

He leans closer. "I'm so glad you're okay. It could have been worse. A lot worse." He kisses the back of my neck gently, warmly. He moves his hand down past my elbows, and then he moves to my thighs, my buttocks.

There's always a part of me that feels resistance in this moment. For one thing, I don't feel particularly attractive right now. Not particularly sexy. For another, while it's been many years since Paul and I went through his having an affair, it never completely goes away. The thought of him touching another woman like this, it's always there. And at times it feels, almost, like someone watching.

But I've learned to let this go, to give in to what I want. Paul and I lead busy lives. And we're no spring chickens. Even though ours is an empty nest — long gone are the days sex was precluded by children always underfoot — it's not become some romance-athon since Joni left for college. We're often working late, often tired, two ships passing in the night.

So we take our chances when they arise. And right now is more than that, anyway. It's about closeness, comfort, intimacy.

I step into the shower ahead of Paul. He removes his clothes and steps in after. I turn to face him, and he presses me gently but firmly against the shower wall. The water pours down. I adjust the temperature so it's not scalding.

We fall into our rhythm. For a few moments, I forget everything. Michael Rand, Arnold Bleeker, creepy Steve Starzyk.

Laura Bishop, released from prison. Just a few miles away.

CHAPTER TWENTY-ONE

After our shower, I'm in the kitchen making sandwiches for lunch. Paul comes through and tells me that he's already procured a rental car to replace the wrecked Range Rover. "It's just a small sedan, less impact-resistant than the Rover, so don't go hitting any more deer."

"Ha ha."

He kisses me, tells me again he's so grateful I'm okay, then leaves to work on his boat in the garage. Once I hear the whine of his electric sander, I lick some mayo off my fingers and pick up the phone. First I text Sean, who is supposed to be arriving this evening. Currently living in Colorado, he decided to drive instead of fly and so set out sometime yesterday.

Hey kiddo. ETA?

I set the phone on the kitchen island and hurry back upstairs. My overnight bag is in the closet in our bedroom. Distraught as I was last night, at least I had the presence of mind to stick the Tom Bishop file in there. I'm able to locate it quickly and thumb through it, looking for court contact information.

There. The judge who oversaw the case was the Honorable Raymond Meyers. I call, knowing I'm likely to get a machine — it's the weekend, after all. But a young woman answers, sounding pert and intelligent. It's the judge's clerk, named Sydney.

"Sydney," I say. "I didn't expect to get anyone."

She explains that she's going over a big deposition on a criminal case. We small-talk a little — she graduated Yale two springs ago, and she really likes clerking for Meyers. She thinks he's a great judge.

I penetrate the small talk with a deep dive. "Well, Sydney, about fifteen years ago, Judge Meyers presided over a capital murder case — David Bishop?"

"Oh yes, I'm familiar with that case."

"Great. Then you probably know that there was a juvenile involved."

"Yes," she says, not quite as pert or bright. "Those records are sealed."

"That's right. So, I was a consulting clinical psychologist on that case. I worked with the New York investigators. They requested I do a mental health evaluation. I did five sessions with the juvenile." I choose my next words carefully. "The work we did in those sessions had an impact on the direction of the case."

"Yes," Sydney says, almost too quietly to hear.

"I have my notes, but it was a closed courtroom, testimony sealed. I really could use a look at that information. Could you put in the request to Judge Meyers for me?"

A pause. Then, tentative, "Sure . . . Can I ask what for?"

"Well, that would be between me and Judge Meyers."

It's a little curt, but I can't give her an honest answer. I want to know who else came into the court, gave statements, etc. Some distant family in Arizona, maybe. Any friends of Laura Bishop. There are all sorts of possible angles to this thing.

I try to sound nicer at the end. "If you could have the judge call me at his earliest convenience, I'd appreciate it."

"Of course."

When I hang up with her, the electric sander is quiet. I wait a few seconds, then it starts up again. My next call is to Candace. Arnold Bleeker's daughter. I have her number in my phone.

A man answers, and he's gruff: "What do you want?"

"I'm sorry, I'm trying to reach Candace."

"She doesn't want to talk to you. And this is my phone, not hers."

I pad down the stairs, feeling a bit of hope. It's something in his voice — he's not as dead-set against me as she is.

"I understand that," I say. "She made that clear, and I'm so sorry to be bothering you. Are you her husband?"

"That's none of your business."

"Well, you grabbed me, pretty hard." If there's a bruise, it's camouflaged by the accident, but he doesn't know that. "I could go to the police and press charges. But I don't want that. All I want is a chance to explain. I know Candace's adopted brother. I can't say how I know him, but . . . Hello?"

I stop in the middle of the living room. So much for my intuition. Candace's friend hung up on me. What is it with these people?

Getting frustrated now, I dial back. No one answers. The call goes to voicemail: "Hi, this is Greg, with G. Force Trucking. I can't answer my phone right now, but leave your info and I'll get back to ya."

There's a beep. My mouth is open to hold forth, but then I close it. I'm standing in front of the floor-to-ceiling windows in the living room, with a view clear down to the lake. Beside the dock, in the clear dark water, is an object. Something floating.

For a moment, I just stand there, too shocked to move.

Then I turn from the windows and run.

CHAPTER TWENTY-TWO

Paul must see me streak across the yard, because suddenly he's just behind me. I almost fall but am able to keep my balance. When I reach the dock, I sprint to the end of the wood. Paul's vibrations follow. I'm on my knees reaching into the water. The white shape is floating just out of reach, but close enough to realize it's a sweatshirt with no one in it.

I know that sweatshirt; it's Joni's. She could have slipped out of it. Or been struggling and it came off. Any number of things.

"Em . . ." Paul says. "What—"

Shoes and all, I jump from the dock. It's August, but Lake Placid is always cold. So cold, it once preserved the body of a missing woman for decades. The lake slopes away quickly from our shore so that just a few feet from the grassy embankment, the water is up to my chest. That's where I land and start swimming for the shirt, just a few yards away.

I grab at it. It billows under my grasp. I push it aside and dive under after hearing Paul call my name a second time.

The cold sharpens my senses. Kicking with my feet to plunge deeper, I open my eyes. The sun penetrates enough and the water is clear so I can see the sandy bottom. I touch it with my fingers and arc my back and start back toward the surface. Then, keeping myself submerged by letting out some air and fanning upward with my hands, I search. I do a complete circle in the water.

Seeing nothing, I break the surface for a breath.

"Emily!"

I'm back under again. Paul knows what I'm doing; I don't need to explain myself to him right now or listen as he tries to dissuade me. I search farther out, going until the bottom disappears beneath me. I swivel back. The metal posts supporting the dock come into view. I swim around them and partly under the dock.

Joni is nowhere.

Breaking the surface again, I don't see Paul right away. Then I spot him — he's fished out the sweatshirt that drifted over to him and is wringing it out. I kick for the ladder on the side of the dock, then climb out and stand, panting, hands on my hips, water pattering down onto the treated wood.

"My first time in since we got here," I say between breathy exhalations. My chest and ribs hurt from last night's accident, but the cool water was exhilarating.

Paul gives me an angry glance. He finishes wringing out the sweatshirt and hangs it from the back of one of the Adirondack chairs occupying the dock that runs along the bank, connecting the two others. Shaking his head, he starts up the lawn for the house. He's clearly upset with me.

"I thought I saw someone in the water," I call after him.

Paul stops immediately. He walks back toward me at a brisk pace. Not much gets Paul emotional. But when it does, he's all in. "I know," he says testily. "I figured you thought someone was in there. But you've just been in a car accident, Emily. You have a giant bruise on your face. I know they said you weren't concussed, but you've definitely had some sort of reaction."

He stands, fuming.

I say, "You could've jumped in."

His nostrils flare and his jaw twitches. "I could see no one was there. Just you, thrashing around."

He turns and walks away again. I open my mouth but close it. It's no use. I know he's upset because he's worried; he's lacking control. It's his self-esteem, I decided long ago. Paul needs to feel capable and in charge, or he fears being rejected — even after all these years.

I watch until he goes into the house — he gives the side door a little slam — and then I take off my T-shirt. We're located in a corner of the lake, a kind of cove, with the nearest neighbor a quarter mile away. Boating activity stays mostly restricted to the main body of the lake. We get the occasional fisherman puttering back into our area, or the kayaker or canoer who's exploring the shoreline. But it's typically quiet and private, like now.

I drop my shirt and squeeze out my hair; it's short and will dry quickly. For now, I scrape it back out of my face. I sit and take my wet sneakers off, remove the socks. As I do, I look at the boathouse.

The boathouse sits in the water. It's like a garage, but for boats. In bare feet now, I rise from the chair. The boathouse is navy blue with dark red trim. There are two windows on my side. I step between docks and peer in the first window. I can see the sailboat and part of the dinghy.

Next to the window is the door. I grab the doorknob, find it locked.

"Paul . . . ?"

My call to my husband is half-hearted; I know he can't hear me all the way up at the house. But it's odd — why is the door locked? We only do that when we're away. I check the first window again, then move to the second. I can't see in much better; the angle is bad and the glass is dirty. Paul has been meaning to connect all the docks with a short piece, one that joins the U-shape inside the boathouse with the U-shape on the outside, but he's been preoccupied building his boat. A gap remains between them. Since the door is locked, that means if I want to get inside, I've got to go back in the water.

I head back for the ladder and lower myself down, push off and do a breaststroke. What's compelling me, I'm not entirely sure. A feeling. Maybe residual symptoms from last night's accident — Paul could be partly right.

I swim for the open mouth of the boathouse. At least there's another ladder in there, a metal ladder from an old boat that we hooked to the inner docks. It's rickety, but I climb up. Now I'm standing next to the sailboat. It's shady in here, and when the wind blows, evaporating the moisture on my skin, I feel a chill.

It's gloomy in the boathouse. The walls are exposed so that the studs are visible, making it feel a bit like being inside a ribcage. There's an old anchor hanging on the back wall. Several bright orange seat cushions. A long run of rope, thick and frayed, hanging from a ten-penny nail. In the corner, a basket filled with fishing poles.

The sailboat is tiny. I remember when Paul bought it. Second-hand, from someone local. Paul had seen it on the side of the road. It's blue and white and a little beat up. We named it *Couchsagrage*, after an Adirondack legend. Paul thought it was funny to give such a small boat a long name. But he taught himself how to use it, then both of our children. The only one who wouldn't know what to do is me.

I continue to inspect everything. The sailboat looks normal, I decide. The dinghy is the same as it ever is, a round-bottom boat with four bench seats and two rowing oars, plus the trolling motor and battery.

As I walk along, I almost trip on a green fishing net. I jam it into the basket along with the poles. Two more windows look over the rest of our cove — the shoreline sweeps around and heads back for the main body of water just yards away from the boathouse. Nothing out there, and nothing in here.

I start back to the other side. Before climbing back down the rickety ladder, I notice something carved into the wood. In between two vertical studs, etched into the exposed plywood, a heart with an arrow through it and two names.

Joni
Michael

And beneath those, today's date. Well, no — yesterday's date. When they were down here together and I heard them splashing around and Joni giggling. They must've been carving this.

My fingers brush the grooves. I'm not sure who had a knife; maybe it's in here. I look around on the dock but don't see one. Then I notice it — a small pocketknife up on the windowsill. Well, not much of a windowsill, but just the framing-in of the window. I hadn't seen it when I peered in. Must be Paul's.

As I turn away, another carving catches my eye. This one isn't as deep, as if scratched out quickly.

Not a heart, not names, but a sentence. Five words.

I want my mommy back.

CHAPTER TWENTY-THREE

I hear the pop of sand and gravel beneath car tires. Joni is pulling her Subaru into the driveway. I hold the door open and smile as she and Michael walk to and enter the house. It's been half an hour since going in the lake and my hair is still damp. I've been able to think of little else since seeing those words carved into the boathouse wall, of how they must've gotten there. But I have to pick my moment.

I'm just not sure when that is yet.

"How you guys doing?"

"Good," Joni says. She stops and eyes the bruise on my cheek. "How are *you*?"

"I'm fine. Come on in. Did you guys eat?"

"Yeah, I took Michael to the diner in town." She walks deeper into the house.

The two of them are the picture of summer: he wears a black V-neck T-shirt and brown shorts. She's wearing a bathing suit, with a breezy pink shirt over top, jean shorts, and brown sandals on her feet. Her blonde hair is pulled back into a loose bun. This is the Joni-look I'm used to.

"Anyone seen my white sweatshirt?" She's looking around in the living room.

"Fished it out of the lake," I tell her.

"Really?" She comes closer for scrutiny. Practically sniffing me as she looks me over. "You went swimming?"

"Just so I could get it. It must've blown off the dock. It's hanging on the line now. Up by the shack."

Finally, she breaks eye contact. "Thank you." I'm struck, for a moment, by how lovely she is.

When she was in her mid-teens, Joni did some modeling, mostly for clothing catalogues. It wasn't something I ever would've sought for her, but Paul's secretary had a sister at an agency.

Her nose wrinkles with a question. "Where's Dad?"

"You probably went right by him. Where else? Working on the boat."

She nods. I smile at Michael. I feel like a psychic reaching for his thoughts, but I ask about their morning, their breakfast. Joni remarks about the diner being redone and about downtown being crowded, and I zone out, thinking about — (*I want my mommy back*) — how Joni hated modeling when she was young. Mostly, it became the perfect cause for rebellion. Only, the rebellion lasted after the last photographer refused to work with her and we called it quits. It went on through two private schools, multiple attempts at running away from home, and sudden disappearances. Times she would venture into the city on her own.

When she was fifteen, we sent her to see someone for her anxiety and depression. She hated that, too. Like Maggie Lewis, Joni didn't want to be on any medication. But when the doctor prescribed Effexor, we decided to try. It was gut-wrenching to me. She was so young, so troubled, but SSRIs such as Effexor had shown efficacy, even in teens.

In the end, she wasn't on it for long. She seemed to grow out of her funk naturally. It doesn't mean everyone does.

Joni walks into the kitchen and opens the fridge and asks Michael if he wants a drink. He takes a can of iced tea. We continue chatting. Every now and again, I catch Michael looking at me. Or maybe I'm looking at him. Either way, it's like we're having this sub-perceptive side conversation. Like telepaths.

Me: *I know.*

Him: *And I know you know. . .*

I sit at the counter extension, where we have a couple of stools. Watching the pair of them slurp their canned drinks and stand around like teenagers, I ask them what they're planning to do next.

"Not sure," Joni says. She glances at Michael, who lifts his eyebrows in deference to her.

The way to do this, I think, is to keep it as calm and pleasant as possible.

"How about dinner? You guys gonna be here for dinner?"

"Um, I don't know." Joni continues looking at him.

"Okay, well . . ." I take a breath. "Sean is coming."

Joni's gaze swivels to me. She's always adored her older brother. "Yeah? You heard from him?"

I check my phone. My last text to him is still there: *Hey kiddo. ETA?*

His response arrived about a half hour later. *Inbound. ETA 7:30 p.m. Sorry for the delay, Ma!*

I show it to Joni.

"Uh-huh," she says, looking. The utterance is meant to demonstrate her lack of faith.

I give her a stern look at first, but then soften. "Listen, this is your vacation, too. I'm not trying to pin you guys down to anything. But we still owe you a celebratory dinner."

"No, you don't," Joni says. "We don't need that."

Michael and I share another quick glance. Who looked at who first?

"Of course you do. You're engaged. The least we can do is take you out."

"You mean ask us a bunch of questions."

"No . . ."

"About the future, about where are we going to live, about what are we going to do for money. About how much is the wedding going to cost, et cetera."

There's marginal humor in her voice, but mostly, she's being petulant. Even Michael seems to sense it. He puts a hand on her back and murmurs something too low for me to pick up on, but she shrugs him off. The most likely explanation is probably the right one: Joni is edgy because she's brought her fiancé to the lake house for our annual family get-together, someone we've never met, and so far, we've been pretty frigging cool about it.

If you discount my antics or what I've discovered, all of which she's unaware of.

So she's defensive, waiting for the other shoe to drop.

At that moment, Paul comes in from outside, breaking the tension.

"Daddy," she says, and trots to him and gives him a big hug. Paul is holding a paintbrush in one hand and a rag in the other, so he's unable to properly hug her back. But she makes a big show of affection for him — letting everyone know he's the preferred parent right now.

I cast my gaze at Michael, who gives me a sheepish smile and looks down, like he understands.

Welcome to the family. You'll fit right in.

"So, Michael," I say. "I have a confession to make."

When he raises his eyes to me again, they seem to dance in the light filling the floor-to-ceiling windows behind me. That incredible green-blue, like a lagoon.

"I checked you out on Facebook."

"I'm not on Facebook," he says.

"I guess that explains why I couldn't find you. There were quite a few Michael Rands, though. I was going through them for a while."

"Sorry," he says. "I should've told you."

I make a face and wave at the air. "No, not at all. It's not something you have to tell people. 'Hi, I'm not on Facebook.' And I'm admitting to snooping."

Joni has let go of Paul. She is not exactly glaring at me, but close. Giving me the stink-eye, anyway. Paul continues toward the sink, where he starts to wash out his brush. "Paul, honey," I say. "What are you doing? Kitchen sinks are for dishes and food preparation, not oily paintbrushes."

"I'm going to put a sink in the garage," he says, still rinsing the brush.

"I'm actually not on *any* social media," Michael says.

Joni moves toward him, tentative. It's clear she has mixed feelings whether he should talk to me.

"Really?" I ask. "No Instagram? No TikTok? Nothing?"

He shakes his head. I'm acting lighthearted, but he seems serious. "You know, what's funny is . . . social media is getting harder to define. We call Facebook and Twitter social media. But so is YouTube, Pinterest, Substack . . . Does that mean online comments sections are, too? I mean, you can get into a debate in the comments section of a newspaper. Even some retailers. Customer reviews can turn into cultural arguments." He steps toward the counter and sets his drink down. He's just across from me; I could reach out and touch him.

"Basically, all of the internet has become e-commerce and social media."

"Paul," I say, "are you hearing this?"

Still rinsing: "Uh-huh."

I ask Michael, both to keep listening to him talk, which is deeply affirming his identity — his mannerisms, his inflections, all the same — and because I'm genuinely interested in his answer: "Okay, so what else do you think the internet *could* have been?"

He shakes his head. "I don't think it could have been anything else. I think it's how human beings are. And what's really interesting is how people increasingly treat social networks like public utilities. Like, if you don't have Facebook, you won't have access to certain information. That might be as part of a recreational group, or school, or work. But Facebook is a private company. It's advertising to you. Can you imagine if you had a landline phone, and every few minutes it would ring, and it would be an ad for something?" He looks around at Joni, behind him. She offers a wan smile and plucks at the frayed ends of her jean shorts. Michael turns back to me. "Or if you answered, and it gives you some tidbit of news . . . and you have no idea where it's coming from, or if it's true . . ."

Did he just make a reference to something specific? Like the strange voicemail on my phone? I'm suddenly nervous, trapped in his blue eyes. But when he blinks and looks away, I remind myself that I'm in control of how I react. Besides, he's just waxing philosophical.

Paul shuts off the tap at that moment and tears free a paper towel to dry the cleaned brush. "Michael studied media literacy at Colgate," he says.

"I was a film and media studies major," Michael clarifies.

"Wow, a carpenter who's an intellectual? I didn't know you went to Colgate. That's a great school. It's right near where Joni goes to Hamilton."

Michael nods. "I had a scholarship. I played lacrosse."

We continue to talk. Gradually, Joni seems to loosen up and even contributes to the conversation and laughs a few times. According to Michael, who says he grew up in Huntington, Long Island (not Sayville), lacrosse was a passion, and SUNY Stony Brook the obvious choice for his higher education.

But then his parents died. His father, who was a successful businessman working in the city, was also a heavy drinker. One night, Michael's father and mother were on their way home from a function in Manhattan. Michael's father swerved into a tractor-trailer on the highway. He and Michael's mother were both killed right away.

Michael was seventeen, he says, a junior in high school.

"After that, everything changed. I didn't want to go to Stony Brook. I didn't want to go anywhere at all. I didn't even want to live, to be honest."

Joni is holding onto him, resting her chin on his shoulder. She kisses his neck and feathers her hand over his chest.

The question just pops out of me: "Who did you stay with?"

"No one. I mean, I didn't go anywhere. My aunt and uncle actually came to stay with *me*."

Interesting, I think. So close to the truth — in reality, Thomas, who lived in Westchester County, *went* to stay with

112

his aunt and uncle on Long Island. In Michael's twisted version — if it is, in fact, an alteration of the truth — he's *from* Long Island, and his aunt and uncle came to stay with *him*.

"They believed that . . . well, that it would be best for me to stay in my house. Stick with my routine."

Even more fascinating, I think, because evidence shows this to be an effective form of managing extreme grief for children — to keep things as consistent as possible. One might think that there would be too many painful reminders, but those painful reminders are preferable and mentally healthier for children than sudden, major change. Like having to move out and live with new people.

Did Michael research that for his story? Or did he just come up with it on his own?

I say, "That was very nice of them."

"Yeah, they're wonderful people."

"I'd like to meet them."

Joni's eyes dart to me, like I'm being pushy. But Michael just smiles. "I'm sure you will."

There is a moment of silence and I clear my throat. "So . . ."

"I did miss a few months of my junior year of high school. But I was able to get back on track and graduate on time." His brow dimples in thought. "I was ready to leave Long Island by then. Colgate was my moonshot school. And I got in."

"And that's how you two met?" I point my finger between them. "Since Hamilton is so close? Because it obviously wasn't social networking . . ."

Joni answers with a sigh. "I was going to save all of this for when Sean got here."

"I'm sorry, honey." Thinking of Sean, I check my phone again. Nothing. In truth, I'm kind of waiting for him, too. What's in the offing is a sort of intervention, and it seems right Sean would be here. He's insightful, kind. He could help with Michael.

"We met at a lacrosse game," Joni says. "Our schools were playing each other. And I went with Liz and some of the others just for something to do. And there he was. I watched the way he played, the way he moved . . . Liz is dating one of the guys on our team, and so we were hanging around in the parking lot, and then Michael came out. And he looked right over at me . . ."

"Wait," I say, cutting into their love-staring. "When was this?"

"Early this spring," Joni says. "Just after Easter."

Paul goes for the fridge. "That's good," he says. "You met the old-fashioned way, in person. That's the best." He gets a glass and pours himself some juice.

Michael's story is forgery — it has to be. But meeting my daughter at a sports game? She just happened to be there? Either he's gone a long way toward making it work — an incredibly long way, somehow timing things for her to meet him — or I'm missing something.

I could also be losing my mind. That's a possibility, too.

For now, one more question: "So, Michael — you graduated this spring?"

He drags his eyes away from Joni and looks at me, shakes his head, appearing chagrined. "No, I, ah . . . Well, I'll just be honest — my grades slipped and I lost my scholarship. Without it, I can't afford to finish. And I need another year to get all my credits."

Money, I think, suddenly and forcibly. *Could this whole thing be about money? Extortion?* Colgate is not a cheap school.

"I'm sorry to hear that," I say.

Paul stands beside me, smelling of wood stain. His knuckles are darkened with it. "Is there a way to get things back on track?"

Michael gives a nod but looks chagrined. "Maybe, yeah. I'm seeing what I can work out. I want to finish."

Joni interrupts before Paul can speak again. "They lost the game," she says. "Colgate lost to Hamilton." It's like she's trying to bring the conversation back to the important part — their impending union.

Michael looks at her. "It was a key game, too."

"But you wouldn't have met me."

"That's right."

And they go back to mooning over each other. This time, Joni takes him by the hand and leads him out of the kitchen. Before either Paul or I can object, she says to us, "Okay? Enough grilling for now? You got the juicy details."

But she smiles, and I see, for the first time since she's been here, real delight in my daughter's eyes. Joni has lots of defenses, but she is a good woman. I remember her often as a baby, who came into the world so quietly, so softly, so watchfully. My little bundle, that tiny face. The preternatural calm she exuded.

"We're going swimming," she calls over her shoulder, and she bangs out the front door, Michael in tow.

Both Paul and I turn to watch them run down the sloping lawn toward the sparkling water. She taunts Michael and he chases her, grabs her, and she squeals with laughter.

"I think we might just have to come to terms with it," Paul says behind me.

"What?"

"Our daughter has found her man."

I watch them continue down to the water, stripping off clothes, running for the end of the dock, then jumping in — her diving elegantly, him launching into a cannonball and making a big splash.

Oh God, I think.

What am I going to do?

CHAPTER TWENTY-FOUR

After their swim, Joni and Michael sit in towels by the water's edge, holding hands. I turn from the window and walk upstairs to find Paul changing in our bedroom.

"The death of two parents," I say, "and no life insurance? At least, not enough to cover a year's tuition?"

Paul pulls on khaki shorts. He looks at me and shrugs. "I don't know. Sounds kind of private."

I roll my eyes. My husband doesn't need to lecture me on privacy. But his comment doesn't bother me. Instead, I approach him and give him a kiss. He has to pause, his arms through his dark-green polo shirt but not yet over his head. Paul is in good shape for a man in his late fifties. Of course, nobody can beat time, and I've never been that hung up on physique, but it's good that Paul is healthy. And right now, with his arms in his shirt, he's my temporary captive. I push against him and give him a kiss.

He studies me, looking into my eyes.

I ask, "Remember when *we* first met?"

"Of course."

"You thought I would never meet your parents. Or your friends. I was too busy with school, then work."

"I remember."

"I told you it would all come with time."

"Yes," he says, sighing. "You were right."

"That's not what I mean. I mean that I'm hoping . . . that's all this is. I just need to give it time with Michael. Like you said. There's been so many false starts with her . . . But we'll get to know him, and I won't have to be anxious."

He cocks his eyebrow at me — a very "Paul" expression. Paul has an angular face, sharp eyebrows, and when he raises his left one as high as the other, it's comical. But he's checking my sincerity.

"What?" I ask.

He pulls his shirt down the rest of the way. "Sounds like a plan."

Dressed, Paul lingers a moment. My little confession seems to have softened him. He touches my face, his thumb near my bruise. "How you feeling? Otherwise?"

"I feel fine. I'm good."

I smile and pat his butt as he walks out of the bedroom. Once he's through the door and out of sight, my smile drops.

* * *

In the closet is my bag from the trip home. I open it and dig out Starzyk's business card. He answers on the second ring. "Dr. Lindman? I was hoping to hear from you."

I'm already feeling regret. Maybe it's just the tone of his voice. "I was wondering if you could help me with something."

"Is everything okay?"

"Everything's fine, I just—"

"Have you been contacted?"

I assume he means Laura Bishop. "No . . . I . . . no."

"Is the boy still there with you?"

"Yes."

"How does he seem?"

I walk to the bedroom window, a dormer to one side of the vaulted ceiling. The view of the lake is the same, just from higher up. Joni and Michael are no longer in the chairs. Their towels are gone.

I move to the door and shut it quickly but softly, speaking in a low voice. "He's fine."

"Has he gone anywhere?"

"No, just with my daughter. Just to lunch."

"Any strange phone calls?"

"Have I gotten any strange phone calls?"

"Him. Has *he*."

"Not that I'm aware of. Excuse me, Detective, but I called *you*."

He's silent for a moment. "I understand that. He could arrange to meet her some other way. But I wouldn't advise following him. I'm not suggesting that. Okay?"

I shut my eyes and give a thought-clearing shake of my head. "The reason I'm calling — did you ever keep tabs on where Thomas Bishop went after everything happened?"

"I believe he went to live with his aunt and uncle."

"But you never kept tabs on him after that?"

"No . . . That's not in my purview."

"I just thought . . . you were at the Bishop house."

Starzyk makes no reply.

"He might be living in Arizona," I say. "This might not be him. This Michael Rand has a very . . . compelling life story. He's been to college. His parents are deceased . . ."

"Have you been able to verify any of that?"

"My daughter met him at college."

"Uh-huh. So, she can verify he's been there for however long?"

"He was playing on the lacrosse team. They said it was just after Easter."

"Lacrosse team . . ." Starzyk mutters. He's writing it down. "Easter . . . And it's which college?"

I almost don't tell him. "Colgate University."

"Uh-huh. Okay. And you say he hasn't behaved in any suspicious way."

I think through every glance, every small moment over the past two days. Michael has admitted some baggage, but he's the picture of a doting boyfriend. Around us, he's neither obsequious nor arrogant, but perhaps just charmingly nervous and typically shy unless talking about a subject which interests him, like social media. In short, if he has a flaw, it's being too perfect.

"Detective, can I ask you — you seem very interested in this. But if Laura Bishop is out on parole, that means she was reviewed. She's had good behavior. And yet you were sitting outside the house last night . . ."

Starzyk is quiet for so long, I think we lost connection.

Then, his voice low: "Dr. Lindman, I think there's a real concern here."

I wait.

"Where you're staying — it's in Lake Placid?"

"Are you checking up on me?"

"You're fifteen miles from Cold Brook Prison."

It's true, and I don't have a response.

"For your own safety," he says, "don't follow this Michael Rand, especially if you think he's meeting her. They could be dangerous. I have to go now. We'll talk again."

He hangs up.

CHAPTER TWENTY-FIVE | SATURDAY
LATE EVENING

I'm not quite done making dinner — I've pulled out all the stops and it feels like I'm on the verge of completing an Olympic decathlon — when Sean shows up early.

"Hey," he says, coming close for a hug. "Traffic was lighter than I expected." His smile fades as he notices my bruises and small cut. "Mom, what happened?"

I put my arms around him, press my face into his chest. My son is home.

But I don't linger; I have to finish cooking.

"What are you doing? Did you get into a fight or something?"

"I hit a deer with the Range Rover."

"You *what*? And you got all banged up?" Sean follows me around the kitchen. "I bet it's that stupid car. You know those things just underwent a huge recall? Why are you making dinner? Ma. You need to sit down."

Sean's complaints and concerns seem to motivate everyone else. Michael offers to set the table, while Joni takes over some of the last of the cooking, warming the bread and plating up the meal. Paul comes in and finally distracts Sean.

Father and son hug and speak quietly, and then both are looking at me. I'm left standing alone in the kitchen, nothing to do. "I'm *fine*," I say, loud and clear.

Once we're all seated, Paul uncorks the wine and everyone takes a glass, except for Michael. He raises his water. We would toast Joni's engagement, except Sean doesn't know yet. She wants to tell him in her own time.

My head is swimming.

"To the lake house," Paul says. "To us all being together."

First, Sean regales us with tales of the West. For six months, he worked a grain elevator at a farm in South Dakota. He wintered in Idaho, mostly skiing and bartending. This past spring, he joined up with another farm, this one operating on one-hundred-percent-renewable energy sources to create organic produce.

Sean is ruggedly handsome, with tanned skin and a two-day beard stubble. He's got the Irish that comes through both my line and Paul's, but also the bit of Italian I inherited from my great-grandfather, who was from Rome. Sean's hair is ruddy brown, his eyes dark blue. There's a bend to his nose from when he broke it — twice. As a boy, Sean was a daredevil. He was always leaping from things: kitchen counters, the backs of vehicles, swing sets — all pretty typical stuff. But then there was the skateboarding, and the snowboarding, with all of the jumps. And when that wasn't enough, hang gliding and bungee jumping came next. His first skydive was at the age of eighteen. Paul and I were both anxious about it, but we had no choice — he was an adult.

Over the last two years or so, Sean has gotten a little calmer. Some of the jobs — like smoke jumping in Arizona — had me up nights. But the move to the grain elevator job, and then to picking organic produce, gives me hope. I may not go completely gray just yet.

Sean and Michael seem to warm to each other instantly. While talking, Sean's gaze connects with mine and he winks. It seems a preliminary stamp of approval for Michael.

If you only knew.

Once Paul and Joni are done bombarding Sean with questions, he asks Michael about himself. Michael hits on all the same points he's shared with Paul and me. Joni glances at me — her eyes convey something much different from Sean's: a reminder that *this* was when we were supposed to learn everything about her fiancé. And maybe she has a point: Now, we're hearing everything twice. But that's good. I've said hardly a word, just listened, and as Michael shares his personal story, I find myself evaluating his performance, checking for inconsistencies. Either it's very well-rehearsed or it's genuine. If it's the latter, then I've got some strange, personal knots to untangle.

From there, the conversation moves to more general topics. The weather, plans for the upcoming week. Sean asks Paul, "When's your boat gonna be ready, Dad?"

"I'm getting close. I'll put the second coat on her tonight."

"What about the sailboat? You guys been out in the *Cootchie*?"

"Sean Anthony," I say with mock sternness.

He grins. "Sorry, Ma."

Paul mentions some repairs done to the sailboat the previous autumn. As they talk, Michael listens raptly. Joni pours herself some more wine and offers it around. Paul and Sean agree to more, distractedly. I decline. Sort of in solidarity with Michael, sort of because I've been maybe hitting the stuff a bit too hard lately. And I've been having those cravings to smoke — even smelling it when there's none around. Remembering the bluish haze of it in the air. The din of voices from a cocktail party, ice cubes ratting in tumblers, people in a hidden back room, noses bent to a glass table . . .

I'm about to excuse myself for an unneeded trip to the bathroom, just to clear my head, when I notice Michael checking his phone.

Any strange phone calls?

I'd almost forgotten talking to Starzyk.

A moment later, with Sean and Paul and Joni in a lively reverie about the time the three of them capsized the boat, Michael says, "Excuse me. Sorry, I'll just be right back."

"Head down the driveway a bit and you'll have a better chance at reception," Joni says.

"Thanks, babe."

She smiles and gives his hand a squeeze and dives back into the conversation with her father and brother.

Michael walks out of the room toward the side door. After a few seconds, I pull together some dishes and head for the kitchen sink.

"Honey, I'll do all that," Paul says, noticing. "You're going to get in trouble with our son."

"It's okay. I'm just puttering." I sneak a glance at Michael stepping outside.

"It's good to see him," Paul says about Sean.

"Yes, it is."

After Paul's absorbed with Sean and Joni again, I head to the side door. Michael stands near the cars in the driveway.

Subtly, quietly, I drift closer. The solid door is open, leaving the screen. His voice floats to me as a murmur. He sounds calm, striking an almost professional tone.

"Mmhmm. No, I understand . . ." His feet crunch across the driveway as he moves farther out of range.

"Mom, what are you doing?"

Joni startles me. She's standing in the hallway, looking so pretty in her white, sleeveless blouse, the flower pattern around the midriff. She holds her wineglass in one hand and holds her elbow with the other, her hips cocked at a slightly sassy angle.

"Just propping the door open. The air is so nice tonight. Warm."

Joni seems to accept this and looks past me, through the open door.

"Sean really likes him, I think," I say.

"Of course he does."

"I didn't mean anything . . ."

"He's a good man."

"I know, honey. I just want to make sure you're okay."

I expect pushback, *why wouldn't I be okay* — but instead see something in the corner of my daughter's gaze, just before she steps past me toward the door. "I'm fine, Mom."

She's fine, I'm fine. Everybody's fine.

F-I-N-E = fucked-up, insecure, neurotic and emotional.

The evening contains that bluish shade, monochrome, as the sun descends and takes the colors with it. Joni stands in the doorway, gazing into the dusk.

I risk closing the gap between us and put my hands on her shoulders. Joni doesn't resist or pull away. "I love you, you know."

"I know. I love you, too."

"I want you to be happy. I want you to be safe. That's all."

"I know."

"You can always come to me. If there's anything. Anything that . . ."

Her shoulders rise and fall as she pulls a heavy breath. Then she lowers her head. Through tears, she repeats, "I know, Mom . . ."

I'm almost whispering now. "What is it?"

"Nothing," she says emphatically, betrayed by her tears.

"All right," I say. Then, tentatively: "You used to talk to me."

"Yeah, when I was ten."

"You still can."

She snuffs and wipes her tears away. "When I was little, I told you that I didn't want to grow up."

"I remember."

"You said that I would still be this little girl forever. That people were like trees. That when you cut a tree you see the rings of its growth, and that's your past, always there."

She faces me. I've left the hallway dark, so we're in the gloom, but her eyes are shining from the kitchen and dining area lights.

"I don't feel that little girl inside," she says. "I didn't for a long time, Mom. And then — it sounds corny, but — Michael came along and I felt okay to let go again. To be me. To remember her."

"That doesn't sound corny at all." My own tears have started.

"Yeah, well . . ."

She starts away and I grab her arm. Maybe too forcibly, because she glances down at my hand and I let go. "You were about to say something else. Just now. What? Honey, just talk to me. Okay? I can't take it anymore."

"Why would you say that?"

I almost blurt it out. It's on the tip of my tongue. And so what if I told her? This is my daughter. My flesh and blood.

But I can't. It's not about me or Joni. If those who seek counseling can't trust their therapists with privacy, then the whole thing goes out the window.

Joni is still staring at me.

"I don't mean anything. But you've got this guy . . . you're standing here with me, and something has got you upset—"

"I just told you why. You don't have to *fix* me anymore, Mom. That's the point. I found someone that makes me feel good. For who I am."

"Then I'm thrilled for you."

"No, you're not. I know you. You think he's just another flash in the pan. You think I'm too young. That I should wait, like you and Dad. You got your careers started . . ."

"Barely . . ."

"That I'm just rushing into things . . ."

She falls silent, looking through the door again. Michael is just a shape in the gloaming, nearer the garage than the house, his voice a faint mumble, his feet scratching against the ground.

Joni says, "You don't trust me because of how I used to be. You think I'm unstable."

"Joni—"

"Let me. You think I'm unstable, but that's not even it. You're worried. You're worried because you think my bad choices will reflect your bad choices. All the shit from when Sean and I were kids."

"Hey," I say in a sharp whisper. "Now listen up."

But she's glaring at me, and I know I've just screwed up. I've got a hold of her arm again, for one thing, which I slowly release.

"We'll just go," Joni says.

She turns on her heel and walks quickly back to the dining room.

"Jo . . ." I start after her, but stop.

Suddenly, I'm incensed. I didn't ask for this. I didn't ask to be in this position. Yes, I have children, and I accept that there will always be burdens that come with having even adult children. But this is something I never anticipated happening, and it's making me crazy and driving a wedge between us. And there's only one way to solve it.

I push out the screen door and march through the gathering darkness in search of Michael.

CHAPTER TWENTY-SIX

DR EMILY LINDMAN
CASE NOTES
MAY 17
Session 2

Met with Tom today for one hour, our second session. He remains quiet and subdued. It's been over six months since his father was killed, but the boy wears it like a shroud. His eyes make him look older; he's seen too much for someone his age. There is a weight in his shoulders and stiffness in his gait.

His demeanor presents similar clues to his burden, his repression. When the body reacts to a mechanical stress — like a back injury — the response is inflammation. The brain works similarly, only the "inflammation" from trauma is a muddying of events. A fog rolls in that leaves certain things in stark relief, while veiling others.

Tom does not elaborate when I ask about his extended family — the aunt and uncle he's now living with. He offers only basic information, sparing detail. They're nice, they take care of him, he has a cousin. When I gently ease toward the past, i.e., how he's come to live with them, the answer is blunt and perfunctory. "Because I had to."

This taciturnity, and the fact that he's given conflicting statements to police, is normal for someone who's endured a trauma. Tom is more than a witness; he's a victim. The murderer took his father's life and also robbed Tom of his childhood. His innocence. I remain, so far, unconvinced there is anything clinically wrong with Thomas Bishop other than the mist, as I call it, formed to protect him from further trauma, from further pain.

I need to help him clear that mist. To find the hidden details of October 27. But the process can't start without him. Without his will. He needs to begin to open up to his grief, and then I can further our trust.

* * *

Michael sees me coming and smiles. When I'm close enough, he must read my features, because the smile drops. He holds up a finger and says into the phone, "Hey, thanks for talking and for everything. I gotta go. I'll be back in touch soon. All right."

It all seems louder than necessary and a bit staged for my benefit, but whatever. I reach Michael and stop. "I think I know you," I say. "I think you were my patient fifteen years ago."

It's more confessional than accusatory. I watch his reaction carefully, though the dark is making it harder to discern.

I wait.

Michael seems taken aback. "I don't know what to say . . . You think I was your *patient*?"

"Yes. An eight-year-old boy I treated named Tom Bishop."

"Like, your *therapy* patient?"

"Yes."

Now I really study him, hunting for any betrayal. Michael blinks at me a few times. He frowns. "Who's Tom Bishop?"

I give the house a glance, sensing we're being watched. Indeed, a silhouette stands behind the screen door. Joni. I take Michael by the arm — gently, so as not to alarm him — and move him farther down the driveway. Passing the garage, we trigger a motion sensor and a light snaps on. The sharp scents of wood varnish and turpentine waft out of the open bay. I push us farther, beyond the reach of the light, back into darkness.

"I don't want to upset you," I say. Some of my steam has blown off, but I'm still determined. I decide to back it up a step and take a new approach. "I'm in a dilemma, and I need your help."

"Um, okay. Absolutely. What can I do?"

"You know I'm a therapist."

"Of course. Yes."

I swallow, tasting remnants of dinner — we had salmon, rice, asparagus — and the white wine. Am I a little drunk? I cut myself off at two glasses. "One of the things I've done as a therapist, though not anymore, was to work with police. You, Michael, look exactly like the older version of a boy I was asked to evaluate during the course of a death investigation. A murder."

I stop walking to gauge his reaction. It's the same, open and inquisitive, devoid of any fear or anger. "That boy was named Tom Bishop," I repeat his name. "He was a key witness in the case." I pause after each sentence, still scanning for signs of recognition, deceit. Anything. "The victim was his father. The suspect, eventually convicted, was his mother. None of this rings any bells?"

A mosquito whines near my ear. I wave it away, keeping a close watch on Michael. He looks back at me with that guileless expression, but then something passes over his features. A moment later, he lowers his head.

"Michael? What is it?"

He gradually raises his eyes to me. His face is lit from the side by the garage light back twenty yards. "I lied," he says.

My body temperature drops. Another mosquito sinks its needle into the skin of my bare arm, but I barely notice. "Okay," I say. "Tell me."

"My parents didn't die when I was a junior in high school."

"Okay . . ." There's a resignation in my voice. Relief.

"I was much younger when things happened."

"That's right," I say.

He takes a deep breath. This is going to change everything. But if he tells Joni about it, then it's no longer my burden. Michael can be the one to broach the subject to the family and set the tone for how little or how much he wants everyone to know. I'll suggest full disclosure to Joni, his future wife, but other than that, it's whatever he wants.

With emotion in his voice, Michael says, "The whole thing is fucked up. Sorry for the language."

"I hear it all the time." Just as I take his hand in mine, the area light blinks off, plunging us into full darkness. The bugs are starting to frenzy. Maybe we can conclude this back inside the house . . .

"My aunt and uncle . . ." he says. "They're . . . they made some bad choices."

I wait.

Michael says, "They spent the inheritance. They squandered it, really. And the whole thing had kind of a reverse effect. They didn't have much. And when I came to live with them, they ended up buying this big expensive house — they said it was better for me, growing up. Better for us as a family. But they were overleveraged. They were up to their eyes in debt even though on paper — you know, when you fill out those financial aid forms — it looked like they had a lot of money. I didn't get any grants, and they had barely anything they could give me. It was scholarship or nothing. So, that's who I was just talking to. A friend at Colgate. I need to get back there. I need to finish."

My head is spinning. It's not exactly the confession I'd been anticipating. I need to pick it apart. "You're saying both your parents died?"

"In a car wreck, yeah."

It's time to stick or move, as my own late father would say. I can't keep waffling. If I'm going to get past this, I have to go through it. I have to try.

"Michael, your father was murdered."

He gives a polite shake of his head. "No. He wasn't."

"Your mother went to prison for it."

More head-shaking. "Dr. Lindman . . . you have me confused with someone else."

"You remember everything? Their car accident? That whole period in your life . . . I don't think you really even remember it, Michael."

He makes no reply at first. I can hear his phone vibrating in his pocket, see the light of its screen showing through the fabric. Then he admits it: "Honestly, it is a hard time to remember. But that doesn't mean it's not what happened. People have talked to me about it my whole life. My aunt and uncle. My cousin. Family friends. It's my life. It's what happened."

"What if — and listen, please, I'm not trying to upset you — like I said, I need your help. What if, as an alternative theory, what happened *is* what I remember? Because of how heinous things were, how painful, certain people took it upon themselves to construct a new reality for you? Something that was less painful, that explained the loss of your parents, but . . ."

I stop myself. For one thing, Michael looks a shade whiter, his face floating before me like a ghost. I'm doing exactly what a therapist is trained to not do: dump massive, life-changing insight onto a patient. It could overload his system. To have your entire reality, your identity, exposed as a lie? Some people can't handle that. *Most* people can't handle that. Especially if it's not done right.

"All right, let's take a breath. Let me just propose this to you — you have a past that's a bit uncertain, even to you. Leaving aside what other people have told you, you just admitted your memory is hazy. I have a belief — one that only grows with each passing moment I'm with you, as much as I've tried to rationalize it or put it out of my mind — you're the boy I knew. And let me try to prove it to you. The boy, Tom Bishop, had a scar on his upper thigh. When he was six, walking along a guard rail, balancing, he fell. The sharp edge of the angle iron caught the inside of his leg and tore it open. He had fifteen stitches."

"I've been in my bathing suit," Michael says quickly. There's an edge in his tone — his defenses are up. His phone chimes, as if with a text. It's probably Joni.

"I haven't been with you, or near you, swimming," I say. "And even standard swimming trunks could hide it. Unless you've been swimming in a Speedo—"

Michael starts for the house, his feet crunching.

"Michael . . ." I follow him.

He turns abruptly and walks past me in the other direction. "I've got to get ready," he mutters. "I'm not even ready."

I hurry to catch him. The farther we venture from the house, the deeper the inky blackness becomes. "Ready for what? Michael — it's pitch black out here. You can't even see . . ."

He clicks on the light from his phone.

"Michael, you don't need to go anywhere. Just wait. Wait . . ."

His legs are longer, his strides powerful; I'm jogging to keep up. "All I want is the truth. For both of us. I know this is a lot. But I'm not trying to hurt you."

It hits me that the text I saw, *Did they buy it?* could refer to anything. He's mentioned his uncle buying the house on Long Island. Though that was a while ago, it could be related. And the number — central New York. Where Colgate is located. It could be a classmate talking about something school-related.

But there are so many other things. The uncanny resemblance. The timing of Laura Bishop's release and her proximity to our home. The phrase uttered on my phone and etched in our boathouse . . .

Suddenly, I twist my ankle on a rock in the road and stumble.

He is suddenly right beside me, his hand at my back. "You okay?"

"Just tripped." By the time I reorient myself, he's surging ahead once again. I call after him, "Listen, what if we tried something? I have a colleague who's great with hypnotherapy. We could call her — she'd fit you right in. We could see . . ."

I trail off, hearing an engine approach. It's still a ways off, but it's there, nearing. Then, through the dense trees: headlights.

Our driveway is a quarter mile of gravel, which meets with a dirt road that runs along part of the lake. I'm several paces behind Michael, who's nearing the driveway's end and the road. It could be anyone out there.

"Watch out," I say; it's the mother in me: "Watch out for that car, Michael."

Starzyk's words fill my head: *Don't follow this person, especially if you think he's meeting her. They could be dangerous.*

I slow while he keeps walking apace, his cell phone light swinging with the pendulum movements of his arms. The engine is louder, the headlights brighter, and soon the vehicle is right in front of Michael. It's a dark color, an SUV — maybe an Escalade. It brakes to a stop, halting me in my tracks.

I'm about to say something — honestly, I'm about to scream for help — when Michael opens the back door.

He gets into the vehicle, shuts the door and never looks back.

I stand there, dumbfounded. The vehicle just idles a moment. There's just enough moonlight to reflect in its black surface.

Then it pulls forward, the white reverse lights come on, and it backs into the driveway. I retreat a few steps, still in shock. The white lights wink off, red taillights flash, and the SUV spins a little gravel as it turns back onto the dirt road and drives off into the night.

CHAPTER TWENTY-SEVEN

DR EMILY LINDMAN
CASE NOTES
MAY 20
Session 3

Met with Tom, one hour, third session. Today felt like we made head-way, despite an interruption from police.

Tom and I began by talking about school, where he is now, and I asked him how school in Long Island compared to school in Bronxville. He said about the same. But I could see it got him thinking about events from six months ago.

I decided to touch on his grief. To share with him that I'd lost my father, too. And it worked. It got him talking. Particularly, it got him talking about the last day his father was alive, and his memory exploded with details.

He remembered that, that day, his third-grade teacher had had a cold, and some of the kids noticed a booger lodged in the teacher's nose. He remembered that he took the bus to his after-school baby-sitter. And from there, his mother picked him up. He recalled that, at home, his mother had gotten out the family boots and winter coats a couple of days prior, in anticipation of the first snowfall.

And he was able to describe his home in detail. I feel like I've been there now: the many clocks in the kitchen and stairwell — including one pig clock with eyes that shifted side to side in time with the seconds. Tom knew the oven mitts hanging from the stove dials. The color of the tile floor was burnt orange, he says, and the kitchen smelled like garlic, because his mother was cooking pasta.

But he says he can't remember what happened after that.

This can be trauma's lasting impact. A darkening of major events, yet a keen memory for seemingly irrelevant details. It's all another part of that misty protection.

On the other hand, Tom may remember certain things and not return to them, or change them, to avoid pain.

In the initial police report with Tom's first interview, Tom says he was awakened later that night by his mother crying. But a second report says he awoke prior to this, hearing his parents arguing.

Police asked Tom if his mother and father argued a lot. Tom either chose not to reply or didn't know how to answer. I'll assume the latter — children do pick up on their parents' stress, but they don't have anything with which to compare it.

But the police think this inconsistency could point to Tom misleading them. So much so that they interrupted our session. They're worried that Tom's mother might be leaving the area, and they need to move to press charges. After three sessions with Tom, I think they could be right about the deception, though it's not deliberate. I believe Tom has not been able to properly process that night. He's living in a limbo, caught between what he can remember and what he can't — or won't.

And I'm close to setting him free.

* * *

The sound of the engine is still fading as I pick up on footsteps hurrying toward me from the house.

A light is bouncing along with the approaching footfalls. It can only be one person.

"Mom?"

"I'm here."

"Where's Michael? What happened?"

"He left."

"He *left*?"

I catch glimpses of my daughter's face in the light from her phone. Before I can say anything else, she's trotting toward the road.

"Jo," I call after her. "Jo, honey . . ."

"Don't, Mom."

And things were just starting to mend between us . . .

When she doesn't speak again, I can see her touching her screen. She puts the phone to her ear. A moment later: "Michael? Babe? Is everything . . ." She listens. "No, I understand. Believe me, I understand." Another pause. "No, I don't need anything else. I'm ready whenever."

At this point, Paul is walking toward us from the house, another vague shape in the darkness. Paul's light is an actual flashlight. "Everybody okay?"

"We're fine, honey," I say, just loud enough.

Joni is still on the phone. "Can you tell me what happened? What did she do to you?"

"Jo, come on . . ." I start for her, reaching out, and she moves away.

"What did she say?" Joni listens, then, "All right, baby. That's fine. I'll be waiting."

She ends the call. Even in the semidarkness, I can see her angry face. Paul has reached us and stands beside me. "What's going on?"

"Mom just freaked Michael the fuck out," Joni says.

"Jo, listen, there are some things we need to talk about."

"No," she says, emphatically. She crunches up the driveway toward me. "We're done talking. I've had about enough of—"

My voice goes up an octave. "Hey! Listen up. You know my life, Joni. You know that in my job, certain things require discretion."

She stops. "What are you talking about?"

"Who did he just get in that car with?"

"What the fuck is going on with you?"

Paul: "Joni, don't speak like that to your mother."

"Is that her?" I ask. "I mean what are you guys doing? I feel like I'm in the goddamn *Twilight Zone*, here, Joni. Time to level with me."

"Level with *you*? Why don't *you* just tell me what you said to him?"

I glance at Paul, then refocus on Joni. "Maybe in a minute."

"Because you look like you want to accuse him of something," Joni says. "You've looked like that since the moment he got here."

Her tone is cutting, and puts me over the edge. "Oh, have I? Have your father and I seemed a little off? Could that be because we've hardly seen or heard from you since Easter — you pulled another one of your disappearing acts, just like you used to. And when you finally grace us with your presence — surprise! You show up with your eleventh boyfriend and — oh — this one, guess what? You're *engaged*. Wow! But don't worry about it. 'Don't worry about it, Mom and Dad — I'm fine. Just fine. That time you found me on the street with a needle in my arm? I'm just *perfect* now.'"

Joni is staring at me. Even in scant light, I can see her face has crumbled. Paul moves closer and touches my arm, but I shrug him off.

"Was that her?" I ask suddenly. "Did he arrange to meet *her*?"

Joni doesn't say anything for a long time. So long that I take Paul's flashlight and shine it in her face. She squints in its brightness but stares back at me. I know I've hurt her; it crushes me.

Her pain turns to defiance, just as regular as the moon and the sun. The defiance forms a wry smile, a pity in her eyes. "Wow, Mom. Your work really has gotten to you. You think everyone is hiding something. Maybe you're projecting? I mean — '*her*'? Who are you even talking about? And maybe there's a reason, Mom. That I did what I did back then. You ever think that?" She turns to Paul. "Either of you?"

"Hey," Paul says, taking back the flashlight, but keeping it on her. "Let's just tone it down."

But Joni is livid now. "And you're out here interrogating him. After everything he's already been through!"

Her raised voice echoes in the trees, off the mountains. Remote as we are, I worry that the neighbors can hear. Sound carries, especially across the lake.

"Do you understand that?" she asks. "I mean, you talk about *me*. Just like always, the focus is on *me*. But you're running around these past two days, hitting animals with the car, acting like a nutcase! We came up here to tell you our plans, and it's just been a wall of skepticism!"

"Keep it down, Jo," I say. I've simmered down some, listening to my daughter while chasing multiple thought strands.

"I don't need your approval of Michael," she growls at me. "I don't need your projection — either of you. Your own shit, your own infidelity issues a million years ago —"

"Watch it," warns Paul. There's ice in his voice.

"Fine. But you're so far gone, Mom . . . I can't even. I mean, I think you need help."

Somehow, in the midst of her tirade, I've found calm. "So tell me who was in the car."

Joni stares at me with that defiant look. She doesn't want to satisfy me with a response.

She doesn't need to.

As if on command, the headlights appear again in the distance, stuttering through the trees. The sound of the engine drifts toward us. Joni starts for the road.

"Hey," Paul calls. Both of us follow our daughter.

She spins on us. "They're our *friends*, guys. Madison and Hunter. Remember Madison Tremont?"

I do. Madison is one of Joni's childhood friends. Stuck for a response, I stammer, "I didn't know they . . . do they live up here?"

"Yes. They live up here. We came up the night before — Thursday night — and stayed with them."

It explains why Joni and Michael had enough time to for a tour before meeting us at the lake house at eleven a.m. "Why didn't you tell me?"

Joni takes a moment. She's calmer now, too, maybe now that she's gotten in a few shots at me — the guilt of that tends to mollify her. We're not so dissimilar. "Because of what you *do,* Mom. Because of how involved you get in everything. If I told you we were going there, you'd have a million questions. A million suggestions. How long are you staying? When did they move here? Why don't they come over to the lake house? I was going to tell you; I just didn't get around to it yet." A moment later, she adds, "They built a yurt."

Paul: "A yurt?"

Joni sighs. She turns her back to us. She says, "Yeah, a yurt," and continues walking.

The SUV pulls up at the base of the driveway. I feel like things have taken a turn for the bizarre, and I'm rushing to complete the thoughts in my head and make sense of what's just happened. Only thing stands clear, one sharp feeling: I want to rush over, to tell Michael I'm sorry. I want to ask when they'll be back. I want to know, *need* to know, but my daughter's words ring in my head: *Because of what you* do, *Mom. How involved you get in everything.*

The back door opens. I peer in and glimpse Michael. The front passenger window comes down, revealing a pretty, young woman. Her dangling earrings sparkle in the light.

Paul waves. "Hi, Madison."

"Hi, Mr. Lindman."

I hear Joni say something quiet which sounds like, "Let's just go," as she gets into the back.

Madison gives us a sheepish smile and a wave, then sends up the window as the car backs into the driveway, turns, and leaves again.

I stand beside Paul a moment, dimly aware of his hand on my upper back. Speechless, I turn and trudge back for the house.

Paul doesn't ask any questions. Relevant ones, at least. He just says, "They have a yurt and drive an Escalade?"

I want to crawl into bed and not emerge for days.

CHAPTER TWENTY-EIGHT

Sean is sitting at the table when we come in. He's bent over his phone, then he looks up and tosses the phone on the table, offering a sympathetic smile. "What was *that* all about?"

"Joni and Michael went out with some friends," I say.

Sean looks at me, reading my body language. He can tell I'm tense. He says, "Joni told me Madison lives up here now on property owned by her parents. She and her boyfriend have a yurt. They built it themselves with steam-bent wood, or something. It's like a house."

I survey the dining area and kitchen. All is sparkling clean. Sean has done all of the cleanup, it seems. Suddenly, I'm on the verge of tears.

Sean hurries to me. "Mom, come on . . . It's okay."

I take his arm. Looking around, I wonder where Paul has gone. Did he come in with me or did I just imagine it? Maybe he's out in the garage, admiring his handmade boat.

Yurts in the woods? Paul's beloved boat? These are the things we're thinking about after what just happened?

I'm seized by the urge to smoke. "Hey," I ask Sean. "You got anything?" I put fingers to my lips and draw air.

"Weed?"

"Just a cigarette."

"I don't smoke, Ma. You know that."

I consider it. "How about the other thing?"

"Just sit down. I'll get you some wine."

I let Sean lead me to the table and sit. He gets the white wine from the kitchen, pulls a fresh glass from the cabinet. He pours me a half glass. I shouldn't, but I take a sip anyway. Then I manage to look at my son. How did this happen? He's barely twenty-five and Joni is twenty-two. But while she still feels like a child to me, he seems mature. Sure, he can be hard to get a hold of, unpredictable, but he's figuring things out.

He takes my hand. "It's gonna be okay," he says again.

"Yeah."

"We've been here before, right?"

"What do you mean? With Joni?"

He shrugs: *Yes.*

"I don't know. I think this is different. I think I really screwed up."

I tell him about it as best as I can, keeping details private. Sean listens, his brow furrowing with empathy, nodding his understanding. But instead of feeling unburdened, a new spirit of frustration rises up in me. How can this be happening? How can someone who seems so much like my former patient . . . how can I be wrong about this person?

He has a credible alternate life from the one I expect him to have. Even if he admits to a hazy memory — surely *something* would spark in him at my prompting.

Or maybe it has, and he's suppressing . . .

Or — wait — maybe he's told *Joni* the real story, not knowing she was my daughter? Is that possible? But then why would she act so bewildered by my suggestion of his mother?

"There I go again," I say.

Sean frowns. "What?"

"Nothing." We change topics. I ask him about his life. He tells me about surfing in the Pacific Ocean.

"You were in California?"

"Just for a couple of weeks."

"I don't remember that."

"I posted a couple of pics. Nothing big." He tells me he was out there looking for work — the fruit-picking kind. But when he got the sense that nearly every farm sought migrant labor, which was cheaper, he moved on. He'd met a girl, though, a young woman, in Venice Beach. She was the one who suggested Colorado. "You wouldn't associate Colorado with organic produce, but it's huge out there."

"Tell me about the girl." I'm happy to be distracted by Sean's life. It's so free and romping, it's like a romance novel. Her name was Chloe, and she was a Colorado girl who made trips to the Pacific Coast in the winter to warm up and stay with friends. "Once we got back to Denver, though, she left my ass," Sean says.

I give his hand a squeeze and stick out my lower lip. "She doesn't deserve you."

"It's all good. We had some fun. I'm not ready to settle down right now anyway."

The notion sends my thoughts back around to Joni. I was never one to pressure my kids to get hitched and give me grandbabies. Of course, grandkids would be great. Someday. For Paul and me, it's important that our children have a chance to live life. To sow some oats. We're believers that this promotes a healthy, lasting union once one is established. There's no *I wish I would have done* . . . before putting down roots and growing a family. I had my time as a young single woman, experiencing the world. Paul had his gadabout days. Other than the one trouble spot many years ago, it's been mostly smooth sailing for us.

Hasn't it?

"I'm happy for you, Sean," I tell my son. "Living life on your own terms. It's important."

I'm about to say something else when I hear a sound: a car. Getting up from the table, I glance at the clock on the kitchen stove — Sean and I have been talking for nearly an hour. There are voices outside, faint but getting louder. Footsteps on the gravel. I walk to the entrance and stand at the screen door. The night air is perfumed with pine and alders. With the sun gone a couple of hours, the breeze is cool on my skin.

Paul is definitely in the garage; the open bay throws out a bleaching white light. Emerging from the darkness into that brightness are my daughter and her fiancé.

I don't know who else I expected, but seeing them suddenly makes me nervous, like a schoolgirl whose prom date arrived. It's because I have some apologizing to do, some divisions to mend.

I watch a moment as Paul comes out and talks to them. He draws Michael into the garage to look at the boat. Joni stays in the driveway. She turns to look at me and I freeze.

Then she raises her hand in a wave.

I wave back. Right after, I hug myself, suddenly chilled by a cool breeze. My emotions are jumbling together — gratitude, suspicion, anticipation. It's all I can do to stay there, not go barging into the garage and demand to know why they're back so soon.

"Hey, look who it is," Sean says. He's moved beside me, sipping his wine.

Paul can be heard boasting about his boat. Michael mumbles his admiration. Then Michael retreats, and Joni takes his arm, and Paul says, "See you inside," from somewhere within the garage.

I move back from the door and enter the kitchen, unsure what to do with myself. Sean returns to the table and sits down.

The dishes are done but for my wine glass, so I scoop it off the table and wash it. By the time I'm placing it in the drying rack, Joni and Michael have come in.

It's a little hard for me to make eye contact. It was such a difficult scene in the driveway. I'm still processing it. Yet the two of them seemed to have come to some sort of consensus about things. It's in their movements, the deliberateness of their demeanor. They both say "Hi" to me, and their voices are whispery, light. Michael pulls out Joni's chair and she sits. Then he takes his seat — where he was at dinner, facing the kitchen, his back to the windows and the dark lake beyond them.

I finally manage to find my voice. "Back so soon? Everything okay?"

Joni answers. "We didn't feel like going out. We were supposed to have drinks with them later. When things . . . when you and Michael were outside, I called them, asked them if they could come a little sooner. That's when they picked up Michael."

"Okay," I say. I lean on the sink, feeling somewhat back in familiar territory: listening to my daughter explain her actions, justify things.

But there's more. And it's written all over Michael's face.

"Dr. Lindman," he begins.

"Emily."

He clears his throat. His eyes dart between me, Joni, and Sean. Finally, they stay on me, beaming sincerity. "I'm sorry about what happened earlier."

"It's okay. Listen, guys—"

Joni holds up her hand. "Mom. Just hear him out. Okay?"

I zip my lips.

Michael says, "You're right. I'm not sure what happened when I was younger. All my life, people kept it mostly quiet. About my parents. But I always knew something was off. I just figured they were . . . you know, sparing me certain details. Like why I never went to a funeral. I thought maybe their bodies were . . ." He clears his throat again, as if on the edge of emotion.

It triggers my maternal instinct, and I leave the kitchen for the dining room. I sit down between them as he finishes.

"Like their bodies were too badly injured, or something." After he finishes the thought, he faces me. I can tell it requires effort. "But there are other things. Things I can't square. I have . . . other memories. They're blurry. They're . . . It's like they're the memories of someone else. And when you . . . When we talked in the driveway, it touched a nerve. That's why I just got in the car and left. I'm sorry."

"It's okay," I manage. "I understand."

And then Michael, after glancing at Joni one more time for support, tells me this:

"I'd like to do what you suggested."

I draw a breath and wait.

"I'd like to try hypnotherapy," Michael says. "You know, regressive therapy. Whatever it is. And maybe see what's there. Maybe I'll get to the truth."

I exhale and say, "I think that's a good idea."

His bright eyes lock on mine.

He says, "But I want you to do it."

CHAPTER TWENTY-NINE

A light rain has started to fall, spitting against the picture window. Our boathouse light reveals white chop on the lake, wind blowing hard on the water.

"There's no way," I say to Michael. "It would be a conflict of interest. You're my future son-in-law, and therapists don't practice on their own families. And anyway, I can't help you because I'd have a preconceived idea. I'd be trying to lead you to what I believe is true."

"But what if you didn't, though?" Joni asks. She's enthusiastic. Joni has always liked a bit of drama.

I shake my head. "I can't."

Michael, who hasn't said anything since asking me to perform the therapy on him, gets up from the table. He unsnaps his pants.

"Babe?" Joni looks between us, her eyes wide. "What are you doing?"

He pulls his pants down. He's wearing red boxer briefs beneath. I can already see it, snaking out the left leg of his underpants: the scar. He rolls back more of the fabric to reveal it all. It has a crescent shape to it, more hooked at one end.

"That?" Joni says. "Why are you showing her that?"

"Because she knew it was there."

Joni gives me a suspicious look. "She didn't just see it?"

"No. Look where it is. She knows because she has a file on me somewhere. Is that right, Dr. Lindman?"

"That's right. Which is why I can't help you with this. I would only be . . ."

I trail off as Michael steps toward me. "You asked me to help you. Outside, you asked me to help you. Now I'm asking. Please. Let's just see. Just one time. If I'm not . . . if it doesn't work or you're uncomfortable, we'll stop and I won't ask again."

He looks at me, longingly, as the rain picks up outside.

Sean has been so quiet, I've almost forgotten he's here. "I think you should do it, Mom."

I look around at him. My voice of reason. And then I wonder where Paul is, but then I hear a creak above my head, the sound of running water; at some point, he returned inside and went to the upstairs bathroom.

"All right," I say. "We'll sleep on it, and if we all still feel the same way, maybe we can try it tomorrow."

But Michael is shaking his head. "I think it should be tonight."

"Michael . . ."

Joni cuts in again: "You've already stirred stuff up in him, Mom. He was remembering things, saying things to me in the car. If we sleep, it could cloud it all over. You know that's exactly what happens with sleep."

I only stand there, breathing. Watching Michael, seeking the truth in his eyes. Looking at my two children, who seem as anxious for me to get started as Michael is.

Finally, I break. "Okay. But I need to do a few things first."

The relief in Michael's eyes is unmistakable.

* * *

We go through it. I've brought Michael into Sean's room on the second floor. Like Joni's room, it views the lake. The rain is coming harder and the wind has picked up. Right on cue, like some kind of movie. But a white noise in the background aids the process. Michael is able to relax. He seems to trust me.

Hypnotherapy doesn't work on everyone; some people are more suggestible than others. It's hardest for those with high situational awareness, those who have trouble letting go, or who are compulsive or obsessive by nature. Michael actually strikes me as easygoing and has since Joni introduced him. Though Tom Bishop was full of anguish — and full of rage — it was the kind you knew to be righteous. Even if it could be toxic, left unchecked. I knew — or sensed — while working with Tom, that a decent, kind boy was there amid the trauma of what he'd witnessed. A boy in a terrible situation.

"Now, Michael," I say, leaning forward slightly in my chair, "you're fully and completely relaxed. You know that you're safe. That you're looked after. You know that everything is in its right place. The rain is soothing you, and you feel completely at ease. Completely comfortable."

He is on the bed, lying down. It's not necessary to lie down for hypnotherapy — in fact, sometimes it's discouraged, lest the patient drift off into sleep — but Michael suggested it. I watch his chest rise and fall, evenly, steadily. The light comes from a small lamp on the bedside table. The room is slightly musky, damp from underuse.

The rain drums on the room. It patters against the windows and streaks the glass.

"Michael, I want you to listen to my voice. Everything around you is quiet and dark. Even the rain is fading away. Hear it fade . . . Just my voice is left, the volume of everything else turned down until it's nothing. Pure tranquil silence. My voice is sort of pulling you along. We're going to go back in time, Michael, we're going to go back to your house on Pondfield Road. Can you see that house? Do you remember it?"

Michael, softly: "Yes."

"Can you describe it to me? What color is it?"

"It's white. With black around the edges."

This is major: He's just described the house in Bronxville, the very one I parked in front of two nights ago. I'm done considering coincidences at this point.

"That's right. White with black trim. Do you like the color?"

"No. I always wished it was red or blue." Michael already sounds younger, slightly childlike.

"Let's go into the house," I say. "Okay? Let's you and I go into the front door together."

"Can I hold your hand?"

For a moment, I don't respond. It was as if his voice even *became* Tom's voice for a moment, a full octave higher. A sweeter, lighter voice. Finally I say, "Of course you can hold my hand. Feel it in yours?" I've not actually touched him, but I can sense his relaxation at imagining it. "All right. Now . . . let's go inside."

"Okay."

I give it a second or two. "What do we see?"

"Boots."

"Boots?"

"By the door. Boots and shoes. And jackets hanging. My red winter jacket."

"Right, it's winter. Is it snowing outside?"

On the bed, Michael gives a little shake of his head. "Not right now."

I consider it. It had snowed the night of David Bishop's murder, one of the first of the season. But it had been later, hours after he'd gotten home. And while visible footprints leading to and from the side door were part of the initial police report, those tracks had melted in the morning sun.

They weren't hard evidence. They were one piece of a mystery. One I can remember desperate police scrambling to solve.

They seemed to have it in for the wife . . .

But these thoughts are galloping ahead of where I need to be.

"Okay. So all the boots and jackets are there inside the door. What's next? What's going on in the kitchen?"

Michael doesn't respond.

"Michael?"

His hand twitches. Then his head — a minor jerking motion, like someone dreaming.

"Michael? Did you fall asleep?"

"No." A child's answer. *Nooo*. Then: "There's nothing going on in the kitchen. The clocks are ticking."

"The clocks . . . Are there lots of clocks?"

"Yes." His words are dreamy, slightly slurred. "They go up the stairs."

"That's right. The clocks are on the wall going up the stairs. Let's go up there together."

He utters a kind of moan, like he's reluctant.

"What do you say, Michael? Can you show me your room?" I want to call him Tom, but he's responding to Michael fine. No need to push.

"Okay," he says, after a pause. "We're in my room."

"Good. Very good. Can you tell me about your room?"

He describes the way it was set up. The toys, the posters on the wall, the Pokémon game. I haven't even specified to *when* we were returning, only that we needed to go back in time, to some point. Michael has selected this. The boots and thick coats point to winter, which could be any winter — but based on Michael's mannerisms, his voice, and the description of his room, he most certainly seems to have chosen the time near his father's murder.

Maybe this very night, in his memory.

It is more than I expected, more than I would have hoped for, in a first session. Honestly, the whole thing raises my suspicion that Michael is faking it.

If so, he's convincing as ever. Or I'm gullible. But I don't think so. And there's no better alternative to seeing it through, anyway.

I listen as he continues to tell me about his belongings — now it's his cherished Harry Potter books on the shelves beside his bed — and yet I'm slightly distracted, knowing that Sean and Joni and Paul are all downstairs right now, surely talking about this. Each of them knows a little something, but so far their knowledge has been disparate. Now, together, they're going to be able to form a more complete picture.

There's nothing more I can do to stop that from happening. The cat is pretty much out of the bag. I could have refused to do the treatment with Michael, could have insisted he wait for my colleague's opening, could have made excuses about needing to update my hypnotherapy license, but I didn't.

Because I have to know.

Even if it's a charade, I have to find out.

Not just whether Michael is Tom — I need to know what he believes truly happened that night.

CHAPTER THIRTY

"Tom?"

It's been a few seconds since I've given him any direction, having gotten lost in my own thoughts. I've said "Tom" instead of "Michael" without intending.

"Yes?"

But he's answered.

"It's time for bed," I say.

"I don't want to go to bed."

"Well, you've had a long day. I think—"

"I don't want to!" he shouts. On the bed, Michael's eyes remain closed, but his forehead is lined with a scowl, his hands closed into fists.

So much for easygoing Tom, I think. But then I remind myself: *The Tom of fifteen years ago is not the same as the Tom — or Michael — in my son's bed.*

Though Michael has brought us back to a time just prior to his father's death, the boy who experienced that murder, who saw it take its gruesome place, is already layered in. The frustrated, sad and angry boy who came to see me — he's here.

Plus, I screwed up. Now that we're here, I've been trying to fast forward to the moment he witnessed the crime, but

Michael's mind isn't video playback. It's too much too soon for him, hence the mini-tantrum.

"Okay, Tom. It's okay . . . how about we read a bedtime story instead?"

He settles. His fists relax and his forehead smooths. "All right," he intones. "I'll pick one."

We get back to it. First, he makes an elaborate show of choosing a book. I marvel that he can remember so many titles. But he spent a significant portion of his childhood in this room and has a vivid picture of this time in his life.

"How about Harry Potter?" I ask, when time has passed.

He doesn't respond.

"Tom? Can we pick a book?" I feign a yawn. "I'm getting tired."

"There's someone," he whispers.

"What?" I edge closer, feeling the hairs on my arms stiffening. "Someone where?"

"There's someone outside."

It's so convincing, so compelling, that I stand up.

"Can you see them?" Even though I realize Michael is talking about the past, I move to the windows. The rain hits the lake at an angle, frothing it white. I hear the boats thumping in the boathouse.

"I can see him," Michael says.

My blood runs cold. "What is he doing?"

"He's sitting in a car. I think he's watching."

The words chill me. "You think he's watching?" I ease back toward the chair, recommitting to Michael's memory. *His* world.

"He's sitting there. Smoking."

Another flash in my mind: two cigarette butts in the street. Cops had found them and bagged them. Along with the tracks in the snow, it was early evidence of an intruder. That theory held for six months, although no one was ever arrested.

But Tom told police he saw his mother.

Right?

"Tom? What's the man outside doing now?"

"I want to read."

"Is he still there?"

"I don't know."

"Can you see him?"

Tom never told me this. Not that I remember. I'll have to go back through my case notes to be sure, but this is all new to me.

"Tom? Can you still see the man?"

"I'm done. I need to leave here." Michael's gruffer tone suggests he's reverting to his present, older self. Trying to come back.

I sit down quickly. "Wait now, Tom. Let's stay in your room. I'll read you a book, and then we can go to sleep."

"I don't want to go to sleep."

"Well, let's go back down to the kitchen and maybe get sna—"

"I don't want to go to the kitchen!" he yells with the rage of a grown man. He smashes his fists down on the bed. The deep scowl has returned. His jaw bulges on the sides.

"Is it fighting?" I remember a phrase Tom Bishop used from his police interviews. "Do you hear bad fighting?"

Michael answers by grunting and writhing on the bed.

"Okay — Tom? I need you to listen to my voice."

"I'm not going to the kitchen!"

"Listen to me. Just my voice. Your house is fading. Everything is fading around you. Can you hear the rain? The rain is starting to come back, like the volume turned up on your stereo. Can you hear it?"

He is relaxing a little, though his fists remain clenched. Finally: "I can hear it."

"Follow my voice, and follow the rain. We're going to go forward in time. Back to the lake house. Back to Joni. You remember Joni?"

The twitch of a smile. "Yes."

"Okay. We're coming back from the past, we're returning to the present. Right here, right now. From Tom to

Michael. You're at the lake house with Joni. With me, Emily. We're in Sean's room. You're lying in his bed. Now, I'm going to count back from five . . ."

Less than a minute later, Michael is sitting up in the bed, legs off the side. He rubs his temple like his head aches mildly, and he wears a sheepish grin. I offer him some water. He drinks it, and I sit back in the chair, watching him.

Frank Mills, in my head: *Everything takes longer than expected.*

Yeah, this is going to take a little while.

CHAPTER THIRTY-ONE

POLICE REPORT
INVESTIGATORS R. MOONEY and S. STARZYK
WITNESS INTERVIEW TRANSCRIPT, LAURA
AVEENA BISHOP
OCTOBER 27

Mooney: Hi, Mrs. Bishop. Thank you for speaking with us. We know things are . . . it's really hard right now. But you doing this, while things are fresh. It can really help.

Laura: Is Tom okay?

Mooney: He's fine. We just talked to him. You'll see him again in just a few minutes.

Laura: Okay.

Mooney: Let's just get right to the hard stuff. Get it out of the way. What can you tell us about last night? If you could start with when you came home. You came home from work . . . ?

Laura: Yes. I came home from work.

Mooney: And where do you work?

Laura: In the city. In New York City. In SOHO.

Mooney: You're an art dealer?

Laura: No. I manage artists.

Starzyk: What is that? If I may ask. Getting paintings sold, or something?

Laura: Sometimes. Arranging gallery shows. Museums. Private events. Coordinating publicity efforts.

[Indistinguishable speaking.]

Starzyk: Anybody I would know about? Banksy or someone like that?

Laura: Kate Morrison. Um, Isaiah Jackson-Smith. Corrine Whitman.

Starzyk: Huh. And you've been doing this how long?

Laura: I've been with United for five years.

Mooney: United. That's United Artists Management?

Laura: Okay. I mean, yes. How much longer is this going to take? My son . . .

Mooney: Not long. Your son is fine. He's just in the other room, playing with some toys. An officer is with him. She's great with kids.

Starzyk: You were out of work for a while, is that right? You had Thomas, and then raised him for a couple of years?

Laura: I got my master's, and a few months later, had Tom.

Starzyk: Your master's. From Cooper's Union. Very prestigious. What about before that? You're from Stamford, Connecticut?

Laura: Yes.

Starzyk: What was your childhood like? You grew up with three sisters, and you're the oldest. Then you did some traveling?

Laura: I went to Europe. To Paris. Italy, England. I spent six months in Costa Rica.

Starzyk: And what were you doing?

Laura: Living. Working. Painting.

Starzyk: Ah, so you're a painter, too. Any success with that?

Laura: How do you mean?

Starzyk: Shows. Big sales, big commissions. I don't know how it works. Didn't Jackson Pollock — didn't he get contracted to do some big painting for a museum?

Laura: I wanted to get out of Connecticut. I wanted to see some of the world before I went to college. It was a structured gap year. It was planned. I didn't intend to sell paintings. I was studying with people. Learning craft and technique, but also representation. Management.

Mooney: Did you spot any talent?

Laura: Everywhere. The world is full of talented people. Everyone has a talent for something.

Starzyk: But not everyone is able to make a success out of it. That's where you come in.

Laura: Not everyone has the same set of circumstances . . . Are we going to talk about who killed my husband?

Mooney: Mrs. Bishop, we're just trying to establish a little about who you are, for the record. I'm sure it's no surprise that, in these types of situations, we have to ask the spouse some questions. It's a very difficult position for you, I know.

Laura: I don't understand. I've told you what happened. I told you I heard David struggling with someone. That they were in the kitchen. It sounded like fighting — like wrestling. My son even said he saw someone sitting outside, in a vehicle . . . Why are you looking at me like that?

Mooney: Mrs. Bishop, Mrs. Bishop . . . please. I understand your frustration. We've got your statement, and we're taking it very seriously. The crime-scene unit is still at your house, gathering evidence. We ask these questions because it's procedure. We'd ask anyone. Hard as it is to ask, or to be asked.

Starzyk: It's also relevant, Mrs. Bishop, that there are eyewitnesses of you slapping your husband at a restaurant—

Laura: That's got nothing to do with this!

Starzyk: —and people who have come forward saying your husband suspected you of having an affair. Someone you met in the city at your art gallery.

Laura: I want to go see my son.

[Chairs scraping. Sounds of movement.]

Mooney: I'm sorry, Mrs. Bishop. I apologize for Detective Starzyk. That was out of line. Let's just get back to the timeline. Okay? You came home from work . . .

Laura: You want the timeline — I already gave my statement at the house. He wants to know all about my life. The two of you bring up something that happened in a restaurant six months ago, out of context, which has nothing to do with this. What kind of police department is this? I want someone else to investigate this. You haven't even asked me who I think it might be.

Mooney: Who you think this might be? You have someone in mind for your husband's murder?

Laura: Jesus Christ, you say it like you've already decided I'm guilty.

Starzyk: Please calm down, ma'am. You're getting very agitated. We asked about the timeline because—

Laura: Fine. I came home from work and picked up my son from the sitter. I took him home. I made dinner in anticipation of David's arrival. He missed the train and arrived home a half hour later. Okay?

Mooney: At eight p.m.?

Laura: At eight. Yes. We ate, we talked. We—

Starzyk: What did you talk about?

Laura: Our son. David's work. My work. A normal conversation on a normal night.

Mooney: And he seemed perfectly okay to you? Perfectly normal?

Laura: He seemed a little overworked. A little tired. But he puts in long days.

Mooney: Okay. So he's a little tired, you're talking. Any drinking?

Laura: Like I said in my statement, we each had a glass of wine with dinner. That's it. I went upstairs and gave Tom a bath, read him a story, and put him to bed. If David drank more, I don't know. It's really just amazing how little you've—

Mooney: Did you go back downstairs at any point?

Laura: Yes! Also like I've said, multiple times. I came down in my pajamas. I finished the dishes. David was outside, having a cigar, talking on the phone.

Mooney: A good conversation? Bad conversation?

Laura: My God. Do you think I'm going to change my story? He was blowing cigar smoke into the air and laughing. And that's the last time that I saw . . .

[Indistinguishable noises.]

Mooney: I know this is hard for you, but you're doing well. Can you keep going? For the tape, the witness has nodded yes. He came upstairs, though, at some point?

[Indistinguishable noises.]

Mooney: Mrs. Bishop, I know this is hard, but I need you to answer.

Laura: I . . . I heard the floor creak. He went into Tom's room. To kiss him good night. I was so tired. I just . . . fell asleep.

Mooney: And then you were awakened . . .

Laura: I heard a noise. A thump. It sounded like . . . at first I thought I was dreaming about a gym. Someone playing basketball. Shoes squeaking. Breathing hard. But then there was another . . . another noise. It was sickening. A living thing being hit with something . . . bludgeoned . . . a cracking . . . oh God . . .

[Indistinguishable speaking. Chair scrapes.]

Mooney: It's okay. Take a couple of deep breaths. That's it. It's going to be okay, Mrs. Bishop . . .

Starzyk: We're almost done, Laura. We know what you saw when you came downstairs. You don't have to go through that again. Your husband was there on the floor. The side door — the door to the mudroom off the kitchen — was ajar. You said the cold air came in. You said that beside your husband on the floor was a hammer. Covered in blood.

[Indistinguishable speaking.]

Starzyk: Can you answer again for the tape?

Laura: Yes.

Starzyk: Yes, you saw a hammer?

Laura: Yes.

Starzyk: What did you think when you saw it?

Laura: Wh . . . What?

Starzyk: Among other things. Everything is going through your mind. But did you think — 'I know that hammer'? Or 'What's that doing here?' Or — 'Whoever did this left the murder weapon'? Anything like that?

Laura: No. I didn't think anything about the hammer.

Starzyk: Except that it had been used in this awful thing. You must've thought that, with some part of your mind.

Laura: I guess.

Mooney: For the tape, images K1a through K1g are being shown to the witness.

Starzyk: Mrs. Bishop, we took inventory of all the items in your garage, and in the small outbuilding — the shed — where your husband kept the lawnmower and other things. Here is a picture of the hammer. Please take a look. Now, would you say, is it your best recollection that this hammer belonged to your late husband, David?

Laura: Yes.

Starzyk: Would you say you had an idea where it was located?

[Silence.]

Starzyk: Mrs. Bishop—

Laura: I think I need a lawyer. Not because I did anything, but because you seem determined to paint a certain picture. I could say something completely innocent and have it used against me.

Starzyk: You can retain counsel. Absolutely. That's your right. But just so you know, my question sought to affirm aspects of the crime scene. Like tracks in the snow leading to the garage. Accessing the garage, which was unlocked. Our belief that the hammer was kept in the garage.

Laura: Sure. Yes. And the man my son saw outside the house, the man who I heard fighting with my husband in the kitchen, he was the one who walked up our driveway, went to the garage, found a hammer, came into the house and beat my husband to death. But you don't have anything on that, do you? Nothing you can use. That's why you're still talking to me. Okay? I'm leaving.

[Chair scraping.]

Mooney: For the tape, Laura Bishop has left the room.

Starzyk: I think we touched a nerve. And who knows where to find a hammer in someone's garage? I don't even know where my own hammer is.

Mooney: That wasn't right.

Starzyk: What? We have it all right here. United Artists Management is on the edge of bankruptcy. She's suspected of cheating on him. Witnesses saw her hit him in the face at that restaurant. That's motive, plus motive, plus violent tendencies. So someone was in a car outside? Who gives a shit? Crime scene wasn't able to determine if—

Mooney: Because the crime scene got contaminated.

Starzyk: Bullshit. We didn't — the tape is still running, Rebecca. Shut it off. Roll back the last minute and erase it. For God's sake. That's not my fault. Not my fault some tech fucked up the scene. Listen, I'm going for a cigarette. If we're going to get done with paperwork by ton—

[Recording ends.]

CHAPTER THIRTY-TWO | SUNDAY

It's late, and I can't sleep. I keep hearing Michael's childlike voice in my head. Or picture him writhing on the bed, grunting with impotent fury. It's just past three a.m. I get up and decide to use the downstairs bathroom to pee, so as not to wake anyone. Afterward, I run the tap for a glass of water.

Now I'm really awake.

I get a couple of things from upstairs as quietly as I can. While I'm in the closet, Paul mumbles something in his sleep. He sounds like he's having a bad dream. After a moment, he rolls over onto his side and mumbles something.

"It's okay," I say. "Go back to sleep."

Back downstairs, I slip out into the night air — cool now, after the rain, everything wet and shining in the moonlight. The lake has calmed and softly laps the shore. I sluice away some water from one of the Adirondack chairs and sit down.

I light a cigarette. It's one of Joni's, and it seems to help me think.

Two minutes later, I text Frank Mills.

You up?

The squiggles pop up almost immediately. Then: *No.*

Smiling, I peck out the next message: *Detective Rebecca Mooney . . . Retired? Where?*

I puff the cigarette. Mills responds: *That's an easy one. She's up near you.*

I text: *?*

Frank's response: *Lake George.*

Okay, well, she's in the general vicinity, but over an hour away. I don't think Frank's ever been north of the Bronx, so to him, everything past Riverdale is in proximity to everything else.

But that's interesting: Rebecca Mooney took her retirement in a similar touristy-but-rural town. I suppose more people than you'd first think migrate up here in later years, where life moves a little slower.

I ask Frank, *Anything controversial about her retirement? Not that I recall. She took the first exit, though.*

He means Mooney retired as soon as she was eligible. Some cops work a little longer, grow their benefits. Mooney bailed at the earliest opportunity.

I mash out the cigarette on the porch. One more text to Frank, and I'll go back to bed.

I type: *Michael thinks he might be Tom.*

A second later I add: *And he saw a man that night.*

I wait but don't see the dots. A minute passes, then two, with the water lapping, making sucking sounds as it jostles beneath the docks. Frank has yet to respond. But that's how it works with texting. You never know.

Only it gives me an uneasy feeling as I climb the gentle hill back toward the house, checking my phone as I go.

On my way, I see a light turn out upstairs.

* * *

In the morning, I knock on the closed door to Joni's room; breakfast is ready. No one answers. I knock again and listen close for a moan, a groan — something. It's ten a.m., but there's no response. The door is unlocked. "Jo? Michael? Coming in . . ."

The bed is empty, the covers mussed. Clothes and shoes litter the floor on Joni's side; the bedside table is crowded with half-drunk glasses of water, wadded tissues, some loose bills and change, a John Sandford hardback book she probably got from the family room downstairs.

Michael's side of the bed is the opposite: neat and tidy. A pair of hard-soled shoes is lined up next to a folded pair of pants and his black duffel bag. His phone is plugged into the wall. They can't be far.

I open a window to get out the musky sleep-smell and linger a moment. Michael's bag is zipped closed, but I bet his diary is still inside.

"Hey," Paul says from the doorway.

I fight the urge to hurry out of the room. I'm done trying to hide any of this. "Where are the kids?"

"They were up early. Ate and put on shoes, went for a walk."

"A walk?"

"I know, right? Who body-snatched our daughter?"

Joni is still young, still figuring out who she is — but until now, our daughter abhorred physical recreation. It was always Sean who was outdoorsy and athletic, while Joni preferred . . . other hobbies.

"Hobbies" such as taking off in the middle of the night as a teenager, leaving no word of where she was going or whom she was with. Bronxville looks like a cozy, wealthy town on the outside. And it is . . . but then there's the side that tourists and casual observers easily miss. It is a home to surgeons and lawyers and finance gurus — as well as at least one network news celebrity and one pro athlete — and people forget that these affluent, overachieving individuals tend to have children. Children with trust funds and private school enrollments and bad attitudes. Kids who get into trouble, and get into it young. Alcohol, drugs, sex. And not like in the eighties, when Paul and I grew up. The world is scarier today, I think. The consequences more dire.

If Joni has emerged from that and is the type to take Sunday morning walks with her fiancé, then good for her. "Maybe we didn't completely screw her up," I say.

Paul nears me. "No, we did, but kids are resilient."

He means it to be funny, I'm sure, but it leaves me cold. I push past him out of the room.

"Hey, so, I need to go into town and get some more stain for the boat."

I stop at the top of the stairs. "Okay. Can you take the pickup?"

"You got something you need? I can grab it for you."

"I'm not sure right now. I'd like to just have the rental on hand, if that's okay."

"Sure."

I flash a smile, say "Thanks," and head down the stairs.

I've been checking my phone all morning for a reply from Frank, but nothing. I tell myself it could be anything — Frank is a grown man, beholden to no one. But it adds to my worries. Why did Frank suggest Laura Bishop was framed by police? Or, at least, that they used desperate measures to close the case?

Furthermore, who sent me the voice message with "I want my mommy back"? Who scrawled it in the boathouse? How genuine is Michael's story, his implication that he's forgotten his real past? Why is Steven Starzyk so interested in Laura Bishop's release? Who does Michael think was the man outside the house?

Did Michael seek me out? Or is that incredibly narcissistic of me?

Does he know about his mother's release? Is that part of why he's here?

Does Laura Bishop believe she was falsely convicted?

I don't have the answers to any of these questions. The only thing I'm sure of is that little Tom Bishop witnessed his mother kill his father. That's what he eventually told me. And that's what he told the cops.

CHAPTER THIRTY-THREE

With Paul gone into town, Joni and Michael out walking, and Sean off somewhere, too, I have the house to myself. I'm searching through Joni's things for another cigarette when my phone rings.

"Frank!"

"It's me."

"It's good to hear from you."

"Listen, I got something for you." His voice sounds funny; a little strained.

"You okay?"

"Doug Wiseman," Frank says. "I'm having some trouble tracking where he is now, but he's a New York guy. Born and bred. And he was — well I don't know if it was dating or what you'd call it — but he was involved with Laura Bishop after the murder. She was gonna leave town with him. Move away and start over, I guess."

"How did you find this out?" I leave Joni's room and enter my own. Close the door.

"That's the thing. I kept looking into the Tom Bishop I found in Arizona, and one of his residences was at a place owned by Wiseman. I don't know if it does anything for you, but there it is."

I don't know either. Ever since Michael came forward, admitting his past, the Tom Bishop from Arizona has seemed to be someone else. But with the Wiseman connection . . . Has Tom/Michael just not shared that part of his story yet? It's possible.

"But listen," Frank says, "I gotta talk to you about something else. That's why I called."

"Something happen last night?"

"Yeah, I'm sorry about that. I, um . . . this is as far as I can go, Em. I'm gonna have to let this one go."

It takes me by surprise. "Frank, I'm sorry. I didn't mean to put you out."

"You didn't. Nah, you didn't. I just had something come up. You know how this business goes. All it takes is all you've got."

He's lying. I can hear it in the pitch of his voice. In the spaces between the words.

"I'm just sorry I can't go any farther with it, Emmy. I want to help you out, but . . ."

"It's okay."

"Yeah, well . . . Listen, you take care, Doc. I'll be seeing—"

I catch him just before he can hang up. "Did someone contact you? Put you off this?"

Frank is quiet a moment. "It's best if we let it go."

Bingo.

"Just tell me if it was Starzyk."

I listen to silence. The faint background noise of a TV.

It has to be.

"How about Mooney, Frank? Were you able to talk to her? You said she was retired in Lake George. Maybe she'll talk to me?"

"I'm sorry, Emily."

"You know, Frank," I say, in a quick whisper, "they were pressuring me. Worried she was about to leave town. Or, as I know now, was about to take off with Wiseman."

This could very well be why Frank is shying away. Corrupt cops framing a woman for the murder of her husband? You

168

hear about planting evidence, but planting, so to speak, a child's statement? Hiding the coercion behind the work of a consulting psychotherapist?

Bad stuff. Stuff cops would do anything to protect.

"Frank?"

But my old pal is gone.

CHAPTER THIRTY-FOUR

I have Starzyk's number in my phone. I think about calling him. But what would I say?

And what am I getting into?

"Mom?" It's Sean, downstairs, having just come in from outside.

I glance at my watch — getting close to noon. I've spent all morning up here getting consumed by this.

"Be right down!"

I wash first, like my hands are dirty. My reflection looks guilty, my brown eyes dark and ringed with doubt.

Sean is in the kitchen, sweating in his tank top and shorty-shorts. He's slamming a glass of water.

I put on a big smile. "Hi — go for a run?"

He nods, wipes his mouth with the back of his hand. "I did the Mirror Lake loop twice. Where is everybody?"

"Out. Your father is in town, and I guess your sister and Michael took a walk. You didn't see them?"

Sean shakes his head and drinks some more water. Sweat beads his upper lip. He's tan and healthy-looking, the ropy muscles of his legs standing against his skin. He must catch me looking. "What?"

"I'm just proud of you."

"Well, don't be too proud, I guess."

"Why not?"

"I don't know," he says.

"Sean, people try to figure it out forever. You're already doing it. You're already living your life. This is it. The future is what we do today. You're making money, you're taking care of yourself. Who cares if you're not sticking to one career path?"

He cocks an eyebrow at me like I'm nuts. "You do something to my mother?"

I hit his shoulder and he cracks a smile, then busses my cheek before heading upstairs, redolent of perspiration and fresh air. "I'm gonna hit the shower." He pauses halfway up: "We got plans for this afternoon?"

"Not at the moment."

"I want to take Mike out on the sailboat," he says.

And then he's upstairs and the bathroom door closes.

Mike.

My son is amazing, I think. Despite the sudden controversy around Michael, Sean seems drawn in, not keeping a distance. But then, Sean's always been that way. Outgoing, friendly. Joni was always the withdrawn one, while Sean went right up to complete strangers. We even joked that he'd go off with the milkman if we weren't careful.

I start pulling things out of the fridge for lunch, and my good humor ebbs. If what I'm about to embark on has any success — showing that Starzyk and Mooney put a frame around Laura Bishop — then my family is going to be dealing with something very different than a young man whose own mother killed his father. It will look like the cops used an eight-year-old boy to put her away.

Plus, if it were me who'd spent fifteen years in prison for a crime I didn't commit, I'd probably be out for revenge.

* * *

It's after lunch, though still no sign of Joni or Michael. Sean has eaten and repaired to the living room, where he's lying on the couch, looking at his phone.

171

"Sean? I have to go out for a while."

"Okay," he says, distracted. Then, "Where you going?"

"To see a friend. It'll take a couple of hours. You need anything?"

He lifts his head up so he can see me over the back of the couch. "I'm good. Gonna just chill here, wait for them to get back."

Perfect. I decide to leave now before I talk myself out of it.

I checked into Mooney this morning and found an address in the White Pages online. Jacob R. Mooney. No mention of Rebecca, but Mooney is a fairly unusual name and Frank said Lake George, so it's probably not a coincidence.

The rental is a sleek little Toyota Camry, black. There are scratches around the ignition from where previous renters tried to insert the key. But it's a good car, drives solidly and speedily, and I make the hour-long trip in one piece.

The GPS brings me to a rustic cabin on the north shore of a large, oblong lake. Lake George is fed by the Hudson River, and the Mooney place is at the end of a winding, wooded road where the river ends and the lake begins.

The rain is back, blowing hard on the water. I see someone in the window as I get out and run for the door. A man about Paul's age, but heavier, greets me with a tentative smile.

"Help you?"

"I'm looking for Rebecca Mooney?"

He has a mostly white beard and penetrating blue eyes. "Yeah, okay — who are you?"

I explain that I'm an old acquaintance. That I consulted on cases with her. "There's one I'd like to talk to her about, but her number is unlisted and cell phone just goes to voice mail."

"We shut our phones off," he says, giving me an up-and-down look. The entrance has an awning, but I'm still getting wet from the raindrops pinging everywhere, back-splashing my legs.

"I'm really sorry to bother you," I say. "I would never do anything like this. But . . . to tell you the truth, it's personal."

"How did you find us?"

"Google."

He shakes his head like the internet is a scourge. He's wearing shorts and sandals but a flannel shirt. His name is likely Jacob, the homeowner listed online. He glances back into the house as he gives the matter some thought. With his attention back on me fully, he asks, "Where did you say you were from?"

"Westchester."

"You just drove all the way up here?"

I tell him about my lake house, much closer. While we talk, I'm hunched over, trying to keep out of the rain. His face softens, like he's taking pity. "Listen, come in. Come in."

"Thank you."

Once we're inside, he closes the door behind me, muffling the sharper sound of rain. Now it's a vibration, a drumming on the roof and eaves. "Nasty weather," I say.

"Yeah. We need it though."

The foyer is nice, sided in knotty pine, with an opening onto a likewise rustic kitchen. I see a cast-iron stove, maple countertops, classic farm-style linoleum that's a ruddy brown. The setup triggers thoughts of the Bishop home.

The man is looking at me. "You said this was about a case?"

"It'll just take a few minutes. Is Detective Mooney . . . is Rebecca here?"

He delays a reply. "She's here. Do you . . . When is the last time you spoke to Rebecca? Or saw her?"

It's a good question; I think back. "I believe we worked together on one more case. Or maybe it was two. Right around that same time."

"Yeah . . ." he says. He runs fingers through his wavy gray hair.

"Can I ask your name?"

"Sorry. It's Jake." He puts out his hand. After a brief, light handshake, he tilts his head. "That didn't come up on Google, too?"

"It said Jacob, but I didn't want to presume anything. I'm Emily Lindman."

I'm eager to talk to Mooney, but she doesn't seem to be around. Past Jake, through the kitchen, a living room with tall windows overlooks the water. The home is more timber-frame-rustic than our modern lake house. It's smaller, but charming. And I can smell something — perhaps liquor. Could be coming from Jake.

"Let me get you a towel," he says. "Be right back."

He walks through the kitchen and turns. I stand there a moment, dripping, then take off the raincoat I'm wearing and find a free hook. That done, I'm less drippy and risk venturing into the kitchen. More smells hang in the air — garlic, basil. I see the remnants of pesto pasta in the sink. On the fridge, a picture of Jake holding up a big fish.

In another photo, a woman in a sunhat. The angle is bad, the sun silhouetting her. She's adjusting her hat, and I can just see the whites of her teeth as she smiles. I inch closer.

A creaking board over my head grabs my attention. I stare up at the ceiling as someone upstairs walks from my left to my right. The rain continues to beat down, but beneath the white noise, I hear muffled voices.

Something about it sends chills down my back. I need to get out of here. This was a mistake. I don't know these people. I don't belong in this house . . .

I start toward the entryway. As I walk, my phone buzzes in my pocket. I stop where I've hung my coat and check — it's a voice mail from Paul. My phone never rang. But that happens sometimes — bad cell service and the call won't come through, only the message indicator. I'm about to listen when someone speaks behind me.

"Here you go."

Jake holds out a towel.

"Oh, thank you." I take it, force a smile, and dab my face and hair with it.

Jake watches. He's a bit awkward. "Rebecca usually takes a nap after lunch. Sometimes she sleeps straight through."

Straight through what? I wonder. To dinner? Not unheard of, but it seems out of character with the Mooney I remember. "Is she . . . upstairs?"

"Yeah. She's up in the bedroom. You can go on up. She said she'll see you."

"Okay. Great."

Jake doesn't move for a moment. He keeps his blue eyes on me. "I'll show you up," he says finally.

I follow him through the house. Curiosity has replaced my sudden fear. The stairs are open to the living room as we ascend to the second floor, providing for an elevated view of the lake. "This place is wonderful," I say.

Jake, lumbering ahead of me, says, "My father and I built it. Thirty years ago. Started as a little hunting camp. Just the kitchen. We kept adding to it."

The upstairs has a carpeted hallway — a kind of balcony. The first door is shut, the second door ajar. He pushes it the rest of the way and stands aside for me to enter.

I hesitate.

But this is what I've come for.

CHAPTER THIRTY-FIVE

I step into the room. It's dim, with one lit lamp on the dresser to my right. Two windows overlook the gravel driveway; I can partially see my car. In the bed, the woman is in shadows. Like in the picture on the fridge, she's backlit, obscuring her features.

"Hello," I say. "Been a long time, Rebecca."

The woman in the bed says, "Fifteen years?"

"About that. Maybe exactly that." There's a chair between the dresser and the bed. I sit down.

Jake says, "Need anything, honey?"

"No, I'm fine."

"All right." He gives me one last look, and I see it this time, unequivocally: He's not thrilled that I'm here. She's obviously sick, and this is their hideaway, and I've just brought the world with me. The past, her career, all of it.

After Jake leaves, I turn to Mooney. "I'm really sorry to intrude."

"He said you seemed desperate."

"I guess I am." As my eyes adjust to the light, I can see her features a little better. She's thin. She's wearing a handkerchief on her head. "I didn't know that you weren't feeling well."

She laughs, and it turns into a coughing fit. I tense, ready to do something, but who knows what. When it subsides, she says, "Not feeling well. Yeah, you could put it that way."

There's the tough chick I remember. The no-nonsense New Yorker personality coming through, even when she's clearly been weakened by a debilitating illness. Cancer, no doubt.

"You're from the city, originally — is that right?"

"Queens. Born and raised. I worked there for almost ten years before I got transferred up to Westchester. Then I did a little over ten more. But I got sick with breast cancer. I retired, I beat it, and then it came back. It's in my lymph system."

"I'm so sorry."

She waves a hand. "That's not for sympathy. That's so you don't have to sit there guessing, and we can get on to whatever it is you're here to see me about."

I open my mouth, but Mooney says, "Well, I know, though. Why you're here. I remember you. As soon as Jake said your name. Laura Bishop is out on parole, right? I got a courtesy email, since it was my investigation. They let her go yesterday. Did she call you? Harass you?" Mooney starts coughing again.

"No, nothing like that." I wait until Mooney's lungs settle down and tell her the story. The whole story. She listens completely and doesn't interrupt. Once I'm finished, I ask her what she thinks.

"Arnold Bleeker," she muses. "I remember, he was a real handful. He and his wife — Annie, I think her name was . . ."

"Alice."

"They made a big stink when their sister-in-law was convicted. Even before that. They said we were harassing her. That she was a grieving widow and we were heartless."

"Did you . . . were you very interested in Laura Bishop as a suspect?"

"Oh sure, we liked her for it. Of course we did. Eighty percent of the time it's someone close to the victim. And we had two witnesses — good witnesses — say that their marriage was on the rocks. That she and her husband were partiers, you know, maybe even swingers. We knew that her business — she was into art dealing, or something — wasn't doing so hot. The life insurance paid her a million and a half. Plus, she had no alibi. What's not to like? But we had no hard evidence. And we had a crime scene that was wrecked."

"Wrecked," I repeat. "What do you mean? Contaminated?"

Mooney's face is cloaked in shadow, but I sense the air tighten with her trepidation. The word *contaminated* seems to have caused it. Good. That's what I'm here for.

"A few things were suboptimal," Mooney finally admits. "For one thing, the first cops to respond to the 911, two local PD, they did a perimeter check, walked all around the house. It's procedure, but they ruined all our tracks. Then the sun took care of the rest the next day."

She sighs. For a moment, I think it's all she'll say. But then she continues. "The other thing — we had a witness say there was someone parked in the street just prior to the murder, and cigarette butts were found, but the tech had a tear in his glove. Cross-contamination."

"I understand."

Mooney says, "*She,* of course, insisted someone else was there, too, Bishop did. But the defense had the same problem — inadmissible evidence. Nothing to build on. Still, her lawyer said she was pleading not guilty, that it was gonna go to trial. And so I met with her again, and the boy again, and got new statements. But the boy's didn't match up. He'd go back and forth from saying his parents were fighting to saying they weren't. That's when I submitted to the DA that we get him evaluated."

"And that's when you brought me in."

"Correct."

I sit for a moment in the dimly lit room, the rain a steady background force. Carefully, I recollect, "You were talking with Tom during the same time period I was. Isn't that right?"

"Well, we had to. We couldn't wait three sessions over a week. Or five sessions over two weeks. Especially not when Laura Bishop was threatening to move."

I remember the two cops coming to my office, effectively telling me to speed it along.

"We were worried because Bishop had linked up with some guy. Someone with resources. Money."

"Doug Wiseman," I blurt.

"Doug Wiseman," Mooney agrees. "That's right. How did you know about him?"

"I, um . . ."

Mooney is sharp. "You hired someone."

Might as well admit it. "I did. An old friend."

"Frank Mills."

Her insight is a little disconcerting. But she says, "It came up when we researched you as a consultant. You'd hired him once before. But you knew him before that?"

I want to ask more about Wiseman, but I quickly indulge her. "Yeah, Frank Mills was a patrol officer when I was in college. We actually met around the time my father died. I was at a really low point; I did some stupid things. Frank helped me. He even had a friend who was a therapist. Sarah Burgess. We lost touch for a while, but he tracked me down years later, found out I was married and had kids. And we've been friends since."

As she watches me, I can see her mind working. "Has he found out anything else for you?"

"Just that you were retired here in Lake George. And that there's a Thomas Bishop in Arizona. Same middle name, birthdate, and physical appearance. A dead ringer. And apparently one of Tom's residences out there was at a place owned by Wiseman. Can you tell me about him?"

She gives me a shrewd look but seems to decide something, and the look dissipates. "We became aware of him about two months into the investigation."

"Aware of him how?"

"Well, we had tags on Laura. What that means is we regularly surveilled her, kept track of her movements. She was going out to dinner with this guy, meeting him at his place, all this. He owned a restaurant. I think he still does — at least partly, and from afar. Like a silent partner. Anyway, he started showing up. And then we found out they were planning a move together. That's when we knew we had to shit or get off the pot."

I'm feeling excited despite the gloomy room, my sick host and the tragedy of all of this. "But maybe Wiseman was with her before you noticed him?"

"Oh sure, it's possible they knew each other prior to the murder. Very possible. He actually retained David Bishop's services. Managing some money for him."

My heart is beating harder now. "So what happened?"

"He had a solid alibi. And it looks more likely he dated her after the murders. Three months or so."

"But if he knew David before the murder, he could have known Laura."

"Could have, sure. But we had no proof. She certainly didn't admit it."

"What was his alibi?"

"He was traveling."

"Where?"

Mooney puts a hand to her head, like she's getting fatigued. "I don't remember. But listen — there's the thing — the thing I *do* remember. It always seemed to me like Bishop had someone to blame. An alternative suspect. But she never said who. It was like she was waiting for the trial, and *then* she'd name someone. But she changed her plea and there never was a trial."

"Maybe because she was guilty," I offer.

"Maybe."

"What was the life insurance situation? Do you remember that?"

Mooney nods. "She was a beneficiary, but since she murdered the insured, she got nothing, of course. Which was also why I felt it was strange she was withholding this alternative suspect."

"How can you be sure she had one?"

Mooney is silent a moment. "I can't. But it was in her eyes."

I'm about to follow that up with more questions when I hear someone approach. Jake returns and asks how she's doing. She says she's fine, but Jake gives me the eyes again. I'm on the verge of overstaying my welcome. Mooney is sick and no longer an active investigator. The space between me and Jake feels heavy.

"I should get going," I say, standing.

"Oh," Jake says. "Yeah, okay." He seems obviously relieved. And Mooney doesn't object.

But I have one last question.

"Before I go. One professional to another. One human being to another. Do you think everything that happened with the Bishop case was . . . ?" I stop short of saying *above board.* "Did it go as best as it could?"

"Was it by the book? Mistakes were made, I'll say that. Multiple mistakes. But do I think we got the bad guy in the end?" She's contemplative. "As soon as we had the boy as our witness, I mean, once he opened up to you, Bishop changed her plea to guilty. What else is there? For the law, nothing."

I am able to see Mooney clearly now. Her gaunt face and sunken eyes. I remember the sassy detective. I remember thinking that she put up a bit of a front — tough, even butch — in order to hang with the boys. To deal with the men surrounding her, to avoid showing any vulnerabilities. I've known women like Mooney my whole life, who take a hard job, who have to work twice as hard.

I can tell when they're scared. I can see through the bravado.

Rebecca Mooney is scared.

* * *

Halfway down the gravel road, I pass by a pickup truck going the other way. The weather is still grim and rainy, and the

181

man behind the wheel is an obscure figure. But his brake lights flash as I pass. And as I descend a small hill, one last glance in the mirror makes me think he's stopped.

I drive distractedly for a few minutes, constantly checking my mirrors. I also pull out the tape recorder in my pocket and rewind twenty minutes' worth of conversation. It's the same tape recorder I've been using for twenty years, analog, not digital.

I hit play.

". . . *were suboptimal*," Mooney says on the tape. "*For one thing, the first cops to respond to the 911, two local PD, they did a perimeter check, walked all around the house . . .*"

I stop playback, feeling that thrill again. If anyone needs convincing that mistakes were made by the police back then, Mooney is the one to admit it. While she seemed scared at the end, I also felt her desire to come clean. Maybe purge herself of her sins before she meets an untimely end?

Back in civilization, I navigate the main drag in Lake George, bustling with tourists in the late summer season. I realize I haven't checked the message from Paul and I'm about to when I catch sight of the pickup truck in my side mirror. It's waiting for the light like I am, about five cars back — I'm pretty sure it's the same one, a gray Ford Super Duty.

Waiting for the light, I check my voicemail.

"Em!" Paul sounds frantic. "Where are you? Listen, Em, there's been an accident."

I almost don't register the words, since I'm so focused on the truck.

But the next words are crystal clear: "Sean is hurt," Paul says. "It's bad, Em. It's bad. Call me back. Try to get here as soon as you can."

The message ends. I'm so stunned that it's not until the car behind me blares its horn that I get moving. I forget about the gray Ford truck, I forget about everything, just focusing on what I have to do — drive the car to the interstate, head north, get to my son.

My boy . . .

PART FOUR

CHAPTER THIRTY-SIX

TRANSCRIPT OF 911 CALL
OCTOBER 27

911: 911, what's your emergency?

Caller: Um, my dad is hurt.

[*Noises in the background.*]

911: He's hurt? What's the matter with him?

Caller: He's dead.

[*Woman in background: We don't know that yet!*]

Caller: He might be . . . he might be okay. My mom says. But he's—

911: Where are you, honey? What's your address?

Caller: Um, it's 2113 Pondfield Road. In Bronxville.

911: Okay. What's your name?

Caller: Tom.

911: Tom, can you tell me what happened to your daddy?

Caller: He got hit by a hammer.

911: Hit by a hammer? Did he hurt himself?

Caller: No, someone did.

911: Do you know who?

[*Woman in background: Tell them to send an ambulance!*]

911: Is that your mother?

Caller: Yes.

911: Is she with your father?

Caller: Uh-huh.

911: You can tell her an ambulance is on the way. Is your father breathing?

Caller [*muffled*]: Mom, is Daddy breathing?

[*Woman in background: unintelligible.*]

Caller: She says he's not. He's, um, not breathing. Is my dad gonna be okay?

911: We're coming, honey. We're coming to help him

. . .

CHAPTER THIRTY-SEVEN

I don't remember the drive.

That's not entirely true. I remember going eighty-five miles an hour, ninety at times, and thinking that if my excessive speed alerted a state trooper, that trooper would have to chase me all the way home. If I'd had ten police cars and a helicopter on me by the time I got there, I wouldn't have cared.

I also recall trying Paul's phone over and over again. Listening to the ringing through the car speakers. Cutting off his outgoing message: "Hi, you've reached Paul Lindman. I'm actually on vaca—"

I've left at least three messages already. *On my way. Call me back. Tell me more. Where are you? Which hospital?*

The sun's just above the treeline as I exit the interstate and speed toward Lake Placid. I need to know where they've taken him — Lake Placid's hospital is small, but it has an emergency room. I went there after my run-in with the deer. Saranac Lake's is larger.

When I finally hear from someone, it isn't who I expected. His voice, coming through the car speakers, is calm. Apologetic even.

"Mrs. Lindman," Michael says.

"Where's Sean? Where are Paul and Joni?"

"They're with him."

"With him where? With Sean? Michael — what happened?"

"We were sailing. He was teaching me. He hit his head and went into the water. I went in after him, but I'm not a very strong swimmer. He was down a long time . . ."

"Michael . . ." I can feel the anxiety rising, threatening to turn into panic. And I'm breathing too fast. I try to slow it down. "Where *is he*?"

"Um, it's Adirondack Medical Center. In Saranac Lake. But they're talking about moving him. He's—"

I end the call. It's impulsive, but another word from Michael and I'm going to lose control. And the last time I came charging along this windy mountain road, I hit a deer.

What's going on? Sean's never had a boating accident in his life. He hit his head?

I try to clear my mind. Think of nothing but getting there in one piece. The daylight is fading. It feels poignant, like my entire life is getting darker.

* * *

Sean is silent, unmoving. A tube in his neck does the breathing for him. His skin has blanched, and his eyes are still beneath the closed lids. I gingerly touch his bandaged skull and plant a kiss on his forehead. "Hi, Seanie. Hi, baby. Mommy is here."

My eyes are dry, probably because I'm in shock.

Paul is just beside me, his hand on my shoulder. Joni sits in the corner, her feet drawn up onto the chair, arms wrapped around her knees. She looks out the window and bites at her fingernail. Michael stands beside her. He's studying the floor, but when I look at him, his eyes come up.

My question is soft but demands an answer. "What happened?"

Paul's hand slips away from my shoulder as I walk to the corner, toward Michael.

"I . . . he was teaching me," Michael stammers. "I've never sailed."

Joni gives me a hard look. "He was tacking to head upwind, Mom. The boom swung around and hit him."

Michael's voice becomes thick with emotion. "He was teaching me . . . showing me. I distracted him."

"Stop it," Joni says, taking Michael's arm. "It's not your fault."

"He was headed upwind? Tacking?" I say. "I'd maybe believe he slipped on deck."

The words are out before I've had a chance to preview them.

Joni's mouth opens as she stares up at me in incredulity. Michael looks slightly confused, his eyes swimming.

But I don't stop. The horse has now left the barn. "Sean's never had an accident like this. Sailing since he was eight, and never once hit by the boom."

Paul pulls at my shoulder. "Honey. Come on . . ."

I yank away, my gaze drilling into Michael. "Then he went overboard? That's what you're saying?"

He nods, and a tear falls from his eyelash. His long, almost feminine eyelashes. His sharp nose and thick eyebrows and handsome face. I want to slap it. He's standing there, while Sean is comatose.

"Why didn't you pull him out right away?"

"Mom, stop." Joni glares up at me. Pure hatred in her eyes. I don't care.

"I tried," Michael whines. "But we were going fast. He fell in and I was alone. I didn't know what to do right away. I panicked. It was just a few seconds, but . . . when I finally jumped in to swim to him, he was already several yards away. I tried to . . . get his face out of the water. And then we had to get back to shore . . ." Michael sobs. Joni stands and embraces him.

I study Michael's face over Joni's shoulder. "I don't buy this act anymore," I say to him, pulling away again from

Paul's clutches. "If you've got something against me or my family, be a man. Come at me head-on. No more games."

"*Emily*," Paul says sternly. "Sean wouldn't want this."

It's what finally gets me. I return my attention to Sean, lying there helplessly. At the same moment, a nurse comes into the room. "You can't all be in here right now."

She's followed by others. She says, "You need to let us work. To let us help your son."

When Paul finally drags me out of the room, at last, I'm bawling.

* * *

I opt for the car in the parking lot instead of the waiting room. No sad people to stare at me in the parking lot; I'm still crying. Paul sits beside me, in the passenger seat. He stares out the window, rubbing his knuckle back and forth across his mouth.

When I can speak again, I ask him where Joni and Michael went.

"They're still inside."

I nod and blot my eyes with a tissue, but it's no good — a fresh bout of anguish overcomes me. "Oh, God . . ." And then, a flash of anger: Laura Bishop is behind this. She's out to take an eye for an eye. I've known it all along.

"He's going to be all right," Paul soothes.

"They said he wasn't breathing for a long time. You heard Michael. They were out in the middle of the lake. Michael swam all the way back to the shore with him?"

"Someone saw them. Some tourist saw them swimming and picked them up."

"Did they see what happened?"

Paul shakes his head. "I don't know. It all happened really fast."

"We need to talk to the police."

Paul faces me. "First, you need to talk to *me*."

189

I sigh, letting some of the tension unwind. Maybe the police aren't the best option right now. Not until I can sort a few things out. I tell him about the meeting with Mooney. "Laura Bishop might know who I am. And about what happened with Tom. What if she sent him to us?"

"*Sent* him? To do what? *Marry* Joni? That seems pretty elaborate."

"Sent him to do *this*." I wave my arms, meaning, everything. "Think about what's happened. I hit a deer — I could've been killed . . ."

"The *deer*?"

"I was rushing home. Once I found out that she'd been paroled. The weird message I got on my phone, the carving . . ." I know Paul's not aware of some of this. "It's to destabilize us."

"I don't know, if anything—"

"Look what just happened to Sean. He doesn't have accidents, Paul."

"Everybody has accidents."

I shake my head. "So this tourist, he drove them back to the lake house?"

"No — they went to the boat launch at the marina. Michael thought Sean needed an ambulance. That they'd have better luck on the town side of the lake then our side, getting an ambulance back in the narrow roads." Paul raises his eyebrows, as if to say, *would a killer think of that?* He adds, "Michael called 911, then me. The ambulance got there first. It was Michael who rode with Sean. He hasn't left his side."

I'm still shaking my head, now shedding more tears, dizzy with uncertainty. I let it all out until it's done. Paul rubs my back.

"I think we need to take a breath here," Paul says.

I nod, trying to pull it together.

Paul says, "This has been a lot. Michael showing up has been a big surprise, in more ways than one. And we're reeling from it. But we need to put our heads together. You know some things, and I know some things. But we've got to come together. We're a team, Em, okay?"

I'm nodding and crying. I want to tell Paul about Doug Wiseman. About what a ready-made villain he is. How even Mooney thought Laura knew who did it or had someone to blame, and Wiseman was likely it. Maybe it's a way out of all of this for us. But my phone rings.

CHAPTER THIRTY-EIGHT

"So you went to see Rebecca Mooney?"

"Detective Starzyk," I say, wiping a hand across my runny nose, "I can't really talk right now. I have a family crisis that—"

"This will just take a minute, okay? Mrs. Lindman, you're free to talk to and see whoever you choose. But I hope you realize that you might not like what comes out of it."

"Detective, if that's a threat, I'm not really—"

"That's not a threat. Not from me. I think we both know where the real threat is coming from."

Paul is watching me with concern. I cover the phone and whisper to him, "Go be with Sean. I can handle this."

He waits, but I nod and give him a gentle push. "I'm all right."

When Paul finally gets out and closes the door, I finish with Starzyk. "I think I might be getting in touch with your internal affairs bureau, Detective."

"Who do you think would suffer the worst consequences in that situation?"

The implication is I would. "That's ridiculous. My case notes and evaluation reflect exactly what happened, by the book. The errors and cover-ups appear all on *your* side of the equation."

"Whoa, whoa, whoa. Hang on a second."

"No. I've heard enough. You know how this looks, and you're scared. Mooney is scared. You know that things could slip through your fingers all over again."

"Boy, you are a piece of work, lady . . ."

"Now, I really do have to go. Please don't call me again."

I hang up, breathing hard. Starzyk is trying to intimidate me, and I pushed back.

The nerve of that guy! Only, I should've asked him about Frank. Not that he'd admit it, and not that I don't already know. Cops and private investigators can have a touchy relationship. Frank relies on good vibes with the police to best serve his clients.

More important: Starzyk is clearly watching me. Showing up at the Bishop home when I'm there, knowing that I visited Mooney . . . He was the gray Ford in Lake George, I'm sure. He's keeping tabs on things because, like I said, he's scared.

I shake it off. It doesn't matter right this moment. What matters now is being with my son.

But when I return to the hospital, Paul has a different idea.

"I'm going to stay with him tonight."

I blink at Paul. "So am I."

"He's in the ICU. Only one other person can be in there."

We're in the waiting area, which is about half full, including Joni and Michael. I keep my voice measured, aware that we're drawing attention, just what I don't want. "Then it's *me*," I say in a low voice. "I'm his mother."

"You've also already gotten the attention of hospital administration," he says quietly.

"What? Why?"

But I know why — because I was loud and aggressive earlier towards Michael.

"So," Paul says in an irritatingly soothing tone, "you can either sleep out here in the lobby, which I wouldn't recommend. Or you can go home and get some real rest. You look exhausted, Em. You've been running all over the place. You—"

"Stop." Fresh tears burn against the backs of my eyes. I don't want to lose it again, so take a deep breath through my nose. "I don't need you telling me about my health when our son is—"

Paul takes my shoulders. "Honey, this is exactly when you need to worry about your health. You know that."

It takes another ten minutes of convincing me; even so, I insist on seeing Sean's doctor. This takes another thirty minutes, until finally we're in Sean's room, and I'm getting a crash course in comas. In Sean's case, it was caused by a combination of traumatic head injury and cerebral hypoxia. As much as I try to pin down the doc to a prognosis, he gives us the "It could be hours, days, or even months. The brain is a mysterious organ . . ." and so on. If Sean doesn't come around in a couple of days, a hospital in Albany will be better equipped to handle his needs.

I stare at Sean the whole time. He looks utterly helpless, a broken toy with the batteries fallen out. In a hospital gown, an ID bracelet on his wrist, the IV going in his arm, the ventilator in his neck. The hissing and beeping of the machines. The astringent smell of the room, along with the suspicion that things are never as clean as they seem in a hospital, and there are dust bunnies and stray hairs, billions of writhing germs.

The heavy gauze wrapping his head.

I finally leave feeling heartbroken, stunned, a failure. I've failed my son, somehow. I didn't protect him. I've been preoccupied by Joni, ever since she was a recalcitrant tween testing our limits. We always put our faith in Sean. He had his head on straight. He was daring and adventurous, but safe and smart. I'd worried he'd injure himself as a boy, but as a man, he instilled confidence.

Now his brain, starved of oxygen, has shut down.

I can't even think about it. I can't think about his chances at regaining consciousness. The possibility that he never returns . . .

No. Don't.

But I walk to the rental car in a daze, picturing his wholesome, handsome face. His hazel eyes — same as his father's. His genial smile.

I'm lost in my love for him, opening the car door, when footsteps quickly approach.

Michael is running toward me. His face replaces the mental image of my son. I feel colder the second I see him; my skin tightens, pupils narrow.

He's slightly out of breath. "I'll drive you," he says.

You're out of your fucking mind is my first thought. But I catch myself.

"It's okay. Go back inside and be with Joni. She needs you."

"Honestly, it was her idea. But she's right. We need to talk."

"I don't think we do. Not unless it's going to be honest, anyway. But I just don't have the strength right now." I let my shoulders drop, releasing some of the tension. "And I'm sorry about what I said in the hospital room. I was just angry and hurt and lashed out at you. I shouldn't have treated you that way . . ." I pause to fight against new emotion. "I just need to go home now."

"And I'll drive you there," he insists. "Joni asked me to get a few things for her at the house, so I'm gonna go anyway. I'll drop you and then I'll come back."

"No." But I'm curious. "How?"

"I'll take Sean's car. Just let me, okay?"

In the end, since it's dark, and I've already had one accident in the past forty-eight hours, I accept.

For Sean.

195

CHAPTER THIRTY-NINE

I feed Michael some leftovers. We eat in silence. My thoughts swing from Sean to the young man seated across from me. Who is he? Why is he in my house? Was what happened to Sean an accident or something else? Is Michael capable of something so sinister? Or maybe it was one of those things that's not quite an accident, not quite premeditated?

He could be mentally unstable.

I have so many questions. *Why are you engaged to my daughter? Was it fate or did you seek her out? Is your mother behind this?*

But neither of us speaks, except when Michael says, "Thank you," and picks up his dishes and places them in the sink. "I'll grab Joni's things and then I'll go."

I face the lake through the windows, watching the column of light from the dock lamp ride the bumpy waves. I don't say anything to Michael. A stair tread pops behind me as he ascends to the second floor.

I hear more creaking over my head as he walks into Joni's room. The door closes, more footfalls follow, then silence.

Who is this stranger in my life? What is his purpose here?

Each time I try to fathom the coincidence, it's as though my own mind spits out the thought undigested. Is it really possible that Michael met my daughter at a college lacrosse game? Part of me says *no way*. But it's contradicted by another notion: anything is possible.

Therapists and former patients do sometimes bump into each other on the street or discover they ride the same daily train. Maybe this is a more complicated version of those coincidences: Former patient dates therapist's daughter.

But — unknowingly?

Even if Michael had full recall of his trauma, it's plausible he forgot the name of a therapist he saw a handful of times fifteen years ago, let alone what she looked like. Or be able to fathom what she'd look like now. At first, he might only have a picture or two to go by, something Joni showed him on her phone.

But once he met me in person, would that have not jogged his memory?

Maybe it did. Maybe this whole thing is a case of Michael, having fallen in love with Joni, becoming mortified at who her mother turns out to be.

Mortified not just because of what *I* might know about him, but because he's already concocted this false narrative for Joni about his parents dying in a car wreck.

Ashamed by what his mother did to his father, he's built an alternate self. For years, it works just fine. By the time he's old enough to care about girls, perhaps, the media have mostly forgotten about him. He's gone through puberty; he looks different enough that the paparazzi have lost the scent. And so now, when it comes to that getting-to-know-you moment in a new relationship, he's free to improvise. He keeps it tragic, with plenty of truth to reinforce the lies. There's only one problem: he ends up dating the daughter of someone who knows better.

The chance is very slim, but possible. For one thing, I'm not the only one who knows. He could've wound up dating the daughter of his ad litem from the case. Or the judge's daughter. Or one of the police officers or crime-scene techs involved. Even a reporter who might still recall the case with clarity.

But instead of any of them, it was me.

And maybe seeing us this weekend wasn't the first time he made the connection. Surely Joni showed him some pictures. And then there's her last name. My last name. Had he forgotten it at first? Or thought nothing of it? The "*aha*" moment might not have come until several months into their relationship. They could've had a conversation about what I did for a living, what Paul did. By the time Michael finally put it together, he was in too deep.

Maybe it's all a sign of how much he loves my Jo. That he didn't run, even after he realized what a horror show of a coincidence this whole thing was.

And so — then what? He comes to visit, and he has to suspect I'll recognize him. But he plays ignorant? Does he really think he'll get away with the lie?

Or is this whole "hazy memory" part of a new deception? Maybe it's a way for him to safely return to the truth without looking like a liar — in my eyes or, more importantly for him, in Joni's eyes.

Instead of coming clean in one fell swoop, he's admitted that his past remains enshrouded. He's asked me to be the one who helps tease out more of his memory. Once we get back to full recall — meaning, once he playacts his way back — he's in the clear. He can be the boy I remember and be Michael, too. His lie to Joni can get explained away by having caregivers implant it when he was young. That, and, having gone through such a traumatic experience, he did some heavy compartmentalizing.

But . . .

But it leaves a few things on the table. Like the proximity to Laura Bishop's prison and the timing of her parole.

Enough. I pick up my own dishes and put them in the sink. The kitchen is a mess. I left for Mooney's in a bit of a hurry, and food was prepared in my absence. The ketchup is still out. Crumbs on the tile countertop. Knives caked with peanut butter. Only my son would have ketchup and peanut butter in the same meal.

Thinking of Sean pierces my heart with grief. He was making himself a sandwich — or *something* — then he took his sister's fiancé sailing, and then . . .

And now he's . . .

I don't know what he is. Or where he is. I know where his body is, but his consciousness seems lost to me. I can't feel it.

I miss him already.

The sudden and gripping sadness soon curdles into anger.

Maybe if I want to get to the bottom of things, I really should call the police right now, explain everything. Maybe it's time. What do I have to be worried about? If it turns out this is truly linked to the past, anyone can see it's a case of police corruption. Coercions and cover-ups. Using a respected therapist to legitimize their case.

Talk about throwing my life into chaos. It's been chaotic before; I'm not sure I could handle it again. There would be media following us around. Nightly news segments about "the case from fifteen years ago."

I just don't know if I could handle it all right now. Cops here, Joni stabbing me with her eyes, Michael nervous but trying to cooperate.

And now I've been *treating* him? Using my tools as a psychotherapist to uncover a past I myself was a part of? The cops would have a field day with me, given such a conflict of interest, such an ethical breach.

My career would be over.

It dawns on me then, as I go through the kitchen, sweeping crumbs into my palm, wiping down the countertops, that I've got to see this through on my own. If Michael is faking to save face — pretending he can't remember to subvert the humiliating truth of his lie — maybe I can help him with that. If, on the other hand, he's part of some grander deceit, I'll be more in control of it than I am now, just waiting for the other shoe to drop.

By the time I've finally worked all this out in my head, I'm already at the top of the stairs. Moving down the hallway, I stop in front of Joni's door.

"Come in," Michael says when I knock. He's on the bed, looking at his phone. He sets it aside and stands up. "Everything okay?"

I pull a slow, easy breath. Looking deeply into those green eyes, I say, "Let's try again."

CHAPTER FORTY

"I really love your daughter," Michael says from the bed in Joni's room. "I think she's amazing."

"She *is* amazing," I say. "She's come through a lot."

He gazes up at the ceiling, contemplative. I drag a chair into the corner. It's the chair from Sean's room. We used his room last night, but I couldn't bear to be in there right now. It's all I can do just to keep my head clear.

Of course, that's impossible. Sean is my son. My first-born. And he's lying in a hospital bed with a machine breathing for him.

But he's going to wake up. He's going to come back to you. Because he's strong. Sean has always been strong . . .

"Joni says you and Paul were a little bit . . . I don't know. Kind of wild? Back in the day?"

Michael's question catches me off guard. I slowly sit down in the chair. "What did she say?"

"Just that you guys used to throw big parties. You know, Fourth of July, that kind of a thing . . ."

"I don't know that I'd call them 'big parties.' We some families over from the neighborhood for holidays. It was hardly all the time."

". . . Joni says she had her first drink at one of those parties."

I place my hands in my lap. "I remember."

"Sorry, I'm just a little nervous."

"Nothing to worry about. I'm right here, and you're safe." The words sound flat to my ears. I always have my patients' best interests at heart, but it sounds less than genuine coming out of my mouth.

Leave it. Call it off right now.

"What else did Joni say?"

"Just that you stopped. No more parties."

"People move on. Families get older, you lose touch."

"Yeah . . ."

His disbelief gets under my skin. Is he playing some sort of game? I play a different hand.

"What about growing up in the Bleeker home?" I haven't used this name yet and want to see how he reacts. "Maybe we can start there. Did they have people over for the holidays?"

"My uncle is a bit of a loner. Maybe an introvert. Very smart guy. He writes technical manuals, plus he's published a few of his own books. And my aunt was a college professor. She worked almost right up until she died."

Michael's answer seems genuine. And the depiction of his aunt reminds me of Rebecca Mooney for a moment, looking dark and desiccated in her bed, the rain spitting against the windows.

I ask, "And how was it having a sister? Do you still keep in touch with Candace?" It's another dig for information.

"Not really. When Aunt Alice died, it kind of broke up the family."

"I'm sorry. The whole thing is very sad." I'm sliding back toward sympathy. Michael once again seems guileless. A man who's grown up in the long shadow of a terrible family tragedy.

But it could all be a trick. I need to keep reminding myself of that.

"We saw each other through the funeral and everything," he says, meaning Candace. "I'd been at Colgate for a year. I mean, we talk every once in a while . . ."

"She has a husband?"

"Yeah. Greg. He has a trucking company or something."

It checks out with what I already know.

But there are things Michael doesn't know. And so I tell him about visiting his Uncle Arnold, and how Candace showed up, and that her husband Greg grabbed me. How they thought I was harassing their father.

Michael absorbs it all, at first looking shocked, but recovering quickly. "Yeah, she's a little high strung. A little fussy. She used to clean all those pigs her mother collected, dust them all off. Pigs everywhere in that house. So . . . you were checking up on me, huh?" A smile edges his mouth.

"I was. I'm probably still checking up on you. This isn't therapy. Not in any clinical sense."

"I know."

"This is me, hoping that unveiling the truth can help you. That it can help us both."

"I understand. How did Arnold seem?"

Small, I want to say. *Shrunken*. But instead I describe him in what favorable light I can, and this seems to please Michael.

What I don't elaborate on is how upset both Arnold and Candace were upon discovering who I was. That Candace accused me of being part of something. How, at first, I thought Arnold was maybe getting senile, paranoid. But that I've since come to think they were unhappy with Laura's trial.

After I'm done describing a highly edited version of my encounter with Michael's family, he stares off for a bit, lost in thought.

"Michael," I say, not knowing how to begin. "If this . . . if you're being honest with me, then this really may not be the setting. To uncover the truth, and a truth as hard as what yours might be . . . It's like surfacing in the water. You know, you can go too fast and get the bends. For your own health, your own safety, this should really be with a clinician, someone other than me."

He locks on me with those preternaturally light eyes. Eyes shining with intelligence. "You still think I'm lying."

"I don't know what to think. I'm trying not to have an opinion, to be objective. But you see how silly that is? I'm too close to this. You could say I have an agenda."

He's quiet. "I want to do this. I think it will help. Please."

I take a slow breath. My gaze wanders to the window, to the lake, growing dark in the eventide. I picture the sailboat cutting through the chop. My son sitting at the back, gripping the tiller, wind in his hair, grin on his face. We taught Sean to sail when he was very young.

This whole thing — sitting here with Michael — it's surreal. I should be at the hospital with my son.

But I am here. For whatever reason, because of whatever choices I've made, I'm here.

Once more, I'm driven by my own need.

"All right, Michael. Lie back now, okay?"

A smile slipstreams across his face, almost too quick to catch. "All right," he says, instantly sobered and ready for business.

"All the way back. There you go. Okay. We're just going to breathe for a minute. We're going to inhale to a count of three, and exhale to a count of five. We're going to slow the heart rate. We're going to calm the mind."

I take a few breaths of my own. I move my thoughts from the lake and my son to this young man. This room. This space in time.

"Good," I say. "Inhale again. And exhale. That's it, breathe. Are you ready?"

"Yes." Michael's breathing is regular and deep. His eyes are closed, but he's awake.

"Then let's begin."

CHAPTER FORTY-ONE

The air is cold but humid, holding the promise of snow. Tom feels the dampness, but it registers further back in his mind; unimportant. What's important is that he's home at last, after nearly eleven hours of school and day care, he's back. He's thinking about the book he's reading. It's a good one — Deathly Hallows — *and he's excited to return to that world.*

"Wash up before you do anything else," his mother says, as if reading his mind.

They walk from the driveway to the side entrance. There's a garage, but it's filled with Dad's tools, an old motorcycle, a hundred boxes of things — no room for a car.

"Okay," Tom says, and his mother keys the lock and lets them inside.

It's warm in the house. He breathes in. It smells like traces of the coffee and bacon from that morning. The leathery, rubbery odor of shoes and boots lining the entryway. Dust and pine and mildew. The ticking of the many clocks — there are fourteen of them.

This is home.

He kicks off his boots and heads for the downstairs bathroom. There's a stool tucked under the sink and he pulls it out so he can look at himself in the mirror. He can't wait to grow taller. His teacher says

he's an advanced reader. He wishes he were an advanced grower too —
he's nearly the shortest boy in his classes.

Hands washed, Tom bounds upstairs.

"Dinner in twenty minutes!"

"Okay!" He doesn't have a watch and can barely figure twenty
minutes, but she'll call again. For now, he's going to immerse himself in
his favorite alternative reality . . .

. . . and lose himself until his mother appears in his doorway.

Has it been twenty minutes? She's holding his plate. Her face is
blank and her eyes devoid. "Do you want an invitation? Or do you want
me to just throw it out?"

"Sorry!" He hops up — he's hungry — and brings the plate back
downstairs. Once in the kitchen at the table where they usually eat, Tom
sits down. (There's a "dining room," but his parents only really use it for
company, for their parties and Christmas and things like that.)

His mother's plate is empty, but her wine glass is full. She sits
across from him and drinks, staring off into space.

"Use your napkin," she says, catching him. He wipes some spa-
ghetti sauce from the corners of his mouth.

Dad isn't there. The fact of it feels big and loud, though neither
of them mentions it. It's a familiar predicament. And Tom knows that
asking about his father will only make his mother more upset; her mood
has darkened like this before.

Besides, Dad will be along eventually. He always comes home. At
least, sometimes, when Tom is in bed before his dad gets in, he'll hear
the footsteps coming into his room and feel the dry kiss on his forehead.

Tom's mother drinks her wine, then gets up. She pours another
glass and stands at the sink, gazing out the window.

"It's going to snow tonight," she says.

"Maybe we can go sledding tomorrow?"

But she doesn't answer or turn around. She only stares out the
window, like she's deep in thought.

* * *

"I want my mom back," Michael mumbles.

I sit up a little straighter. "What's that, honey?"

He delays a response. "She's just angry."

"What is she angry about?"

But he doesn't answer.

Carefully, I ask, "Tom . . . where are you right now? Are you still sitting with her at the table?"

"Yes."

"Tell me what happens next."

* * *

Dinner is awkward and silent. At one point, his mother leaves and doesn't come back until after he's finished. He waits for her return before taking his dishes to the sink — this way, she can see he's cleaned his plate.

She barely notices. She has a funny smell, like car exhaust. But when he drops his plate in the sink a little too harshly, it rouses her. She looks around, as if coming out of a dream, then focuses on him.

Wonderfully, she smiles.

He cautiously approaches — has she been crying? Her eyes are glassy, and there's a faint black smudge under each. Like her makeup ran.

"All right, let's get you ready for bed, mister."

She's back. Mom is back.

They go through an evening ritual. Since dinner started late, it's nearly bedtime now. First, she runs the bath for him and fills it with suds. She lets him play, crashing his toy plane into the water. But he doesn't feel much like playing. He reads long chapter books now. His teacher says he's an advanced reader. What other third grader reads whole Harry Potter books?

Soon, he's toweling off with his mother's help, and then, on his own, getting into his pajamas. She has him get in bed and promises she'll be back to read some of his book with him.

But she never comes. He starts to read on his own. Part of him wants to call out to her, but he's reluctant. She's acting this way because Dad still isn't home. Tom knows they've been having problems. Shouting, sometimes. Mom going off into her room and crying.

Dad is always working late. He said once that their marriage was a "sham." Tom knows what a sham is. But he doesn't know why his parents don't love each other anymore. He can only suspect it has some-thing to do with when his mother first started acting like an imposter. Like someone else was sharing her brain. Which was — hard to say for sure — maybe a year ago.

* * *

"How was she acting strange?" I ask.

Michael rolls over on the bed. He draws himself up into a fetal position and pulls one of the pillows to his chest. In a light voice, he replies, "She picked me up from Miss Diana's one day and she was different."

"Did she look different? Act differently?"

"She wore different clothes than usual. A dress. And she smelled like perfume."

"Tell me what happened next. After she left your room . . ."

* * *

He's in his bed, reading, when he hears a noise. A car engine. A moment later, the front door opens and closes.

It's hard not to get out of bed and rush downstairs to see his father. But he holds fast — and a moment later, he hears voices. He's pretty sure it's his mother and his father.

At first, they're normal — the deeper voice of his father vibrates through the floorboards. The higher pitch of his mother drifts up the stairs. She's unhappy, and letting it be known.

I made dinner for us. Tom and I sat here and waited.

Tom guesses it's what she's saying. The shape of her words sound close, anyway.

I'm sorry, *his dad replies,* I told you I had to work late . . .

Tom wants to hear more clearly. He slips out of bed and creeps to his door, opens it quietly and props it ajar.

Their voices carry up the stairs.

"I don't want to have the same argument," his dad says.

"So don't, David. Let's just not talk at all. Just keep punishing me."

"I'm not punishing you, Laura. You do that to yourself."

"Oh, isn't that convenient for you. So you're passive-aggressively punishing me. Bravo."

"Just let me eat."

"Why don't you divorce me?"

"You're drunk, Laura."

"I'm not drunk. Why don't you? I think you're afraid to. I think you're afraid to be alone. You don't love me, but you can't bear to be alone. But really, what it is, it's better for you to punish me. You like having something on me. Something you can feel superior about. This is right where you like to be. Because you're mean, David. You're—"

"Enough!"

His father's bellow seems to shake the house. Tom hears David get up from the table and stride to the sink, dump in his dishes with a clatter. A moment later, he's moving toward the stairs. Tom closes the door and hurries to his bed, diving back under the covers as his father's heavy footfalls ascend the stairs.

They fade down the upstairs hallway. He must be going into his room to get changed. He probably still wears his suit and tie.

What are they fighting about? Why would Tom's father want to punish his mother? What does that mean?

Tom lies there wondering, listening to the sounds of the house. His father running the water in the upstairs bathroom. His mother moving around in the kitchen. For a moment, he thinks she's speaking. But to whom? Herself?

The tension between his parents forms a deep ache in his heart. A splitting in his mind. If his parents don't love each other, what does that mean for him? They made him — they came together and made him; he knows that much. They loved each other, and he grew in his mother's belly. Now that they don't love each other, does he cease to exist? No, he's still here. But what does it mean when he's one part his father and one part his mother — and they're so divided?

* * *

Michael's eyes are wet. He lies on his side, holding the blanket.

He won't talk for a long time. I have a hundred questions. And I want to press on, to go deeper into the night of the murder.

But I'm getting simultaneously pulled toward my own son. I need to call Paul and Joni and check in with them.

Just when I'm about to end the session, Michael speaks again.

"There's someone else here."

CHAPTER FORTY-TWO

As Tom lies there worrying about his parents, he hears a familiar sound: a car engine. But Dad is already home. And this car doesn't turn into the house driveway. Instead, it comes to a stop somewhere outside.

Tom dares to get out of bed and go to the windows. Below the windows is a radiator, wafting heat. He climbs atop it for a view down on the street.

The vehicle idles just beyond the light thrown by a streetlamp. A figure sits behind the wheel, and a white curl of smoke rises up from a slightly open window.

The bathroom water shuts off. Tom rushes back to bed as some-one approaches his door. He's just gotten the covers right when his door opens.

His father enters — Tom knows it's his father by the smell of soap and the creaking of the floor beneath his weight. He keeps his eyes closed, feigning sleep. But when his father places a gentle hand on Tom's chest, then kisses him on the forehead, Tom stirs.

"Dad?"

"Just me, buddy. Go back to sleep."

"Everything okay?"

David opens his mouth, then closes it. He sits on the side of the bed. Tom feels his weight; the mattress sags toward his father, pulling Tom closer as his father asks, "Did you hear us? Talking?"

"Yeah. A little."

"It's all right, buddy. Every couple has arguments."

"But you and Mom . . . for a long time . . ."

"We'll work it out. How was your day?"

Tom describes some of school and day care, but he has a hard time taking his mind off his worries. Divorce? He knows a little about that. But he can't bring himself to ask his father. David kisses his forehead again and wishes him a good night. At the door, he turns.

"I love you, Tom."

And then he leaves.

* * *

"Tom?" I try to remain calm, but inside I'm filling up with anxiety, about to spill over. "Who is outside? Can you see him?"

"No."

A name comes to mind, bright and clear. "Is it Doug Wiseman?"

"Who?"

The question spilled out of me before I could stop it, but Tom's response gives me pause. That angle might be moot because Tom doesn't know Doug Wiseman yet. Both Frank and Detective Mooney thought he came later. Even if they're wrong and David Bishop is "punishing" his wife for having an affair, it's still highly unlikely Tom knows Doug at this point in his life, even if his mother does.

"Never mind," I say. "Just tell me what happens now."

* * *

His father and mother talk some more in the kitchen. It sounds less fraught, and that eases Tom's mind. He hears her walk up the stairs — her footfalls are as distinct as his father's — and listens as she moves down the hallway to her bedroom and shuts the door. Now it's just his father downstairs. Probably finishing up his meal.

His mother is going to bed and his father is eating a late dinner. All is right with the world.

Relieved, his mind wanders to school and some of the kids there, and then to Harry Potter and the story he's reading.

With that, Tom drifts off to sleep.

For a little while.

His rest is disturbed when the side door to the house opens and closes.

It, too, is a distinctive sound he knows well. Has his mother gone out to smoke? Has his father left?

Tom checks the window: The car in the street remains parked there. Only now, it's unoccupied. Something smolders on the snowy road, too small to see. A cigarette, maybe.

Nimbly, he hurries to his door. Before he even gets it open, a voice rises from the kitchen. His father.

"What are you doing? Are you fucking crazy?"

Tom freezes, thinking it's him David is talking to. But it can't be. His father can't see him yet. And he'd never speak to Tom that way.

But from downstairs, there's no response. Maybe just the rustle of a coat, the groan of the floor beneath solid weight.

"I'm calling the police," David says.

Heart beating harder now, Tom pushes his door open farther and eases out to the stair landing. He starts down, mindful of the noise.

"I'm calling them," David says. "I'm calling them right now. You better put it away. Hey — put it away!"

There's a noise — a wet, smacking sound — like the sound made when his mother hits the chicken with a studded mallet, and his father cries out in pain. Tom freezes in place. He's halfway down the stairs, listening as two people wrestle. Bursts of grunts. Feet scuff the linoleum in an obscene, aggressive dance. The sounds reverberate in the stairwell, past the clocks, up to Tom's ears.

Bad fighting . . .

There's another wet-smack sound and a soft noise, almost like a kitten's mewl.

Something hits the floor.

A second later, Tom sees a bloody hammer tossed aside, hears it thump against the lower cabinets.

Then a figure, its back to Tom, runs for the side door.

* * *

I've temporarily forgotten everything else in my life. I'm leaning toward the bed, barely seated, straining toward Michael, who has drawn into an even tighter ball. The tears stream down his face sideways. His body shakes. I want to stop this, but I can't. Not now. We're too close.

"Michael . . . who was in the kitchen?"

* * *

Snowflakes not yet melted stand out in crisp white contrast on the person's black jacket. Tom sees this as the person leaves. Slipping back out into the night, where more snow swirls in an updraft.

The moment is so shocking, so unfamiliar, that Tom doesn't move. Can't move. It's as if he's become disconnected from his body. There's just the thinnest sense of existence, of being loosely tethered to reality.

Finally, after what seems like it could be either seconds or hours, Tom continues down the stairs, until his father comes into view.

And his mother, who cradles his father's bloody head in his hands.

She looks up at Tom, tears streaming down her face, her mouth open in a frozen scream.

* * *

Michael is moaning on the bed. The sound has a different tone and pitch from his regression to Tom. This is distinctly feminine; the unsung howl of his mother.

"Tom," I say quickly, sensing the danger, "it's time to come back to the here and now. It's time to return to our time. Where you are called Michael. Return to where I am. Where everything is safe and sound."

"No," he says sharply. His eyes stay scrunched tightly closed, though the tears have stopped. Determination resounds in his words. "I'm staying."

"You can't. You can't stay there. It's not even really a place or a time. You're *here*, with me, Dr. Lindman. This is your rightful place. It's time to wake up."

"No." It's a softer protest now.

I try to pull him out of it. I tell him to focus on my voice. To let everything else fade away. He's been suggestible up until now. "When I count backward from five, you're going to—"

"No!" Michael bolts upright as he screams. The force of his voice tightens my defenses. A second later, he's off the bed. His eyes are still closed, unseeing, but he's flailing with his arms, as if fending off attackers.

As if he's reenacting the fight in the kitchen.

He picks up the lamp from the bedside table.

As soon as I see what he's about to do, I'm out of the chair. I take refuge in the doorway, watching.

Michael swings the lamp, yanking the cord from the wall. The room darkens. He breathes and grunts and swings. The lamp strikes the bed post, exploding the bulb with a terrific pop.

"Michael," I say, from the door. "Michael, please stop . . ."

But he's got to work it through.

I stay out of harm's way as Michael destroys my daughter's bedroom. Using the lamp as a bat, he clears the perfumes and bric-a-brac from the dresser. He hurls it at the white walls, leaving jagged scrape marks where it shatters. He beats at the bed and pillows until the down feathers fill the air. Finally, he runs out of energy. Panting and sobbing, he drops to his knees, head hanging. He collapses onto his side.

For one terrible moment, I'm sure I'm going to have two young men in my life who are persistently unconscious. But Michael rolls over onto his back.

Moaning, he then opens his eyes. Staring up at the ceiling, he says one sentence. It is a crisp utterance, sharp and clean with discovery.

"It wasn't her."

CHAPTER FORTY-THREE

I don't know what to do first. Or who, if anyone, to call.

After a moment's indecision, I start by getting Michael a glass of water from the upstairs bathroom. He's still in Joni's room. Both the space and the man in it are demolished. He sits on the edge of her bed, his hands on his knees, his head lowered. He's covered in down feathers. They cloak the room, like snow.

"Here. Drink this."

He takes the water from me but doesn't look up. I wait while he drinks — greedily, in one go — and then carefully, I sit beside him.

"Okay," I say softly. I need to speak to my husband. And with Joni. And to check on Sean. "Are you okay?"

Michael nods, silent.

"You did really well, Michael. We just covered a lot of territory. It's normal to be feeling upset. Drained, even. All completely normal."

He nods some more.

"You've got a lot of new information — well, it seems like new information — crowding your brain. And all the emotions that come with it." I ask the question quietly, but boldly: "Do you remember?"

His head slowly rises, and his eyes connect with me. I see a depth I hadn't seen before. A sorrow that breaks my heart.

He says, "I remember."

"You didn't see your mother hurt your father."

He slowly shakes his head. Tears fill his eyes. He swallows. "No."

"It was a confusing time. A terrible time. Things get jumbled up."

He doesn't respond to this.

"We're going to have a long road ahead now. But it's important we stay the course. Don't you think?"

He nods.

I say, "If these memories we unearthed tonight, if you're sure they're the truth, then we're going to have some people to call. A lawyer, for starters. We'll need to figure out our next steps."

He looks at me for a moment, unspeaking. Then: "Okay."

Finally, I say, "And because some of these people are going to ask, let's try and get to it right now — do you think you could identify your father's attacker?"

Michael crosses his arms and takes a shuddering breath. It's as if he's drawing inward, protecting himself. The thought of his father's attacker still out there . . . In addition to everything else, obviously including the possible false conviction of his mother, it's got to be scary. A murderer walking free.

I rise from the bed when it's clear he can't — or won't — identify anyone now. I don't even have a picture of Doug Wiseman to show him. Maybe in an email from Frank? But that can wait.

"The important thing is," I say, "you've taken this important step. You've—"

"Why did I say it was her?"

The question stops me cold. It's so innocent, carrying such guilt and shame with it, I almost lose the ability to stand. But we can't get into that right now. Going charging after the cops before we have the whole story will only make matters worse.

I tell Michael, "What you need to do now is get some rest. Don't worry about any of that. Just let the new information take its time to soak in. Let the thoughts and feelings come up; don't try to suppress them. You'll be able to relax soon, I promise you. Go ahead and use Sean's room."

Michael shakes his head. "I can't. I can't stay in there. It's my fault what happened to him."

"No, it's not. Sailing accidents happen. Now you're conflating two things."

"He was out there because of *me*."

"He would've been out there anyway. You feel responsible for your mother, and so now you feel responsible for Sean. But you're *not* responsible for her. You were a child. So stop."

He looks up and studies my face. Then he lowers his head again. His shoulders jump with a single sob.

"Michael," I warn him softly. "I need to know if you're going to be okay. Are you worried you might hurt yourself?"

His face tilted down, he shakes his head.

"Are you worried you might hurt someone else?"

He looks up and frowns. "What? No."

"I have to ask. I'm not your therapist, but I have to ask. And listen, if you're not comfortable in Sean's room, take the couch downstairs."

Michael sniffs and swipes at his nose with the back of his hand before glancing around the room. "I'm going to clean this up."

I surprise him, and myself, by grabbing his shoulder. "Leave it. Just go downstairs. Lie down on the couch. Drink some more water, try to unwind. I'm going to make some calls."

And I leave the room, afraid my own emotions are going to tear loose in front of him.

Enclosed in my bedroom, I pull out my phone. Calling Paul first isn't right, either. I can't be present for my family until I take care of my needs. I'm a dam about to burst.

I call the only person I can think of. The person who's known me for over twenty years, the one who's seen me through the roughest parts of my life.

I call my old therapist, Sarah.

CHAPTER FORTY-FOUR

It's her machine. Not her voicemail, but the landline machine she still keeps in her home office. I start to leave a brief, if vague, message — "Hi, Sarah, it's been so long and . . . the timing is strange, it's late, I know . . . I'd really like to speak to you. One professional to another . . ." but the message grows until I'm pouring my heart out.

I tell Sarah about what happened from the time Michael showed up to the revelation just minutes ago. I tell her about Arnold Bleeker and Candace. About Rebecca Mooney. I even mention Maggie Lewis's suicide.

By the end of it, I'm fully sobbing. Every other sentence is an apology. For calling her, for calling late, for not keeping up with my therapy these past few years. Through it all, I picture Sarah the way she was twenty-five years ago, her silver hair back in a braid, her large hoop earrings, the smell of jasmine in her office. A real hippie.

God, she has to be in her mid- to late seventies now. Poor Sarah, getting dragged into my mess. But therapists are great with boundaries, and she'll know how to process it. And so I unload and talk for so long that the machine cuts me off with a shrill beep.

A bit dazed, I put my phone away. I find the Kleenex on Paul's dresser and wipe my eyes, clear my sinuses. Paul is my next call. He talks very quietly at first, as if he'll disturb Sean. But Sean can't hear him, of course. There's been no change. The doctor came back briefly about an hour before and then went off shift.

Our son's future remains in limbo.

I ask Paul where Joni is.

"I don't know. I assumed Michael came back and the two of them went out."

"It's almost eleven . . ."

"Yeah."

I sigh and say, "Michael is actually still here with me."

"Oh. Okay. Why?"

"We . . . I'll talk to you about it in the morning. It's too much right now."

But Paul knows. "You did it again. You regressed him."

"Let's just wait until tomorrow."

I hear a door close downstairs. Alarmed, I leave the bedroom and start down. "Michael?"

Paul, on the phone: "What? Did he leave? Emily, I think you need to be careful now. We don't know how he's going to act . . ."

I come into the kitchen first, then check the living room. No one on either couch. "Michael?" Moving to the windows, I see a figure walking across the darkened front lawn, toward the docks. *Oh no.*

"Paul, I've got to go. He's on his way down to the water."

"Let him. Listen to me. Maybe you need to stay away from him complete—"

But I run for the door. It doesn't matter what Michael has gotten us into. He was an innocent child. Now he's out there, riddled with pain and guilt. Because of me. Because of choices *I've* made.

I can't let anything happen to him. I can't have another Maggie Lewis.

"Michael!"

I run across the yard, down the gentle slope toward the water, flailing my arms as I go, as if trying to flag down a truck. Michael turns as he steps onto the dock. It's hard to make out his features in the darkness.

But then I realize something. He's not alone. Someone else is on the dock with him, farther out. The moon back-lights her long hair.

I slow myself down and stop.

"Michael . . ."

"What's the matter?" he asks.

I'm focused past him on the woman. Unable to see her clearly, my mind fills in the blanks. I picture Laura Bishop. She takes a few steps toward Michael. "Wait!" I call out.

Then the woman puts her hand in Michael's and stands close enough that the light of the house can just reach her.

* * *

Joni says, "Mom — just stay there. Calm down."

"What are you doing here?"

She says something to Michael too quietly for me to hear. He nods. The two of them start up the lawn, giving me a wide berth. In my rush to reach Michael, I missed seeing the vehicle in the driveway. The two of them head for Joni's Subaru.

"Jo, honey . . ." I start after them. "What's going on?"

"Mom, just leave it alone."

"Leave it alone?" They must have been texting. While I was unburdening myself to Sarah, then talking to Paul. But the hospital is miles from here. Joni was already on her way, then. Of course she was. Michael never returned to her, so she came looking.

I call to him. "Please talk to her, Michael. Tell her that we did what we had to. That we need to deal with this."

He stops, and then I stop. He stands looking at me in the semidarkness, his face glowing a bit from the house lights, like a phantom. Joni is pulling on his arm. "Michael. Leave her."

Joni's distance, her coldness, is painful. I don't even know where to begin to address it, so I face her fiancé.

"We have to fix this, Michael, or it will only get worse. And we're getting close."

Instead of resentment, I see resignation on his young face, his squared features. "It's okay. We can do more later. But I've got to go now."

He turns and lets Joni lead him by the hand. She only releases him in order to get behind the wheel of the Subaru.

The motion-sensor light pours onto the scene. My daughter is just a shadow, sitting in the car. The sight of her prompts me to run after her. I'm feeling old feelings — the hunt for my wayward girl when she was just a teen.

Joni hits the gas and reverses the Subaru, then does a tight turn around and tears down the long driveway, out of sight.

I listen until the engine noise has completely faded. Until the chorus of crickets has returned, the occasional burp of the frog down along the water's edge.

I know she loves me, but whatever she's doing, whatever she knows about Michael, it's clear she's on his side.

In a way, I admire it. You have to side with your partner if a marriage is going to work. You have to protect them.

I wonder at the state of my own union. Paul hasn't even texted after I hung up on him. I'm alone here, at the lake house, feeling like everything in my life has come crashing down in just a few short days.

As if I'm being punished.

CHAPTER FORTY-FIVE

Mena.

Her face floats to me out of a dozing haze. Her cheeks flushed, like she's had a drink or two. The nervous energy she emanates.

Thoughts of her blend into memories of Maggie Lewis. Young, beautiful Maggie. Not much older than Joni. Stricken with some of the same issues, in fact. Full of guilt, like Michael.

Even like I was, at that age.

A thought occurs to me, some edge of a grand pattern, but it eludes sharper focus. Something about how humans repeat behaviors? I know it's true. We tend to recreate our childhoods, for one thing. We also tend to attach ourselves to a mate similar to our opposite-sex parent.

Even more bizarre, we also like to create the same situations for ourselves again and again. You've heard the saying — insanity is doing the same thing and expecting different results. It's a truism, not a real definition, but there's no question that we can be our own worst enemy — our own greatest obstacle.

Mena. My faithful and long-time assistant. She's only ever helped and supported me. And she's seen everyone that's ever come into my office. And knows about every police case I've ever consulted on . . .

Why am I suddenly wondering about her?

Her behavior the night we met at my office, for one thing. The way she seemed nerved up over the Bishop case. Oh, she tried to pass it off as her grief for Maggie Lewis, but I knew.

Everyone seems afraid of what happened fifteen years ago. As if the hammer that struck David Bishop delivered a blow to us all. At least, it reverberated deep into our lives.

It's even affected Sean. Whether Michael did something consciously, unconsciously, or not at all, my son is vegetative, for God's sake.

None of us are in our right minds, I suppose. We're beside ourselves with shock and worry.

Poor Joni.

My daughter is protecting herself the best way she knows — she's retrieved her fiancé and taken control. She's not answering my text messages, and neither is Paul. Hopefully because he's getting some rest.

It's what I should be doing. It's after midnight.

So I lie back again. I try to shut off my mind. To end the parade of faces and din of voices. To stop myself from reliving Michael's outburst in the bedroom. His gut-wrenching recall of his family history, of the night his father died.

I push it all away and try to focus on my breathing. On the crickets, and the distant slopping of water against the boathouse docks.

I want my mommy back . . .

No, push it away, push it away . . .

It takes a knock at the door before I rise up from the couch to see the red-and-blue lights flashing in through my windows and feel the frantic buzzing of my phone against my leg.

PART FIVE

CHAPTER FORTY-SIX

First, the phone.

It's Paul.

"I can't find Joni."

"She was just here."

"At the house?"

"She took Michael and left."

As I'm explaining things to Paul, I'm headed for the door. The flashing lights are from a police car in my driveway. I rake fingers through my hair and shake it out. "I have to go now. Police are at the door."

"Police?" He's alarmed but also sounds angry.

"Everything is okay. I'll call you back."

I end the call and open the door to a beefy young man in a dark blue local police uniform. Another officer, female, is halfway between the entrance and the garage, shining a light around.

The male officer gives me a close look. "Ma'am? Is everything all right?"

I pull my light sweater around me tighter, though the night is still warm. Memories of Joni continue to surface. Christmas, when she was fifteen and missing. She'd run away from home and was found the next day by a New York City transit cop, passed out on the subway.

When I speak, my voice is dry, the words broken. "What happened? Did something happen to her?"

"Happen to who?"

"My daughter. Joni Lindman."

The young cop's gold nametag reads Fletcher. He's maybe twenty-five or thirty. Ginger-haired, cut short, with neat sideburns. The type of kid that was doing keg stands at his frat just a few years before turning law-and-order.

"Ma'am," he says, "We're here because of a disturbance call. Someone on the lake said they heard lots of noise coming from this direction. Screaming and shouting and things breaking. They weren't completely sure it was your house, but with the stuff that just happened yesterday . . . Was that your son?"

"Yes. My son, Sean. But that was an accident."

"Sure. But that's what caused us to zero in on your house when we got the domestic call. Ma'am, are you all right? You've got a bruise there on your face . . ."

"Oh, that . . ." I start to explain, but I'm distracted by more headlights coming up the drive.

Thinking it might be Joni, I walk past the local officer.

"Ma'am," he says. When I don't respond, he whistles.

The other cop, who's been wandering around the property with her flashlight, is a little closer. She gets in my path. "Ma'am, let's just sit tight for a minute, okay?"

"This is probably my daughter," I say. But it's not. The vehicle comes into view. More police. This one is a state trooper's car, darker with a yellow stripe. Two figures inside. Good grief.

"That's our backup," the female officer explains. "The caller dialed 911, and 911 sends it out to everyone in the vicinity. They're just checking that everything's okay."

The state troopers exit the vehicle, each sliding a nightstick through their belts once they've stood. One's a little taller, but both are fit and dark-haired, like brothers. They each give me a glance, then start to chat quietly with the female officer.

"Ma'am," says the other local cop, Fletcher, easing up behind me. "Who else is in the house?"

"You can call me Emily."

"Okay, Emily. Who else is home?"

"No one is here. Not right now. My daughter just left."

"And who's your daughter?"

It goes on like this until they have the basic details down. Fletcher says, "And so it was you and Michael here in the house about a half hour ago?"

"Yes."

"Were you fighting?"

"No."

They're waiting for an answer. I tell them the first thing that springs to mind. "I'm treating Michael. I'm doing regressive therapy."

The woman, identified on her uniform as Coyle, speaks up. "He's your daughter's fiancé, and you're treating him?"

"Not formally. It's a long story. I can't really discuss it all, because of patient confidentiality."

Coyle nods. "I see." She glances at the others.

One of the troopers says, "Ma'am, we'd like to just take a look around. Make sure everything is all right. Is that okay with you?"

"No one is here. I'm not hiding anything. I used to work with law enforcement. As a consulting clinical therapist."

"That's great," Fletcher says. One of the troopers goes past him, and past me, inside. The other starts around the back of the house.

Coyle asks, "Have you had much to drink tonight, Emily?"

"No. Why are you asking me that?"

"Just getting a sense of things. And the bruise on your face?"

"I hit a deer."

Coyle and Fletcher trade looks. Fletcher: "You hit a deer and got a bruise on your face?"

Coyle points at my forearm, which shows some black and blue. "You got that, too?"

It's likely from Candace's husband, Greg. But they don't need to know that. "Yes. I hit a deer two nights ago. No, three nights ago . . . I'm sorry. My son is in the hospital. He's in a coma. And my daughter . . . We're in the midst of a family crisis here, really."

"You feel like you're in crisis?" Coyle looks concerned.

"That's not what I — I mean, we're dealing with some major things, like families do. When it rains, it pours. I'm sorry that we were loud, that Michael was loud . . ."

I trail off when Fletcher pulls his phone, as if checking a message. After he reads it, he levels a look at me. "Ma'am — Emily — did you have an altercation on the second floor? The room is torn up pretty bad. Should we go have a look?"

I take them inside. Coyle and Fletcher are clocking everything as they walk through my house. In the bedroom, both seem to have made up their minds — this is more than family problems. "Did your daughter's fiancé do this?" Fletcher puts his hands on his hips. We stand in the mess with Coyle and the taller trooper.

"I told you, this was part of his regression. He acted out."

"And his name? You said Michael Rand? Could you maybe find out where he and your daughter went? I think everything's going to be okay, but we might just like to have a quick talk with him. Then we can leave you to your business."

I'm trembling slightly. My words have a bite I can't quite control. "I don't know where they are. I can't keep track of my daughter every five minutes. She's a grown woman."

The three cops in the room give each other knowing looks, then Fletcher leads them out.

After we return downstairs, I try to make amends by offering them all something to drink. Each politely declines.

It's after one in the morning when they finally have filed out of my house and returned to their cars. The last one, the trooper, is coming up from the boathouse. He stops and talks to Fletcher and Coyle, his words lost under the sound of the idling engine. Fletcher gets out. He and the trooper approach me. The trooper says, "Mrs. Lindman, can you come with me for a minute?"

"What is it?"

"Just come with me, please."

* * *

The state trooper walks me to the boathouse. Our feet make hollow noises on the wooden dock as we walk to the door and open it.

The dinghy and the sailboat are bobbing in the water. The water gently slops against their hulls and the wooden boathouse foundation. The trooper snaps on a flashlight and shines it on the sailboat.

The blood is dark, having mostly dried. It spills over the wales and then smears alongside the hull. I can almost discern a handprint.

"That's my son's blood," I say, answering the unasked question. "That's Sean's blood."

The trooper: "You said this happened out over the water?"

"Yes. Sean took Michael sailing. Show him a few things."

"Uh-huh. And Sean was hit in the head? By . . . that big thing there?"

"Yes. The boom."

"Is that a common accident in sailing?"

The resentment starts to build. I'd already had these feelings, these suspicions, and put them away. Now it's being re-litigated by the police. "Common enough," I say.

"Uh-huh. And so the boom hits your son in the head, and he goes into the water. Is that right? Michael then gets in the water, swims to him, and then what? Keeps his head out of the water? Tries to get him to shore?"

"They were picked up." My voice sounds slightly muffled. My eyelids flutter with momentary lightheadedness. "Picked up by someone passing by."

Officer Fletcher grabs me. "Whoa. Emily. Are you okay?"

"I'm fine."

Didn't Paul say there was someone? Someone who took Sean and Michael aboard, called 911, and brought them to the boat launch? My thoughts are fuzzy. So much has happened in just a few days.

The trooper asks, "Who returned the sailboat to the boathouse?"

"My husband must've . . . he would've gone out in the rowboat. And towed it back." But I doubt my own words. Would Paul have gone out on the lake to retrieve the sailboat before rushing to the hospital? That doesn't make any sense.

My gaze seeks the symbol scratched into the wood near the boathouse opening. The heart with the arrow through my daughter's name. Michael's name. I can't quite make them out from here. I want to move closer, verify them, and take another look at the words etched into the windowsill just above.

But the next question from the state trooper causes me to forget all about it.

"Mrs. Lindman, do you know Laura Bishop?"

My skin starts to crawl. "Yes."

"In what capacity?"

A pause. Then: "She was part of a case I consulted on. Years ago."

The trooper pauses, looks at Fletcher, then back at me. The boats bob in the water; the water makes its hollow sounds. "We're notified when an inmate is about to be released from state prison."

"Okay . . ."

"We also receive a cross-report on anyone that inmate may have contacted on the day before his or her release." The trooper nods to Fletcher, who leads us out of the boathouse and up the hill.

The trooper says, "Laura Bishop is going to be out in a few hours. Eight a.m. this morning. And the last phone call she made was to a Michael Rand. Your daughter's fiancé."

CHAPTER FORTY-SEVEN

So they've been in touch.

Or maybe she just left a message? The police weren't able to tell me more. No specifics on the time. But I know calls from prison are recorded, so it's got to be on file somewhere.

What matters more: Michael knows who he is. That seems definitive now. He knows he's Tom Bishop — why else would he be in contact with Laura? And if he's been in touch with her, it strongly suggests that the whole "memory loss" thing has been a charade.

I remember him in our driveway, right after I told him I believed him to be Tom Bishop. How he said, "I'm not ready." Now it makes sense. He wasn't ready for me to lift the veil off his identity just yet.

I manage to convince the police that they can go. I'll be all right. They're skeptical, but since I'm not about to press any charges, and they're not going to arrest me for a noise complaint, they eventually leave.

As soon as they're gone, I light a cigarette. Not Joni's brand. I can't seem to recall when I bought them or where they came from. But the crackling burn of the tobacco soothes. The smoke cycles through me as I text Joni. *Where are you?* A familiar pull of frustration and despair is settling into my neck and shoulders. An old feeling. My intractable daughter. Rebellious, unresponsive.

I text Paul, too, apologizing for my earlier abruptness, explaining what happened; the watered-down version. *Police checking on things. Everything is okay.*

Nothing could be further from the truth. And the fact that I'm withdrawing from Paul, rather than banding together with him in this time of multiple crises and uncertainty, makes things all the bleaker.

Resolving to start anew in the morning and get my life back, I put out the cigarette in the driveway and return to the couch. After a few fitful minutes, I say a prayer. I'm not a particularly religious person, but I ask that my son be looked after. My daughter. And Michael, too.

He lied to you.

But why? Maybe there's a good reason? Are there things he may be genuinely in the dark about? He might know he's Tom Bishop, but he might be seeking answers to genuine questions.

No. He's been messing with you this whole time.

It occurs to me that the simplest solution is usually the best. Occam's razor. I consider it: Either Michael fabricated an entire life, complete with a college experience that enabled him to meet and woo my daughter, so that he could come here to our lake house to beguile and disturb us — and then to nearly kill his fiancée's brother — or he's a lost soul with a hazy, troubled past. Between his subconscious leading him in certain directions and a dash of fate, he's here.

Which seems more likely?

Unable to answer, I finally fall into a troubled sleep.

* * *

When the phone rings, morning sunlight is streaming through the southeast-facing windows overlooking the lake. My mouth feels cottony, my head wrapped in wet gauze. Almost like the old days. When Paul and I still cut a rug.

What day is it?

Monday.

What time?

8:23 a.m. Laura Bishop is officially out of prison.

The thought then goes right out of my head when I finally realize who is calling.

I sit bolt upright, wipe my eyes and answer. "Sarah?"

"Emily . . ." Her voice is soft, weathered. Exuding concern. "Are you okay?"

"I'm okay. Thank you for calling. How are *you*? It's been so long."

"I'm well, thank you. Emily, how can I help? Your message was . . . urgent."

A laugh escapes me that sounds more manic than I'd prefer. I'm up off the couch and headed for the door to check the driveway for Joni's car. "I know, I just unloaded on you. And I'm sorry."

"No, it's all right. It's fine. I want to talk to you . . . How are you?"

I reach the door and push aside the curtain. Both the rental car and Sean's car are there. But not Joni's Subaru. The disappointment feels like a weight. I turn and sag against the door, pinching my temples. Shutting my eyes. "Well, Sarah . . . Joni is . . . She took off last night."

"You said in your message. And I'm so sorry about Sean. What an absolute tragedy. Oh, my . . . how is he? What are they saying?"

We talk a little bit about his condition, his prognosis, and about the accident. Sarah listens. She absorbs it all quietly, with the occasional *tsk* or sigh. When I'm finished, she asks, "And Joni hasn't come back?"

"No. She hasn't." I move into the kitchen and take down a glass, run the tap. "She's angry with me. So angry."

Sarah is quiet.

I force some water down. "Do you remember? I was still seeing you sometimes. And Joni would disappear. She'd just take off."

That soft voice: "I remember."

"She didn't even have a phone then. When she first ran away. She was twelve. And then when she did have a phone, she just ignored us. I'd be up until four in the morning, waiting for her to come home. We were so helpless."

"It was a difficult time for you."

I shrug off the bad memories. I need to get moving. Take a quick shower to clear my head. Maybe some coffee. Then I need to get to the hospital, see my son. Maybe find out if Paul knows who brought our sailboat home. It seems like a small thing, but now I need to know. Maybe Paul has the phone number of the Good Samaritan who helped.

"Emily?"

"I'm sorry. Sarah, can I ask you a hypothetical?"

"Hypotheticals are my favorite. Metaphors, too."

"I remember that." I'm transported to her home office, looking at her kindly face, the large earrings catching the afternoon light. "I wonder if someone might . . . Well, I'm wondering about your experience with severe repression. Someone pushing something down so far that it becomes unconscious. But then it . . ."

"What?"

"Comes out in other ways."

Sarah is silent for a moment. "Freud warned that something like that would always come out. And the longer a person waited, the worse it would be."

"Wasn't he talking about something you knew? Suppressed consciously, not repressed."

"They're not very different, in the end."

I think about it for a moment.

"May I ask *you* a question, Emily?"

"Of course."

"Do you remember your reason for first coming to me?"

It takes me a moment. I'm partly aware that I've drifted back into the living room. The sun is shining hard on the lake, jeweling the small waves with a million scattered diamonds. "It was my father. Well, it was Paul. It was . . . I'd hit him. I felt like I was going to be . . . My temper was going to be a problem."

"You were very concerned."

"Is that what you wanted to know?" I sit down on the couch to await her response.

Sarah is silent a moment. I can hear a white noise background, like ocean waves. "You'd had your rock bottom, you said. You'd struggled with your guilt to the point you'd considered suicide."

"Yes." I'm getting that floaty sensation again. Five hours was not enough sleep, apparently. I lie down on the couch.

"But then you picked yourself back up. We worked on it. You processed your emotions about your father — he'd died in his forties, isn't that right?"

"Forty-nine."

Something clicks in the back of my mind, like pieces coming together. Wasn't David Bishop forty-nine? I'll have to check my case notes.

Sarah says, "You got yourself going in the right direction again. You married Paul. You went back to school and studied to be a therapist yourself."

"That's right," I say, sensing that Sarah is leading me somewhere. Her voice is comforting. My eyes feel heavy.

"But we might've been too hasty to reduce our sessions. Do you think?"

My eyelids pull open. "What do you mean?"

But I can sense it, hear it, smell it — people crowded in a room, laughing. The sweet scent of alcohol, thick and pervasive. The heat of bodies. Outside, smokers under a cloud of nicotine. In the bathroom, a few furtive lines of cocaine.

"I mean that when we think we have it all together, we have to be careful. We have to stay on guard. Especially when we have destructive tendencies."

I sit up again, the comforting spell having been pierced by anxiety. Guilt. Was there a young face somewhere in that crowd of people? A young girl?

"Sarah, what are you saying?"

"I'm saying that you had pressures. You weren't seeing me as much, but you had pressures. From work, from parenting, from your social life." She takes a breath. "And then there was the affair."

The affair.

Of course there was the affair. It's not like I've forgotten *that*. We were young, the kids were young; we'd built up a lot of pressure, like Sarah is saying. Paul worked long hours in the city, while I listened to people's problems all day. When he came home, I was often tired, grouchy. I was at my limit and didn't have the mental bandwidth to listen to his woes too.

Eventually, Paul sought comfort elsewhere. It's not that I blame myself, but I had a role to play. Paul's affair was brief, and we worked it out. Without a doubt, divorce was on my mind for some time. But we stayed together. For the kids. Until, eventually, we found each other again.

"I should've seen you more," I confess to Sarah. "I know that. It probably would've made things easier."

"I'm not saying anything is your fault," Sarah says. "But I think it's important to remember these things. To have someone else help you. When we remember, we're not actually going back to the same event each time in our minds. We're remembering the last time we *remembered*. And so things can get distorted over time. Bent one way or the other, toward our preference." She adds, "All we really have is the present."

"Of course." I'm up again, ascending the stairs, resolved to get my day started. "But if we fail to remember the past . . ."

"We're doomed to repeat it." She laughs. A light, papery sound. "It's a conundrum. Which is why I brought it up. I think what you're going through now . . . It's important to have your memories at full avail. This is as much about you as it is anyone else."

That stops me. "Joni, you mean? The parties we had when she and Sean were little . . . ?"

"Well, that. You didn't tell me everything, of course, but I think the affair took a lot out of you. Putting your marriage back together."

"We always put the kids first."

"Kids know."

I tighten up in defense. "Well, yes . . . kids know. They know they're loved."

"Of course . . ."

"Sarah . . . thank you. Your calling me back is so appreciated. It means so much. But I might need to go now."

She hesitates. "Of course. Call me anytime."

"Let's talk again very soon."

She doesn't respond.

"Sarah?"

"You were very good at closing things off," Sarah says.

The words unnerve me. Tickle the back of my neck. Like electricity. "What do you mean?"

"I shouldn't have said that. Listen, Emily, you can call me back if you need to. I'll be here."

"Thank you, Sarah. I will."

I toss the phone onto the bed. *Kids know.* What is that supposed to mean? Of course *kids know.* But we loved our two children. We raised them right, and they never wanted for anything. I can't go around blaming myself for Joni's recalcitrance as a teenager. Without question, our home life factors in, but Joni is an individual. She made her choices; she makes them still.

I can't be held responsible for every one of them, can I?

But it gets me thinking. Thinking about affairs. I sit down at the laptop and pull up my email, then find the last email from Frank Mills.

Frank is good at what he does. Not only does he have Doug Wiseman's info, he's got pictures. Both candid photos, like you'd see on social media. One of them is from a few decades ago, Wiseman looking younger. In that one, he's on a boat, wearing a white-and-blue polo shirt. His hair is curly and a bit unruly. In the second photo, he's sitting at an outdoor table, laughing. His hair is shorter. He's holding a beer in his hand. It looks imported.

I study the first photo more closely. In it, he's got a cigarette pinched between his fingers.

I wonder what brand Wiseman smoked. Did the cops ever question him? They say he didn't factor in until later. But if Laura was having an affair? If there was a man outside the night her husband was killed?

It makes so much sense it gives me chills. It feels like I'm on the verge of solving a criminal case the investigators got wrong. If I can just convince the people who need convincing, this whole thing will be over.

* * *

The shower feels good and helps me straighten out my priorities. Joni is a grown woman, and I can't go chasing after her. And whether Michael has been in touch with his mother this whole time — I can't control any of that. What I can do is talk to the state police professional standards bureau and give them everything I've got, but after I do one thing first.

I'm going to visit my son. Spend some time with him. Be with him in the present, in the *now*, just like Sarah said. I'll even read to him.

The rest of it all can wait a few hours. Sean needs me.

I dress casually but comfortably. Denim shorts. My good sandals. A blouse from one of my aunts — white with a charming pattern, like beaded necklaces surrounding the wide neck. It's a fine temperature in the house, warm outside, but the hospital can get cool, I'm guessing. I haven't spent much time in one. I'm lucky. Besides my two pregnancies, the only lengthy stay at a hospital was when my father had his heart attack. At any rate, I grab a sweatshirt to bring and stuff it in a tote bag.

I seek out a book to bring, something to read to Sean. And I should bring my husband something to eat, I suppose.

I'll make him a sandwich. And I'll bring it to him at the hospital where he watches over our injured son.

This is my life.

Do I resent it? Or is it what I deserve?

I'm about to answer myself that question when a fast shape on the lake catches my eye.

The boat is cruising along, a nice motorboat, the kind you see water skiers behind, and it's headed into our cove.

As I watch, it steers toward the dock, then slows, splitting the water in frothy waves.

There's a lone man behind the wheel.

CHAPTER FORTY-EIGHT

I almost don't venture down. I nearly hurry to the rental car and leave. Because one more thing and I might have a nervous breakdown.

But I can't help but think this is quite likely the tourist who helped Sean and Michael. I can see it in his face, in the pity and concern beaming at me over the distance.

Once I wave, and he waves, his worried look transforms into a smile of relief. He's bearded, in his late forties or early fifties. Fit for his age. I see diving equipment on the boat as he putters up to the dock.

"Can I help you?" I ask.

"Hello — so sorry to just stop by like this." He speaks with a heavy French-Canadian accent.

"It's okay. Toss me your line."

He throws me a thick short rope attached to his bow, and I give it a couple of wraps around the dock cleat. But I'll have to make this short — Sean is waiting.

The man hops onto the dock and ties off the back end in the same way. He's wearing beige shorts and brown sandals. His white T-shirt is well worn, the neck wide, gray chest hairs curling out. I can smell the suntan lotion. "I'm Luca," he says. "Luca Marceau. You must be Mrs. Lindman."

"I am. Are you the, um . . . ?" It's hard to finish the question.

I don't have to. Luca Marceau gets a somber look and nods his head. He rubs his calloused hands together, as if nervous. "Yes. I was the one to take your son and his friend to the boat launch."

"Thank you for what you did. Mr. Marceau. I am just so grateful . . ."

"How is he . . . is the boy who . . . ?"

"He's hanging in there. Right now, he's still unconscious."

The sorrow in Marceau's eyes threatens to spill over. Seeing this stranger about to burst into tears on my dock is almost too much to bear. He covers his mouth. "I'm so sorry."

"It's okay. Just . . . I can't tell you how appreciative I am for what you did."

"Anyone would have. I was just there."

"My husband and I would like to properly thank you. Are you going to be around the area for long?"

"Only until tomorrow. Then we return. We are from Quebec." His fluency in English seems to waver with his emotion.

I nod and sort of shake my head in disbelief at the same time. "We're so grateful, Mr. Marceau. I was going to try and track you down. Did you bring the sailboat back as well?"

He's nodding. "Yes. I hope this is okay."

"It's very okay." I bite my lip, running my next questions past my internal censor. But I have to know. "Mr. Marceau . . ."

"Luca."

"Luca. Can I ask you what you saw?"

He regards me silently for a moment with his dark eyes. Then, "I didn't see. My family was in the boat. My daughter, she pointed — she said, 'Daddy, there's two men in the water.'"

"Okay."

"They were several meters from the boat. The sailboat. I look and I see, clearly, the men are struggling."

He must see the question in my eyes because he clarifies.

"One man is swimming, holding the other. Pulling him through the water, like this." Marceau demonstrates holding someone around the chest.

I nod some more. It's hard to continue this line of questioning — we're all programmed for social cohesion — but I have to know. "And your daughter, did she see what caused the two men to go into the water?"

"No, I don't think she did. We're divers. We like to scuba. The lake here is deep, one of the deepest. I take them; I show them where the Lady in the Lake was found."

The Lady in the Lake. The murdered woman sunk in the water and discovered decades later. Preserved by the frigid temperature of its depths. A bizarre and macabre activity for a family, but to each his own.

Marceau continues, "We had just surfaced. We were heading back, everyone talking, laughing, you know. Having some snacks. And my daughter, she look over—"

"Who else was with you?"

He seems surprised by my interruption. Or, perhaps more accurately, he is starting to wonder at my questions. If I suspect something.

"My wife, too," he begins slowly. "Our son. He's eleven. And our son's friend, who we brought for the trip."

"So the five of you."

"*Oui*. Yes."

I give it just a few beats, but if anyone saw anything untoward — and as a family, they surely would have discussed it — Luca isn't offering. I thank him again and ask him to please leave me his number.

"You don't have to do this for me. Dinner and so on."

I don't have anything to write on, but I have my phone. "Please," I say.

"Okay." Marceau gives me the number and I input it into my phone. When I finish, we stand there a moment and then he gets moving, untying the lines.

"Luca?"

He's been waiting for my question. "Yes?"

"How did he seem? The young man who was helping my son."

Marceau blinks several times. Then he asks, "Your son was swimming with the boy in the water, yes?"

"Well, my son was sailing. They weren't swimming, they were sailing."

"Yes, sailing . . ."

Marceau appears confused, and I wonder if something got lost in translation.

"What I mean is, the young man helping my son, what was his demeanor? I'm sure he was shocked. Did he seem . . . ? What is it?"

"I'm sorry," Marceau says. He offers an embarrassed smile and shakes his head. "I think I don't understand. Your son helped the man who was drowning . . ."

"No, my son *was* the man who was drowning."

We're both quiet for a few seconds. Marceau's eyes dart around. He scratches at his chin.

I start to feel a cold sensation. It forms in the pit of my stomach and spreads. "Luca, did the man who was swimming — did he tell you he was my son?"

"I must be confused . . ."

"Wait. Dark hair. Light blue eyes. That's a young man named Michael, my daughter's fiancé. My son, Sean Lindman, was the one in the water. I've been told the boom struck his head and he went in. Then Michael jumped in after him . . ."

Marceau is backing away. He steps wide into his boat. "Of course. Yes. That's right."

"I'm sorry, I don't mean to make you uncomfortable. We've just . . . It's been a difficult few days. Please just tell me if you assumed that Michael was my son, or he *told* you he was my son . . ."

Marceau meets my gaze. "It was all very fast."

I grip the boat. I'm not letting go without an answer.

"I think I might assume. Because he say he live here. On the lake. And I take the boat back, and see the house, so . . ."

"But my husband arrived at the boat launch. Didn't you talk to him? How did you know which house? I'm sorry. It sounds like I'm—"

My buzzing phone interrupts me. A quick glance at the screen reveals an unfamiliar number. I'm not even sure of the area code. It's vaguely familiar, but I'll wait for the voicemail.

Marceau, meanwhile, shakes his head. "Your husband? I did not meet him. Your son — or the young man — he describe the house. Back in the cove. Big gray house, the windows, the boathouse. Because he was going in the ambulance. He said if police came, or someone needed to know about the boat."

"But you just turned around and brought it back."

"Yes, I have the tow rope and the sailboat is small, so . . ." Marceau shrugs. He's uncomfortable, trying to leave.

Somehow, Michael gave him the impression that he was my son. If Michael came right out and said that, Marceau can't say with certainty.

I let go of the boat. With his tie lines aboard, I give the bow a little push as he ignites the engine. He putts backward into the gunmetal water, then changes gears. He waves and then forwards the throttle, pushing waves until the speed lifts the boat out of the water to plane the surface.

CHAPTER FORTY-NINE

Sean is as I left him. The machine does his breathing. Paul is asleep in the chair. I don't wake him, but instead spend some quiet time with my son. Already, he smells like the hospital — sterile and stale. I pet his blond hair, run my fingers against his cheek and jaw. "I love you."

I begin to read. Eventually, Paul wakes up. He blinks at everything, getting his bearings, and sees me. For a moment, we only look each other. Then he lifts his eyebrows in question, asking silently about Joni.

I shake my head.

Paul asks, "Where do you think she went?"

"I don't know, and I don't care."

He stands, stretches, grimacing as he tips from one side to the other, hands on his hips.

I apologize to him for the previous night. "There was a lot going on."

He waves it off. "I understand."

Looking at Sean again, whose serene face is the same, whose arms are down at his sides, the bedsheet taut across his chest, I'm reminded that he's not going anywhere. I don't want to miss it if he wakes up, but I can't hold my breath. Paul and I need to talk.

* * *

We're outside, behind the hospital where the parking lot extends, and I'm smoking a cigarette in the shadow of the building. "I can't help it, Paul." I'm on the verge of tears. "I keep thinking about one of my clients."

"The one who died?"

I nod.

"When is the funeral?"

"It was today. But that's not . . . I keep thinking about her situation. That she left her child. Gave him up when she was young. She would talk about him. She'd tell me about leaving him. About what it was like, how she felt empty. How she felt nothing."

Suddenly I'm shivering. I step toward the sunlight. "Paul, I just . . . I feel like I'm coming apart. Did we abandon Joni when she needed us most? Sending her to prep schools? Signing her up to model for those stupid magazines? Did we rob her of a . . . ?" I can't finish, and my body goes limp as I cry.

Did we rob her of a childhood?

Paul takes me in a hug. He rubs my back. "This is a hard time. This is so hard. Our son is in there. But he's going to be okay. And Joni is tough."

Pulling it together, I gaze into Paul's eyes. "Yeah?"

He smiles faintly and nods. "You've just got to relax. Our daughter is forever a source of drama. We have to pace ourselves."

I laugh a little through the tears. "Yeah."

Then, after a few breaths into Paul's chest, I lean back. "You don't think we fucked her up?"

"No."

I nod, trying to accept it. Part of me knows I'm focused on the wrong issue. But that's how the mind works sometimes.

"Something else I need to tell you," I say. "The man who brought Sean to the boat launch, his name is Luca Marceau. We need to thank him properly somehow."

"How did you find out?"

"He came to the house. I was just leaving, but he rode up on his boat and we talked."

"Weird, but okay."

"Well, the whole thing was weird. He also met Michael. And he seems pretty sure Michael said he was our son."

Paul is quiet.

I end up being the one coming to Michael's defense. "It's possible he was just being efficient. Michael is practically our son-in-law. And in a crisis, it's best to keep things simple."

I pull farther away from my husband to get a better look at his face. Paul stares off into the sea of parked cars, sun-spangled in the late August morning. I shield my eyes as I look there, too; it's nearly blinding.

Paul says, "Are you going to tell me about the police?"

I take a deep drag of the cigarette, then let it out. "Okay."

He looks at me, waiting.

"Maybe Michael didn't have anything to do with what happened to Sean. I'm not sure. But he's been in touch with her."

"Her *who*?" Paul's jaw is clenched, his eyes distant. "Laura?"

I nod. I explain about the police being notified of her last call. That it went to Michael.

Paul listens, his eyes drifting back to the parking lot. He holds out his hand, his first two fingers extended. I pass the cigarette to him and he drags on the cigarette. The smoke issues from his nostrils.

He hands it back to me, and I mash it out on the ground.

"I'm going back inside," Paul says.

I nod, but stay put.

"Em, you coming?"

"In a minute."

He squeezes my shoulder as he walks away. Watching Paul recede, I think about Doug Wiseman. I'm not sure Paul is going to be able to help me push forward in that department. At least, not right now. He's too hurt, it seems, too offended by Michael's apparent deceit.

As I'm contemplating it, my phone rings. It's Michael, as if on cue.

"I was just thinking about you," I say.

"I think I'm remembering more." It sounds like he's been crying.

"Michael? What's wrong? Is everything okay?"

"Dr. Lindman," he says. "I think I'm remembering more. I think I'm remembering all of it."

CHAPTER FIFTY

I know it's wrong.

I'm finally convinced that my daughter's fiancé has been manipulating me. Not just to save face, but for much graver purposes. Revenge, most likely.

But I'm going to play along. I'm going to play along, because that's all I can think to do. I have to know what Michael is going to say next. What the next move is, the next overturned stone.

Only when it's all finished, all on the table, can I make the best decision about how to proceed.

Because at this point, whatever the truth is, there's every chance it could ruin my career, my reputation, everything I've built. I have no idea what the police will accept, or — in this day and age — how the media will spin it. Even if coercion by police is the ultimate conclusion, I'll still be the hapless therapist who let it happen. My name will get out there, I'm positive.

Unless, maybe, I can get out in front of it.

I step on the gas and skirt the edges of Saranac Lake, hoping to beat the little snarls of summer traffic, knowing that despite my plan, this is the very essence of human frailty. This is the classic dilemma everyone faces at some point in their lives — to bury a darker reality or let it come to the surface.

It's a dilemma that hounds you, pursues you. It takes shape — it's a big, hulking truck, and it's bearing down on me as we speak.

I'm only able to glance at it in the mirror as I drive, but it looks familiar: a gray Ford Super Duty.

A moment later, a red light starts flashing from its dash.

I slow and pull over on a side street in front of a ramshackle home with a massive porch. The street is lined with them.

I know who it is before he even steps out of the truck, puts on his aviator sunglasses, and walks up alongside my car.

I buzz down the window.

"Emily Lindman," Starzyk says, putting his hands on my door. He looks down at me through the glasses. "How we doing, Doc?"

Of all the emotions going through me, all the possible responses, my brain seems to select one for me: "Did I do something wrong?"

"Well, not answering my calls isn't necessarily *wrong*, but it sure doesn't feel right."

I pick up my phone. "Sorry, I had your card, but didn't have you in my phone, so I didn't recognize the number. There's just been a lot happening."

"I hear you." After glancing up and down the street, he marks me again. "So, where you going?"

"Detective Starzyk . . . can you tell me what this is about?"

"People always want to know what they did," he says. A car vehicle is coming the other way, a van, and Starzyk watches it pass. He tips his head to the driver and continues talking. "You know, before I was an investigator, I was a trooper. Lotta guys out of BCI started that way. They like you to have some experience as a trooper. And I got some, I was able to do a few investigations on my own. But you got to put in your time running radar, too. Catching speeders. And it's the same thing, whether you pull someone over for speeding or knock on their door — guilty faces. 'Did I do something wrong?' Everybody is guilty of something. Everybody's got an unclean conscience. That's what I've seen, my whole career."

Not knowing where this is going, I seek to be assertive. "Detective, I have to get going."

"You going to see Michael?" His tone makes it sound like we're all the best of friends.

"Can you please tell me why you've pulled me over?"

Starzyk hesitates. Then he leans down and removes his shades. His dark eyes seem to quiver in their sockets. "Lots of questions being answered with questions. Here's mine. Why do you think I'm here, Doc? For my fucking health?"

"All right," I say. I look away from him. My heart is beating, my hands shaking. I put them on the wheel, 10 and 2. All I have to do is grab the shifter and put the car in gear. This is unlawful. Starzyk needs to be reported.

But I don't move.

Starzyk asks, "Have you seen her?"

"Who?" I stay looking ahead, out the windshield. Lawn after lawn, porch after porch, house after house. Each the same, each with unique character. Tucked between maples and oaks, the homes are former cure cottages, holdovers from when city people like me sought refuge in the rural north.

"Come on now," Starzyk says. "You know who."

I finally look at him. "You're asking me if I've had any contact with Laura Bishop? No, I haven't. I've been busy with my family. My son is in the hospital."

Using one finger, Starzyk pushes his glasses back in front of his eyes. "Terrible accident, I heard. Your boy out there on the water. Michael Rand right there with him."

We're starting to draw attention — someone in the window of a house two doors down. Farther up the street, a kid stands astride his bicycle, gawking.

Still shaking, I swallow. *It's now or never.* "Detective, if there's something you want to tell me, something about what

happened with the David Bishop case . . . with Tom Bishop
. . . maybe I'm not the person to talk to about it. Maybe you
need to speak to your superiors. Now, if you don't mind . . ."

"But you'll speak to Michael about it, won't you?" Starzyk
asks. The friendliness is gone from his voice. The words are
cold. "Yeah. You'll talk to your little buddy there. Bet he's
telling you some nice stories. Just like he did fifteen years ago."

That gets me. I take my hand off the shifter and give
Starzyk my full attention. "Whatever you think I'm doing,
whatever you're afraid of . . ."

But Starzyk leans in so close that I can smell pastrami on
his breath. "*You're* the one who needs to be afraid."

I can barely move. Being talked to like this, and by a
police officer — I've never experienced anything like it. The
men and women I worked with over the years were always
outstanding individuals. Starzyk is a different breed. He
scares me in deep places. It's all I can do not to scream and
flee.

But he pulls his head back a little. He glances up and
down the street one more time. He says, "You go ahead and
run along. You have your little times with Michael. See what
he has to say about the whole thing. Just know that I warned
you."

"What does that mean?" I manage. My voice is choked,
my whole body trembling.

Starzyk doesn't answer me as he walks away. I watch him
in the side mirror as he gets back into his truck. I want so
badly to drive away first, to be in control, but I'm shaken to
the core. I feel the same way, almost, as when I hit the deer.
It's another impact.

Instead, I sit there as Starzyk pulls away from the curb
and roars past in his truck. He doesn't look at me as he goes
— I just have this quick image of him in profile, sunglasses
on.

How dare you, I think, as the truck heads down the road.

It's like I've been violated. And that's what this is: an
abuse of power. Cops can't just pull people over willy-nilly.

This is obviously personal for him — he's using his personal phone to call me. And his personal vehicle too — when I saw him in Bronxville, he was in an unmarked police car. Now he's been following me around in his pickup truck.

I grab my phone, wondering if I should call 911, or if I can just google the number for BCI headquarters in Albany. The former seems a bit dramatic but might more readily connect me to the right people once I explain the situation. The latter, though, just seems more reasonable.

But I sit there, looking at my phone, not moving.

The person in the window is gone. The kid has mounted his bike and rides circles in the road, focused on childhood things once more.

Call.

But I don't.

It's still not a complete picture yet. Right now, all I've got is a cop acting weird. Maybe abusing his authority, sure. Getting pushy with his power. And it might be enough to get him in trouble, but what are we talking about? A reprimand, most likely, a slap on the wrist. I'm a respected doctor with a long history of working well with law enforcement, but Starzyk is also decorated. A call from me, no matter how earnest, would have far less impact on his life than he's had on mine.

This isn't about an eye for an eye. This is about justice. *That's* how it's got to be. I've got to be ready with everything — I need Michael's whole story, need to know what and who he saw — and then I can make the move.

CHAPTER FIFTY-ONE

I follow the directions Michael gave me, because once I've gone off the main roads and am deep enough into the woods, there's no more satellite guidance. First the LTE indicator blips off, then the tower signal strength fades down to one bar as I pilot the Toyota rental over a narrow, bumpy dirt road. Finally, the phone claims *No Service*.

It's even more remote and rustic out here than at our home on the lake. The sunlight shines bars of light through a high canopy of trees. Douglas firs and red birches make up the lower scrub. Deer flies nose-dive at the car as I make my way in. Deeper and deeper.

Seven-tenths of a mile later, I'm looking at it. A yurt. But like Sean described, it's well-built, wooden. A real house.

I see a small chicken coop and a vegetable garden. A grouping of solar panels. A decent-sized generator with a large can of gas beside it probably serves as their backup power. As I drove in, I went up in elevation, where there were fewer larger trees to form the canopy; the unfettered sun burns down onto the panels. Nearby, a sturdy shed most likely holds the batteries. The other small outbuilding looks like a bathhouse.

This is where Madison Tremont, a childhood friend of Joni's, has made her home with her boyfriend, Hunter. While I commend them for their spirit of adventure and the effort toward renewable energy, as Paul pointed out, the dark gray Escalade parked next to the pine trees seems a bit antithetical.

But I'm not here to judge.

The door to the yurt opens, and Michael takes the two steps down to the ground and approaches as I exit my car.

His eyes are puffy and reddened, as if he's been crying. As he gets closer, his lip trembles, and he throws his arms around me in a big hug. "Thank you for coming," he says into my shoulder and hair. "I'm sorry. I'm sorry I left last night."

"It's okay." I've gone rigid at his embrace but force myself to squeeze him back before pulling free. I glance around. "Where is everyone else?"

He wipes his eyes and sniffs. "They're hiking. They wanted to give us some space."

I step back and keep looking, seeking any signs of danger. I don't know what. Maybe someone lurking at the property's edge. But all I hear are the clucking chickens and the songbirds; all I see are the white butterflies dancing amid the bright green ferns.

"We're halfway up a mountain," Michael says. "Madison and Hunter hike to the top all the time."

For a moment, I think I catch the sound of an engine, but then it's gone. I've been here five minutes. I checked the mirrors as I came. If Starzyk followed me, he's keeping a distance.

You're the one who needs to be afraid.

A warning? Or a threat? Well, Starzyk can't know what Michael has told me in confidence. Even if he could, anything Michael has said so far is dubious as new evidence. No judge would hear of it — Michael's mother-in-law-to-be eliciting memories through regression therapy, fifteen years after the fact?

What's on the record, too, would be unbearably hard to budge: a young Thomas Bishop admitted to witnessing his father's murder. He made a final statement to the cops naming his mother as the murderer. Laura then pled guilty. End of story.

At least, I hope so.

So what does Starzyk think he knows?

Michael is looking at me. I notice a smile playing at the edges of his mouth, a glimmer in his eye. "You need this as much as I do," he says.

I take a breath, let it out slowly. "Maybe I do."

* * *

We get started. In anticipation of my arrival, someone, probably Michael, has lit candles. There is a couch in the center of the room.

I've never been in a yurt. I expected it to be just one round space, but they've built two additional side rooms: a bathroom and what looks like a pantry. The ceiling is dome-shaped, with two skylights letting in the scattered sunlight. It smells nice, like earthy spices — cumin, maybe. Cinnamon. Hippie smells.

I ask Michael if he's comfortable. He is. He lies like a corpse on the couch, his eyes closed.

I begin to talk him into deeper relaxation. I watch as his chest rises and falls, and his breathing slows. Not everyone is suggestible, not enough for regressive therapy. Michael seems to slide into it like a lake of oil.

We're similar that way. Sarah had me under hypnosis a couple of times, and it seemed to go smoothly enough. It's something fundamental about certain people, that they can be so persuaded. It doesn't mean we're weak-willed, but it's something in the brain. A different way of processing stimuli. Paul, for instance, could never be hypnotized. Probably Joni would be resistant, too.

Sean would be susceptible. He's more like me.

The thought of my son temporarily derails me. "Okay, let's keep breathing, keep relaxing . . ."

I struggle to find my place again. I think about Joni, hiking up the mountain with her friends, leaving us with the space to do this. Kids are so much more accepting these days. Nothing surprises this generation.

"Michael? Can you hear me?"

His voice is monotone, slightly slurred: "Yes, I can hear you." His eyes remain closed, his fingers folded over his stomach. He took his shoes off to lie down — for a moment, I'm distracted, thinking he's wearing Sean's socks.

Stop it. Stay focused.

"You've come a long way, Michael. We've done a lot of work already. I want you to feel all of the space you've created. Can you feel it?"

"Yes."

"Look around you right now. What do you see?"

"My house."

"Your house. You mean your house as a boy?"

"Yes."

"Can you describe it to me?"

He describes the house on Pondfield Road with even more clarity and detail.

"Michael, I want you to go to a mirror. Can you find a mirror?"

"Yes."

"Now, feeling all of the space you've created, all of the air breezing through, I want you to look in the mirror."

"I'm looking."

"And what do you see?"

"I see me."

"Are you a boy?"

"Yes, I'm a boy."

"How old are you?"

"Eight."

"Okay. Good. And . . . what's your name?"

He starts to say Michael, starts to form the "M" sound, but the sound elongates and becomes, "My name is Tom."

"Very good," I say, feeling that little rush of adrenaline. We're back. Locked in. Michael's voice has taken on that higher, youthful pitch again. From there, we go through the evening. It's as before. He remembers his mother's cold, distant stare at dinner. Drinking her wine. Sending him up to his room. He recalls lying in bed and reading.

He also recalls the car outside, parked but running, smoke issuing from the tailpipe.

His mother and father argue. His mother goes upstairs.

"Then what do you hear?" I ask.

"Nothing. I fall asleep."

"But something awakens you." I don't mean to be pushy or to guide him, but I can't help it. I have to know.

"Yes. Something wakes me up. The door."

The door to the kitchen. Someone has left, or someone is here. Tom thinks to check the car in the road, now empty. His father speaks loudly in the kitchen below. *What are you doing? Are you fucking crazy?*

Then there's fighting. David Bishop fearfully threatens to call the police. Tom makes his way down the stairs . . .

"Your mother's bedroom," I interrupt. "Is the door open?"

"It was closed."

David shouts for the intruder — or Laura, if it's her — to put something away. It must be the hammer he or she is wielding.

It's not Laura.

No. Michael made that clear in our last session. He hears more of the *bad fighting* and then a body drops to the floor — his father — before he sees a man flee out the door.

"Is it a man?"

"Yes. It's a man."

"I need you to see him, Tom. I need you to freeze this picture right now. Like a movie. Press pause."

Michael's voice is high, whispery: "Okay . . ."

"Did you freeze it?"

"Yes."

"Now zoom in. You know how to zoom in?"

"Yes."

"Really get a close look. What color hair does the man have?"

Michael says nothing. His brow has furrowed. His lips work against each other, as if struggling to form the word: "Brown."

"Brown hair. What is he wearing?"

"I don't . . . I can't . . ."

"You told me you were ready. You *are* ready. You're ready to remember."

"He has a black coat. A little snow on it."

"What about any part of his face? Can you see — does he have pale skin? Or darker? Is he tall? Short?"

I might be pressing too hard — Michael sits up on the couch. But his eyes are shut tight, his scowl deepening. He's straining to see inside his memory. "The reflection in the door," he says.

"Yes?"

"I can see his face in the reflection of the door."

"You can see him . . ." Gooseflesh erupts across my arms, along the back of my neck, like I've just touched a low-voltage live circuit.

"I can see his face in the reflection. The glass that's in the door. He's looking at me . . ."

Michael's face contorts in fear. He wraps his arms around himself. I break from protocol — I've violated a million rules already, why not — and move beside him and take him in my arms, rub his shoulders. "It's okay. He can't hurt you. This is just a picture. But listen to me now. I want you to keep that picture. I want you to imagine you can print it out. Okay? You know what a printer is. I want you to print it out in full color. And then I want you to imagine putting it in your book bag. Like your school book bag."

"Okay . . ."

I pause only briefly, knowing that the mind works fast in these situations, like in a dream. "Okay? You got it?"

"I got it."

"Now, put it in your backpack. I'm going to bring you out, bring you back here with me now, and you're going to take that backpack with you, okay?"

"Okay . . ."

I ease Michael back down into a supine position and return to my chair. Then, slowly, so he doesn't rise too fast, I talk him out of his deep regressive state. I describe the yurt and the woods and remind him of Joni and his life here. After about twenty minutes being under, Michael blinks open his eyes. He slowly sits up on the couch. He looks around, then at me, and he smiles.

"Michael," I say, having a little trouble speaking. "Did you bring the picture with you?"

He just stares a moment, then nods and taps the side of his head. "I got it."

I let out a held breath. As I do, I take my phone out of my pocket. There's no service here, but a call isn't what I'm after. It's the picture I saved. Two of them, actually. The older Doug Wiseman and the younger version. I hold up the younger one in front of Michael.

"Is it this man?"

Michael looks at it, squints, then shakes his head. "No."

I hold my breath a moment. Then: "Are you sure? Look again."

He does, but it's clear he's not recognizing the face in the picture. "He must look at least familiar to you." I flip to the older version. "Here, how about now?"

"Oh," Michael says. "Okay. I think I remember him."

"From that night?"

Michael shakes his head. "No. Not from that night. It's not him."

"Michael, your mother was involved with this man. His name is Doug Wiseman. He's the man in the image."

Michael continues shaking his head. "It's not him. He looks familiar — I think I met him once, before Mom went to prison, but that's—"

"Listen to me," I say. "We're going to try again. You might need to take a second look at that reflection. Michael? Are you listening?"

Michael has stopped looking at me. His gaze is set over my shoulder. And he begins to look worried. Even scared.

"Michael? What is it?"

"Behind you," he says.

CHAPTER FIFTY-TWO

Paul is standing there, breathing hard, sweat beading his brow.

I get to my feet. "What are you doing here?"

His eyes move to Michael, then back to me. He says two words, and they go right through me; they seem to reverberate in my skull: "Sean's awake."

In the next instant, Paul is leading me out of the yurt. I glance back at Michael, who remains sitting there, a look of pure terror on his face.

I barrage Paul with questions.

"When? How? Has he spoken? What did the doctor say?"

"Just an hour ago."

"I haven't even been gone that long."

"About twenty minutes after you left. Maybe a half hour."

"Has he said anything?"

"No. But he's responsive." Paul is still using the old pickup to get around. He opens the passenger door for me.

Before getting in, I cast another look back. Michael is standing in front of the yurt. His arms hang at his sides, and he's making fists with his hands, gripping and releasing. He looks nervous. More than nervous — he's completely overwhelmed. My heart hurts for him. But the fact that he looks so nervous can only mean one thing . . .

"Sean is definitely conscious?"

"Yes."

"But he hasn't spoken?"

"No, but he's responding to commands — moving his arms and legs . . . What?"

I glance at Michael.

Paul looks there too. "Did you regress him?"

I nod.

"Already? Jesus. What did he say?"

I don't answer Paul. I stand, looking at Michael, thinking that, no matter what, none of this is his fault. He was just a boy, caught in the middle of things. Adults, people who were supposed to protect him, failed to do so. Instead, they sought to protect themselves. To get what they needed.

I start toward him.

Paul calls after me, "Em — there's no time for this!"

Of course there's time.

I reach Michael and study his face. The worry, the fear. "Michael," I say, "I can't believe the timing. But I'm not just leaving you, okay? I'm not abandoning you. We'll get back to this, and we'll get to the bottom of it. It's just that right now, I need to go see—"

"Don't go," Michael interrupts.

"I have to. It's . . . my son."

Paul gets in the pickup truck and starts it up. He revs the engine.

Michael's gaze moves from the truck to me, those green eyes dancing. "Don't go," he repeats.

I've had enough. "Michael, I have a family. Sean is my son."

"Emily!" Paul calls. "Come on!"

I stare into Michael's eyes, then I turn and leave.

CHAPTER FIFTY-THREE

We barrel down the bumpy road out of the woods. Michael disappears from my side-view mirror.

The forest thickens as we descend in elevation. Paul isn't speaking, he's just concentrating on the road. He's going a bit too fast, grinding the axles.

"Paul . . ."

"What did he say?"

"Paul, slow down . . ."

"Why won't you tell me what Michael said?"

I shut my eyes, tight. "We didn't get a chance. He was about to tell me something when you showed up."

"Bullshit. You still think he doesn't remember? He's been stringing you along."

"I don't know. I think he remembered more than he let on at first. But it did take my work to get to the bottom of it."

"Why? Why would you even do that?"

"To *know*, Paul. Why else? We have to know. For his sake and for ours."

"I already know what he said." Paul is gripping the wheel hard enough to whiten his knuckles. His jaw twitches as he grinds his teeth. "He asked you not to go. Not to leave him, right?"

I sigh. "Yes."

Paul makes a sound between a laugh and yell. "And why would he say that? Because that son of a bitch did something to Sean. He doesn't want us going to see Sean because of what Sean might say."

"I never said Michael hurt Sean . . ."

Paul looks at me like I'm crazy. "Have you forgotten? Of course you did. That was the first thing you thought." He shakes his head.

We reach the end of the dirt road and turn onto a paved one. I check my phone — one bar.

"We don't know his angle," Paul says. "Or what this whole thing really . . . Listen, I love Jo. But this is too much. There's too much to deal with."

"I'm handling it."

"Oh, yeah? Going to find some ironclad proof that the police coerced him? You're ready to go to trial with that? Spend the next four, five years of your life wrapped up in this?"

"I almost had him seeing the person who did it."

Paul gives me a sharp look. I show him the picture of Wiseman. "I think he recognized him," I say. "He was fuzzy about the specifics, his timing is a little off, but this could be the guy."

"You're serious . . . You think he was going to name him?"

"I don't know. I was close. I was right on top of it. And then you showed up. That's my point."

"Well, I had a good reason, didn't it?" Paul shakes his head in anger and disbelief. "*Fuck* this guy," he mutters. "Fuck him. I'm tired of this shit."

"Calm down, okay? I can't take it when you're like this."

Paul mumbles something else and pours on the gas.

"Slow down, please." My head is spinning. "Paul . . ."

"What?"

"I said, *slow down!*" It's a piercing shriek. I normally don't yell. I'm a together person. People rely on me.

Paul suddenly hits the brakes and pulls over onto the shoulder. Even though we're on a paved road, we're a ways between anything. Just a few cars coming and going in either direction.

"What are you doing?" I ask. Paul is scaring me.

"I slowed down."

"Paul . . ."

"No, listen to me. You think this is the way forward. With you rushing off to save Michael from his horrible past. But you're forgetting something. If this comes out, and this all gets re-examined, the police will see things they didn't before. They always do."

I don't want to admit it, but Paul is right.

"Do you know what I'm saying?" Paul asks.

It's difficult to form the sentence. As if the words won't quite fit in my mouth: "That we knew the Bishops."

"Yes," Paul says. "That we knew the Bishops."

CHAPTER FIFTY-FOUR

I look at my husband as if seeing him for the first time today. He's wearing a white T-shirt that says *Snapshot Regatta.* Some sailing competition, years ago. He's in chino shorts and boat shoes. Dressed for the late summer vacation. Just another day at the lake house.

He's staring at me now. Into me. Breathing hard, chest rising and falling. "We knew the Bishops, and you took the assignment anyway. That's a conflict of interest."

I'm close to tears. I fight them. Nothing wrong with emotion, just not *now.* Not here. "We didn't know them that well . . ."

"We knew them well enough to socialize at their house. To drink with them. People saw us. It was before anyone was on Facebook, before Instagram, but people still took pictures. There's likely evidence of us and them, together. How do you think that will look? What judge will listen to any of this? I mean, did you forget?"

Sometimes, I hear myself saying, *trauma causes us to close off certain areas of our minds.*

"No," I say. My voice sounds small. I take a breath and better express it. "No, I didn't *forget.*"

Paul gradually softens his penetrating stare. After a moment, he's gazing out the windshield. More cars pass, the slipstream pushing against the pickup, rocking it on its worn-out shocks. "We even went to one of her shows, Em. In the city."

The sentence triggers a domino effect in my brain. I'm suddenly just like Michael, experiencing an onrush of memory, filling a vacuum: faces, voices, places, moments.

Laura Bishop, a gallery in SOHO. Paul and I going in. He's in a suit, I'm wearing a dress. We're given flutes of champagne. Laura Bishop works the room. She's very pretty in her black dress, dark earrings, like leaves, dangling from her perfect little ears. A far cry from the woman with frizzy hair and glassy eyes staring out from her mugshot.

We knew them . . .

"I'm surprised no one looked harder in the first place," Paul now says. "We all lived in Bronxville together. It's not a big town. One of their friends knew one of our friends, and that was it. When we all met for the first time, you were pregnant with Sean."

Paul suddenly nears me again and takes my hand. "Emily, listen to me. So, you took a case and it was someone you knew. So what? No big deal. But what's not going to fly is thinking you can navigate this anymore. This kid's mother is out, and they're obviously up to something. He hurt Sean and doesn't want us to know. And now he's, what? Begging you not to go? Why? He thinks I'm lying? Why would I lie? This is all just his way of implicating me. This is him coming after us, trying to fuck us over. Don't you see that?"

I don't answer.

Paul sighs and retreats from me. He puts the truck in drive and starts pulling out onto the road.

A vehicle blares its horn and swerves around us. It causes a car coming in the other direction to veer over to the shoulder. Everyone is blowing horns and screeching tires.

"Paul!"

He hits the gas and drives on. I watch in the mirrors as a vehicle gets back on the road. The people who passed us are just ahead; the driver flings a hand out the window, as if to say, *what the hell?*

"Paul, you gotta ease up."

He doesn't respond. We ride in silence. When we reach a stop sign, he makes a left. Now we're on the main road between Lake Placid and Saranac Lake. Ten minutes from the hospital.

Have I lost my mind? Is Paul right? Am I doomed in all of my efforts because we knew the Bishops? Why didn't I consider that sooner?

The phone vibrates. I check if Paul noticed, but he's fixed on the road.

It's Mena calling.

I let the voicemail pick it up. I'm so distraught right now I can't imagine talking to her, or anyone. I don't even know what I'd say. Maybe:

I think I'm having a nervous breakdown.

CHAPTER FIFTY-FIVE

We arrive at the hospital. Paul stops at the main entrance. The pickup truck is idling — rattling, really, like it's about to collapse. Paul only looks straight ahead.

"Paul. I'm sorry."

"Uh-huh." He's unmoved. "Go on in. I'll park and be right there."

"Can you look at me?"

"No."

Paul accelerates, engine grumbling, and I jump back from the vehicle as the door swings closed. A nurse helping an elderly man along sees and gives me a look. I flash her a smile, but inside, I'm in knots.

The doors slide open and I hurry into the hospital, trying not to run. I'm just sort of trotting along, but already realize I don't have my bearings. Someone at the front desk is able to point me in the right direction. I get moving again, realizing it's been all day since I've eaten. Realizing that I must look like hell.

But it's coming to an end. My son is coming back to me. That's all that matters.

How long will he have to stay in the hospital, I wonder. What was he doing that he might be eager to get back to? He told me stories, but I forget if he has a job to return to. That's the funny thing with memory: we accept misremembering things, because it's so common. One neuroscientist estimated that we forget 99.9% of everything that happens to us.

It's all stored somewhere, though. We just don't have the means to access everything.

Everybody expects to remember the big things. Only, that's not the case, either. You don't remember but one or two of your birthdays. Or one or two holidays. And that's only if you keep thinking of them again, for some reason. Between short-term memory and long-term memory is a kind of bottle neck. In order to squeeze something through, you need to revisit it many times.

So we assume that profound experiences — especially things we did wrong — will get stored in long-term memory. And for the most part, we're right.

Except for when something is so troubling that we seek to block it out. Like Michael, perhaps, having witnessed his father's murder. Making him malleable, susceptible to outside influence, planting a false memory. Such as seeing his mother do it. Why not? She was acting strangely that night and had been for weeks. Even young Tom himself said it was like she was an imposter at times.

I want my mommy back . . .

I push through a set of double doors and round a bend. Now I'm running, and I don't care how it looks. A doctor sees me and opens his mouth as if to warn me to slow down, but I run right past. One more turn and I'm in familiar territory. This is the hall Sean is on.

I see his door, the number on it — 312 — and push open.

"Ma'am," someone says behind me. "Did you sign in?"

I step into the room. My son is in the bed. The lighting is dim. The machines are breathing, whirring, making their noise.

His eyes are closed.

I step beside him, trembling, letting the tears fall.

"Sean?"

"Ma'am." The doctor is in the doorway.

Someone else joins him. "That's the mother," she says.

"Seanie?" I squeeze my son's hand. I pat it. "Sean, honey. Mommy's here."

Sean makes no response.

I look up. The doctor and nurse are watching me. "When did he . . . Is he just sleeping?"

They trade concerned glances. "Mrs. Lindman . . ." The nurse walks closer. "Your son is in a coma."

"I know. He *was*. But he woke up." His hand feels limp in my grip. "Didn't he?"

Another look passes between them. The nurse mouths something silently to the doctor, who nods and leaves. The nurse then turns to me, her face filled with compassion. "Mrs. Lindman, this is a difficult time. But Sean is stable. His condition is stable. Okay? We're doing all that we can."

"He didn't wake up?"

"Ma'am, I'm sorry, but no."

I give Sean one last look. The tears dry in my face as deep, hot fear winds through my nervous system. My head tingles, like a mild electric current. I kiss Sean's hand. I whisper into his ear: "Mommy loves you."

The nurse reaches for me as I hurry past. She's calling me as I run down the corridor.

"Mrs. Lindman!"

But I can't stop. I think my husband is about to kill someone.

CHAPTER FIFTY-SIX

I make it all the way outside to the parking lot before I realize one crucial fact: I don't have transportation. Paul dropped me off.

And as I swipe through my phone to call him, I notice my battery life is at just under 20 percent. In all the running around I've been doing, I've forgotten to charge it. Searching for a signal, as the phone was likely doing while in the woods, also drains the battery.

Paul's line rings until his voicemail answers. In his usual upbeat, affable-sounding voice, my husband says, "Hi, you've reached Paul Lindman. I'm actually on vacation right now, if you can believe that. I'll be back in the office August 26. If it's an emergency, call my office . . ."

I wait through the rest of it. Then, "He isn't awake, Paul. Whatever it is you think you're doing . . ."

It's impossible to know where to even take this. My brain is stuck on the craziest fact of all: Did my husband actually just lie to me about our son waking up? It's such a low blow, such a horrible thing to do in order to get me away from Michael.

The midday sun is hammering down. It's hot out here in the parking lot and I'm feeling heavy on my feet. So much so that I almost lose consciousness. I walk to the edge of the parking lot, where some trees provide shade. My whole body is vibrating, like I'm in shock.

I try Joni next, but her phone goes straight to voicemail — it seems she's lost service.

Does that mean she finished her hike and is back at the yurt? Would Paul do anything to Michael with our daughter there? Or does he have some plan to get rid of her too? Lie to *her* about something, drive *her* a convenient distance away? What about her friends?

Dear God.

This is my life.

An unraveling nightmare.

My next call has to be to 911. There's no other way. I mean, I don't even know the address of Madison and Hunter's place — it's a yurt in the middle of the woods, for God's sake — but I know the vicinity. And the police will likely have them in the system.

Get real.

You haven't done it yet, and you're not doing it now.

It's true. I hesitated in the past in order to gather more information. To find out what Michael saw. But even if he said it was Doug Wiseman, no one is going to believe how he arrived at that conclusion. Not when the woman who led him to it lied about knowing his family fifteen years ago. Paul is right.

But . . .

There could be one thing. One way through this.

Because this has to end.

My hand slips into my pants pocket. I feel the stiff card, press my thumb against its straight edge.

I pull it out and stare at the name. The number. Then I key it into my phone.

Starzyk answers on the second ring. "Hey, Doc. I was hoping you'd call."

* * *

The state investigator pulls into the hospital parking lot just ten minutes later. He leans over and pushes the door open wide. "Get in."

Seconds later, we're speeding along, taking the same route I took earlier in the day, skirting along the edge of town. "Talk to me," Starzyk says.

"Like I told you on the phone, I think Paul could hurt Michael."

"Because your husband thinks Michael hurt Sean. On the boat."

"Maybe."

Starzyk waits. "You're not telling me everything."

No, I'm not. But first, I need to level the playing field. "Mooney says mistakes were made. Do you admit that?"

He sniffs, delaying a response. "I wouldn't be here if mistakes hadn't been made. You know that."

"Tell me, please; just tell me. You said Doug Wiseman wasn't a suspect. That he came later. But there was someone else there. You have to know who. If it wasn't Wiseman, then who?"

Starzyk takes a deep breath. "Yeah, we knew there was someone else there. We had the witnesses, the car in the street, the cigarette butts — you've heard all that. Crime scene made mistakes. *We* made mistakes. We allowed the kid in the room when we first questioned Laura Bishop, for one thing. We shouldn't have done that — it contaminated her statement and his. But we went through everybody. We talked to all of David Bishop's work contacts."

I'm just quiet, listening, waiting for the point when he tells me he knows about me and the Bishops.

"We had half a dozen theories about someone else being there. Someone David owed money, maybe. Or someone who was screwing his wife. That was the other big one. We even had a witness, a friend of David's, tell us he suspected an affair. But we couldn't stick that to Doug Wiseman, because there *was* no Doug Wiseman at that time. He literally did not exist in Laura Bishop's life. He came later, this older guy

277

who got kind of obsessed with her, I think, wanted to save her from the whole thing, move her away. It never happened. We got her before she could run off."

Starzyk has driven us through the residential area, and we merge onto a highway that takes us through the trees, between Saranac Lake and Lake Placid.

He looks over at me. I feel those reflective bug eyes on me again, but I don't look at the investigator. I'm facing the window, marshaling the will to do what comes next.

"There's something else," I say to Starzyk.

"What?"

"I knew the Bishops. *We* did. Paul and I."

He drives in silence a moment.

"How? We looked at everything and—"

"Just socially. It's not a big place. 6,400 people. Not everyone intermingles — it's the uptight suburbs — but we did. We went to their place for at least a party or two. Maybe even had them over. It's a hazy time in my life. Paul and I were going through a difficult patch. There was lots of drinking."

I stop there, not wanting to go any further. *Afraid* to go any further.

But I have to. I'm so deep in an ethical breach I don't know if I can ever crawl out anyway.

"I knew the Bishops when I agreed to evaluate their son."

"Why would you do that?"

My lips feel numb. Maybe I'm in someone else's body. Maybe I'm asleep.

"I'm not proud of it," I say. A single tear slips down my cheek. I make a vow that it's the last. "But I think I just wanted to be a part of it. I didn't want to read about it in the paper. And I wanted to help."

"Jesus," Starzyk says.

I place my hands on the sides of my head again. I feel like I'm going to be sick. "Can you pull over?"

"We're almost there."

278

I try to breathe through it. "Why are you even here? You're here because you're covering your own self. For coercing Tom."

"Hey — we made mistakes, we let a guy get away, but I didn't *coerce* anybody. I don't know why the kid named his mother. And it doesn't matter — she pled guilty. Case closed. I'm here because I could never let it go. *Who* was the guy we all knew had been there? That's the same question you're asking. The medical examiner looked at all the wounds inflicted on David Bishop. He looked at Laura, her size, her reach, and he said, no way. This was done by someone much bigger than her. David Bishop struggled with this guy."

Bad fighting.

Starzyk makes a turn onto a secondary road. "All right. Now you got to tell me where it is."

"Just up ahead. It's a dirt road. I'll show you."

My head is buzzing. It's hard to ground myself, to really make sense of anything. What are we going to find halfway up this mountain? How can anything go back to normal after this? Can I find my way out, or is this the end of everything?

It all started with that fucking affair. Paul and his lover. It took forever for us to get over it. There was lots of shouting and crying and drinking — not the best chapter in my life.

To have an affair, you have to have some sort of duality in you. You have to be able to live a separate life. To keep those emotions completely walled off. It's not an easy thing to do. If you've had trauma, certain things can get buried at the back of your mind. But it's unintentional. When you're sleeping around and hiding it, *that* kind of compartmentalization seems more sinister. And Paul was capable of that.

Maybe I'm a therapist who's been living with troubled men her whole life. Maybe I've married my father without realizing it. Knowing psychology doesn't protect you from making your own terrible mistakes. That's the big joke. You can't escape what life has in store for you.

"There it is." I point to the dirt road up ahead.

Starzyk slows and makes the turn. He starts up the bumpy road. As he does, he reaches between his legs. He pulls out a gun.

"Oh God," I say. "What is happening?"

I want to jump out and run. Just run. Back to a time and a place when things made sense.

A time of a blissfully forgotten past.

CHAPTER FIFTY-SEVEN

"Aren't you going to call some backup?" The closer we get, the higher my anxiety becomes.

"I want to know what this is first," Starzyk says.

I can only hang on for the bumpy ride until it comes into view. Madison and Hunter's pretty little off-grid property. Where no one can hear you scream.

Starzyk gives me one of his looks. "You all right?"

I realize I'm laughing.

"No, I'm not all right." I think I've left sanity back at the hospital with my son.

The pickup is parked off to one side of the clearing. The rental car is still there, and so are the Escalade belonging to my daughter's friends and Joni's Subaru. Things are getting crowded.

Starzyk puts his truck in park. "Stay here."

He gets out, gun in hand, and moves toward the yurt like the cops in TV shows. I see no one. The chickens are softly clucking. The wind rustles the tops of the trees. It's getting later in the day; my phone says five thirty. The battery is down to fifteen percent. No signal.

Of all things, my stomach growls.

"Hello?" Starzyk is at the front of the yurt, standing to one side of the door. "Anyone home?"

He glances at me, then starts to circle the building. Once he's out of sight, I exit the truck. Stay put? If I sit there another second, I'll lose my mind.

"Michael?"

No response. I start for the yurt, picking my way past a stack of lumber, a battery-powered drill sitting on top. "Hello? Anyone?"

I'm sure Starzyk is cringing right now at the sound of my voice. But we never had the element of surprise — anyone here would've heard us drive up. I open the front door. Before I even step through, an odor hits me.

Sticky, coppery. A sickly sweet smell.

My breath catches in my throat. My hand doesn't leave the door knob. I am frozen in the threshold, looking at the two bodies on the floor. Madison, Joni's childhood friend. Her boyfriend, Hunter, someone I've never even met.

It looks like they've been beaten to death with a hammer.

* * *

The two dead people are sort of flopped over one another, arms and legs akimbo. Blood has splattered everywhere. A violent, messy death. The urge to vomit hits me. I turn from the scene and step down to the ground and puke into the dirt and weeds.

I'm vaguely aware of footsteps behind me, coming fast. "The fuck are you—?" Starzyk stops when he sees me, when he sees the open door. He takes the three wooden steps and looks in. "Ah, God. Ah, shit . . ."

I'm bent over, breathing, trying not to pass out. "That's my . . . Those are . . ." I try to explain the people in the house, but before I can choke through the words, a scream rises from the woods.

I look up that direction, feeling frozen.

Starzyk tenses, aims his weapon. "Shit," he says again. It's a woman's scream.

* * *

Starzyk is trying to make a call. "Nothing. Christ. Nothing . . ." He mutters something about how if he had his official police vehicle he'd be able to communicate.

I'm still staring into the woods.

I'd know that scream anywhere.

It's the sound of my daughter.

I start moving that direction.

"Hey," Starzyk whispers harshly. "Hey — hey . . ."

"Do whatever you gotta do," I tell him. "My baby is in trouble."

I see a path in the woods. It might be the hiking trail Michael mentioned: the one that leads to the mountaintop. There have been no more screams. Just the one. I walk a ways and stop and listen. The forest is quiet; even the birds have fallen silent. The only sound is the faintest soughing of the wind. The subtle breeze stirs scents of pine and alders. Crisp, clear smells. Autumn around the corner.

I grew up with woods like this in my backyard. Places to explore. Places to hide.

"Joni!" I hadn't even planned to call her name.

The response is more silence.

I press on. The trail is mostly discernible, though narrow with overgrowth in some places. It's starting to become hilly, and I'm panting as I climb, pressing my palms against my knees to overcome the bigger obstacles.

Without some other sign, I can't be sure this is the right direction.

"Jonieee!"

I stop to listen, but now the only sound is my labored breathing. I think about turning back. I have my bearings, at least — the sun is lowering into the trees to my right, so that's west. Which means I'm headed north. I'm unsure what good the orientation does me. But it makes me feel like I have some scrap of control—

The gunshot from behind me is a thunderclap that rolls through the woods, reverberating in the trees, echoing off the distant mountain.

Starzyk.

Who is he shooting at?

I'm torn. If I press on, I'll not necessarily get any closer to my daughter. The answers could be back where I came from. Maybe Starzyk fired a warning shot.

But if I continue up the path — Michael said there was reception once you gained enough elevation. I can finally summon help.

Of course, now that I'm ready to call the cops and let the chips fall where they may, my phone still shows *No Service*. And I have a mere eleven percent of my battery left.

I plow forward, calling my daughter's name. Someone brutally murdered her friends. And now maybe they've dragged her out here.

My head spins with all that has happened. Michael showing up in our lives. Maybe an accident. One in a million, but still possible. Michael meeting Joni. Michael hiding his dark truth from her until he realizes she was my daughter. Michael trying to fix it by feigning memory loss, getting me to help him with the retrieval.

A terrible lie, but maybe understandable.

But it wasn't true. Maybe Michael didn't know who the true killer was, but everything else has been in his grasp. This has been a way to exact revenge. To ruin my life for being his therapist fifteen years ago.

Maybe he's after all of us. He's after the police, too.

One thing is for certain: he wants us to pay. Both of them do, Laura probably most of all.

I call for Joni again as I hoist myself over giant tree roots and scramble up rocks. The trees are thinning, the sky opening up. I check my phone again — one bar!

A twig snaps.

Off to my right, something is moving through the brush. I panic, ducking to hide in the brush. I wait; watch.

A figure moves through the fir trees, coming toward me.

One arm hangs to his side while he uses the other to swipe at the branches in his way. My heart beats into my throat. I can hide, but any movement now and he's going to see me. I choose instead to face him, and step to where he can see me more clearly.

"Michael."

At first he doesn't react, just keeps moving along with that strange, wounded gait. Then he focuses on me. His look of blank concentration morphs into sorrow. "Dr. Lindman," he says.

"Don't come any closer," I warn. "Where's Joni?"

He stops walking and looks around. "She . . . She was with me." His voice has that light, almost boyish quality to it. The bewilderment makes him seem even younger, more innocent. Naïve. "They came back from the hike and . . . Mr. Lindman was here. He just showed up."

"Where is he now?"

Michael swallows. He looks at me and shakes his head. "I don't know."

It's only now that I see the blood. It drips from the fingertips of his limp arm.

"What happened?"

"He . . . Everybody was here, and Mr. Lindman wanted to talk to me alone, but no one would let him. He had a hammer. Hunter said it was his, from his shed. Hunter tried to talk to Mr. Lindman, to calm him down. He approached him and . . . Mr. Lindman swung."

I shake my head. My body is trembling. "No, Michael. I pushed you too hard too fast. You're transferring things from your past to your present. Superimposing Paul on the man who killed your father."

Michael shakes his head. "No. He beat up Hunter. Madison screamed and attacked him. He killed her, too. Joni ran, I ran. We tried the cars — he took the keys . . . What?"

"If you're not delusional, then you're lying and trying to hurt us."

"I'm not. I'm trying to explain! We came up here for the cell service. It's closer than getting to the road. Mr. Lindman chased us. I finally stopped and turned around to face him. And he hit me with it. With the hammer. I think my arm is broken."

I don't want to look, but I do. There's a bend to the forearm that's wrong.

I consider the gunshot back at the property. Between Starzyk and Paul? It's the only thing that makes sense. But I squint my eyes shut and shake my head. "No. I don't believe you."

"Dr. Lindman, I promise you it's the truth."

My eyes fly open. "*But where is Joni?*"

"Maybe she went back up the trail to get better reception. Maybe she's hiding. After I got hurt, I don't know . . . I think I'm in shock . . ."

"Why did she scream?"

"She saw it all happen. Everything. She saw him. What he did to them. What he did to me."

Still shaking, I open the keypad on my phone and dial 911. It takes a few seconds to connect, but the call finally goes through. Relief washes over me.

"What's your emergency?"

"This is Dr. Emily Lindman. Two people have been killed. The killer is still . . ." The tears fall as I finish the sentence. "The killer is still here."

I give the 911 operator the location. Or, someone does, someone in my body, with my voice, operating on her own.

"Ma'am? I'm seeing that there's been another call, just a few minutes ago, from about the same location."

"Who?" I'm frantic. "Was it a young woman? Joni Lindman? Hello—?"

But the call is lost. My battery is dead.

CHAPTER FIFTY-EIGHT

I make a decision and grab Michael by his good arm. He needs medical attention. The police will send an ambulance. "You need to get back down to the property."

He nods, then looks up the trail.

I hear the footfalls and rustling brush before I see the person. *Joni!* My heart lifts as my daughter comes into view. When she sees me, she instantly bursts into tears.

She reaches me and falls into my arms, sobbing. I hug her tight, stroke her hair. Shush her.

"It's okay, honey. It's going to be okay."

After a moment, the three of us make our way down. It's a little easier going once the terrain levels out. I find a nice-sized stick as we near the edge of the woods and pick it up.

Once we reach the property, I tell Michael and Joni to get behind me.

"Paul?"

We're met with silence.

"Detective Starzyk?"

But there's no sign of my husband or the state police investigator. Only the vehicles that remain.

The door to the yurt hangs open. "Don't look in there," I whisper to the kids, knowing they've already seen it.

I steer them toward the rental car instead. We have to get out of here. Get away. I have no idea if Paul is still here. The police must be on their way by now. If we leave now, we might meet them coming up the long dirt road.

Paul has anticipated this. I reach for the door handle, and he jumps up from the seat and throws open the door.

Joni screams.

Paul looks like Paul, but he also looks like someone else. Almost unrecognizable to me. As if his skin is tighter.

He holds a bloody hammer. But as he pushes us back toward the yurt, I see a gun tucked into the waistband of his chino shorts.

"Dad, stop!"

"Paul," I say. "What are you doing?"

"Get up to the house."

"Paul, stop it. The police are coming."

Talking to my husband this way feels like an act. Like we've decided to roleplay different people. This is real, though; my husband is actually holding a bloody murder weapon. There are two people inside. People he killed in cold blood.

I've been covering for Paul, but I've also been in denial. That it could ever happen again. That my husband is psychotic.

I guess there are a lot of things I've been denying.

My stomach rolls when I see the feet sticking out from behind the pickup truck; Starzyk is on the ground. He's unmoving. The closer we get to the yurt, the clearer the view of the detective. I can see blood coming from his ears.

"Oh, God . . ."

The sight of him hits hard. I've been protecting myself, half-lying and half-joking to myself about what's going on. Any sense that I might get out of this is gone now, replaced with a stark, empty fear. There is nowhere to go from here. There is nothing else to hide from, or repress, or try to fix.

Paul pulls the gun from his shorts. Joni moans beside me. I'm still backing up toward the building, my arms spread out, one covering Joni, the other Michael.

"Paul . . ." I almost choke on the word. "Please stop. It's me. We're your family."

Paul's mouth twitches, like he might speak. His eyes seem to shrink to even denser, darker points. He flicks the gun, indicating we get inside the yurt.

What choice do we have?

Joni goes first, followed by Michael. I'm last.

"Come back to me," I say, staring at Paul as I stumble inside. "Come back to me, Paul . . ."

He takes one of the steps, his face inches from mine. "You had your chance," he says. "Now we do it my way."

He slams the door in my face.

I back away from it. Joni is whimpering in the center of the room. Michael holds his arm and stares dumbly at the floor. The bodies of Madison and Hunter have started to draw flies. "Cover them in a blanket," I whisper.

Something thumps against the door. It's followed by a soft, high-pitch whining and some minor vibration. By the time I realize what's happening and rush toward the door, it's too late. I hit my shoulder against it, but it doesn't budge.

Paul has locked us in. He's boarded up the door.

I rush to one of the octagonal windows and peer out. Seeing nothing, I try the next one. I'm kicking furniture out of the way; a lamp falls and the bulb shatters. I glimpse Paul outside. He's over by the backup power generator.

He's got the can of gas.

He unscrews the cap as he walks toward the yurt.

CHAPTER FIFTY-NINE

Paul splashes the gas around the yurt, circling the entire building.

Joni screams and pounds the door, then the windows, following him as he goes, pleading.

How can he?

His own *daughter*?

Michael has placed a blanket over the two dead people. He stands, watching as his fiancé beseeches her father. *Please don't burn us alive.* Something in his expression reads that he's been here before. A family horror like this. He's come full circle.

I run to each window, searching for a way out. There are six in all, each double-hung, but none of them will open. Paul has already engineered it. He's nailed boards across them to prevent any from sliding up.

There's got to be something. My attention turns to the skylight. I find a stool and drag it over. It's enough to reach the hand crank and open the window, but there's no way to remove the glass, the screen, let alone pull myself up there and shimmy through.

We all end up on the floor, huddled under it, breathing hard, trying not to panic. Michael has gone pale, his skin beaded with sweat. Holding his arm, he lies back, moaning. He's going to pass out from the shock and pain. Joni moves beside him. She curls up into a fetal position.

Then Joni speaks. "It wasn't supposed to go like this."

Michael opens his eyes and looks at her.

Joni faces me. "I'm sorry, Mom."

"For what?" It feels breathless.

"Michael told me who he was. Early on when we were dating." She looks at him. "I almost left him, but then I didn't. He told me about his mother, and about you."

The betrayal slides over my heart like a dark hand. It squeezes.

"I thought he deserved answers," Joni says. "And so did I. Laura suspected it was Dad. She deserved to know, too." Joni looks at the covered bodies of Madison and Hunter as her eyes well with tears. "But this was never supposed to happen."

I look there, too. I'm about to say something — I don't even know what — when I hear a noise outside.

I rise to my feet. And I move to the nearest window in time to see Paul light the match.

* * *

Within seconds, the flames are licking the windows from the outside. Looking through, I can see Starzyk, still on his back, blood around his head. *Maybe you got off easy*, I think, already feeling the temperature rise.

Death by flaming yurt.

I can't help it. It's just where my mind goes.

Frantic, I look for something to break the glass. I hesitated before, expecting Paul would cover a breaking window with his gun and shoot us. But now there's no choice. I consider a small end table, but it's too wide. A chair? Everything is too big and heavy. In the open kitchen, I riffle through the drawers and consider a few items until Joni says, "Mom . . ."

I see her holding up a bloody hammer.

291

"Don't touch that!" It's just an instinct — she's holding a murder weapon. But what does it matter? We'll burn alive if we don't do something.

I take it, our eyes briefly connecting. I see pain there, and love, but she'll never ask for forgiveness. She knows she doesn't need to.

I rush at one of the windows at the back of the yurt. The glass shatters but remains mostly in place. I hit it again, this time dislodging a huge, jagged chunk.

A figure runs past the window. The sight momentarily paralyzes me, then I chase the movement from window to window until the figure stops. It's Paul. He stands there looking in at me, his face a blank.

I want to shriek, pound on the glass, scream at him that he'll have his own personal bonfire in hell. But there's nothing left in me. I'm a shell of a person at the end of her life.

And the flames are getting higher.

Paul stares at me — his eyes reflect the flames climbing the wooden walls between us. His image shimmers in the rising heat.

But then he turns to look at something outside. His expression changes to a look of surprise. He is raising the gun when he's struck by a two-by-four that sends the gun flying from his grip and Paul stumbling backwards.

The person wielding the lumber is fast — not only does she manage to get the gun, but she darts far enough out of his reach that when he lunges for her, he nearly goes sprawling.

She aims at his head. Paul freezes.

It wasn't Paul that I just saw running. It was her.

Joni speaks behind me. "Mom? What is it?"

I can hardly believe the words. "Laura Bishop is here. She just took the gun from your father."

CHAPTER SIXTY

Paul met Laura Bishop at one of our house parties. She invited us to an art show in Manhattan. After that, he kept seeing her.

When David Bishop was murdered, and word leaked of a male suspect, I feared the worst. Paul had been acting strange, flying into rages for no reason. I hounded him until he admitted to the affair. He never named her, but I suspected.

Six months went by, and no arrests. The news articles dried up. It seemed over. Then Rebecca Mooney and Steven Starzyk asked for my help. Not knowing of my marginal connections to the Bishops or my suspicions, the investigators asked me to meet with Tom. He had given conflicting statements, they said. Could I help them get to the bottom of it?

How could I say no? Not just for Tom's sake — I wanted to know what he saw. If it had anything to do with my husband.

Nothing Tom told me would be directly admissible in court. I would discuss things with him and then submit my formal evaluation at the end of five sessions. At that time, he would give Mooney and Starzyk a new statement. A final statement.

Five sessions.

Midway through our second session, Tom was describing a vehicle in the street. By the third session, a man in the house. But then, everything changed. The police asked me to hurry. I focused more on the hard details of that night, and Tom admitted to his parents arguing. In our final session, he boldly proclaimed his mother was the killer.

The rest was history.

And then, fifteen years later, a young man showed up at our door with our daughter. I had my immediate fears; Paul didn't think it was possible.

The rest is history.

I'm pulled out of the past when I notice Laura is yelling something to Paul, but I can't hear it; the crackling flames smother the sound. Sweat is running down my face.

We watch as Paul, presumably doing as Laura instructs, picks up a tool from the ground. The drill I saw earlier, on the lumber pile.

"Hurry," I say under my breath. It's become too hot this close to the window, and my view is at last obscured by flame and smoke and quivering heat.

The three of us retreat to the center of the room where it's coolest. We stand, huddled, watching the door. All we can do now is hope.

No, not all we can do. I must've dropped the hammer somewhere when I first saw Laura outside, but I search for something else that can be used as a weapon, and settle on the lamp that fell. It's heavy enough, and I can swing it like a baseball bat.

Noise comes from the other side of the door. A vibration. A muffled whine.

The smoke is filling the room now. "Cover your mouths," I tell the kids. I pull my shirt up over my nose and stand just inside the door, wielding the heavy lamp. The noise stops. A board falls away. Then the door opens.

CHAPTER SIXTY-ONE

Beyond the open door are leaping flames. I don't have any idea what awaits on the other side, and I'm not letting Joni through first. But before I can dive through, Michael grabs me.

His eyes lock on mine, alive with determination, then he's gone.

I grab Joni and we go together.

Searing heat, the smell of singed hair — my own — a sudden suffocation. My foot misses a step coming out and I tumble to the ground, losing grip on Joni and the lamp. But I'm on my feet an instant later, screaming into the inferno, screaming for my daughter.

She's in my arms a moment after that, her own hair smoking, one of her sleeves aflame. I smother it with my body. Someone shouts — it's Michael. Paul has grabbed him, and the two of them wrestle. Joni screams and jumps on her father's back and claws at his head and neck. He sends her flying.

Laura Bishop is on the ground a few yards away, curled into a ball. When she looks my way, I catch her eye. She's bleeding from the face, as if Paul hit or scratched her, but she's okay. She unfurls her body just enough to show me that she's still got the gun; she's clutching it like a football against her midsection. Paul tried to get it from her in the moments before we made it out of the yurt.

He is still grappling with Michael. He's got his hands around the younger man's throat. Michael is trying to fend him off with one arm. His legs kick at the air. His face is turning bright red.

I move to Laura, and she hands me the gun.

There is no thinking.

There is only action.

I step toward Paul. I've never fired a gun, never even held one. But it looks modern, the point-and-shoot type.

I aim it at Paul. He looks over at me. His eyes are inhuman, his lips pulled back in an animal's sneer.

The gun kicks in my hand — I wasn't expecting that. The sound is explosive and crisp and reverberates throughout the hardwood forest. I miss Paul; the shot is only meant to shock him, and it works: Michael manages to get away.

Paul is tense — the bullet went wide, but my inexperience with shooting means the next round might go anywhere. And he knows it. He stands there, hands clutching the air, glaring at me.

The yurt is almost completely engulfed by fire now. Flames shoot up nearly to the tops of the trees. I aim the gun again, this time directly at Paul's face.

His expression changes. He appears sorrowful, scared. "Honey," he says. I can barely hear him over the crackling inferno. "Emmy . . . please . . . what are you doing?"

"You tried to burn us."

His face contorts in agony. He points at Laura Bishop, like a child might. "She's the one who locked you in."

"Stop it, Paul. I saw you light the match."

He's shaking his head. Blood oozes from his clavicle. "Honey, no. Ever since your accident . . . hitting the deer, you haven't been the same. You've got things all twisted around in your head. Honey . . . Emily — you need help."

"*Stop it*, Paul!" I'm shaking again. I've still got Starzyk's gun trained on him, but I'm trembling. Uncertain.

Sirens wail in the distance.

Paul holds out his hand. His eyebrows are knitted in compassion. He shakes his head. "Emmy, you've had issues your whole life. It's your father's fault. We'll get you some help, okay? We'll call Sarah. We'll get everything straightened out, and this will all be okay. But right now, we need to get away from these two people." He casts angry eyes on Michael and Laura. "They're con artists, Emily."

He looks at our daughter. "Joni, you'll understand as you get older. People like this, they—"

His words are cut off as the entire roof of the yurt collapses. It sends up a huge plume of black smoke and hot embers scattering in the air like fireworks. A couple of them land on me, burning like miniature meteors.

Everybody backs farther away from the blazing structure. It's a skeleton of a building now, oddly like a carousel.

Around and around.

We stand there, watching, mesmerized.

Until I remember Paul.

Amid the distraction, my husband has slipped away.

CHAPTER SIXTY-TWO

"He won't get very far," the cop says to me. "Especially if he doesn't have anything with him — provisions, tools, things like that."

The place is surrounded; I've never seen so many police and firemen and emergency service workers. Since the location is so remote, the dirt road is nearly unnavigable; the fire department could only arrive in smaller vehicles called brush trucks. They had to let the structure burn while keeping it from spreading, shoveling dirt and spraying water to create an impassable perimeter.

Seeing them work in their heavy gear, in all the heat and danger, uplifts my heart.

Once Paul disappeared, I hustled everyone into the rental car. I'd barely put the shifter in drive when the first state trooper showed up. Starzyk — alive, but barely — was whisked away by the first ambulance, and then Michael in the next. Joni went with him.

I almost forget that the cop is still standing beside me. He gazes into the woods. "This property abuts state land. Lots of wilderness out there. He doesn't even have any water, you said?"

"Not that I saw."

I feel weak in the knees and find a stump near the chicken coop. The chickens were mercifully — miraculously — saved from the blaze. Only one got a bit singed, its white feathers blackened.

"Are you all right?" The cop, a state trooper, looks worried.

"I'm fine."

"Can you keep going?" He has a notebook and has been taking my statement.

"I can go on."

"Okay. So at what point did you discharge the weapon?"

Discharge the weapon. That's police talk, always so formal. Always so calm and detached. The way I'm supposed to be, too, when administering therapy. Objective. Unattached to outcome.

"I shot at him when he was on top of Michael. Well, near him. To scare him."

What if you're wrong? What if Paul is *the one being manipulated? Joni, too? What if Paul took you back to Sean just to get you out of harm's way?*

"They were wrestling, you said? Can you show me where?"

"Right over there, I think. There was a lot of smoke."

"Mmhmm."

What plans had Laura Bishop made with her son? How long had they been in communication? How can this possibly be my life?

"Let's move back in time a moment," the trooper says. His phrasing is so close to what I'd said to Michael during our sessions, it chills my skin. "What about the officer who suffered the gunshot wound? Investigator Steven Starzyk. Were you able to see who fired the weapon?"

No. I wasn't. I assume it was Paul, but I'm having trouble keeping everything straight.

"Ma'am?"

I try to answer the trooper but am overcome with a coughing fit. I'm sitting here on this stump, wrapped in one of those silver blankets, being interrogated, and I probably have smoke inhalation. Another trooper intervenes. I think I recognize her — but from where? My house the other night? Events are jumbling together.

The first cop says, "Trooper Kane, let's get her the attention she needs. I'm seeing second-degree burns, and she's having trouble breathing."

They help me to my feet. The next thing I know, I'm on a stretcher, breathing in pure oxygen, being lifted into the back of a waiting ambulance. I see a helicopter overhead and feel it cutting through the air. Beside it, a massive column of blue-black smoke.

Poor Madison and Hunter. What am I even going to say to their loved ones?

Sorry, my family is a little fucked up.

The doors to the ambulance close. It's a tumultuous ride back to the paved road, and I'm wincing with each bump.

"Are you in pain?" a paramedic asks me. "Can I give you anything for it?"

I nod gratefully. A moment later, I ask, "Where are we going?"

"Adirondack Medical Center. Saranac Lake."

At least, I think, I'll be back with my son.

CHAPTER SIXTY-THREE

It's getting late, going on nine p.m. The hospital room is quiet. Just the sound of my heart monitor, the mumble of people in the hallway.

It doesn't last.

Two detectives come into the room saying they're from state BCI. They ask me all the same questions the state troopers did at the scene.

I ask about Paul. They assure me that they're looking for him, that it's a full-on manhunt. He's a fugitive from justice. But I also get the impression that, for them, my husband is just one piece of a mysterious picture.

"We're trying to reconstruct events," one of the detectives says. His name is Parker and he has a scar over one eye, splicing his eyebrow. The other detective is just inside the room, by the door. He stands like a marine.

"We've got a lot of information," Parker says, "but it's a matter of putting it all together."

I get it. The fire erased any ironclad evidence that Paul killed Madison and Hunter. And whether he shot Starzyk can't be corroborated. Neither can the fact of him locking us in the yurt, attempting to burn us alive. It's just my word. And Joni's. And Michael's. Are our stories the same?

The detectives inform me that Michael and Joni are in the same hospital. Michael has been treated for a broken arm, as well as minor cuts and bruises and some smoke inhalation. Joni is in better shape and will be released presently. But until all their questioning is complete, the police are asking that we remain separate. Someone from the state troopers has even been posted outside my door as a gatekeeper.

My injuries are apparently more extensive than Joni's. At least, the doctor I saw about a half hour before the detectives told me that he wanted to check on a few things. He asked me if I'd had any other accidents prior to the fire, because he suspected a recent concussion. I told him about hitting the deer.

The detectives ask me about that, too. They want to know why I'm driving a rental car. Explaining about the deer makes me feel like I'm on less stable ground with them than before. Once again, an unreliable — or at least questionable — witness.

"What about Laura Bishop?" I ask.

They exchange looks. "We're talking to her, too," Parker says.

I worry that's all he's going to say, but then he adds, "Mrs. Bishop gave us quite a story."

The detective by the door, Reynolds, speaks up. "According to Laura Bishop, she's innocent."

"But she pled guilty."

Parker arches his spliced eyebrow. "She says she pled guilty only to spare her son. She didn't want to contest his statement to the police, to fight it in court, to drag the family through a lengthy trial."

Bullshit, I think.

What I say is, "She doesn't seem like the type to spare her family."

"No, I agree," says Parker. "I think she knew she was cooked. She may have hoped to sell a jury on an alternative suspect, but there was no evidence to support it. And the DA had witnesses that she might've been cheating on her husband. Plus, there was the kid. If she went to trial, it would basically be his word against hers. And who was a jury going to believe? A sweet eight-year-old kid, or his unfaithful mother who threw swanky, drug-fueled parties in the city?"

"And who had a temper," Reynolds adds.

"Right," Parker says. "A temper. Plenty of witnesses to say she was a feisty character. So? Her counsel advised her to take a deal. She pled to a lesser offense and got twenty-five years with the possibility of parole. I guess she's been an angel inside, but that doesn't mean she hasn't been stewing. About what happened, about the cops, her son . . ."

"*You*," adds Reynolds.

"You," Parker agrees, looking at me with a kind of pity in his eyes.

"Me," I say.

"And your family. Your daughter."

Reynolds comes forward. "We think that Laura Bishop got herself back in her son's good graces some time ago. A couple of years—"

"And what?" I ask. "They concocted some whole elaborate thing? Joni met Michael at *college* . . .*"

Reynolds nods. He's taller than Parker, with a mole on his jawline. Short, dark hair gelled to perfection. "We think he was already enrolled. That's the one true bit of serendipity in all of this. He met your daughter there and told his mother. Otherwise, every bit of this has been calculated. Laura and her son have conspired to . . . well, essentially break into your life, for some time."

"Why?"

The detectives trade another look between them. Parker picks up the thread. "To mess with you. It seems as simple as that. To mess with you and your husband. The way it seems, to kind of tear you apart. The way it seems to us, she blames you for her conviction. We know Thomas, or rather Michael, has been visiting with her for years. We think she sort of sent him in to destabilize you and your family. Put you through all this business about remembering his past."

Reynolds chips in, "Of course they must've figured you would, you know, recognize Michael, which is why he did the whole partial amnesia thing."

"They're just messed-up people," Parker adds.

I'm shaking my head with disbelief. My throat is so dry. I ask for a drink.

Detective Parker tilts his head. "I'm sorry? I didn't catch that."

"I need water," I whisper.

Parker glances at Reynolds, who leaves to run the tap in the bathroom. He brings me back a plastic cup and I drink from it greedily, water running down my chin.

"Easy," Parker says. "Careful."

I set it aside and wipe my mouth. My mind goes blank with overload.

"Listen," Parker says. "Why don't you get some rest? We'll come back and follow up with you a little later."

"Where is Laura now?"

"In custody," Reynolds assures. "We're keeping an eye on her."

"And we're still talking to her," Parker says.

For some reason, that scares me more than anything.

CHAPTER SIXTY-FOUR

When the detectives leave, another pair of investigators enter, this time a man and a woman. They're better-dressed in more expensive suits. They tell me they're with PSB — the Professional Standards Bureau — and start asking me questions about Steven Starzyk and Rebecca Mooney.

Now's my chance. I tell them about the transcripts I was given prior to evaluating Tom. Transcript of his interviews. And one of them which, toward the end, has Mooney and Starzyk talking about contamination of the scene. On the tape, Starzyk tells Mooney to erase the last minute, but she never did.

"Interesting," the woman says.

Once I've told them everything else I can, I ask them to do me a favor.

"It depends," the man says.

"Can you check on Frank Mills for me? He's in Yonkers — he's a private investigator. I asked him to help me out when . . . when this thing all began. And then he stopped responding to my texts or calls."

"Do you have a phone number? Address?"

I give them what I have for Frank.

Once they're gone, I try to get some rest. I doze for perhaps fifteen, twenty minutes. When I wake up, I'm briefly disoriented.

Then:

Mena . . .

She called, way back when Paul was driving me out of the woods to see Sean, and I let it go to voicemail. Then my battery died. Someone at the hospital was nice enough to loan me a charger, so I can now return her call.

She answers on the second ring. "Dr. Lindman?"

"Mena . . . how are you? Is everything all right?"

"I heard about Sean . . . I'm so sorry. How is he?"

We go through it, with me giving her the abridged version of events, and Mena gasping and sighing and worrying about me. To divert her, I ask about things at the office. "It's been quiet. Everyone knows you're on vacation."

Vacation. Is that the word for what I'm on?

"Maggie Lewis's funeral was today," Mena says, tentative. "I didn't want to bother you. I sent an email to remind you but didn't call . . ."

"It's fine, Mena."

"I went," Mena says. "I hope that's okay."

"Really? You went?"

"People saw that I was there. I thought maybe it . . . I'm sorry. I think about it now, and it was the wrong decision . . ."

"No, Mena. Not at all."

"People will understand," she says. "With everything you have going on. Your own family . . ."

"Mena, it's okay. I'm not worried about appearances."

Silence follows. I sense Mena is stuck on something. She was acting strangely when I saw her during the past weekend, too. Mena has always been introverted, even skittish. But this is something else. "Mena? Is there anything you want to talk to me about?"

"No."

It sounds like a yes.

"Mena, it's okay. There's been a lot going on. Maggie Lewis's suicide, then everything that's happened up here, with Sean . . . I think it's best we talk. So there's no more surprises."

"They sent over the sealed record for the Bishop case," she blurts. "I think the clerk for Judge Meyers forgot you weren't at your office. I . . . I have the records."

"Okay. That's okay, Mena. Things are kind of . . . well, they're pretty much over up here now. You can't even believe the things that . . . I'll have to explain later. It's been a crazy weekend. Craziest of my life."

Mena sounds close to tears. "I know."

"You know?"

"I figured it might be."

"Mena?"

"I would never do anything like this. But when you called me a few days ago, asking about . . . you know . . . and your case notes, it brought some things back to me."

I sit up a little in the bed. I'm dimly aware the rain is streaking the dark windows of my room. That I can still smell smoke from the burning yurt — maybe my clothes are somewhere in the room? "Okay — what wouldn't you do?"

"I'd never go through your files. Your notes. But I just thought . . . Oh God . . ." She sobs, unable to finish.

"Mena. It's okay. Really. What about my notes?"

"I read them."

"Why would you do that?"

But it's already ignited a memory. And the process of remembering feels a bit like the flames that threatened to consume me not hours ago. I'm hot, and I push down the sheet of the hospital bed.

"Why would you do that?" I repeat to Mena, my mind racing. If I said or did anything wrong, it wouldn't be in my case notes. Even though what I sent was a formal evaluation, a judge can subpoena case notes, or anything else.

"Because I wanted to be sure," Mena says, sounding like she already is.

"Sure of what?"

"That you lied in them."

"Mena . . ." I feel my insides turning cold. "I don't understand what you're saying."

Yes, you do.

"Being in this office all these years, I know the good you've done, Dr. Lindman. You're an incredible therapist. You truly care about people. And you're good at what you do. So good that . . ."

"Mena—"

"The truth is I've always admired you. I know you think I've never aspired to more than this, but I wish I could do what you do. And so I listened in. I eavesdropped on your sessions with Tom Bishop. I'm not proud of it. But I know what you said to him. *How* you said it to him. Because, at first, it was just about getting him to doubt what he saw and heard. Getting him to doubt his own certainty — because his certainty was never really there in the first place. And then it was planting the seed that his mother did more than argue with his father. And that he — Tom — just didn't want to believe that. But sometimes the truth was hard. So hard to bear." Mena pauses to catch her breath. "And then he told the police exactly what you coached him to say."

I think it might be over, but Mena isn't finished. She's fully crying now. But I can understand her. I don't want to, but I can.

"I've always thought you did what you did to protect your family," Mena says. "And I told myself I didn't know what I heard. Maybe I was wrong. Maybe it was some new technique you were using. I tried everything. And then you were seeing your own therapist. I thought it was to get through the stuff with Paul. But you were dealing with what you'd done. Weren't you?"

I don't have an answer. I'm too stunned to speak.

Mena stops talking, only sobbing. Then, tear-choked words: "I'd only been working for you for three years. I thought about leaving. But I stayed. I convinced myself it wasn't my business, that I didn't know everything. And then she was convicted. Laura Bishop. She pled guilty, which must've meant she did it. So I thought I must've really misheard things, really screwed up. And I let it go . . . Until you called me and you told me what was happening. Then I knew. I knew it was true!" Her voices rises at the end to a shrill pitch. Mena is hysterical.

"Mena . . . Calm down."

It's all coming out now. Yes, it's finally coming out. Like a hatch underwater, it's opening. The trapped air is rising to the surface.

Too fast . . . too fast.

But maybe it's for the best.

"Mena," I say. "I'm sorry . . ."

As she continues to sob, the door to my hospital room opens.

CHAPTER SIXTY-FIVE

Parker and Reynolds are back. Parker is the more nor-mal-looking one, less soldierly anyway, but it's hard to read even his expression. Perhaps he's stoic like this when he's about to arrest someone.

"How are you feeling, Dr. Lindman?"

"I'm okay. Hoping to get out of here soon." An odd thing to say, considering. Maybe it's best I don't speak.

Parker nods. As I watch, he pulls a small recording device from the phone. He puts it on the food table beside me.

"We had another talk with Laura Bishop tonight," he says.

Reynolds adds, "She continues to have interesting things to say."

Parker asks, "Would you like to hear it?"

I swallow over raw bones in my throat. My eyes are grainy, unblinking. "Okay," I rasp.

Parker hits play. Then he folds his arms and steps back. Reynolds keeps post at the door.

Laura Bishop's voice emanates from the small device. She sounds like I remember her, a kind of smoky, debutante air about her. Like some old movie starlet from the fifties. "About sixteen years ago, I had an affair with Paul Lindman," she says. "Back then, my husband was kind of a socialite. So were the Lindmans. We'd make excuses to dress up and have parties and so would they. It seemed respectable at first. But there were drugs. There were people swapping spouses. The Lindmans weren't into that — they weren't swingers — but that didn't stop Paul from seeking me out."

I close my eyes. I don't want to go back there, to those days, but it's like I've been found at last. I've been hiding out from the past, but now its bright lights are on me.

"Paul found me in the city, where I work. He said he was interested in buying some art. He wanted some paintings for his office and the lobby of one of his buildings. So we started to meet. One of his buildings, one that his firm built, was a hotel. He showed me the penthouse suite. And that was it. We met there to 'discuss art' several times for over four months. Many times. Four months and two weeks, to be exact. And then I broke it off. Because Paul was getting weirdly possessive. He was jealous of David. I was still sleeping with my husband, and Paul knew it, and he hated it. And when I broke it off with Paul . . . Let's just say he didn't handle it well."

She pauses. I don't dare look directly at Parker or Reynolds but see them peripherally, standing like statues.

"I don't believe he thought it through," Laura says about Paul. "I don't know how he imagined we could be together afterwards. Maybe he didn't. Maybe he just wanted to kill what he thought prevented us from being together. Because he went back to his life."

Her voice changes subtly in pitch. "Paul is good at hiding things," she says. My skin tightens with panic. It feels like she's speaking to me directly, knowing I'd hear this. "He's hidden an entire part of himself from public view."

Then Laura's voice changes again, as if she's faced away from the recorder. "She's the same way. Emily. They're two peas in a pod. Because she knew. She knew about the affair, and if she didn't know for sure it was me, she suspected. And that's why, when the police called her to evaluate my son, she didn't admit to knowing me, or knowing David. She didn't inform you. Okay, she said she'd heard our names, it's not a very big town. But that was it. She lied about her conflict of interest because she wanted to know what my son had to say. *My* son. And when he described a man outside his window, sitting in a car, smoking, that's when she knew. She knew it was Paul, and that she needed to steer my son away from that. Give him something else. Someone else. *Me.*"

I can hardly breathe. The room seems to shrink around me, Parker and Reynolds sliding toward the bed. I can practically feel the cold steel of the handcuffs sliding over my wrists. Picture myself being walked out of the hospital and put into the back of a waiting police car.

Parker ends the playback. He returns the recording device to his pocket. For a moment, he stares into the corner, as if marshaling the right words.

You have the right to remain silent.

He shakes his head, as if mournful. Then his eyes slide to mine. "She keeps going on for a while longer, but basically — that's the gist. Laura Bishop claims that you brainwashed her son. That the whole thing — his statement to police that he saw his mother do it — it was all you. You kind of gave him the old Jedi mind trick."

I search Parker's eyes. Is this a time to be joking?

He looks back at me and then at Reynolds, by the door. Parker says to Reynolds, "Fucking ex-cons, right? Doesn't matter if they're out, they're still working an angle. Every time."

When Parker faces me again, it takes me a moment to realize what I'm hearing: He doesn't believe Laura Bishop.

"As far as I'm concerned," Parker says, "It's just a matter of time before the truth comes out about what she did up there at the yurt. Just need to piece it all together. Then she's going to go right back inside."

He shakes his head some more, as if he's sorry. "It's a shame, you know, what these institutions do to people; they don't know how to function on the outside."

I swallow dryly. I try to nod. I try to look normal.

Parker says, "Maybe when I retire, I'll become a penologist. Try to get some reform going. Because right now, we're just putting people back on the street who . . . Well, I'm bending your ear here." He pats my leg beneath the sheet. "Dr. Lindman, I just thought you should be aware. This woman plans to sue you."

He shakes his head one last time. "What a world. People coming out of prison and getting into lawsuits. Going after law-abiding citizens. But listen, we've got her under wraps; she's not going anywhere. You're safe. And we'll keep you posted. All right?"

I can only stare at him dumbly.

Parker then drifts toward the door. Reynolds opens it and leaves without looking back. Parker stops and turns back with some final words. "Oh, and we're looking hard for your husband, ma'am. I wanted to ask you — does he have any woodsman skills? Survival skills? Knowing that might help us in our search. Lot of acres out there, lot of wild forest."

Paul? Survival skills? Maybe in some twisted way, yes. But not as a wilderness survivalist.

Barely able to form the words, I say to Parker, "No, I don't think so."

He gives the wall a rap with his knuckles; a superstitious gesture, perhaps. "All right, well. Rest up, Dr. Lindman. Take care."

The door closes, and I'm alone again in the quiet.

Just me, and my thoughts.

Just me, and the abyss.

CHAPTER SIXTY-SIX

They don't find Paul.

CHAPTER SIXTY-SEVEN

It's mid-September. The first signs of autumn nibble the edges of summer. A cool breeze, a smattering of red and orange in the trees. Here and there: purple.

I have not returned to Bronxville but have stayed holed up in the lake house. I'm waiting for my son to wake up. I'm waiting for the endless parade of cops and reporters to come to an end. I feel like it's close.

No, they never found Paul. They think he died in the forest. And they still don't believe Laura Bishop, even though she's following through with her threat and her lawyer just filed papers in court yesterday. She's going to sue me. Psychological damages, years lost in prison, plus all the unrecoverable grief of missing her son's childhood, and the stigma of being a felon. A murderer.

You'd think she'd seek a new trial. An exoneration.

My lawyer explained why not. "You've got to consider what that entails. There's a higher bar for criminal cases than for civil suits. There's no new physical evidence, for one thing. She'd have to have her son up there to recant. And who's the one who brought the truth out of him? You are — the exact same therapist she's claiming was criminally corrupt in your therapy fifteen years ago. And who knows if

315

Michael would be even *willing* to testify, anyway? I have my doubts. You said he's still with your daughter?"

"Yes," I say, and my gaze drifts to the lake. They're not down there, of course. I've seen neither my daughter nor her fiancé for almost a month. I think Joni is trying to sort it all out. Now that the charade is over, and her part in this has helped Michael unveil the truth, she's examining how she feels about me. Which she should.

And how do *I* feel about me?

Disgusted. Horrified.

"Michael and Joni are still together," I say to my lawyer. His name is John Blakely.

"Well," Blakely says, "from what I'm hearing, Michael is not on Laura's side."

"Her side?"

"I know, it's a . . . touchy situation, Emily, and I don't mean to . . . Look, at this point, there are sides. Once there's a court case, it's binary. Us versus them. So, I'm asking you — do you think he would testify? To say he was . . ."

"Coerced by me? Manipulated? Would he say that a therapist, a professional, a woman who was supposed to be there to protect him, to help him, instead manipulated his mind in order to hide what her husband did?"

My lawyer doesn't respond. I've answered his question with a question. He's talking about sides, because people have made up their minds. It's right there on social media. People who believe Michael Rand and Laura Bishop are con artists who took advantage of a family, and people who think Michael is a victim. That Paul and I are the bad guys. But to what extent they think Paul is a murderer and I covered for him greatly varies.

What do I care, anyway? I know what I did. And I know what Paul did, though I was, for a long time, repressing the very thought of it. I was in denial at the same time I was trying to work the situation, cover myself. To steer Michael toward thinking it was the cops who coerced him. Steer him toward seeing Doug Wiseman as the killer.

All these years later, and I was still manipulating.

I am a horrible, subhuman person.

"Well?" Blakely asks. "How much exposure do you have here? What about your case notes? Things like that?"

My case notes . . .

My case notes constitute a clever covering of my tracks. A subtle throwing of shade on the New York State Police. And they show certain truths: it was true Tom heard his parents arguing that night. And it was true that the police urged Tom to consider the possibility of his mother's guilt. But these were facts I exploited. Facts that formed a hole in Laura Bishop's innocence, one I kept widening until it gaped, until it was wide enough to push through the reality I chose.

I chose to psychologically manipulate a young boy into believing his original assessment — seeing someone outside, hearing two men fighting — was just his way to protect his mother. That, in reality, he saw her do it. I took that emptiness he'd seen in her eyes and drew it out and enveloped him with it.

It wasn't hard. He was eight.

No, I don't regret the fifteen years that Laura Bishop spent in prison as an innocent woman, because I don't consider her innocent. She was an adulteress. A would-be home-wrecker. Because of her, I spent that same decade and a half in my own prison: the horrible lasting impression of what I did to her son in order to preserve my marriage, my family. To keep my husband from going to jail, I pushed Tom toward a truth favorable to me. Again, it wasn't hard.

But I shouldn't have done it. Of course I shouldn't have. I should've let Paul rot in state prison, instead. My family would have recovered. If anything, maybe Joni wouldn't have had it so rough. And little Tom Bishop wouldn't have grown up believing such a lie about his own mother.

I abandoned him and my duty to protect him. That's why Maggie Lewis's death and her story affected me so deeply. That's why I've spent the last fifteen years looking over my shoulder. Because, like Freud said, what we repress just comes out in worse ways.

317

_?"_

,oout my case notes," I say.

Michael?"

t going to let the question go unanswered.

.iichael will tell on me, essentially? Throw me

us, like he should? If not to a jury, to reporters?

.l memoir that makes the Oprah Book Club?

ntinue to stare out at the lake. Dark today, slate gray, with angles of choppy waves. I think of the love I witnessed between Michael and Joni. No doubt, Michael did some acting. But there were things he couldn't fake. Like getting his own full picture of the truth.

And his love for my daughter. He truly fell for Joni, even if he never intended it. I am convinced of that.

"No," I say. "I don't think Michael will speak against me."

Blakely is dubious. "How can you be sure?"

"You're the one that just said _you_ were sure."

"Well, I know she's not going to seek a new trial for a number of reasons. Michael's unwillingness to testify is possibly one of them. But it's the one I'm least sure of."

"You can be sure of it." My words convince even my own ears. I don't have to explain to Blakely how I'm so certain; I don't even know if I _could_ explain. No one knows, but Michael and I, what it was like the three times we tracked into his past. Those feelings belong to us.

"All right," Blakely says. "Listen, you just keep doing what you're doing. I've got things under control down here. The way this civil thing plays out — you're never even going to have to see a courtroom. I'll make sure of—"

"How much is she asking? What's she suing me for?"

Blakely is quiet. I can hear the muffled honk of White Plains traffic. "Fifteen million," he says.

I laugh, just a sound that escapes me, almost a bark. "What makes her think we have _fifteen million dollars_?"

"It's just the opening bid. One million for every year spent in prison. But what they're aiming for is ten. And I'll get them even lower."

"How much lower? Paul's an architect and I'm a therapist. We're not the Waltons." I look around, imagining having to sell the lake house. Well, if so, it's only the beginning of what I deserve.

Blakely asks, "What about Paul's life insurance?"

I've actually thought about it. "He's got to be missing for longer, or found. But if it kicks in, it's two-point-five."

And if that's the case, it's going right to my children.

"Okay," Blakely says, sounding relieved. "Then we've got something to work with."

No, we don't.

We talk a little more. He gives me the same advice he's given me twice already about staying quiet in the press. Looking solemn and remorseful if caught on camera, but not to engage. A judge can be swayed by public opinion, Blakely says, just like a jury.

"Laura Bishop still has to prove this thing," Blakely reminds me. "Even if it's not a new criminal case, she's got to — well, her lawyers have to — convince a judge that she was wrongfully convicted. She's got to do it without her son being involved, if it's true that he's going to stay on our side. The first thing they're going to go after, probably, is—"

"John?"

He clears his throat; I've derailed him. "Yes?"

"Can we pick this up later?"

"Sure. Of course." He asks, "You doing all right?"

"I'm going to lie down for a little bit."

"All right. Listen . . . all right. Take it easy. We can talk again whenever."

I thank him and hang up and toss my phone onto the kitchen island. I sip from the glass of red wine there and carry it to the window and look out, watch the lake for a little while.

The couch feels especially soft when I lie down. For a moment, I think I might weep, but then nothing comes. I'm empty.

After a while, I drift off to sleep. I dream of the Bishop home and the blood on the kitchen floor.

Only it's Michael with his head bashed in. It's Joni who sits at the table where his mother sat, drinking her wine. And it's my reflection in the door window, fresh snowflakes coming down behind the glass, hammer in my hand.

* * *

Something wakes me.

The first thing I notice is the light has changed. Evening is coming on. The lake has turned silvery to match the sky.

I hear a noise. A high-pitched whining. Coming from outside the house.

I know that sound.

Moving slowly, quietly, I get up from the couch. I take my phone from the kitchen and walk to the side door. From here, I can see the garage.

A light is on. Something or someone moves in front of it, casting a long shadow over the gravel driveway. In the next instant, the high-pitched whine resumes.

Paul's sander. Someone is working on the boat.

I get my sweater down off the peg and open the door, drawing the garment around me. I walk to the garage with the sound of the sander going.

When it stops, I'm standing just two yards away from the open garage bay. Wood dust floats like pollen. The man standing there waves at the dust. His back is to me; he's hunched over. He runs his hand along the smoothed wood. Then he sets the sander down, brushes his hands together, and straightens up. Finally, he turns around and looks at me.

"Hi, honey," Paul says.

CHAPTER SIXTY-EIGHT

He's unshaven. His hair is oily. He looks malnourished, cheek bones stretched against too-thin skin. When he smiles, his teeth are darker. He's wearing different clothes since the last time I saw him — jeans, a gray T-shirt promoting the Syracuse Orangemen football team — but the boat shoes are the same. Everything is filthy, pants stained and shirt torn. The last thing I notice are his hands, dark with mud. Or dried blood.

He takes a step toward me, and I take a step back.

"What are you doing?" I ask.

He looks from me to the boat, as if it's obvious. "Gonna finish it up. It's overdue."

"Work has been calling for you." I try to keep from trembling. "When they couldn't get you, they tried me. But by now . . ."

His eyes narrow. "I plan to go back as soon as I can. Maybe the end of the week. But I figured, as long as I'm here, I should put the final coat of varnish on her." He nods at the boat. "Just needed to give it a light once-over with the sander first."

We stare at Paul's project for a few moments.

"It looks good," I say.

I can hear a slight wheeze in his breath.

Still watching the boat, he asks me, "Did Sean wake up?"

"No. Not yet."

"And Jo? Where's she?" Paul's head slowly turns. "She still with *him*?"

"I don't know. I think so."

"What about her? Are they with *her*?"

He means Laura. "I think they went to Long Island. To the Bleekers. It's possible she's there."

I add, after a considered pause, "She's suing us."

Paul grunts. He shakes his head and kicks at the gravel. "That fucking bitch."

At least he's not pretending anymore.

After a long silence, he says, "I didn't ask you to do what you did."

"I know, Paul."

"If anything, what I did was a cry for help, right?"

Murdering in cold blood is not a cry for help; it's a sign of psychosis. But I don't say this. "We're all in the grip of some emotion or another at any given time," I tell him. "You were jealous."

"I wasn't jealous. I was *sickened*." Paul's upper lip tugs into a snarl as he takes another step toward me. "Sickened by everything. Sickened by what we'd become. Those parties and those shallow people. The pursuit of . . . nothing."

I stand unmoving, trying not to antagonize. His anger gradually abates, and he gives me a wistful look. "Remember what we were like? When we were young? When we met?"

"I do."

"We were a good team, Em."

"I know."

His bloodshot eyes linger on me. Then he spreads his arms. He wants a hug.

I go to him, trying not to give away how terrified I am. It's just instinct, to keep him calm, make him think everything is okay. But as he takes me in his arms, my gaze falls on a workbench in the garage. The tools hanging on the pegboard. The empty place for the hammer.

Paul smells like BO and fresh air, mixed. I feel his breath in my hair. "I was in the woods, Em. I've been out there, this whole time. Three weeks, right?"

"Yeah." The word is muffled against his neck.

He rubs my back absently. "Helicopters, dogs — I evaded it all. I found a hunting camp and broke in, had some food for a while. I had no idea where I was. And then I found a logging trail that led toward the lake. I knew my way back from there. But I didn't want to. I wasn't ready yet. So I stayed right around here. Right on the lake. I raided the neighbors' place." Paul laughs, and I can feel it vibrate through his protruding ribs. "I knew they were gone and their security's shit. But there's other places; they don't even lock up. So I just stayed here and there, moving around by night. Took a shower once or twice, stole some clothes. I kept going until I figured the cops gave up looking for me. They had to wind it down some-time, right? They had to figure I was more likely dead."

Paul pulls away from me. Out of the hug, he looks in my eyes. "The detective — Starzyk — did he live?"

I nod. "He had a surgery. Left the hospital about a week later. He doesn't remember much."

"Seems to be catching," Paul says distractedly. He looks at the lake house. "I watched the house. I watched everybody coming and going. Lots of cops. But they've been gone for three days. Just the ones that come in and check on you."

He's right.

"So what are you going to do?" I ask.

He gets a thoughtful look. It's almost as if he's consid-ering it for the first time, but of course, that's not true. He's had weeks to think about it. "What I did is something that happens," he says. "At any given moment, there are millions of people feeling murderous impulses. We resist because we're scared. But I just stopped being scared."

He's talking about pleading insanity? A fit of passion, being out of his mind?

"And then you protected me. I didn't even plan for that. You just did it. Because we were a team. We're *still* a team, Em."

323

"That sounds a little bit like a threat."

He makes a face, like I'm being silly. "No, it's not a threat. I mean you protected us then, our family, and you can do it again, now. We can get it all back. We can be a family."

I search his eyes. If I'm totally honest, yes, there's some part of me that wants to believe we can make this better. But I realize that's just attachment. I've spent almost half my life with this man. The idea that it was all a lie, well — that's hard to accept.

"If we're a team," I say, "then you need to admit what you did."

"Admit what? What are you talking about?"

"I'm just saying, admit it to me. If we're going to get through this, we need complete honesty, from this point forward. Nobody needs to know about Madison and Hunter, because no one saw it, or can prove anything anyway. And without new evidence, nothing can be done about David Bishop."

Paul's face is getting hard to read in the gathering dusk, features blending together. Does he think I'm trying to trap him?

"As far as anyone knows," he says, "Michael could have killed the Tremont girl and her hippie boyfriend. And as far as David Bishop goes, you're the only one who knows anything about that, wouldn't you say?"

It's true. Other than Paul, I'm the one with the most information. I've been desperate to stuff it back into the closet ever since Michael showed up, but it didn't work. It couldn't work.

His eyes find me. Just points of light in the semidarkness. "I wanted to get my family back, Em. That's why I did what I did."

I let the statement hang there a moment. "No," I say next. "I need honesty, Paul. Or you get nothing from me." I'm trembling from the inside out, but this is it. This is the moment. I look into Paul's face — he's feigning ignorance — and let him have it. "You cheated on me. On all of us. But she didn't want you. She wanted *him*. So, you killed him."

He starts shaking his head emphatically. "She was a mistake. All I ever wanted was *you*, Em. You and only you."

"You're not going to admit it? That you at least thought about it?"

"Fine. In the haze of our shitty lives back then, I thought I did. I thought I wanted her."

"You wanted her so bad you killed her husband. It's not because you were sickened. You were enraged with jealousy. Admit it."

He stares at me. "Yes, Emily. I killed him because I was fucking jealous."

There.

He said it.

He scowls at me. "This is what you want? This is what will bring us back together?"

"Well, we ought to try it," I say. "We ought to try the truth."

"That goes both ways."

"Okay. Sure. What have you got?"

"You were a shitty mother. A neglectful mother. Always off working. Always hosting parties. Our daughter just wanted a mother."

My voice goes up. "I know our daughter blames me for her problems. That she feels we loved Sean more than her. He was adventurous and outgoing; she was introverted and shy and resented everything we tried to get her into. I know she was insecure. I know that she felt unsafe. Because of how you and I were, how we fought. But, Jesus Christ, Paul. You tried to burn her. Your own *daughter*," I say. "Jesus, Paul. And Madison and Hunter — what did they do? They were just in your way. Just like David had been in your way. Because something is missing in you. I thought maybe it was a crime of passion, something that just overcame you. Once. But it's not. You're sick, Paul. You need help."

Paul is staring at me, his eyes gone glassy and distant. I know I've gone too far. But I can't stop.

"Michael played me. I know that. He faked the amnesia. He faked a version of himself living in Arizona at the address of Laura's old boyfriend, Doug Wiseman. He left me that voicemail, he wrote a message on the boathouse wall. That was all him, trying to throw me off. To throw us off. A little fun and games, as a prelude to Laura's real revenge, a massive lawsuit. And you know what? We deserved it and worse. But you . . . they were just all in your way. Just something to get rid of. You're sick, Paul. The very definition."

Paul's face twists with contempt. He's not hiding it anymore. "Oh, like you're so virtuous, Emily. You know what I did? You want to know? I called Frank Mills. After your accident with the fucking deer. You were passed out at the hospital and I went through your phone, and I saw your texts with him. I told him to back off. And not just because of the whole Bishop situation. But because I *knew*."

"You knew what?"

"I knew how you felt about him."

"Are you kidding me? Frank Mills was a cop. He was there for me during a difficult time."

"You're telling me nothing happened? All these years? You just keep in contact with some random cop from your past? Come on."

"He's a friend."

Paul snorts and shakes his head, incredulous.

I want to tell Paul the real reason that this all unfolded the way it did. That, though Michael was following a plan made with his mother, he diverged from it. He followed his own course.

Why?

Because he fell in love with our daughter.

As sick as Paul is, I want to tell him this because it's about our daughter. I want to tell him that while Joni may have sided with Michael and Laura against us, Michael sided with Joni against Laura. He wouldn't have actually hurt me, or Sean, because he came to love Joni. Initially, she surely gravitated to Michael the way she's gravitated to other young men in the past. But then the two of them fell in love. And her love changed Michael, changed the course of everything.

It's normal to want to share the glory and joy in your children, even with an ex-partner. But I don't.

And I'm not telling him about Sean, either.

Sean, who has been awake for over two weeks now. Sean, who remembered the sailing accident and cleared Michael of any wrongdoing.

Sean, my son, who is now gone again, just a couple of days since he fully recuperated. Gone, since I confessed everything to him. Gone back west, considering whether he'll ever be able to forgive me for what I've done.

"Where are you going?" Paul asks. He seems to gauge the distance I've opened up between us.

"Nowhere," I say.

We stand, watching each other in the twilight. The lake laps against the docks and makes those hollow sounds in the boathouse. The crickets sing in the high grasses and ragweed. Bugs dart through the air.

No, there's nothing more to say.

It happens quickly, then. Even in the scant light, I can see Paul's features change again, going from that look of incredulity to a smoother, eyes-wide look of revelation.

He's just worked it all through. That's what's happening. He's decided on the reason I've stood here with him, talking. Why I asked him about David Bishop.

And the fact that he admitted to killing him.

Paul lunges for me, and he's fast as a snake. He grabs my shirt and rips it open, popping the buttons, revealing the wireless microphone taped to my chest.

For a moment, everything seems to stop. Paul stares at the small device, then at me. After that, he checks his surroundings. He's expecting the cavalry, but there is none. Like Paul said, he's been watching the house. I don't know my husband as well as I should, but that was something I banked on — if the police were here waiting, Paul would never have shown. This was the only way. And once I glimpsed him in the woods three days ago, the time had come.

The next thing I know, Paul has a hammer. It was tucked into the back of his pants. Now he holds it in a fist, and he stares at me.

"What did you do?"

"I loved you," I tell him.

His face is ghostly, an apparition. But I can see the anguish that ripples over his features before they harden into mindless hate. Paul raises the hammer, ready to drop it on my skull.

Instead of running, I just stand there. I close my eyes.

I deserve this.

The sound of footsteps sends my eyelids flying open. Paul is still standing in front of me, but he's just turning his head to the side. Michael comes lunging out from beside the garage. His face is a blur of wide eyes and gnashed teeth.

The hammer goes flying as Michael slams into Paul, tackling him to the ground. A moment later, the two men are grunting and fighting and rolling in the gravel. I step farther back, just as Joni comes running out of the house. She stops beside me. She screams: "Michael!"

Michael manages to get on top of Paul. He straddles Paul at the waist. Paul grabs for Michael's throat, but the younger man is quicker, stronger. He bats Paul's hands away, then lands a punch on his cheek. Another on his mouth. And another. And another.

Paul killed his father. This is the payback that's fifteen years in coming.

"Michael!" Joni runs for him. I grab at her but miss.

She reaches Michael and grabs his shoulders. His head whips around to her and he stares up, murder in his eyes. His fist hangs in the air, blood on the knuckles. Paul is a beaten mess beneath him.

Michael sees Joni. Really sees her. Lowers his fist. His eyes and mouth soften. He lets her help him off Paul and gain his feet.

They stand there, the two of them, looking at each other. Then Michael glances at Paul one last time. He spits at him.

Finally, the two of them turn their attention to me.

My tears are flowing. My body vibrates like I've been electrified. Slowly, without intending it, I drop to my knees. I stare up at these two children who've inherited this mess. Who never asked for it.

"Please forgive me," I say to them.

The two of them gaze back at me impassively. Joni has her arm around Michael's waist. Now he puts his arm around her shoulder. Like this, they turn from me and start walking away. They move down the long driveway, disappearing into the darkness.

My chin drops to my chest. I kneel there and sob. It all just comes out of me. I have no bones. I have no breath. I am just this repentant soul on the ground.

After a moment, I feel a hand on my shoulder. I look up, sniffing back the tears and the snot.

Frank Mills looks down at me. "Hey," he says. "You want me to go pick them up?"

I shake my head. "Let them go for now."

"Okay."

Frank checks Paul, who's not moved from where Michael left him. I can see the rise and fall of Paul's chest. I can hear the bubbly quality of his labored breathing. He's alive, which is more than he deserves.

Frank kicks the hammer farther away. He stands, looking down at Paul a moment, then back at me.

He's been staying with me for the past couple of days; I met the three of them in town and smuggled them to the lake house, being sure to keep out of sight in case Paul was monitoring my comings and goings.

It was Frank who convinced Joni and Michael to come back. Once I saw Paul in the woods near the house, I called Frank and we were able to put it together. Paul was obviously intending to see me. To talk to me. This man I'd married, who'd once had an affair and killed the husband his mistress wouldn't leave. A marriage I'd tried to save by ruining the lives of at least two other people — Michael and his mother.

Only to have Paul, fifteen years later, descend even deeper. Once he'd known he was capable of murder, all bets were off. There was no coming back, if there ever even was.

I stand up. I walk to where Paul lies.

"Be careful," Frank says.

I stare down at my husband, his bloody face. There's just enough light from the house to see him by. "Call 911, Frank."

"Okay." Frank takes out his phone. Even though the coverage is spotty here, 911 always works. I had ample opportunity to call and never did.

But now is the time. It's finally over.

I hear Frank explain the situation to the emergency operator.

Paul reaches up for me. I decide to risk it and take a knee beside him. His gaze falls on the microphone still taped above my breast.

The recording will go a long way toward a conviction. Paul will spend the rest of his life in prison.

It should also help Laura Bishop to sue us.

Which is fine with me. I prefer to be left with nothing once it's all over.

As Frank finishes up the conversation with the emergency operator, I look up the driveway. I can just see Joni and Michael rounding the bend out of sight. And for a moment, just a moment, a warm and brilliant light banishes all the darkness from my soul. As they walk away, the high summer grasses waving in the breeze beside them, cicadas buzzing in the humidity, I see two people who have made each other their highest loyalty. Leaving me and Paul, the messed-up older generation, behind.

And then they're gone.

THE END

ACKNOWLEDGMENTS

Remember that first summer after the pandemic hit? My wife and I needed to get away, and so we rented a tiny, cheap cabin in the middle of nowhere. There, with only a few donkeys to keep us company and a murky pond to escape the heat, we came up with the basic storyline for this book. So, first and foremost, I have to thank my spectacular wife.

After I wrote the thing, I needed some feedback, and that's where a few brave men and women come into the picture. Veronika Jordan. David C. Taylor. Trena Stooksberry. These brilliant people read the story after I'd given it all I could and their feedback made it better. From more lifelike characters to revised endings; if there's a part you like, credit surely goes to them.

Thank you to Joffe Books for taking it on; to Jasper for always keeping the door open and the light on. Thanks to the reader who gave it a first look and pushed it through the gate. Thanks to Emma Grundy Haigh for shepherding it through the entire process from there, for the excellent cover and blurb and all the fine-tuning, for her enthusiasm. For loving this story and truly caring about it — I couldn't ask for more. And thank you to Jodi Compton, who's been my editor for several books now. Also a writer, Jodi knows how to use a soft touch while making all the right points. She's like a ninja, really, or a Jedi, deftly getting the job done while you're oblivious to her magic.

Finally, thank you, reader, for taking a chance on this book. There's a lot out there, and your choice to read this one means the world to me. Really; it's everything.

Thank you for reading this book.

If you enjoyed it, please leave feedback on Amazon or Goodreads, and if there is anything we missed or you have a question about, then please get in touch. We appreciate you choosing our book.

Founded in 2014 in Shoreditch, London, we at Joffe Books pride ourselves on our history of innovative publishing. We were thrilled to be shortlisted for Independent Publisher of the Year at the British Book Awards.

www.joffebooks.com

We're very grateful to eagle-eyed readers who take the time to contact us. Please send any errors you find to corrections@joffebooks.com. We'll get them fixed ASAP.

Printed in Great Britain
by Amazon